HOW TO SURVIVE
SURVIVE
a MODERN-DAY
FAIRY
TALE

HOW TO SURVIVE a MODERN-DAY FAIRY TALE

ELLE CRUZ

Entangled Publishing, LLC
10940 S Parker Road
Suite 327
Parker, CO 80134
rights@entangledpublishing.com

Amara is an imprint of Entangled Publishing, LLC.

Visit our website at www.entangledpublishing.com.

Edited by Liz Pelletier and Lydia Sharp
Cover design by Elizabeth Turner Stokes
Cover illustration of woman © Medesulda/GettyImages
Interior design by Toni Kerr

ISBN 978-1-64937-081-5
Ebook ISBN 978-1-64937-115-7

Manufactured in the United States of America

First Edition November 2021

10 9 8 7 6 5 4 3 2 1

For Oliver

NOTE FROM THE AUTHOR

Dear Reader,

Thank you so much for picking up a copy of this book! This story is very special to me. It's one of the few adult romance novels to center around a Filipino-American protagonist and her family.

Growing up as a second-generation Filipina in Southern California was an amazing experience. I cannot even begin to imagine the sacrifices made by my parents and relatives, who left their homeland and traveled seven thousand miles to a strange, foreign land, with the hope of creating a better life for their children and future generations.

Although I had a wonderful childhood, I grew up never quite knowing where I belonged. I never felt fully American because I wasn't white. I never felt Filipino enough because I wasn't born in the Philippines, and I did not speak or understand the language. As a matter of fact, I would sometimes be ostracized and marginalized by my fellow Filipinos for not knowing the language, or for lacking an intimate knowledge of the culture.

It took a very, very long time for me to understand my place in the world. When I finally had this epiphany, it was like a curtain being lifted to show me this amazing, wondrous world that had been hiding within me all along.

My experience as a second-generation Filipino woman is unique. It is mine and mine alone, and I take immense pride and ownership of it. I have grown up with my feet straddling both worlds, and I do not allow others to define whether or not I am American or Filipino enough. By writing this story, I am taking ownership of my experience and showing the world that Filipino-Americans *exist*, we are here, and we have rich and beautiful and emotional stories to share that everyone can relate to.

With that being said, I wanted to point out that I did my best to do justice to the complex dynamics of a Filipino-American family, while maintaining respect for the culture and avoiding harmful stereotypes. It was not my intention to speak for all Asian or Filipino-Americans. Rather, I am adding to the diverse collection of other Asian-American stories in hopes of uplifting the voices of more diaspora who deserve to be heard.

Above all, I hope that you as a reader enjoy this story, get swept away by the romance, and find nothing but joy and hope in the love story of Claire and Nate.

Sincerely Yours,
Elle

lola— *grandma*

ate (ah-teh)— *a term for an older sister or respected older female*

tita— *aunt*

tito— *uncle*

kuya— *a term for an older brother or respected older male*

lolo— *grandpa*

anak ko— *my child*

pancit— *Filipino dish with noodles, veggies, and meat*

lumpia— *Filipino deep fried egg-rolls*

adobo— *Filipino chicken dish made with soy sauce, vinegar, and bay leaves*

ube— *Filipino dessert flavor made from bright purple yam*

At Entangled, we want our readers to be well-informed. If you would like to know if this book contains any elements that might be of concern for you, please check the back of the book for details.

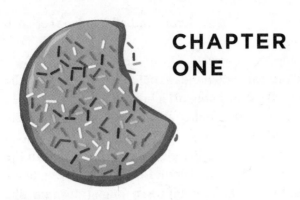

CHAPTER ONE

Some people chased a high by doing drugs. Claire Ventura had never understood that. The best high she'd ever experienced was seeing peoples' reactions to her homemade sugar cookies.

It was Friday morning. Everyone at her grandmother's assisted living facility knew what Fridays meant. The staff's faces lit up as Claire came striding in, rolling her fold-up cart full of goodies. She was going to knock their socks off today.

"Good morning, Miss Claire," the receptionist said.

"Good morning, Rose," she replied as she signed in. "You sound cheerful today. I wonder why?" Claire removed a cellophane-wrapped cookie from her cart—and she got the reaction she was hoping for right as Rose's eyes landed on it.

"Oh my goodness, Miss Claire, I can't believe it," she cried. "It's a rose! I couldn't eat this. It's so pretty. I am never going to eat this."

"You have to eat it," Claire said. "That's part of the magic. Not only do you get to enjoy how pretty it is, but you get to taste how delicious it is, too."

"Thank you so much," Rose gushed again. She clutched the cookie to her heart like it was a long-lost family heirloom. "You are the sweetest thing."

"It's the least I can do for you and the rest of the staff. You are always so nice every time I call, and everyone takes such good care of my lola."

Her first stop was a success. On to the next.

She rolled her cart down the carpeted hallway toward the nurses' station. After dropping off a box full of flower-shaped cookies and receiving the "oohs" and "aahs" she lived for, she headed off toward her grandmother's room.

Claire rolled her cart to the elevator and punched in the secret code to access the second floor. Lola had only been living there for about three months, but it was a tough transition. She was diagnosed with Alzheimer's a few years ago, and it had gotten steadily worse. No one in the family had been prepared for how drastically it would change her. It all came to a head a few months ago when the caregiver at Lola's house called Claire, frantically screaming that Lola had disappeared. It turned out Lola had decided to go for a walk. She was found five miles away at a strip mall.

Five miles.

How she'd gotten there was beside the point. Afterward, Lola wasn't the same. She stopped having conversations. She stopped acting like herself and became a complete stranger. Lola couldn't live alone in her house any longer, so they moved her into the locked Alzheimer's unit at the assisted living facility. This sudden change scared everyone in her family, but not Claire. Lola was still Lola, despite whatever illness she had. Claire had never given up hope, and she came to visit her every single morning.

The elevator door slid open. Claire stepped off and walked across the vestibule to the locked doors. She punched in another code, and the doors slowly opened. The Alzheimer's unit was decorated with accents of love and nostalgia. Old black-and-white photos of the residents who had served in World War II and Korea adorned the walls. Vintage wedding pictures and photos of smiling family members also hung there, paying homage to the residents who'd left their lasting impression on the world.

Ornate red paisley paper covered the walls. The carpet was a plush, dark-green shade with deep gold accents. The woodgrain paneling along the walls might have seemed outdated, but Claire liked the personal touch. It seemed so much more like a home than a facility.

She rolled her cart down the hallway and around the corner to the right. Lola's door was wide open.

"Lola, I'm here," she called. Claire walked into the room and stopped short when she saw her favorite nurse there, studying the picture frames on Lola's dresser.

"Oh. Hi, Allison," she said. "How are you?"

"Fine, thanks. I just finished giving your grandma her meds."

Lola was clean and dressed, sitting primly in her armchair like a faerie queen upon her throne. Her eyes were trained on the TV talk show host, but she showed no signs of engagement or comprehension. A green-and-white crocheted blanket was draped over her lap. The pointed tips of her brown snakeskin flats peeked out from the hem of her pink-and-blue floral dress.

"So how has she been?" Claire asked as she took a seat at the edge of the bed beside Lola's armchair.

"Pretty stable so far. She woke up once last night and started to wander, but she was easily redirected. She went right back to sleep. Do you mind if I ask you a question?"

Claire paused, then said, "Not at all. What is it?"

"I never took the time to look at your grandma's pictures before," she said. "They're so interesting. She has a huge family."

"She sure does," Claire said with a smile. "She gave birth to eleven children at home. Sometimes the midwife couldn't get to her in time and she had to birth them on her own."

"Wow. How many grandkids does she have?"

"Thirty-five."

The nurse's face lit up. "Amazing."

"It's Friday, Allison. You know what that means." Claire plucked another cookie out of her rolling cart and handed it over.

"Oh my God, is this an orchid?" she exclaimed. "You made this all by yourself? How in the world do you do this? It's gorgeous."

"Yes, it's a dendrobium orchid," Claire replied. "My lola's favorite flower."

"I can't accept this. It's too nice. This must have taken hours to make. How much is this? I can pay."

"No, it's a gift. It was no trouble at all, really. And it's the least I can do for all the great care you give to my grandmother."

"This is professional-grade work," Allison said, admiring the cookie. "Is this what you do for a living?"

Claire *aspired* to become a full-time cookie decorator, with plans to sell her creations online and offer tutorials and classes. But two little obstacles stood in the way. One: mustering up the courage to actually leave her day job and follow her dream. And two: breaking the news to her traditional Filipino family that she would *never* pursue a job in medicine or science.

"No," she said. "It's just a side hustle."

"Side hustle?" Allison asked in disbelief. "No way. You've got talent. This could seriously be a full-time business. I'm sure people would pay good money for this kind of work."

Claire shrugged dismissively, even though Allison had given voice to her greatest unspoken dream. She might have played it cool on the outside, but the idea of earning a living from her passion made her happy beyond words.

"Did you want me to stay to help your grandma finish her breakfast?" Allison asked.

"No, I can do it." She waved her off. "But thank you."

"Out of curiosity, what's inside your cart?"

"Magazines. She loves the tabloids." Claire hefted out a stack of magazines with bold, bright headlines across the covers.

"Really?" Allison said with an amused laugh. She picked up one of the magazines and started flipping through it. "How funny is that?"

"I know. I've tried reading a lot of different things to her, but the tabloids with the short, snappy articles and all the pictures of celebrities seem to engage her on some level."

"Uh, yeah, I know exactly what engages your grandma," Allison said with a hearty laugh. "Look at the headline on this one. *Summer Special: Hollywood's Hottest Hunks at the Beach.*"

"Oh my gosh, how ridiculous." She couldn't help but laugh at the outrageousness of the title and the pictures of half-dressed male celebrities across the cover. "You know what they say. There might be snow on the roof, but there's still a fire in the furnace."

Claire and Allison burst into laughter. Lola flicked her eyes over to them for a brief second, then stared back at the TV.

"Oops, I think we startled her," Allison said. "I don't blame her one bit for liking these stories. They're trashy, but so much fun."

"Go ahead and take it," Claire said. "There's plenty more where that came from."

"Are you sure? You don't like to read these?"

"No." She shook her head emphatically. "I can't stand the tabloids. I get them strictly for Lola."

"What's not to like? Look at that six-pack. Working in a place like this makes me appreciate this kind of male beauty."

"You are so funny," Claire said. "But I'm not really fond of celebrities."

"Why not?"

"I'm not into all of the glamour and pressure, and being in the spotlight constantly. I'm an introvert. I just don't understand that lifestyle. And all the wealth makes me uncomfortable. Those celebrities have enough money to end all kinds of suffering, but they'd rather put it toward something ludicrous, like a collection of private jets, or handbags the price of a house."

"I never looked at it that way," Allison said. "I still think they're fascinating, though. Thanks for the cookie and the magazine."

Allison left, and Claire eyed the breakfast tray set up beside Lola.

"Are you hungry?" Claire asked.

No response.

"Okay. Here's what's on today's agenda. I'll help you eat breakfast, then we'll read some magazines. Then we'll watch some TV, and I'll go home. Does that sound good?"

No response.

A little twinge of hurt speared through Claire's heart. She tried her best to keep up a cheerful appearance in front of Lola, but sometimes the reality of her disease hit hard. Claire's memories of Lola pre-Alzheimer's were so vivid. She was a warrior spirit in the body of a tiny woman who once chased down a chicken thief with a huge bolo knife back in the Philippines. She was also a gentle soul who read stories of Filipino folklore to her grandchildren to share her heritage and keep it alive in their hearts. She was so full of life, Claire wondered how there was enough energy left over for the sun to light the skies.

It was beyond difficult seeing her reduced to this sick, frail shell, but Claire wouldn't give up. She imagined Lola trapped inside her body, watching everything happen all around her, helpless to interact with the world the way she used to. Claire always believed the real Lola was in there somewhere, and that she understood and appreciated everything Claire did for her.

Claire picked up a spoonful of oatmeal and held it up to Lola's lips. She took a tentative bite.

"Good job." She hated patronizing her, but she had to admit it worked sometimes. "Here—keep eating. It tastes so good. Oatmeal is your favorite." Claire smiled in excitement when

Lola took the spoon and slowly began to feed herself.

"Progress is progress," Claire whispered, happy to accept any victories having to do with Lola, no matter how small. She picked up one of the magazines. "I have some good ones for you today. Allison took the one with the half-naked hunks, but it's okay. Here's one with all the attendees of the MET gala. You'll love it."

An hour or so later, Claire was almost ready to go. She placed the magazine pile in a corner of the room beside the dresser. There was no use in rolling her now empty cart out of the facility. She folded it up and tucked it flat underneath her arm.

"I'm going now. I'll see you tomorrow, okay?"

"Nahanap mo?"

Claire dropped the cart. It struck the carpeted ground with a muffled crash. The shock of hearing her grandmother speak for the first time in weeks stole her own words for a brief spell.

"Oh my God. In English, Lola. English. I can't understand Tagalog."

Lola paused and leaned forward. After a painstaking minute, her lips finally found the straw, and she took a very slow sip of orange juice.

"Did you find it?" Lola asked finally.

"Find what?"

Instead of answering, Lola sat back in her armchair, settling into the comfortable cushions. She pointed toward the nightstand with her lips. Claire whipped herself around, scrutinizing it for anything unusual.

"What are you looking for?" she asked as she walked to the nightstand. She was so excited she thought she'd explode in a cloud of sparks.

"The key," Lola replied. "You open the box inside my closet."

"But...there's no box inside your closet." Claire opened the door and peered inside at her clothes all neatly lined up on hangers.

"Ay nako," Lola said with a sigh. "Look there."

Bewildered, Claire turned toward the nightstand again. Sure enough, there was a small rusted key on top that she hadn't noticed before. It was partially obscured by a white crocheted doily. Excitement ran through her as she picked up the key and scurried back to Lola.

"What is this for?" she asked.

"To open the box."

"What kind of box?"

"Treasure," Lola whispered. "It's a treasure chest."

Claire hesitated. At first, she was excited about her lola talking again, but if all her words were delusional, there'd be no use in hoping she'd get better.

"Why so sad?" Lola asked. "Stop frowning. You go find it now."

As Claire drove down the jacaranda-lined street to Lola's house, she slowed her car to scan the driveway. Good. None of her family had arrived yet. She wasn't sure why she didn't want her family to know about what Lola said today. Maybe she was scared of what they'd think. Or maybe she wanted it to be a secret between her and Lola, in the unlikely event there was some truth to her bizarre words. Claire still had some time to get to the bottom of this little mystery.

The family had plans to sell Lola's house to help pay for her rent at the assisted living facility. It was the end of an era, and her family was going to meet up there today to finish clearing out the rest of the house.

Sadness loomed over Claire again as she parked the car.

Memories of her and her sisters chasing each other up and down the porch steps, the decades of holiday parties, and the rich aroma of lumpia and pancit lived in her mind so vividly, as if it took place just yesterday. But it was all in the past. Time's powerful hand had changed everything, taking away her childhood and the grandmother she once knew.

Forcing away the sorrow, Claire got out of her car and zipped up the porch steps, then unlocked the door and shut it quietly behind her. The aroma of vanilla and lavender clung to the air—remnants of Lola's favorite candles her family still lit out of respect for her.

She headed into the hallway, her bare feet padding softly against the hardwood floor. Most of the home had been emptied already. Only a few pieces of furniture made it over to Lola's new apartment. The rest had either been sold or divvied up amongst the family members. Only the garage and storage shed needed to be cleared out now.

Stepping up to Lola's old closet in her empty room, Claire confirmed her suspicions—it was empty, too. She didn't know why she'd even bothered. She and her sisters had emptied this room themselves, sorting everything out into two piles: "stays with Lola" and "stays at home." Lola was probably hallucinating.

Unless…

Claire rushed toward the back of the house and quickly slipped her feet into an old pair of flip-flops. The garage was in a separate structure behind the house, faithful to the design of the old Craftsman-style homes in this area of Long Beach. Lola and Lolo (may he rest in peace) bought the house about forty years ago. Since then, the only home modification was adding a second story to the garage structure, turning it into a little studio apartment. It was the only other place Lola could have been referring to…and it was the only place that hadn't been emptied yet.

She rushed up the stairs on the side of the garage structure and opened the door to the apartment. Claire sighed at the huge piles of Lola's belongings still gathered there. This would certainly be a beast to sort out. She skirted around the stacks of sheet-draped furniture and opened the closet.

"Oh my God," she breathed. The closet was full. It was going to be nearly impossible sorting through all these boxes and clothes and—

"Oh my God!"

Her eyes landed on a small chest fashioned from a dark-stained wood. It was almost obscured by a pile of crocheted shawls. For some reason her eye went straight to it—as naturally as it would have been drawn to a beam of light in the darkness.

Claire leaped toward it, shoving a stack of plastic containers out of her way. It toppled to the ground like a crumbling tower. Could there be something in there that Lola wanted only her to see? Did she break free from the shackles of her illness for just a moment to give Claire a special message?

She placed the key into the lock and twisted it. The lock must have been broken, because the key fit loosely inside.

The day Lola had taken a sharp decline from Alzheimer's was the day a part of Claire's heart died. The woman who'd loved and guided her was not the same. She would never be the same. The possibility of disappointment was almost too much to bear. Could the contents of this chest give Claire some sense of reassurance?

Steadying her hands, she slowly opened the lid and saw...

Nothing.

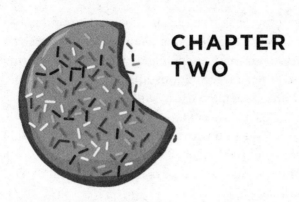

CHAPTER TWO

"Ate, are you up there?"

The sound of her younger sister's voice jarred Claire. She wasn't sure why the emptiness of the treasure chest devastated her so much. Lola had dementia, for goodness' sake. Was it realistic for her to expect something to come of her words? Lola could not even remember the date. Sometimes she didn't even recognize her own children. Running her palms over the chest's smooth surface, Claire traced her fingertips over the grooves, trying to get a grasp on her sadness so she could chuck it far, far away.

"Ate!"

Claire shut the lid and covered it with the shawls.

"I'm up here, but I'm coming down."

She put on a cheerful face and bounded out of the apartment like there was nothing wrong. As the second of three sisters, Claire found herself forced into the role of the peacemaker. The diplomat. The voice of reason and the calm in the storm while the two opposing forces, youngest sister Rochelle and eldest Samantha, rocked the boat whenever they saw fit to do so. Despite their differences, they loved one another fiercely. It was one of the things Lola had insisted upon. Family first.

The Lord only gave you each other, Lola would say. *That's why you should not quarrel.*

Ro was standing inside the back door to the main house with a plastic grocery bag dangling from her arm. Oversized square-framed sunglasses were perched on her nose, flattering the oval shape of her face. She looked absolutely chic in her loose, short, white Bohemian dress with puffy long sleeves.

"Nice dress, Ro," Claire said.

"Thanks, Ate," she said with a big smile. She stepped aside so Claire could enter the house. "It was on the clearance rack at Urban Outfitters. Seriously, it pays to be an XX-small. Did you see Lola already?"

"Yes. Why?"

Ro pouted in disappointment. "Aw," she drawled. "I went to the store and bought her a whole bunch of magazines. I even got her the *In-Touch* exclusive. The one with the hot guys at the beach? I paid extra for that special edition."

"You know how I feel about celebrities," Claire said.

"Yeah, and you are the only straight female in the whole world not affected by this smoke show. Did you see how sickeningly *hot* Nate Noruta looked on the cover? There should be a law prohibiting him from going anywhere wearing clothes. Not only is he hot, but he's rich as hell. There's an article in here about the latest vacation home he bought. It's this sprawling estate at Lake Como in Italy. It cost him twenty-two million dollars."

"Good for him."

Claire was used to Ro's larger-than-life personality. Ro was by far the most outgoing and charismatic Ventura sister. When they were kids, she always stole the spotlight and wanted to be the center of attention. Yes, she did hog the karaoke machine at every family party. And yes, she did strive to snag every lead role in their school's dance and theatre productions. Clearly the birth order theory won out with this one.

"Oh, it looks like everyone else is here, too." Claire headed toward the front door where there was a commotion on the porch.

"Ate, wait."

The abrupt change in Ro's tone stopped Claire in her tracks. "What?"

Ro pushed her sunglasses up over her forehead. Her brow furrowed a bit as she studied Claire.

"Are you okay? You seem…kind of sad."

She scoffed, conjuring a smile that she hoped didn't seem fake. Damn. Her little sister was good. Either she had magical powers of empathy, or she knew her ate far too well.

"No," she said, feigning cheerfulness. "Trust me. Everything's fine."

Claire turned brusquely away from Ro's dubious eyes. Fortunately, the entrance of the family put the impending interrogation to an end. They came streaming into the home in the familiar hustle and bustle that filled her heart with comfort. Claire's mother, Irene, and three of her sisters came in carrying plastic bags full of food. They headed toward the kitchen in a flurry of Tagalog chatter. The two youngest cousins ran into the living room, excited to play in an open space unimpeded by furniture.

Claire and Ro greeted each of the aunties with a polite kiss on the cheek. They tried to kiss their youngest cousins, but they darted out of the way, far more concerned with their game of tag than the business of properly greeting adults.

"Your Tita Chriss is here, too," Mom said, her lips stretched into a tenuous smile.

Claire's heart dipped in dread. She loved the woman about as much as a niece was obligated to love her aunt. Tita Chriss had always considered herself the unspoken matriarch of the family, even when Lola's mind had been intact. The reasons? Because one, she was the eldest. And two, most importantly, she was rich. Tita Chriss was self-made, investing in real estate and making risky financial moves that proved to be very lucrative. Along with the wealth came a sense of entitlement—her unspoken designation as head of the family, and that everyone was subject to her rules, judgments, and expectations.

"Really?" Claire asked. "I thought she was in Italy."

"I know. It surprised me too," Mom replied. "She ended up coming back early."

Tita Chriss made an entrance and whipped her sunglasses off. The whole atmosphere seemed to shift as she surveyed the room, and her younger sisters immediately approached to greet her. Even though Tita Chriss was rich, she dressed modestly and even drove a sensible car. Chrissandra Ilagan Santos showed the world her wealth through her extravagant handbags and homes.

That was one of the many places where Claire and her aunt differed. Claire had never been into fancy accessories. The most expensive purse she owned was a black leather Coach bag she received as a high school graduation gift twelve years ago. She bit her lip as Ro strode up to Tita Chriss and fawned over her new designer shoulder bag.

She squashed her nervousness and approached Tita Chriss just as her older sister Sam walked in. Claire's chest tightened at the hard look in Sam's eyes. Something was off, but now was not the time to address it. Claire kissed her aunt and knew she was obligated to make pleasantries, even though she would rather be doing anything else.

"How was Italy?" she asked with a smile.

"Oh, same old, same old," Chriss replied with a dismissive wave of her hand. "I was getting a little tired of my house in Positano. I think I'm going to sell it for something bigger and higher up on the cliff. But it was nice and relaxing. A good change of pace after working like a dog for all these months without a break. And what about you? Have you found another job yet?"

Claire's jaw tightened. Her fight-or-flight senses tingled, but the obedient niece in her stayed glued to the spot.

"No, I'm not looking for another job," she replied lightly. "I already have a job."

Tita Chriss scrunched up her nose. "You still work at that little bookstore?" she asked incredulously. "But you graduated with an English degree. Shouldn't you be doing something better, like teaching? Or maybe you should try to get into nursing school. I'd be happy to help. I've already put so many of your cousins through nursing school. I can do it for you, too."

And there she was, coming in red-hot. Tita Chriss always targeted Claire and made her the focus of her haughty disappointment. For some reason she never really bothered Ro, even though Ro didn't have one of the "pre-approved" professions in Tita Chriss's mind. Maybe it was because Ro refused to take any of her shit and wasn't intimidated by her. But Claire couldn't help being intimidated by the woman. And perhaps that was why she was always the target.

"Thank you, but I'm fine for now." She shifted uncomfortably as two of her aunts turned their attention to the conversation. "I'm a senior seller at the Book Nook. It's one of the most famous indie bookstores in Northern America."

"No offense, but that's a high school job," Chriss said. "I can't believe you poured so much money into a college degree and you ended up doing absolutely nothing with it. You should take life a lot more seriously. Like me. I'm a strong, intelligent, independent woman. I utilized my talents and resources to the max, and now I'm a millionaire. If you worked hard, you could be like me. Lola and Lolo didn't come all the way to America to see their future generations waste their time. Lola would be very disappointed in you."

For a moment, Claire could do nothing but gape. It was like getting her heart and words ripped out through her chest. Tita Chriss had always been hard on her, but today she went too far. If Claire had the courage, she would have told her aunt she didn't give a shit about her money, and that she'd rather be poor than get her kicks out of harassing others. But she wasn't brave enough. The fire in her sputtered and the words lodged deep in her throat.

"Tita Chriss, that's not fair," Ro said. "You're not giving Claire enough credit. You don't know it yet, but she's thinking of starting her own cookie decorating business. She's really talented, and she's drawn a lot of interest online already. Right, Ate?"

Heat flared up Claire's neck and into her cheeks. Ro was trying to be helpful, but Claire knew this information would do nothing but trigger Tita Chriss.

"Cookies?" Tita Chriss giggled, and the sound of it tied Claire's stomach in a knot. "You can't be serious."

"I'm...kind of considering it," Claire mumbled.

"Ate Chriss! The food is ready," her mother called.

Claire almost collapsed with relief. Her mother would never outright disagree with Tita Chriss, but she still had the sense to swoop in and save her daughter when she needed help.

"We'll talk more about it after lunch." Tita Chriss pasted on a grin and swept into the kitchen to dig into the Chinese takeout laid out across the pale blue-tiled counter.

While the rest of the family converged on the food as well, Claire hung back. Tita Chriss's words stung so badly, Claire would be surprised if she woke up the next morning without scars somewhere. And the last thing she'd said hurt the most: *Lola would be very disappointed in you.* How could Tita Chriss say something so cruel and careless?

Something came over Claire, and she found herself backing away from the kitchen. She didn't know if it was shame or fear, or some combination of both. But after all that had happened today, the last thing she wanted to do was wait for more berating from her disapproving aunt.

Without a word, she turned and left through the front door.

· · ·

Claire needed to clear her mind. First, the harsh reality check of her grandmother's illness, and then Tita Chriss—it was too much for her to handle.

She turned on her signal as she waited for crossing traffic to pass. It was summer in Southern California. The temps were high, and the sun blazed bright enough to beckon throngs of people to the beach. She loved the excitement and liveliness of this season, but she couldn't enjoy it after everything that had happened.

Suddenly Claire's phone rang with Ro's familiar tone.

Claire considered ignoring it, but she knew her sister. Ro was not the type to be ignored.

"Hello?"

"Ate, where did you go?" Ro demanded. "We were supposed to help clear out the garage together."

"I'm sorry. I can't right now. You heard what Tita Chriss said. Would you want to stay around all that negative energy after she unleashed it on you?"

There was a pause and the sound of a closing door.

"Sorry, I had to sneak out through the back," Ro explained. "I know! What the hell was her problem? It pisses me off that Mom and the other aunties don't speak up whenever she acts out."

"It's not their fault. She's the eldest sister, and she's practically bankrolled our whole family. Nobody can speak against her without sounding ungrateful."

"I guess that's true."

Claire drove out of the neighborhood and made another right. She really had no direction in mind. She was just driving to clear her head.

"Actually, I wanted to ask you something," Claire said. "Did you notice something off about Sam today?"

Ro didn't answer.

"Do you know what's wrong with her? Did you talk to her?"

Silence again.

"Hello? Why aren't you answering me?"

"Because I'm eating lunch," Ro said innocently.

The tone in her voice sparked Claire's suspicion.

"Ro..." she said in her big sister voice. "What did you do?"

"I didn't do anything bad on purpose," Ro whispered urgently. "I— It's a long story, but basically, I *might* have hooked up with a guy she liked."

Claire gasped and almost ran through a red light. The car lurched against its squealing tires.

"Tell me you're joking."

Shameful silence once again.

"How did this happen?" she demanded. "How could you do this? She only got divorced six months ago, and you sweep in and take away her new guy?"

"That is not how it happened at all!" Ro retorted. "Ate Sam was the one who introduced us. He's some kind of financial guy at her company. I went on a blind date with him, and I told her that he wasn't my type. But then I ran into him again at a club, one thing led to another, and we hooked up. It was just a one-time thing. But from the way Ate's been acting, it seems like she has a thing for him. If that's the case, why the hell would she introduce us?"

An incoming call interrupted the conversation.

Sam.

"Wait, is that Ate Sam?" Ro squeaked. "Please don't hang up on me. All she's going to do is talk shit. You know how she is."

"Ro, you're being disrespectful." Claire sighed, exasperated. "And you know I have to hear both sides of the story. I'll call you back. And aren't you two at the same house?"

"Yes, but she's inside and I'm in the backyard. Wait—"

She took a quick, calming breath before she switched over to Sam.

"Hi, Ate."

"Did you talk to Ro yet?" Sam asked.

Claire's stomach clenched again. She usually had no problem getting along with her sisters. It was easy because she was a people-pleaser. A yes-woman. She might have described herself as a pushover in secret. But whenever her sisters got into fights, she found herself caught between them, so it was up to her, and her alone, to re-stabilize the pillars of peace holding them up.

"Yes," Claire said.

"What did she tell you?"

"She said she had a lapse in judgment," Claire replied carefully. "There was a misunderstanding, and she feels terrible about hurting your feelings."

"Ro is out of control," Sam whispered harshly. "She's twenty-eight going on twelve. She's made my working environment very difficult due to her immature shenanigans."

"Is it true you set her up with a guy you have feelings for?"

"I didn't..." Sam released a loud sigh. "It's complicated."

"You would really let a man drive a wedge between you two?"

"It's not just about some guy," Sam said. "This is about Ro's complete disregard for other peoples' feelings. She's like a one-woman wrecking crew. Everything she touches turns to rubble."

"Listen, Ate," she replied. "I'm not sure what transpired between you two, but you can't let a guy ruin your relationship. Our family takes precedence. Remember what Lola always told us? She—"

"Oh, give it a rest," Sam interrupted. "I appreciate you, but stop with the 'Lola this' and 'Lola that' stuff. You can't keep hearkening back to advice from someone who has lost their wits."

Those words stunned Claire like a taser shock. Sam kept going on and on about Ro, but Claire couldn't hear past the pain. She couldn't understand why this day had taken an awful turn and flipped her once secure, cozy world upside down. One side of her brain told her to be the good sister—to hear out Sam's side of the story and validate her words. But the strange, new side of her—a broken, hopeless girl—made her do something she usually lacked the nerve to do.

She hung up on her big sister.

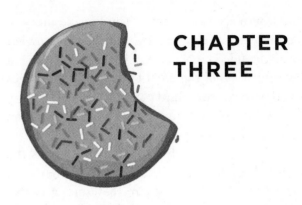

CHAPTER THREE

Claire didn't do sadness. When she felt it creeping up on her, she coped with it the only way she knew how.

She ran.

It was the reason her sisters freaked out. They called and texted her numerous times, asking if she was okay, and if she would come back—*we need you Claire!*—but she knew her limits. The empty treasure chest, Tita Chriss's insults, and Sam's disregard for Lola pushed her over the edge. She needed to distance herself.

Claire kept on driving. She parked briefly to put an end to the deluge of texts by sending off a curt message—*I'm fine. Just needed some space*—which seemed to infuse a sense of temporary calm into her sisters.

She wished Ro hadn't brought up her fledgling cookie business. *Claire's Enchanted Confections.* It was new and sacred, meant to be fostered away from the prying attentions of her family, but her younger sibling couldn't keep her big mouth shut. Claire figured she couldn't be *too* angry, though. Ro had only meant to defend her. She might be the tiniest Ventura sister, but she more than made up for it with her no-bullshit, tough-as-nails attitude. It was one of the reasons Claire loved her to pieces. Ro wasn't afraid to stick up for her, even when it came to Tita Chriss.

Claire turned onto Ocean Avenue. The blue serenity of the Pacific failed to ease its way into the tension gripping her body like it normally did. The beach was her usual haven, but not on a Friday afternoon at the end of June with the shores absolutely packed with people. Hard pass.

She drove past the glimmering round structure of the massive convention center and made a right on Palmetto Boulevard. Her fried nerves started to simmer down as the familiar sights of the neighborhood greeted her. There on her left was The Old Pancake House, where they served twelve different flavors of homemade syrup (her favorite was maple pecan). Across the street she spied the row of charming businesses including a Pilates studio, vintage clothing store, and an art studio where you could do everything from learning to sculpt to constructing miniature furniture.

In two blocks, she would reach the Book Nook, where she had worked for the past three years. Tita Chriss's words came rushing back like a punch to the gut. Claire wanted to believe her aunt's advice was coming from a place of love, no matter how twisted it seemed. Being a bookseller wasn't on anyone's dream list of high-powered, high-income careers, but it didn't matter to Claire. She didn't make a ton of money, but the job made her happy, and it helped support her side gig.

She braced herself for the construction traffic in this area. It had been this way for the past month or so, causing the narrowing of the street to one lane. But to her surprise, there wasn't a bulldozer or orange cone in sight. Claire let out a sigh of relief, grateful they were done. However, she was still annoyed at whatever antiseptic, commercialized business they'd built that would no doubt ruin the unique small-town beach vibe of her neighborhood. She slowed down to check out the new monstrosity...and ended up at a full stop in the middle of the street.

What in the world is this?

A gorgeous storefront of pale granite and modern brushed chrome accents met her eyes instead of the austere, gray concrete she was expecting. The red-lettered sign across the top said FEAST AND FESTIVAL. And there was no mistaking the decadent smell of grilled meats, garlic, and sesame oil wafting through the air.

Someone behind her honked. Claire lurched forward to park in an empty spot set at an angle on the main street, right beside a big truck. For some unknown reason this place gave her a sense of hope. Maybe it was a sign of good things to come. Once she got a chance to peruse the menu and fill her belly with the foods exuding those delicious smells, she'd feel a lot better. It was time to get rid of negative energy and refuel.

When she rounded the back of the truck and headed into the parking spot, she didn't see the man standing there until it was too late. She screamed at the top of her lungs and slammed on the brakes. The man leaped out of the way, landing hard on the sidewalk.

"Oh my goodness, are you all right?" Claire said as she stumbled out of her car and ran over to the man. She picked up his cell phone and baseball cap, which were lying a few feet away from him. "I'm so sorry. I feel like such an idiot. Are you in any pain? Do you think something's broken? Here, let me dust this off for you. It's got a little dirt on it, but I think it's fine. But your phone—goodness gracious, there's a crack in it. Was this crack there before I hit you? Actually, it doesn't matter. I'll pay for it anyway. You've got a scrape on your elbow. Why are you rubbing your leg? Maybe you should take off your pants so we can see if you're injured. Are you comfortable removing your clothes? Because if not, I can drive you to the ER. It's only a mile away. If you're worried about waiting too long, my cousin is the charge nurse there and he can probably get us to the front of the line."

The man stood up and dusted himself off. He hadn't lost his

sunglasses, but they sat a little askew. Claire handed the baseball cap to him. He stuck it back on his head and straightened his sunglasses. Although the shades partially obscured his features, a jolt of recognition made Claire quirk her head.

"Thanks for the offer, but I think I'll be fine," the stranger replied. A short, full beard covered the sculpted angles of his jaw. Claire suddenly noticed he was grinning at her. Not grinning, exactly, but he had an amused expression on his face. She wished his glasses had fallen off so she could see his eyes.

"I'm, uh...I'm willing to pay for the damages to your phone and any injuries you might have." She reached into her purse and pulled out her crumpled checkbook and a pen. There was little money to her name, but she felt so bad she was willing to give up a lot to help the man she very nearly killed.

Then she paused as her skin started to tingle. The stranger was studying her. Carefully. It was as if he was trying to deconstruct her, layer by layer. If he didn't stop looking at her like that, she would either move a step closer, or drop everything and run like hell.

And then the truth hit. He was standing there because he wanted to exchange information so he could finally get away from the girl who not only almost killed him, but also didn't know how to shut up.

Claire cleared her throat and wrote the date on the check. Her hands were shaking. The stranger's lingering stare was not helping the situation at all.

"Um...I don't... Why don't I just give this to you?" She tore the check from the book and held it out. It was an epically bad idea to give a blank check with all her personal information on it to a complete stranger, but she did it anyway. Her pulse picked up when he hesitated for a second. But then he reached out and took the check without a word.

"Okay," Claire said, taking a step back. "Well, if you're fine, I'll be on my way. Bye."

She gave him an abrupt, painfully awkward wave before she spun around and scurried into the restaurant without a backward glance.

It took a while for Claire's heart to slow down to a normal speed. Her encounter with the bearded stranger left her shaken. She was equal parts horrified and humiliated. Thinking back to the things she'd said made her cringe. *Maybe you should take off your pants to see if you're injured.* She suddenly had the urge to crawl under a rock and stay there the rest of the summer.

Her appetite was officially ruined. But she was already here, so she might as well give it a try.

After the host seated her, she perused the menu. The price points were pretty damn high. She settled on a glass of tap water and the most basic dish: pad thai. This place should have been called *Feast or Famine* instead.

After the server took Claire's order, her thoughts went straight to Beard Man again. Why couldn't she stop thinking about him? Was it his magnetic presence? Maybe if she had taken a moment to think, she would have come to her senses and gotten his information so she could call him and make sure he was really doing all right. Yes. She'd messed up big time.

Her shame factor flew off the charts. Claire didn't know if she had the courage to face him again. It was best they went their separate ways.

She gazed around the restaurant. It was nearly empty when she first came in, but now more people were being seated. She was surprised at how many, actually. Did they all know how expensive this place was? The owners really should have considered adding a lunch special to the menu. This was probably going to be the last time she ever ate here—

"Holy shit," Claire said under her breath.

She blinked several times in disbelief. Beard Man was back, and he was *here*. Inside the restaurant. She zeroed in on him from a distance, observing as he took off his glasses and exchanged pleasantries with the host. Her heart went into a full-on gallop as the host led him inside…and she thought she would die when he sat at the bar, with nothing but ten feet of floor space separating them.

She abruptly turned her head away, hoping he wouldn't see her. What the hell was he doing here? She'd assumed he was leaving because he was in the parking lot earlier. Why did he have to come back?

Claire took a deep breath that did nothing to slow the frantic pace of her heart. As nonchalantly as possible, she pivoted in her seat, keeping her head straight while trying to spy him to her left. He was perched on a stool, chatting with the bartender and another employee. His back was toward her, and he gave no inkling that he noticed her.

Heaving a quiet sigh of relief, she turned away and relaxed her tense shoulders. She could still make a clean getaway.

The server arrived and set a steaming plate of shrimp pad thai in front of Claire. The aroma of the fresh ingredients made her stomach growl, but there was no way she was going to eat here now. Not with Beard Man sitting only a few feet away.

"Excuse me," she whispered, catching the server's attention just as he was leaving. "Can I get the check please? And a to-go box."

"Oh, was this supposed to be a takeout order?" he asked.

She cringed and shushed him. He stared at her, taken aback.

"I'm so sorry," she whispered. "But could you keep your voice down a little?"

"Why?" he asked, at the same volume.

"Because— I— Well, it'll take too long to explain. I need the check and a to-go box please. As quickly as possible."

"All right." The server left, but not before giving her a look like she was someone who shouldn't be mingling with society.

Claire threw another glance at Beard Man to confirm he still hadn't noticed her, and she turned away again. She put her hand up to shield her face, just for good measure.

The seconds ticked by. One minute turned into two. One second past two minutes and Claire was ready to crawl out of her skin. Beard Man was still there, and it was just a matter of time before he spotted her. She scanned the restaurant, but her server was nowhere to be seen.

Suddenly Beard Man turned in his seat. Claire gasped and turned away, putting her hand back up to cover the side of her face.

Her heart thundered in her chest. Her foot jiggled nervously as if it had a mind of its own. Thank God the man didn't appear in front of her. Instead, she heard the footsteps of the server approaching.

"Oh my God, thank you so much. I've gotta go, so please keep the change."

"Where are you going?" a new voice said.

Claire physically jumped in her seat when she saw Beard Man standing right there, gazing down at her with the same amused expression that made her feel like spontaneously combusting on the spot.

CHAPTER FOUR

Chatty Claire had left the building. In her place sat a stunned woman who had trouble stringing two words together.

"I—I thought—um, nowhere," she stuttered.

Beard Man smiled. Up close and without sunglasses, she finally got a good look at his face...and it was even better than she remembered. He was certainly of Asian descent, but the green and gold flecks of his hypnotizing hazel eyes hinted at mixed ancestry. If she had to guess, she would think he was Japanese or Korean. But did it matter when his entire being exuded pure hotness? Good Lord, this man was beyond beautiful. She swayed in her seat and gripped the edge of the table, barely managing to grapple her ferocious attraction into a chokehold.

"I'm sorry. I should really introduce myself." He offered his hand. "I'm Nate."

She stared at his hand for a second. *What the hell is your problem, Claire? You've lost the ability to think clearly just because the man standing in front of you is quite possibly the hottest man you've ever seen? Get it together!*

"Hi," she replied, finally shaking his hand. "I'm Claire."

"Do you mind if I join you?"

"I'm sorry, what was that?"

"I said, do you mind if I join you?" Nate repeated.

"Yes, of course— I mean, no! What I mean to say is, I don't mind if you join me. And yes, please do."

Nate took a seat across from her. Claire noticed the dirt smudges on his baseball cap and his shirt, and a wave of humiliation hit all over again. He reached into his pocket and pulled out the folded-up personal check she had given him.

"Oh," she said as he set it on the table. "That's for you. You don't have to give it back."

"It's fine," Nate replied, his hot-as-sin smile still burning a path of destruction through her. "I don't need it. I'm pretty sure you weren't trying to hurt me on purpose. The way I see it, it was my fault. I shouldn't have been standing in the parking spot next to such a large vehicle. Not a smart move."

The server made his return, to-go container and check in hand. Claire tried to withhold her look of disapproval. *So much for "as soon as possible."*

"Thanks," Nate said, taking the container. "I'll take care of it."

The server nodded, tucking the check under his arm and high-tailing it out of there before she could get a word in.

"Wait, where is he going?" she said. "I still have to pay the check."

"Don't worry about it."

Claire froze. "I don't understand what happened just now."

"Why didn't you come over and say hello?" Nate asked instead of explaining.

She hesitated, not knowing how to answer at first. Something about him had her thoughts scattering like a house of cards caught in a tornado.

"I don't know," she said. "I guess it's because I'm still embarrassed. It's hard to face you knowing what I did."

She paused once again, waiting for Nate to respond. He searched her face. There was candor in his eyes—a breath-stealing openness of expression. If she were an expert on the human condition, she would have described his expression as one of discovery, or of wonder. But why? For all intents and purposes, she was the reckless woman whose parking skills were literally lethal.

"Here. I have something for you." she said. She opened her purse, rummaging through it until she found the little cellophane-wrapped cookie and held it out to him. She had been looking forward to eating the tiny cookie replica of the Eiffel Tower herself, but she would rather it go to someone way more deserving than her.

"For me?" he asked, hesitantly reaching for it. "This is beautiful. Where'd you get it?"

"I made it."

Nate's lips quirked up in a smile again. "Seriously?"

"Yes, seriously."

Nate stayed silent for a spell, his fingers playing gently over the edges of the cookie as he stealthily observed her.

"Okay," he said. "I'll keep the cookie, but you can take your blank check back. There is only one way to make everything even between us."

"Really? How?"

"Stay here. Have lunch with me."

"What?" Her heart stuttered on its next beat. "Oh no, I couldn't impose," she said.

"It's not an imposition." His hazel eyes held her gaze, and she felt the floor slip from beneath her. "I'm the owner of this restaurant. I'd love to treat you."

She blinked in surprise. He was the *owner*?

Claire struggled to focus. Nate had the strange ability to incite emotions on the opposite ends of the spectrum within the span of a few seconds. She went from humiliated to intrigued to…some emotion perched between pleasure and excitement. She was not familiar in the least with what was happening, but for some strange reason she wanted nothing more than to get swept away by it.

"Okay," she said.

He spooned a big helping of the pad thai onto an extra plate and slid it across to Claire. She picked up her fork and twirled the noodles around it, but there was no way in hell she could eat. Not when Nate was having that polarizing effect on her. For example, right now she was veering from excitement to awkwardness. How could he be so at ease while she stewed in discomfort?

She suddenly felt very self-conscious. Was she dressed too casually? Showing too much skin? She never gave any thought to the shorts and tank tops she wore every day during the summer season.

Flicking her eyes up, she caught Nate glancing at her. Well. If he was going to look at her, she'd do the same to him. Her gaze strayed to his forearms: tanned and corded with lean muscle. And his hands—they looked strong, but deft and graceful at the same time. She imagined they were the kind of hands that could build a house during the day, then give a woman all kinds of pleasure during the night.

Claire blinked rapidly, surprised at her wayward thoughts.

"Do you live nearby?" Nate asked. "I'm not really familiar with Long Beach."

She cleared her throat. "Yes, I do. My apartment's only a couple miles from here. I actually work at the Book Nook. It's one of the biggest indie bookstores in California. We host a ton of author events and book clubs." She smiled. "I love Long Beach, and I love my neighborhood. It's such a wonderful community to be a part of."

"So, you like to read," he said. "Do you belong to any book clubs?"

"I used to belong to a lot of book clubs," she replied. "But it got too overwhelming. Now I only belong to one: The Dashing

Duke Diehards, or the Triple Ds. It's for fans of Regency romance. When I first joined, I thought I wouldn't really fit in because I was the youngest member. Boy was I wrong. We have so much fun."

She paused as the heat of embarrassment stole up her face. "I'm so sorry. I tend to ramble. It's something I'm working on with not much success, I'm afraid."

"Don't be sorry," he said. "It's one of the many things I find very...charming about you."

One of the many *things?*

Claire suppressed a look of disbelief. When was the last time someone showed this kind of interest in her? Her last serious boyfriend was way back in college. They'd dated for only two years. Since then, she'd dated a few guys here and there, but was never really interested in what they had to offer. She always found other aspects of life—reading, working, family, hobbies—much more worth her time.

Until now.

"I think you've learned more about me than you wanted to," Claire said with a chuckle. "Let's talk about you now."

"What would you like to know?"

"Anything. Your family, your job—anything important to you."

"I live in L.A.," Nate said. "I grew up in the Pacific Northwest, then moved down here for college. I liked it so much I decided to stay. I hated the rain and gloom up north. In terms of my job—I'm an entrepreneur. I dabble in different tech industries. Hobbies? I guess the only things I really have time for are swimming and working out. Aside from that, I'm working all the time."

"And what about your family?"

Nate paused for a second, then said, "What about my family?"

"Family is important," Claire said. "I belong to the typical extended Filipino-American family. I'm the second of three girls. My mom and dad immigrated here thirty years ago. I have a boatload of aunts and uncles on both sides of the family, and even more cousins. I kid you not—there are about fifty cousins in my family from both sides. We had a blast growing up."

Nate stayed silent, his face unreadable. A sense of regret crept up on Claire. It seemed as though his family was a touchy subject, and she wished she could take back her question.

"The details of my family aren't all that interesting," he finally said. "Have you ever heard of the app called *Break the Ice?*"

"Yes," she answered. "My sister Sam told me about it. It's an app that randomly generates thought-provoking questions, right?"

"That's right. Let's try one." He took out his phone. She cringed when she saw the cracked screen, but she maintained her composure.

"If you had the opportunity to take an impromptu vacation anywhere in the world, where would it be?" he said.

Claire pondered in silence as Nate gave her a thoughtful gaze.

"Um…I'm not sure," she said. "Why don't you answer first?"

"This one's easy for me. Cappadocia in Turkey. I love ancient monuments and cities. Everyone who goes there sees old skeletons built thousands of years ago, but I see the innovation and human life in every brick and pillar of those places. It's so inspiring."

A warm sensation filtered across her. She didn't know exactly what she'd been expecting him to say, but it certainly wasn't something deep and profound.

"That's incredible," she said. "Now I feel embarrassed to admit where I wanted to go. It sounds so petty now."

"I'm sure it's not," he insisted. "Tell me."

"Well…it's always been my dream to go to Paris. It's cliché, but I don't care." She shrugged. "There's romance and magic everywhere. I imagine it's the kind of place I can go to escape the stress of everyday life. I want to get caught up in every beautiful thing, even for just a moment. There was a scene in one of my favorite rom-coms—it took place in Paris. The son of a French duke fell in love with an artist, but they weren't allowed to be together because they were in different social strata. The man didn't care, and he and the artist ran away together to Paris. He surprised her with a beautiful gown and a rooftop dinner. They gazed at the romantic city lights, with their hands held tight because they didn't know if they'd ever see each other again after that night."

Nate's gaze was unreadable. Claire held his stare, wondering what was on his mind. The man had just said he described her rambling as "charming." After her discourse on one of her deepest fantasies, she wouldn't be surprised if he changed his mind and asked to be excused.

"What are you doing tomorrow night?" he asked.

"Tomorrow night?" Claire repeated in surprise. "I'm closing at the bookstore."

"What time do you get out?"

"Seven."

"Let me pick you up after work."

Claire thought she was hallucinating. "I'm sorry. What did you say?"

Nate smiled. "I'm asking you out on a date," he clarified.

There must have been some kind of strange, summer magic at work in the air. Or maybe Nate had hit his head on the pavement harder than she thought.

"Okay," Claire said. "Where are we going?"

"You already mentioned it. I'm taking you to Paris."

Her smile faded. "Paris?"

"Yes."

She let out a nervous laugh. "What are you talking about?"

she asked, her disappointment thinly veiled. "Are you joking?"

"No."

Claire blinked. He couldn't possibly be serious. "I don't get it," she said.

A commotion of giggles and screams erupted in the restaurant. Two young women who looked young enough to be teenagers excitedly approached her table.

"Oh my God, can we get a selfie?" the shorter blonde one asked, her voice so high it sounded like a squeal. Claire stared in shock at her outfit: a pair of extremely short shorts and a tiny bikini top that strained precariously against her large breasts with every excited hop. Her companion, a taller blonde girl in a slip of a dress designed to expose at least 95 percent of her body, eagerly thrust her phone out to Claire.

"Can you take a picture of us?" she asked.

Perplexed, Claire took the phone and snapped several photos of the two blondes and Nate. She was a good sport and took a few in both portrait and landscape mode. Flash and no flash. The two girls looked like they were about to die of happiness, and Nate…he wasn't scowling, but she could tell in his eyes he wasn't nearly as joyful about the experience as they were.

Claire sat back down as the girls gushed over him and interrogated him on his life.

"Ladies, thank you for stopping by, but I was having a private moment with this young woman," he explained in a deep, soothing voice. "It was so nice to meet you, though. I appreciate your kind words."

The girls swooned and practically fell over themselves, complimenting Nate and saying they loved him as the host escorted them out of the restaurant.

"Sorry, Mr. Noruta," the host said. "They got past me. It won't happen again."

Claire's eyes went wide as all the clues came together.

Nate fucking Noruta. Her enigmatic lunch date was none other than the thirtysomething tech mogul billionaire CEO and founder of *MyConnect*, one of the most widely used social media platforms in the world. He also owned Trance Media, a mega-corporation that developed and owned wildly popular social media and gaming apps. The extent of her knowledge of him only went as far as the tabloid articles she read to Lola. She was painfully aware that the sales app she used to sell her cookies, *Eclectix*, was developed and maintained by Nate's company.

"Oh my God," she groaned. "*You're* Nate Noruta? I should have recognized you. The beard threw me off. I saw you on the cover of *In-Touch* magazine. The one with Hollywood's hottest hunks at the beach. There was a picture of you wearing teal board shorts. My sister even mentioned you today."

"What did she say about me?"

"She said—" Claire caught herself just in time. There was no way she was going to tell Nate about Ro saying he was so hot there should be a law against him wearing any clothes. Instead she cleared her throat and composed herself.

"Nothing," she replied, not bothering to suppress a cringe. "And I really wish you could have said something earlier. I feel like such a fool. Ugh. I gave you a blank check."

Nate's phone started buzzing.

"I'm sorry, but I have to take this." He turned to the side and spoke discreetly into the phone.

While Nate was distracted, Claire turned her attention toward another commotion going on near the front of the restaurant. A group of excited people congregated by the entrance. They appeared to be led by the blonde duo, and all eyes were turned excitedly on Nate. It didn't take long for Nate to notice what was going on. Once he did, he calmly ended the call.

"I have to get going," he said. "I'm sorry to cut out so soon, but things are escalating out there. We're still on for tomorrow, right?"

She stared at him, emotions churning like a ball of rocks in her stomach. Today's events were so out of her sphere of experience. Her M.O. consisted of three things: calm, quiet, and serenity. The idea of attracting crowds made her shudder. If this was just a small taste of Nate's life, she wasn't sure she could handle it.

Would it be like this in Paris, too?

"I'm not really sure," she replied. "I'll have to think about it."

Nate started to head down the hallway toward the back exit. He didn't respond to her uncertain answer. Instead, he flashed her a mischievous grin that gave her the impression he wasn't going to give up easily. Then he winked at her and darted outside.

What the hell had just happened?

CHAPTER FIVE

Claire lay in bed that night, replaying the events of the day over and over again. She almost convinced herself that her encounter with Nate wasn't real—it was just a figment of her over-active, romance book-riddled imagination. The container of leftover takeout from *Feast and Festival,* however, proved otherwise.

She shared a two-bedroom apartment with her younger sister. When Ro finally came home that evening, Claire debated whether or not to tell her about Nate, especially when she flipped out over the amazing pad thai. Even though it was hard, she kept her mouth shut. For some silly reason, she believed divulging the encounter with Nate would somehow break the spell and make him disappear forever.

Claire didn't want him to disappear. Part of her wanted to see Nate again to confirm it wasn't all a dream. She couldn't deny he was sweet and fascinating. But on the flip side, she wasn't sure about getting involved with a super-famous man who had throngs of people thirsting over him. She didn't even like celebrities. And what kind of person offers to take a total stranger on a first date to Europe?

And he was a B-word. *Billionaire.* They were from two totally different worlds. She wasn't sure his lifestyle and hers were compatible. Crossing paths with him at all was a total fluke.

Or maybe this could be the fairy-tale romance she always dreamed of. Granted, Nate wasn't an English duke, and she was light-years away from being a ball-gowned socialite shattering hearts throughout the *ton*, but it was still the stuff fantasies were made of.

The next morning during her daily visit to Lola, Claire had trouble concentrating. She kept flipping to the magazine articles featuring Nate.

Nate exiting the grocery store.

Nate smiling as the lecturer of a TED talk.

Nate at some black-tie event...with a gorgeous woman on his arm.

Claire frowned. She flipped the page harder than she'd meant to, and it tore. None of this made sense. What made Nate so attracted to Claire that he would fly her halfway around the world? She wasn't a tall, blue-eyed, statuesque beauty like the woman in the photo. She was a short girl who sported a messy top knot and loved to browse discount stores and thrift shops. She drank chamomile tea out of chipped ceramic mugs, not Cristal out of diamond-encrusted flutes.

The thought of Nate's other women halted Claire in her tracks. She was never the type to be jealous or self-conscious. If the thought of Nate made her question her own self-worth, maybe he wasn't right for her anyway.

Nope. He was no good for her. He probably thought she was an easy lay, or something. But even as the thought crossed her mind, she knew it wasn't true.

Why, why, why would he be interested in me?

The question burned through her head all day long. Even when she started her shift at the Book Nook, she kept thinking about Nate. Even though he confused the hell out of her, she had to admit it was nice to be preoccupied with something other than Lola's advancing illness and the fight between her sisters.

Claire finished ringing up a customer and glanced at the clock. Five till seven. She surreptitiously glanced at her phone. No texts or missed calls.

"Something's been bugging you."

Claire shoved her phone back into her pocket. Todd, the handsome young man she considered her work spouse, gazed at her with a suspicious look in his dark brown eyes.

"What gives you that impression?"

"You've been checking your phone all day, risking the wrath of manager Margie catching you violating her workplace policy. You've also been staring off into outer space more times than I can count. Lastly, you've been quiet all day. And if Claire Ventura ain't talking, something is *wrong*."

Claire bit her lip. If there was anyone in the world who could see through her besides her sisters, it was Todd. Plus, the temptation to spill the beans about Nate was killing her.

"Where's Margie?" Claire whispered.

"She's in the back room, taking a break," Todd replied.

Claire made sure there was a cashier at the front, then she pulled Todd over to the corner of the nonfiction shelves.

"Something really weird happened to me yesterday, but I didn't say anything because it's kind of a secret."

"What happened?" Todd demanded, his eyes wide.

"I met someone famous." Claire braced herself for Todd's reaction. "His name is Nate Noruta."

Todd's face lit up.

"Nate Noruta?" he gasped. "I adore him. He's the hottest philanthropist I've ever seen. Where did you meet him?"

"At this new restaurant down the block. Feast and Festival. He owns it."

Todd's full lips stretched into a perfect "O" of astonishment.

"Oh. My. God. Nate Noruta was *here?* On our street? Girl,

I can't believe you were holding out on me. Take me over there! Maybe we can catch another glimpse."

"Actually, there is a possibility you'll get more than a glimpse." Claire's stomach lurched at the thought of seeing Nate again. "He might be showing up here at the bookstore. After my shift."

Todd frowned. "Are you pulling my leg? It's not nice to build up my hopes and then dash them to the ground."

"I'm telling you the truth," Claire whispered harshly. "It's kind of a long story, but I ran into him at the restaurant and... one thing led to another and he asked me out. He said he would pick me up today after my shift."

Todd's eyelids fluttered for a moment. He slowly leaned away from Claire and folded his arms over his chest.

"You're fucking with me, right?" he asked, his voice calm.

"Todd. When have I ever lied to you?"

He shrieked, and Claire jumped back.

"You're totally not fucking with me," he breathed, his hand pressed dramatically to his chest. "Have you told Ro?"

She pursed her lips and shook her head.

"I cannot believe you didn't tell Ro," he admonished. "She is going to kill you. Sam, too."

"I have good reason," she retorted. "Do you even know how meddlesome my sisters are? Any time I start dating anyone, they interfere. They start nitpicking on what's wrong in our relationship, and it makes me nervous. That's one of the reasons I don't date much. It's not worth the hassle."

"Girl, I'm not even gonna go there," Todd replied. "I refuse to get in the middle of you three. But anyway, back to the situation at hand. I'm so proud of you. Who knew there was a little seductress in our Claire?"

"About that...I'm not really sure why he liked me. It doesn't make any sense."

"You're not giving yourself enough credit," Todd said.

"You're a little hottie. Straight guys totally dig this whole thing you've got going on. Slender, clear skin, nice rack, sweet smile."

Her lips twisted in doubt. "Compared to the gorgeous models I've seen him with, I'm nothing."

He gave her a soul-melting glare that rivaled Tita Chriss on her meanest day. "I don't ever want to hear you talk that way about yourself," he said, wagging a finger at her. "Toxic thoughts have no place here. What do we do with negativity?"

"We tell it to fuck off," Claire replied obediently.

"You're damn right. Has he called yet?"

She checked her phone again. "No," she said, her heart growing heavy with disappointment.

"Your shift is over," Todd said, shooing her out of the store. "I can close up myself. Get your little booty out of here. He's probably waiting for you outside right now."

Despite her doubts, Claire followed Todd's advice. Her skin tingled with excitement as she stood on the curb and studied the street. After a few sweeps, she realized Nate wasn't there.

She waited a minute. Then two. On the third minute, she received a text.

Hi Claire, it's Nate. Sorry for the late notice, but I'm running behind at work. Not sure if I can make it tonight. In case I get out early enough, do you mind if I drop by?

She read the message multiple times, and her mind went spiraling into dozens of different directions, trying to find meaning between every word. Late notice? Shouldn't he have been courteous enough to tell her earlier that he would be late? Were these the actions of someone who respected her time and took her seriously?

Claire shook her head, frustrated with herself. What in the world was she doing? Here she was, waiting for a guy who could snap his fingers and have any gorgeous Instagram model show up at his door. She felt like an idiot.

Her feet dragged every step toward her car. She wanted to wait for him. She really did. But the part of her carrying her wounded pride won out. As she drove back home, she received a few more messages:

Hello? Did you see my last text?

Claire?

She convinced herself she was doing the right thing, but she still felt like shit. Was she seriously blowing off Nate Noruta? She didn't like to think of it in those terms. It was more like self-preservation. Plus, it was for the best. She kept repeating her reasons like a mantra:

He attracts too much attention.

Our worlds aren't compatible.

My sisters will sabotage our relationship.

He'll probably just break my heart.

When she got home, Ro had already headed off to work. Claire plopped down on the couch, sighing in relief. Ro might have been the goofy, attention-seeking younger sister, but she was wise beyond her years. She had a knack for reading people, even when they tried to hide everything. In fact, the more you tried to hide something, the more Ro could smell it out.

Claire changed into comfortable sleep shorts and a white camisole. It was only about eight in the evening. Other women her age were probably getting glammed up for a night out on the town, but she was happy to get into her jammies and hop onto her laptop to check her cookie sales.

She went directly to her storefront on *Eclectix*. *Uh-oh...* Nate owned *Eclectix*.

She surveyed her account, which listed five new cookie orders and fifty positive reviews. *Eclectix* was the most popular by far, and her sales were gaining momentum. There was no way she could distance herself from the app. She barely knew

Nate and already his presence was manifesting everywhere.

It would do her no good to keep ruminating on Nate, though. Instead, she started working on her cookie orders. The first step: turning off her notifications. Interruptions were the enemy of work flow.

Aside from that, everything was already prepped: the royal icing was done, and her supplies were all set up in the kitchen. The only thing she had to do was prep the dough, make the cutouts, bake the cookies, and let them cool. The baking process would take about an hour total, and by the time she woke up in the morning she'd have enough time to decorate the cookies and still visit Lola by their daily nine-thirty appointment.

Claire played a few old pop songs on her Bluetooth speaker to get in the right frame of mind for cookie decorating. Anything from the Britney and boyband heyday made the cut. Once the beats started thumping, Claire found herself in a more balanced and comfortable work flow. There were few things more therapeutic than turning a lump of shapeless ingredients into delicious, mouth-watering cookies. Watching the transformation of a plain piece of dough into a mini-masterpiece never failed to amaze her.

She'd barely started gathering her ingredients when someone knocked on the door. The sound was firm and commanding. It reminded her of someone she met not too long ago.

Claire froze. Certainly this was a coincidence. Maybe it was her elderly neighbor, Mrs. Garcia, who occasionally visited to request little things like light bulbs or plastic grocery bags.

They knocked again.

"Claire?"

Her throat went dry. She'd known the man less than a day, but she was willing to bet she'd be able to pick his voice out of a crowd.

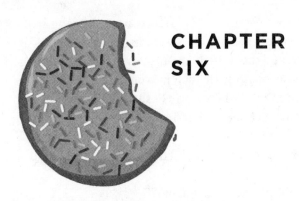

CHAPTER SIX

Claire gasped. She pressed her back to the door, her mind and heart racing each other at the speed of light.

"Hello, Claire? It's Nate."

She held her breath for a second, hoping he was just a figment of her imagination.

"Hello," he said again, his voice rich with amusement. "I heard you in there."

"What are you doing here?" she asked.

"Didn't you see any of my texts?"

Claire grabbed her phone. Sure enough, the texts were all there, hiding obediently because the notifications were turned off.

Good news, I'm free for a little bit.
I'll drop by real quick. Hope you like pizza.
Be there in fifteen.

Claire peered through the peephole again. A sexy rich man was standing outside her door. There was no protocol for this type of situation. But what really threw her was the fact she didn't mind. Sensible, introverted Claire who had an aversion to dating wasn't bothered by Nate showing up practically unannounced in the middle of the night.

Who could blame her? Even through the fish-eye lens, he was fine as hell. She admired the way the shadows of the hallway light fell in relief around his sculpted features, strengthening his bearded profile. His shoulders were broad beneath his dark blue polo shirt, and the hard, lean muscles of his arms bunched and shifted underneath with each movement.

"How do you know where I live?" she asked.

"You gave me a check earlier," he said.

"Oh."

"Are you going to let me in? The pizza's getting cold out here."

"You brought pizza? Where from?"

"It's right around the corner," Nate replied. "I'm sure you know it. They sell pizza and donuts."

Without further hesitation, Claire opened the door. Sure enough, Nate was holding the signature pink-and-green pizza box from her favorite twenty-four-hour neighborhood eatery, Donizza. There was almost nothing she wouldn't do for her favorites from this restaurant.

Her eyes flicked up to Nate's face. She did her best to resist the hypnotic effects of his sexy grin, and opened the door wider to let him in.

Invisible trickles of heat skittered up Claire's skin. She turned slightly to glance at him, and just barely caught him checking her out. The man was slick. The moment he sensed her turn toward him, he turned his glance back to her face.

"This way," she said.

They walked the short distance to the kitchen together. There was practically no surface that wasn't covered with cookie-decorating materials.

"It looks like you've been busy," Nate said. "Where should I put this?"

"Um…on top of the stove," Claire said.

She sidled up beside Nate and opened the box. The aroma of Italian sausage, bacon, and sundried tomatoes instantly invaded the room.

"Oh my God, it's the House Pie," she marveled. "This is the best."

"I got dessert, too." Nate gestured to the small pink box of half a dozen donuts that came with the House Pie special.

Is this man even real?

Claire handed a paper plate and bottle of water to Nate. As they each served themselves a slice of pizza, she had a hard time suppressing a smile. Nate was the definition of good vibes. Sure he was a little bit—okay, actually quite forward and bold, but she couldn't help feeling intrigued. The heat definitely kicked up a notch when they took seats at the tiny, round dining table, and their knees made brief contact. Claire's pulse started beating erratically, and she tried to play it off like he didn't set her soul on fire.

"I had no idea you were so serious about cookies," Nate remarked. "Look at all this. You've got a professional setup in here."

She nodded, unable to respond due to the mouthful of heavenly House Pie. She surveyed her small apartment along with Nate. There were several huge rolling-tray shelves taking up an inordinate amount of space in the living room. Multiple plastic bins and sorting shelves full of cookie-decorating supplies were stacked up against the walls.

"Well, it's kind of a hobby for now," she replied. "Decorating cookies is a lot of fun for me. The fact I'm able to make a little money is like—pardon my pun—the icing on the cake."

Nate's eyes crinkled in amusement, and Claire practically swooned.

"Can I see more of your work?" he asked.

Claire's inner spirit started hopping around in excitement. She simply could not believe he was taking a genuine interest in her *and* her passion.

"I don't have any finished cookies here right now," she said. "But I can show you pictures from my storefront."

"Which one do you use?"

Claire picked up her phone. A sheepish grin flashed across her lips.

"You're very familiar with it," she replied, scooting her chair closer to show him her phone. Her bare arm brushed against his, and he drew in an audible breath. Sitting this close, she could breathe in the alluring scent of him. It was strong enough to wake all the parts that had been sleeping inside Claire for a long, long time. She was playing with fire, but she didn't care. She wanted to see his reaction to her cookies.

"*Eclectix*," Nate said approvingly. "Good choice."

Claire tapped on her sales screen and started scrolling through the orders.

"Wow," he said. "You made these yourself?"

"Yes."

"With no help?"

"None."

He stayed silent as Claire clicked through the orders, showing him her various creations, from themed cookies like the ones she had made for Lola's nursing home, to custom creations for sports teams, employers, and parties.

"I'm blown away," Nate said when she finished. "You are definitely talented. I'm impressed, Claire."

"Thank you," she said. His words made her lighter than air. She turned to look at him again, but this time something was different. The air was charged. The looks they exchanged could have ignited water. Her gaze drifted down to his soft lips, and her hand twitched with the overwhelming urge to run her fingers across the texture of his beard. Her neck grew uncomfortably warm. She was about to sweep her hair to the side, but then she remembered she was wearing a camisole sans bra. She took a shaky breath and scooted her chair a couple of respectable inches away from Nate.

He shifted in his chair and took a deep breath. Claire held hers as she waited for his next move.

"I should get going." His voice was gruff, and he cleared his throat. "I told the board members I'd be back soon."

Claire's breath left her in a quiet rush. God, she didn't want him to leave. He was nothing—absolutely nothing—like she expected a celebrity to be. He was sweet, charismatic, and most important of all: *normal*. She could not figure out how the hell this was possible, but then again she couldn't understand most of what was going on between them.

They hesitated at the front door. Claire fiddled with her hands, and Nate stood there, looking at the ground. A part of her was charmed by him, and the other part wondered why they were both acting like a couple of inexperienced teenagers afraid to even look at each other. Maybe it was because she was trying to hide how strongly she felt about him after knowing him for less than a day. It was so sudden, and so powerful, this feeling he stirred up inside her. It was both thrilling and frightening. Another part of her—the naughty, hidden part—wanted him to drop the gentleman act and do something the opposite of gentlemanly to her. Repeatedly.

"Let's try this again," Nate said. "Do you want to go out with me tomorrow night? This time we won't be interrupted. I promise you'll have a great time."

"I would love to, but tomorrow night I'm busy." The regret stung. "I have a big rush order of cookies I have to prepare."

"Oh. Okay, how about the day after?"

"I'm available."

"Great." He reached for the door handle.

Claire's lips curved into a teasing smile. "Where are you taking me? Bora Bora? The Antarctic?"

Nate's gaze set the butterflies fluttering in her belly.

"You'll see. Good night, Claire."

He turned and left, shutting the door quietly behind him.

She sank slowly down onto her sofa, her mind lost in a fantasy-filled daze.

...

Claire didn't sleep well that night. She kept seeing images of Nate against the dark glow of her closed eyes.

Even on the drive to visit Lola the next morning, she couldn't get Nate out of her mind. So far he hadn't done anything wrong. Every single one of her ex-boyfriends had waved a red flag by now. But even if he seemed perfect, Claire was sure Ro and Sam would be able to find something critically wrong with him.

He's rich and hot. He could have any woman in the world, and he seems to have a thing for me. A basic Filipina who works at a bookstore and decorates cookies. It's too good to be true!

As Claire got out of her car and headed into Lola's assisted living complex, the possible truth finally hit her.

"Of course," she muttered, striding down the hallway. "He's probably not exclusive. There's got to be a bunch of other women he's dating. It makes sense now."

Claire really needed to talk to someone. Preferably someone nonjudgmental and who wouldn't inundate her with bad, unsolicited advice.

So clearly she couldn't tell her sisters.

There was only one person she could confess to. Someone who wouldn't make her feel bad about herself. Even though Lola had been stern in her lucid years, she was always kind and supportive, whether or not she fully understood the problem. Lola might not be the same person she was before, but Claire felt better knowing she could tell her anything.

She knocked and opened the door to Lola's room.

"Hi Lola, it's Claire—"

She gasped when she saw an unexpected woman in the room. It was her older sister, Sam, in tears, kneeling beside Lola's armchair. Dread exploded in Claire's heart.

"Ate Sam? Oh my God, what happened? Is Lola okay?"

Claire rushed over and kneeled in front of Lola, too. She

was dozing in her chair, which was odd. She was usually awake at this time and staring blankly at the TV.

"There's nothing wrong with Lola," Sam replied, carefully swiping a tear away with her thumb. "She was napping when I got here. I just came to visit her."

"Oh." Relief crashed through Claire, but the feeling quickly subsided when she realized Sam was in distress. She couldn't even remember the last time she saw her cry. Claire was convinced Sam had a heart of steel. The woman didn't even get teary-eyed when they watched *Up* and *Coco*. The most shocking of all: Sam didn't shed a tear when her husband Dylan filed for divorce. "But if Lola's okay, why are you crying?"

Sam blew her nose into a tissue.

"Dylan is dating again," she replied, gazing down at the floor. "Janice told me her cousin got matched with his *VioLit* profile."

"What's *VioLit*?" Claire asked.

Sam furrowed her brow.

"You're a single girl in the city and you don't know what *VioLit* is?"

"I've heard of it here and there, but I'm really not familiar with it."

"It's a hookup app, like *Tinder* and *Bumble*," Sam replied. "It's only been six months and Dylan's moved on already."

Sam paused as silent sobs shook her body. Claire gently guided her to sit on the side of Lola's bed. Claire wasn't surprised Dylan had already moved on. She knew he and Sam were already having problems more than a year prior. Pointing out the obvious wouldn't help her sister, though, so Claire offered consolation instead.

"I'm so sorry, Ate," she said, wrapping her arm around Sam.

"I'm the one who's the sorriest," she said. "I can't believe I ever loved that jerk. And Ro still hasn't apologized for what she did. Seriously, everything is happening all at once, and I can't handle it."

"Well…haven't you moved on, too?" Claire asked gently.

Sam shot her a glare. "No," she said, affronted. "I haven't dated anyone."

"But I thought you had feelings for that guy Ro hooked up with."

Sam grimaced and fidgeted with the tissue. "Nothing ever came of that," she grumbled. "Besides, having the inklings of feelings toward someone is vastly different than trolling for multiple people on dating apps."

"Ro told me she tried apologizing to you, and you won't accept it."

"You wouldn't accept it, either, if it wasn't sincere," Sam retorted.

She stood up and started pacing. Lola stirred in her chair, but did not wake up. Despite the tears, Sam was still beautiful in her fashionable fawn slacks and cream-colored blouse shot through with gold thread. Her Jimmy Choos made sharp taps against the wood floor with each step. Claire couldn't help but think Sam was more the type of girl Nate should be interested in, and it made her chest ache.

"Ate, you already know Ro can be rough around the edges," Claire replied. "She doesn't have the best delivery, but she's really trying her best to mend the fences with you."

"No she's not. Your judgment is clouded because you two live together, and she can influence you against me. It would have been nice for the both of you to reach out to me after Dylan left."

Claire stared at Sam in shock. All Claire could remember were the long phone calls and countless hours she and Ro had spent comforting Sam from the moment she started having problems with Dylan, to the day they divorced. Where was this coming from?

"What are you talking about? We wanted you to live with us, but you said you wanted to move in with your friend Janice instead."

Sam scoffed and averted her gaze. "You really didn't want me to live with you," she muttered. "You and Ro have had this little partnership going on since we were kids. You two always played together, and I've always been the odd one out."

Claire gaped at Sam. She'd never acted this way before. Claire had no idea Sam was holding on to so much pain.

"I didn't know you felt that way," Claire said gently. "Let me assure you: Ro and I never meant to exclude you. We're all sisters. No one is left out."

Sam didn't respond immediately. Instead she folded her tissue up and dabbed at her eyes again.

"I have to go." Sam picked up her laptop bag and leaned down to kiss Lola's cheek. "Bye, Lola." She strode out of the room without a backward glance.

"Wait, Ate. Wait!" Claire hurried after her but stopped cold at the threshold of the door. Her outburst had startled a few elderly residents walking by. She smiled apologetically and closed the door, aware she would have to hash this out with Sam at a later time.

Claire kneeled beside Lola. She watched her shallow but steady breathing as the brown blanket draped over her moved back and forth, back and forth.

"Lola? Lola, wake up. It's time to get up now."

Not even the slightest response.

Claire put her hand on Lola's, expecting the familiar warmth through her thin skin. But not today. It was almost cold as ice.

"Oh my God." Fear shot through her veins as Claire jumped up and raced out of the room toward the nursing office.

CHAPTER SEVEN

"Your grandmother is going to be fine," the doctor said. "We ran the UA and discovered she has a urinary tract infection. We're starting IV antibiotics around the clock, and after a couple days she should feel better."

Claire, her mother Irene, and her two aunts Lianne and Bernice stood in Lola's room listening to the on-staff physician explain what had happened. After the initial scare, Claire wanted the nurses to call the paramedics. To her frustration, they didn't, and instead went to the room to assess Lola. Since all her vital signs were normal, they decided not to call the paramedics and instead called Dr. Tran. The doctor ordered some tests, got the results, and ordered medication. It all seemed to go fine, except one thing.

"I want to go home."

Every pair of eyes in the room swung toward Lola as she feebly attempted to stand up from the chair on her own. Claire's mother and aunts tried to calm her down.

"Sit down, Mom, you're okay," Irene chided.

"You're already home." Tita Lianne grasped Lola's hand and attempted to push her back down into the chair.

Big mistake. Lola must not have liked what Lianne said, because she launched into a tirade in her native Tagalog, punctuated with an impressive array of curse words.

"Why is she acting like that?" Bernice asked worriedly.

"It's the infection," Dr. Tran replied. "It's common for UTIs to manifest as behavioral changes."

From the way Lola was shaking her fists and trying to punch her own daughters, it was more than a behavioral change. She was quickly spiraling into a full-blown meltdown. Fortunately, Claire knew what to do. While Lola shouted and fought, Claire turned on the TV and raised the volume. She quickly hit the play button on the Blu Ray player and waited a few seconds until the beginning notes of the intro song to the movie *Ten Things I Hate About You* filled the room. Bernice and Lianne froze in puzzlement.

And so did Lola. She still looked mad as hell, but she wasn't fighting anymore. Claire approached Lola and gently eased her back down into the chair.

"Let's watch a movie," Claire said softly into Lola's ear. "Remember Kat and Patrick? They went to the dance together and he sings to her. Let's watch."

Claire's words were like magic. Lola's fists relaxed, and she sat down in her armchair, her eyes glued to the screen. Irene smiled with pride, and her sisters crooned with approval at Claire's ability to calm Lola down like no other.

"You're amazing," Lianne said.

"Good job, anak." Mom reached out and stroked Claire's hair in approval.

Claire stared at her mother for a moment, unable to return her bright smile.

"It isn't hard, Mom," Claire said. "You have to understand Lola and what sets her off. You can't grab her and force her to do things against her will. You have to distract her."

Claire turned her attention back to Lola, wondering why her mother and aunts had such a hard time coping. Maybe it had something to do with how badly Lola had deteriorated in such a short time. Claire could understand that part. But she couldn't stand it when they treated her like a stubborn child. It took time and patience to learn the ways Lola changed as a result of the Alzheimer's—time that no one except Claire had, apparently.

Tita Bernice walked over and gently nudged Claire.

"Your Tita Chriss wants to talk to you," she said.

Claire fought the urge to cringe as Tita Bernice handed her the phone.

"Hi, Tita Chriss."

"Claire. Your Tita Bernice told me you were able to calm Lola down."

"Yeah. Like I was telling Mom, it isn't hard. All you have to do is—"

"I think you should stay the night with her," Chriss interjected. "I'm worried about her. I'm out of town on business right now, so I'm not available."

Claire hesitated. If she agreed, she'd lose a whole night's worth of cookie decorating, but she knew better than to bring that up to Tita Chriss. "I don't think that's necessary. Lola is getting antibiotics now, and the doctor says she'll be doing better in no time."

"But she is sick and you're the only one who can calm her down," Chriss replied. "What will happen if she starts acting up again? You don't want us to have to call the paramedics again, do you?"

"No. They don't have to call the paramedics. She's already being treated—"

"Stay." Tita Chriss's voice was stern. Final. "Just one night, Claire. Lola needs you."

Claire clenched her teeth. She'd never won an argument with Tita Chriss before, and it looked like now wasn't the time to break the pattern.

"Okay," she said.

"Good," Chriss replied. "Now let me talk to your Tita Bernice again."

Claire handed the phone over, then fumed in silence. To this day she couldn't understand why she allowed Tita Chriss to boss her around. To be honest, Chriss bossed everyone else around, too, and they all seemed content to kiss her ass. Being the richest and eldest in the family didn't mean she deserved to control everyone's lives. If she ever felt brave enough, Claire vowed to let Tita Chriss know her real feelings. Maybe. She wasn't sure.

Her inability to fight back resulted in a lost night of working on her cookies...which inevitably meant she had to cancel her date with Nate.

She closed her eyes and shook her head. She truly was her own worst enemy.

With a sigh of defeat, she picked up her phone to ask Ro to bring her a change of clothes and her toothbrush. Her day took an even sharper nosedive when she saw a couple text messages from Nate.

How are you today?

Can't wait for tomorrow night

Claire excused herself from the room as she stepped into the hallway and pressed the call button. She owed him an explanation.

"Claire. Hey, how are you?"

There went the butterflies again. His voice was so sexy he'd make a killing narrating romance audiobooks.

"H-Hi," she stammered. "I, uh...can I talk to you for a minute?"

"Of course. Hold on a sec."

"Okay."

Nate exchanged brief, muffled words with someone.

"I'm back," he said a few seconds later. "I'm glad to hear from you. What's going on?"

Claire suppressed a groan. She wished for one second he would stop being so nice. It would make letting him down so much easier. But who's to say she was even letting him down? He probably had a mile-long queue of beauties lined up, all ready to take her place.

"I'm really sorry to say this, but I have to cancel our date tomorrow night."

"Why?"

She let out a steadying breath. It wasn't easy discussing her personal family dynamics, but deep inside she knew she could trust Nate. And there was only one way to find out whether or not he would be understanding.

"My grandmother is sick. I have to stay the night and keep an eye on her. I was supposed to use my time tonight to finish a rush order of cookies, but since I won't have the time tonight, I'm going to be busy on the night of our date. I'm so sorry."

"Oh," Nate replied. Surprisingly, he didn't sound annoyed. "What happened to your grandma, if you don't mind me asking? Is she all right?"

"Yes, she's going to be fine. It's a long story, but basically she has a UTI, and because she has Alzheimer's, it's making her act a little more combative than usual. She's getting treated, but my family wants me to stay with her because I'm the only one who can calm her down. I might be her favorite grandchild, but that's not the only reason I can handle her. I actually spend time with her and I've come to know what sets her off and what calms her down. If my family would put in the effort and stop being so scared of upsetting her, they'd be able to calm her down, too."

Nate made a small sound of acknowledgment in his throat. "Tell you what. I can arrange for someone to stay and take care of your grandmother tonight. That way, you'd have time to make your cookies and be able to make our date tomorrow."

Claire tilted her head in puzzlement.

"Wait, what do you mean?"

"My Aunt Vickie is a retired nurse," Nate explained. "She specialized in geriatric psychiatry for almost forty years. She's my godmother, and she'd be happy to help out."

"Are you serious?" A spark of hope flared to life inside Claire. "That would be amazing. Wait…I couldn't ask that of your aunt! She doesn't even know me. No. I feel bad. She's retired. She probably wants to be left alone so she can finally enjoy herself."

"Don't worry about it," Nate said casually. "Aunt Vickie won't mind. Trust me. When you meet her you'll see."

Claire's jaw dropped, but the words wouldn't come. She had a hard time believing Nate was real. He had to be a hallucination. There was no way someone could be so absolutely…perfect.

Nate arrived right in the middle of Lola's dinner. When Claire heard the gentle knock, her stomach immediately tied into a big knot. She helped Lola take a sip of apple juice, then she got up and answered the door.

Oh, Lord almighty.

Nate got better looking every time she laid eyes on him. He stood there at the threshold with a Dodgers baseball cap on, wearing a heather gray T-shirt that draped flatteringly over his lean but incredibly fit body. And his beard…Claire had no idea bearded guys were her thing. After meeting Nate, they were not only her thing, they were stuff her forbidden fantasies were made of.

"Hi," Nate said.

Claire quickly blinked away the images of her and Nate entwined in creative positions. A flush stole into her cheeks when she noticed an older woman standing beside him. Her wry gaze twinkled at Claire as if she had an inkling of what was going on in her mind.

"This is my Aunt Vickie," Nate said. "Aunt Vickie, this is Claire."

Vickie stepped forward and smiled, giving Claire a firm handshake. Although Vickie was rail-thin and old enough to be her mother, there was a vivacity in her eyes and an inexplicable zest in her presence. Claire liked her right away.

"It's so nice to meet you," Vickie said with a sly grin. "Nate, I can see why you're so fond of her. She's a gorgeous girl."

A mortified look stole into Nate's eyes, but then it disappeared. Claire caught it, and she thought it was adorable.

"Vickie, I want to thank you so much for doing this," Claire said. "Are you sure this is okay with you?"

"Of course it's okay with me," Vickie said. "I'm retired, darling. I'm bored out of my mind most of the time. Plus, there's nothing I wouldn't do for this sweetie pie right here." She nudged Nate in the ribs. "Do you have the schedule I asked for, honey?"

Claire fished a folded piece of paper out of her pocket and handed it to Vickie.

"History, med list, code status…you should have been a nurse," Vickie said, impressed with Claire's thoroughness.

"I don't have what it takes to be a nurse," Claire replied. "I don't do well with blood and needles."

Trepidation set in. Tita Chriss would be irate if she found out Claire left Lola with a stranger. Even so, her gut told her she could trust Vickie. Claire knelt beside Lola and patted her hand.

"Lola, this is Vickie," she explained. "She's your nurse. She's going to take care of you for a little while, then I'll come back. You'll be safe with her. I love you."

"Have fun, you two," Vickie called out as they left, her eyebrows rising suggestively.

Claire chuckled and walked with Nate out of the room.

"That was so nice of her," Claire said. "And you. Obviously. You're the one who made this happen. Thanks to you, Miss Nicole's School of Dance will receive their order on time."

"I'm glad it worked out," he replied. "So…do you want me

to follow you, or do you need a ride home?"

"Follow me? It's okay. I'll be fine going home alone."

He shifted his stance and gave her a knowing grin.

"I have a surprise for you," he said. "I want to make sure you finish on time so we can go on the date you promised me tomorrow night...so you've got yourself an assistant."

"Who? You?"

He nodded.

It was a good thing there was a wall against Claire's back, or else she might have fainted.

"Are you sure?" she asked. "Aren't you busy?"

Nate took a step forward. There was heat in his gaze and an energy all around him that she could only describe as...electric.

"Yes," he said. "But never too busy for you."

CHAPTER EIGHT

Claire's heart beat furiously in her chest as she parked in her spot and sprinted up the stairs to her apartment. Fortunately, Nate was a couple minutes behind, which gave her time to tidy up the place and get supplies ready.

She twisted the key in the lock and swung the door open. Just as she suspected: Ro wasn't home. She usually left around this time for her shift at the bar. Claire heaved a sigh of relief. She was nowhere near ready to tell anyone else about her and Nate, let alone her sisters.

The thought of spending time with Nate alone for the next few hours set her heart racing and her fingers turning to butter. She dropped a cookie rack on the floor with a loud *clang* and probably scared the hell out of her neighbor downstairs.

Focus, Claire. You have a big rush order. Your business is important. Don't ever let a man get in the way of your dreams.

Dreams. The word made her lips quirk in a rueful grin. She had always wanted to be an entrepreneur, ever since she was a little girl. It wasn't until a few years ago she finally realized what kind of entrepreneur, but to do something like that took grit. Tenacity. Courage.

All the things she never saw in herself.

Shoving aside her self-doubt, Claire went to work. As she set up her work station, she couldn't help thinking about how happy cookie decorating made her. Her new passion fueled the fire of creativity in her blood, and it became an inseparable part of her. She often fantasized what it would be like to actually have her own full-time cookie decorating business, and planned to set aside time to take actionable steps toward it. And then fear of failure would set in, along with the "I told you so's" from Tita Chriss, and she'd abandon her plan all over again.

A sudden knock on the door derailed her thoughts.

"It's open," she called out.

The door opened and Nate poked his head into the apartment, giving her a smile that threatened to scatter her thoughts even more.

"Reporting for duty," he said.

"Come in." She tied her teal apron around her waist and handed an extra one to Nate. "Put this on. It can be a messy process."

He slipped the apron over his head. It was far too small on him. She pressed her lips together to suppress her laugh.

"What's so funny?" he deadpanned. "You don't think this is hot?"

"I'm sure someone out there thinks it is," she quipped, trying to banish images of him wearing nothing but the apron.

"I hope you don't feel I was being too pushy earlier," Nate said. "About getting my aunt to watch your grandma."

"No, not at all," she replied. "That was amazing, actually. I'm really grateful. It's one of the sweetest things someone's ever done for me."

Claire's heart skipped as Nate's eyes danced with obvious delight. And that was her cue to shift right into business mode.

It's not professional to try and bang the help, Claire.

She tried to keep her hormones at bay as she stood close to Nate, showing him how to flood the white royal icing onto the surface of the round sugar cookies meant to serve as a background for the dance school's logo in edible spray paint.

She demonstrated how to use a toothpick to get rid of the tiny imperfections and bubbles across the iced surface, giving the cookies a smooth, matte appearance when they eventually dried.

"Hmm. Doesn't seem too hard," he said, taking the bag of icing. Nate bent over the counter and copied the way Claire held the bag of icing. His first attempt was awkward, and his hands shook slightly as he painstakingly flooded the cookie.

"Not bad," Claire said with a raised eyebrow. "Your border is kind of crooked here, but aside from that, it's not bad."

"Not bad?" he said. "This is one of a kind. You can charge extra for it."

He smiled and gave Claire a panty-melting wink right when his phone rang.

"Excuse me," he said as he took the call.

Claire continued icing the cookies, but she perked her ears up in hopes of catching a few words. She wasn't typically interested in the life of a celebrity, but Nate fascinated her. She was definitely not immune to his charming and charismatic ways. She wondered about all the different facets of his life, and if any of it was just an act or was all the real Nate.

"I know," he muttered into the phone. He ducked into the small bathroom in the hallway. "Mm-hmm. Yeah. I won't. You already know the answer. Yes. Thanks."

When he returned, Claire noticed a new tension in his shoulders and hardness in his jaw. But when he looked at her, the tension seemed to melt away, and he was Nate all over again.

"Ready for action," he said, as he picked up the icing bag.

Nate resumed his work on her cookies with a precision and dedication that made her heart simmer in pleasure. It was difficult to imagine this was the tech genius behind the world-famous *MyConnect*, and hundreds of apps used by millions of people across the globe. She couldn't even begin to imagine the pressures placed on him every day, but he somehow made time for her. He barely knew her, and yet he was showing her more commitment in these few days than her last boyfriend showed her in their entire two-year relationship.

Claire glanced at the clock. Then at Nate. It was going to be a long time until Ro came home. She could practically see the muscles in Nate's back shifting and flexing through his shirt as he hunched over the cookies with the icing bag, looking like a hunky baking assistant straight out of the collection of her naughty fantasies.

"May I help you with something, Miss Ventura?" His teasing grin jarred her out of her thoughts.

A sense of shame washed over her. Here she was, casually undressing Nate with her eyes, when they had a ton of work to finish before morning. *What do guys think about to get rid of their erections? Bus accidents. Maggots. Sugar-free chocolate.*

"I was just critically observing your technique," she replied, avoiding eye contact. "You're improving. I think this calls for some drinks."

Claire opened her fridge and grabbed two spiked seltzer cans. If she was going to survive the night without spontaneously combusting, she needed a little liquid courage.

"Do you want black cherry or kiwi strawberry?" she asked.

Nate's phone started to buzz, but he ignored it.

"Black cherry," he said.

"Why black cherry?"

"Well...it was my favorite Jell-O flavor when I was a kid."

Claire handed him the can, satisfied with the cute explanation. They popped the tops and bumped their cans together in a little toast.

"To the success of your business," Nate said, as they both took a sip.

"And to the...continued success of yours," Claire replied, a little ashamed at her lack of knowledge about Nate's tech world.

She turned around and started icing the cookies on top of the kitchen counter. Nate resumed his own work behind her at the dining table.

"I can't work very well when you're behind me," he finally said after a few seconds of silence. "I think you should sit next to me. It would be best for our work flow."

Claire smiled and picked up her tray of cookies. She set it next to Nate and sat in the chair beside him. His phone buzzed again.

"You sure do get a lot of calls," she said as she resumed icing.

He glanced at his phone, then stuck it back in his pocket.

"It's my assistant Craig," he replied. "He's sending me reminders. Sorry for all the interruptions."

"Reminders about what?"

"Work. He's constantly reminding me about all my meetings and events. Like tomorrow. I'm booked solid for fourteen straight hours. I had more meetings scheduled, but I told Craig to cancel for our date."

Claire took a large swig of her seltzer. She hadn't drunk alcohol in quite a while, and it was going straight to her head. Sober Claire took a back seat and watched in amusement as Tipsy Claire took the stage.

"So...do you take a lot of women out on dates?"

Nate finished icing a cookie and paused. "Do you really want to know?" he asked.

"Of course I want to know," she replied, even though she was deathly afraid of the answer. "Otherwise I wouldn't have asked."

"No, I don't take a lot of women out. At least not now. Work's been too busy."

"Oh. So you *used* to date around a lot?"

He nodded.

An awkward silence ensued. She had no idea what she wanted to accomplish with that question, but she sure wasn't banking on the jealousy squeezing her gut.

"It's my turn to ask a question," he said, smoothly switching gears. "Have you ever seriously considered turning this into a full-time business?"

"Yes. I have. But I don't really have any immediate plans."

"Why not? I took a look at your storefront on *Eclectix*. You're one of the highest rated sellers in your category."

She could write an entire dissertation on the self-doubt and fear standing in her way, but she wasn't about to open that can of worms. Instead, she boiled her explanation down to a few simple words.

"Yeah. I just don't think it's the right time."

Her eyes drifted away when Nate glanced at her. He could probably tell there was much more behind her answer, but he knew well enough to leave it alone.

"Let's go back to my question," she said. "You say you don't have time to date around, yet here we are. How do you explain this situation?"

"You consider this a date?" Nate asked. "I thought of it as a business collab. You needed help fulfilling a rush order, and I own the storefront you're using to sell your goods."

"Alright," she replied. "If this is a business meeting, I'd like to submit a request to lower the listing fee. It's too high. How are you going to compete with Ebay and Etsy with those fees?"

"I can't lower the listing fee," he said. "But you're very persuasive. I'll waive it for you, and you alone. Don't go telling your friends I'm doing this for everyone."

She narrowed her eyes and swayed closer to him.

"If you waive the fee for me, I think you're going to expect something in return," she said. "What's the term you business guys use? 'Quid pro quo'?"

"You're on to me." Nate gave her a sidelong glance. "In exchange for waiving the fee, you have to agree to go anywhere with me tomorrow night. No matter where it is."

"Oh, that's right." She shifted in her chair and accidentally brushed her knee against Nate. He went still. Claire cleared her throat. "You said our first date was going to be a surprise. Fine.

I won't ask any more about it. But I am looking forward to it."

She stood up and grabbed a bottle of water, resisting the urge to cringe. The liquid courage was supposed to save her, but it was doing the exact opposite. It not only made Nate more enticing by the second, it turned her into an awkward mess. How? By shoving her inhibitions out the door. This teasing banter bouncing between them was spiking her desire more than the seltzer would do to a bowl of punch. If she didn't switch her focus and try to sober up, they'd probably end up naked in her bedroom. It was exactly what she wanted, but now was really not a good time.

Goddamn you, Miss Nicole and your School of Dance!

Taking a deep breath, she played some upbeat contemporary pop songs on the Bluetooth speaker. They needed to finish icing, detailing, and bagging sixty cookies before Ro came home at around five or six in the morning.

And if they hurried up and finished *long* before Ro came home… Claire bit down on a sly smile as she ran a lascivious gaze over his body. Maybe they'd be able to fit in some other activities she'd been imagining.

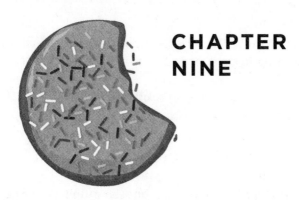

CHAPTER NINE

At one thirty in the morning, Claire was proud of herself for two reasons. One: they were almost done with the cookies. And two: she managed to keep her mind on the straight and narrow, pouring herself into her work with a focused resolve she'd never experienced before. It wasn't easy when the guy sitting inches away from her turned her blood into lava.

As she chattered on incessantly like an obnoxious soundtrack on endless repeat, Nate worked at a brisk but precise pace, seeming to enjoy her company. All the while, he kept receiving texts, and another phone call. He ignored most of them and fulfilled his worker bee role, just as he'd promised.

"Has my aunt contacted you?" Nate asked.

"Oh my God, how could I forget?" She shook her head. "It's been a while. Thanks." She shot off a quick text to Vickie, who replied back within a minute.

"Lola's fine," Claire said with a relieved smile. "She got a little agitated, but Vickie was able to calm her down. She's sleeping now."

Claire turned toward Nate. It was time to say goodbye to him, and she was surprised at the sadness weighing her down.

"I guess you have to get going?" She threw him a grin she hoped looked casual, even though she longed for him to stay.

He didn't respond right away, but his eyes told her he was

reluctant to leave, too.

Claire's phone rang. Her heart went into a frantic rhythm, thinking something had happened to Lola. Instead, it was a text from Sam.

I'm sorry I left so abruptly. But you don't understand what it feels like to be abandoned by your only sisters when you need them the most.

"Claire? What's wrong?" Nate asked.

"Hold on," she muttered, rushing into her room.

It was one thirty in the morning, but she didn't care. She immediately hit the dial button. Her frustration mounted when the call went to voicemail.

"Damn!" She started typing up a text, but an incoming text from Sam interrupted her.

I don't feel like talking. Please leave me alone or else I'll block you.

Claire's heart collapsed like paper in flames. Once Sam built the wall, it wasn't coming down until she was good and ready. It killed her to see Sam hurting so badly. Why did she have to shut people out when she was upset?

"Are you okay?"

Nate stood in the doorway of her bedroom, gazing at her with eyes full of worry. Claire stared back at him in silence. She'd never seen a more beautiful man. But it was more than physical. He was caring. Considerate. He seemed to know what she needed even before she did. It should have been impossible to find someone so perfect for her as he was. It scared her, but the fear was worth whatever was happening between them.

His proximity sent sparks of pleasure skimming across her skin. Nate's eyes changed, too. In real time his gaze morphed from concerned into something darker—hungrier. She dreamed of him looking at her this way countless times, but now it was real, and he was standing before her, filling her doorframe with his searing presence.

"Come in," Claire said.

He kept his intense gaze on Claire as he approached, stepping into her bedroom and stopping an inch away from her. She looked up at him, her eyes gliding across his jawline to his lips. Her fingers moved of their own accord, lightly tracing along the rough texture of his beard. His breathing quickened, and the heat of his warm breath splayed across her hand.

Rivulets of pleasure ran up her arm as she finally cupped Nate's jaw in her hand, just like she dreamed dozens of times. The contact alone set her heart racing. She thought her heart would stop altogether when his hand came up and rested upon hers.

"Claire." His voice was a gruff whisper as his fingers caressed hers.

"Can I kiss you?" she asked.

His lips came down on hers with no hesitation. The sweet melding of their mouths sparked something inside Claire. She had never felt this level of desire for anyone before. It was as if the stars finally aligned to bring her deep-seated dreams to vibrant life.

Who was she to put all that time and effort to waste?

Claire deepened the kiss. She parted her lips, opening herself up to Nate as her arms wrapped around his neck. Excitement leaped in her belly as Nate grasped her waist, pressing her body into his with heated urgency.

Nate abruptly ended their kiss. Disappointment surged into Claire, but quickly vanished when Nate took a moment to bury his face in the crook of her neck. He paused, his entire body going rigid as his hands reverently stroked up and down the small of her back. Claire shivered and bit back a groan as Nate took a deep inhale of her hair and planted little kisses against her collarbone.

"I've been wanting to do this since the first time I met you," he whispered, tasting the hollow of her throat. "You're just... so beautiful."

A wild sense of joy shot through her body. His touch made her feel worshiped. Adored. Her smile disappeared against the soft heat of his mouth and caresses of his tongue as she kissed him once more. Their embrace spiraled even higher, and Claire's knees went weak. She eased down to sit on the edge of her bed. Nate followed her and kneeled between her legs, holding her slender body flush against him.

That's when she felt it—the hard ridge of his arousal pressed against her core. She ran her hands over his firm pecs and around his muscular back, grinding herself into him.

"You feel so fucking good," Nate groaned.

His hands swept down and firmly palmed the curves of her ass. She gasped as he gave her a firm squeeze, then skimmed his hands down until he reached the undersides of her thighs. He pulled her legs farther apart and wedged himself more firmly against her. She gasped again in surprise when he picked her up and turned them around, settling her astride his lap on the bed.

Claire rose up on her knees as Nate ran his hands under her shirt, casting it up over her head. A moment of horror dawned on Claire as she realized she was wearing her oldest, most worn-out bra. She'd bought the once-white bra at least five years ago, and it was now little more than a dingy piece of lingerie lined with frayed lace. If she had any inkling she'd be hooking up with Nate Noruta today, she would have put in a lot more effort.

An unwelcome image flashed through her mind. Gorgeous supermodels all decked out in golden Gucci underwear encrusted with jewels, shimmering under the custom lighting in their outrageous mansions, posing seductively on satin sheets as they waited for Nate to plunder them.

"What's the matter?" Nate asked, gazing up at her.

"My—I wasn't expecting..." Claire stumbled over her words and subconsciously covered her breasts with her arms.

"Do you want to stop?" he asked.

"Stop? No!" Claire paused, taking a moment to compose herself. "No. It's just...ugly underwear."

As soon as the words left her mouth, she died inside. *Ugly underwear? Bravo, Claire. You're practically the genius of dirty talk.*

Instead of answering, Nate kept his face turned up toward her. She got lost in the stark adoration in his eyes as his hands gently roved around her back and unclasped her bra. He slipped the straps down, and Claire lowered her arms, resting them on Nate's shoulders.

"You're perfect," he breathed, his gaze skimming over her naked breasts. "I could look at you all day."

One hand came up to palm her breast, and the other one wrapped around her back to press her closer so he could take her nipple into his mouth.

The flick of his tongue drew a ragged moan out of Claire. Her head sagged against him as his thumb teased her other nipple into a hard nub. Pure pleasure throbbed in her pussy as she grew moist and hot between her legs.

She tried to say his name—to tell him to never stop and go as far as he wanted and to do anything he wanted to her. She wanted to speak, but her mind shattered into a thousand pieces when his fingers eased her shorts and panties aside.

"You're so soft and wet," he whispered against her ear. "Tell me what you want. Anything you want, I'll do it for you. Do you want me to make you come?"

The feel of Nate's fingers stroking up and down her slick cleft, gliding across her clit almost made her pass out. She tried to say "yes," but Nate's skilled fingers artfully severed the connection between her brain and her mouth.

"Claire," he said. "I want to hear you say it. Tell me what you want."

"I...yes," Claire whispered.

"Yes what?"

"I want you to make me come."

"Do you want my fingers or my mouth?"

"Both."

His fingers started working faster. Claire cried out, digging her nails into his back.

"Say it."

"I want you to make me come with your mouth and your fingers on my pussy," she whimpered. Even before she was done talking, Nate was striding across the room with her in his arms. He set her down against the wall, yanked her shorts and panties down, and hitched her leg over his shoulder.

There was nothing hotter than the sight of Nate down there, his mouth on her, going to town like she was his favorite dessert. Claire tried to remember every single vivid detail of this moment, but the mind-blowing sensations of his tongue against her clit made her eyes flutter, and her mind turned to one huge firework ready to go off.

The pressure spiraled higher and stronger in her core. With every flick, lap, and swipe of his tongue, her body seemed to melt more and more into a warm pile of jelly. Her hands searched in futility for purchase against the flat wall, so she reached for Nate instead, burying her fingers into his hair.

She was seconds away from climaxing, but she wanted more of Nate. She wanted to see him naked, too, and feel him moving inside her.

"Nate, I—"

He robbed her of every word when he slipped his finger inside, finding the sensitive bundle of nerves on the front wall of her pussy. He stroked it in time with the frantic movements of his tongue, sending Claire into another time and dimension where nothing existed except the unreal sensations only he could give her.

Claire tried to hold off the orgasm as long as she could. This complete and utter bliss cascading over her was too amazing, and she wanted it to last forever. But the feel of Nate's lips sucking at her clit and his restless and deft fingers were too much. With a few more vigorous strokes, he sent her plunging over the edge. Waves of pleasure coursed through her body, pulsing between her legs and running over her skin in little sparks of electricity.

Her head lolled back against the wall as Nate stood up, grasping her around the waist. As the rush of the orgasm subsided, a delicious, languid giddiness overcame her. She wrapped her arms around Nate and kissed him deeply, tasting the slick heat of her own pleasure as his tongue invaded her mouth.

When she started to settle back down to earth, Claire finally began to grasp her thoughts. They hadn't known each other for long, but there was no denying the powerful, visceral connection between them. He gave her a feeling of safety and of home, where they had their own little world with them alone. She had no idea where this was going, or if they could ever fall in love in the future, but she knew one thing: he made her happy. An unbridled, pure, and incandescent happy she never knew existed.

The front door of the apartment slammed open suddenly, followed by a burst of feminine laughter. Claire gasped and Nate rushed toward the bedroom door, closing it carefully.

"Ro's home!" Claire whispered as she frantically threw her clothes back on. "Get in the closet."

"You don't want to introduce me?" Nate teased, spreading his hands imploringly.

"Not right now. Please hide, I'm begging you."

He wedged himself into the closet and pulled the door closed as much as he could.

"Ate? Are you home?"

Claire had barely yanked up her shorts and sat on the bed before Ro opened the door without knocking. Claire was sitting innocently on her bed, legs crossed, phone in hand. She prayed

Ro wouldn't suspect anything.

"Oh. Hello," she said as casually as possible, belying the racing of her heart. "You're home early."

"Yeah. Listen." Ro walked toward Claire. She made a move to sit beside her, but Claire stood up abruptly and headed toward the door. She couldn't let Ro sit on the bed because if she did, she'd be facing the closet and might notice Nate hiding there.

"I know this is kind of weird, but I brought a guy home." An apologetic look flashed through Ro's eyes.

"Oh," Claire replied in surprise.

"I'm hoping you're okay with it just this once," Ro said. "Please, Ate. We'll stay in my room. Put on your headphones or something. I really, really like this guy."

Claire hesitated. The disapproving big sister in her wanted to admonish Ro for bringing a guy home. It was against the unspoken rules of their apartment. Although Ro hooked up with a lot of guys, Claire never judged her for it, except to tell her to be careful. But Ro always made it a point to never bring someone home. This time was a surprise. And after what she just did with Nate, Claire would be a hypocrite for making Ro feel bad about it.

"Okay," she said, gently guiding Ro outside of her room. "Try not to make a habit of this, all right?"

"Thank you, Ate!" Ro threw her arms around her, giving her a fierce hug. She loosened her grip and scrutinized Claire's face.

"Ate. You're practically glowing. Did something good happen to you today?"

A rush of heat gathered in Claire's cheeks. "You should get back to your guy," she said, gently pushing Ro forward. "He's waiting."

Ro flashed her a megawatt smile, then darted away with a giggle. Once the door to Ro's room slammed shut, Nate cautiously rolled the closet door to the side and stepped out.

"Should I go?" he asked.

As much as Claire wanted him to stay, she didn't feel comfortable with Nate and Ro being in the same place. Plus, it would be really weird to have Nate stay the night while her little sister was having sex with a guy in the other room.

"Yeah," she agreed. "I mean, I don't want you to go, but it's really awkward with my sister and her guy here."

"I see what you mean." Nate sauntered up to Claire and wrapped his hands around her waist, pulling her close. "You don't want your family to know about me. I'm your dirty little secret."

"Well…" Claire smiled, wrapping her arms around Nate's neck again. "I kind of like this. Just me and you, with no one else intruding in on us. Do you understand?"

Nate gently rested his forehead on Claire's. She closed her eyes, content in the circle of his strong arms.

"Of course," he murmured. "We're still on for tomorrow night? You promised no more rush orders, remember?"

"Yes," Claire replied with a laugh. "I removed the option from my listings."

Nate leaned down and kissed her again. They said goodnight to one another, and she made sure the coast was clear before he left the apartment.

Even after she closed the door and leaned against it, her mind lost in a passion-filled daze, she couldn't stop reliving the feel of Nate's caresses and his worship of her body. She couldn't remember the last time she had been this happy, and hoped with all her heart this feeling would last.

CHAPTER TEN

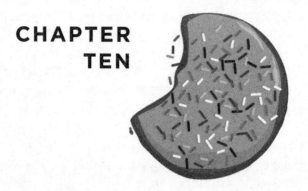

The next morning, Claire was still sailing on cloud nine. The events of last night were enough fantasy fuel to last her entire life. She still couldn't believe she was dating Nate Noruta—a man who was not only hotter than an active volcano, but could make her come like one, too. She had no idea what she'd done to get in God's good graces, but she vowed never to miss a single Sunday mass ever again.

After she shipped off the rush order of cookies, she went to visit Lola. Vickie had left a couple hours before, but reported all was well. Lola had several more confused episodes, but Vickie had been able to calm her down with no problems. Claire had begged Vickie to accept payment for watching Lola, but she adamantly refused.

"Don't be silly," Vickie said. "It was a pleasure. There's a reason I stayed in geriatric nursing for forty years. Like I said before, there's nothing I won't do for my Nate. He is the most generous boy you'll ever meet. I don't take it lightly when he asks for a favor. It must mean he really likes you, because he *never* asks favors from anyone."

Vickie's revelation fascinated Claire. The more hints she picked up, the less he seemed like the stereotypical billionaire. And the more she thought about it, the more she realized she was open to the possibility of being with him, even though there were three facets of his life she wasn't too crazy about—the excessive wealth, fame, and lack of privacy.

As she drove to the Book Nook that afternoon, she knew something had to give. If they were lucky, their relationship would last longer than an average fling. But Nate was a celebrity. Sooner or later, Claire would be thrust into his chaotic world, and she had to be ready. The thought was sobering. How she wished for Nate and her to stay in their own hidden, private world away from intrusive eyes.

Claire parked near the bookstore and scoffed. Why did her brain like to go off on unrealistic tangents? Maybe it was better to forget all this and cross that bridge when she actually reached it.

Right before she got out of her car, she had to take care of unfinished business. Her heart fluttered in trepidation as she shot off a text to Sam.

Hi Ate. Happy Monday! Can we talk pls? Let's have dinner during my break? My treat :-)

Claire stared at her phone. With every second ticking by, her heart sank lower and lower. She was so worried about her sister. Sam was fiercely independent and insisted on doing everything her own way. Claire and Ro had understood this from a young age, and strove to respect her wishes. Claire had no idea Sam felt left out, and she desperately wanted to make things right between them.

To Claire's great relief, Sam replied back.

Ok.

Claire let out a little squeal of joy. Sam was open to talking now. This was the best possible outcome.

Final phone check: *Claire's Enchanted Confections.* She opened up *Eclectix* and checked for any new updates. She saw two new orders and an alert in her seller's account:

Listing fees: +$25.28

Her jaw dropped. The listing fees for all her current

inventory had been refunded. After further investigation, she discovered that the listing fees were no longer applicable to any of her listings going forward. She shot out another text, but this time to Nate.

I was just kidding. You don't have to waive my listing fees!
He responded right away.

*I'm sorry. Who is this? *winking emoji**

I'm not asking for any special favors. You really don't have to do that.

You're right, I don't have to. I want to.

Claire was at a loss. She put her phone away and headed into the bookstore, brainstorming ways to try and thwart his attempts at waiving her fees. Still, excitement over tonight's date put a hop in her step as she sauntered back into the bookstore.

Claire met with Sam at a hole-in-the-wall tapas place down the road at six p.m. sharp.

"I know this doesn't seem like my kind of place," Sam said as they took a seat by the window. "But my employees swore up and down they serve the best street tacos and margaritas here."

The server came by and took their drink and appetizer orders.

"Claire, I want to apologize," Sam said, apropos of nothing.

Claire's eyes widened at the words she never expected. Sam was stubborn and rarely ever admitted when she was wrong. But then again, Sam usually had a good head on her shoulders. She was rarely in the wrong.

"Apologize? Why?" Claire asked.

"For how I reacted earlier. I'm sorry, and I hope you can forgive me."

"Of course I forgive you," Claire replied. She shifted in her chair, trying to choose her words carefully. "But is there anything else you want to talk about? Maybe the split with Dylan is finally hitting you and you need to unpack some of these feelings?"

"There's nothing to unpack," she said, avoiding eye contact. "I was feeling cranky that day, and finding out about Dylan dating again pushed me over the edge. But I'm fine now. It's time to move on. I need to start dating."

"Are you sure?" Claire asked. "Have you considered going to therapy? I'm worried about you. What if you're depressed? The same thing happened to Tita Marlene when she got divorced. She tried hiding her feelings for a long time, and then finally she couldn't take it anymore and she had to get treatment."

The server came by to drop off their drinks.

"Just because that happened to Tita Marlene doesn't mean it's going to happen to me," Sam said, then took a sip of her whiskey sour. "We're two different people in different circumstances. Sal was a deadbeat, and Dylan wasn't."

What difference does it make who the man was? Your marriage broke up. That's the heart of the matter.

But Claire didn't have the nerve to voice her thoughts.

"Please consider counseling, Ate," she insisted. "Don't close the door."

Sam took another swig of her drink and made a dismissive gesture with her hand.

"I don't want to talk about anything sad tonight. I'm going back into the dating pool, and you're going to join me."

Claire's Shirley Temple was halfway to her lips when she paused. "What?"

"I'm going to put our profiles into *VioLit*," Sam said as she pulled out her phone. "Right now."

"I—I don't think that's a good idea," Claire argued. "You can make your own profile, but I don't need one—"

"How long has it been since you've been on a date?" Sam asked calmly, turning on her persuasiveness.

Images of Nate on his knees flashed through Claire's head, but she kept her mouth shut.

"Exactly," Sam said, turning her attention back to her phone. "You haven't been in a real relationship since what's-his-face in college, and you haven't brought any guys home since. Have you ever tried a dating app before?"

"No, but—"

"It's settled then." Sam set her phone down right as their appetizers arrived. "I sent you an invite to create a *VioLit* profile. Come on, Claire. Please do this? For me?"

Claire's insides churned in trepidation. Dating apps turned her off. And why did she need to search for another guy when she had already found the perfect one?

The thought sent another jolt of surprise through her. Already found the perfect one? Claire had only known Nate for four days. Four. Days. Maybe Sam was right. It wouldn't hurt to set up her dating profile to show her support of Sam.

"Okay," Claire said hesitantly. "But do you know who'd really enjoy doing this with us? Ro."

Sam's grin vanished.

"I have nothing to say to her," Sam replied stoically. "Period."

Claire stirred her drink in silent frustration. At the very least, she'd gotten an apology out of Sam. Claire dreaded the uphill battle they faced when it came time to really reconcile Sam and Ro's relationship.

At a quarter till eleven, Margie finally went home, leaving Todd and Claire alone at the bookstore to finish closing. As soon as Claire finished restocking the shopping bags, Todd sidled up to her with a sly grin.

"I have been dying to talk to you all night," he said. "So what happened with Nate? What's the deal? Have you two been seeing each other?"

Claire nodded.

"We actually have a date tonight," she replied with a smile.

Todd squealed and fanned himself.

"Oh honey, I am so happy for you," he said. "What does your family think?"

"I haven't told them yet."

"Not even Ro?"

Claire shook her head.

"Girl, how could you not even tell your own sisters? This is *huge*."

"Have you forgotten everything I've told you about them?" Claire said in her defense. "The last thing I need is them interfering in my personal life, no matter how well intended. It's best I don't say anything for now."

"Well, if it were me, I'd be blabbing to everybody and their cousin about it. I have no idea how you're keeping this a secret."

"Exactly. I don't know what *this* is," Claire replied. "We've only known each other for four days, and already it's so intense between us. I can't explain this wild attraction we have to each other. To be honest, it's a little scary. This has never happened to me before, and I'm not sure how to handle it."

Todd's expression turned serious. He leaned in and gently grasped Claire's hand between both of his own.

"Here's how you handle this, honey," he began. "He is a smoking hot, filthy rich man who wants you bad. All you need to do is sit back, relax, and revel in his attention and affection. Accept this beautiful gift the universe has given you. Don't overthink it!"

Claire's phone rang. Todd dropped her hand like a hot coal.

"Is that *him*?" he whispered.

She put a finger to her lips and answered the phone. "Hello?"

"Hey."

The sound of Nate's voice was enough to turn her on. A

flush of desire spread across her cheeks, and she smiled.

"Hi," she crooned. "How are you?"

"Great," he said. "There's just one thing. I won't be able to pick you up, like I planned. A few things changed last minute, so my assistant Craig will pick you up."

Claire's smile faded. "Really? Why? Are we not going to see each other?"

"We *are* going to see each other," Nate reassured her. "Craig will pick you up at eleven thirty. Make sure you have your passport."

"Are you kidding me?" Claire asked with a nervous laugh.

"You promised me you'd go anywhere," Nate said. "Are you going back on your word?"

"No, but—"

"We won't be gone long," Nate continued. "If there's an emergency back home, or some other obligations, I can get you back right away. What do you say?"

Claire's heart sputtered in her chest, caught in between feelings of excitement and fear.

"I don't know..."

"Please, Claire. I promise you'll have the time of your life. Come with me."

Envisioning Nate Noruta *begging* destroyed all of her reservations. The man was ready to move mountains for her. How many times in her life would she have the opportunity to take advantage of this exact situation? For once, the answer was clear.

"Okay," Claire said. "I'll go with you."

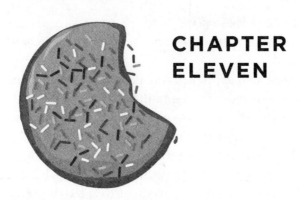

CHAPTER ELEVEN

When Claire got home, she immediately started packing. The very first day they'd met, Nate had mentioned Paris. Was he really taking her there? Rational thought dictated this was not likely, but when it came to Nate, all reason flew out the window. He certainly had the means to take her literally anywhere.

She grabbed her passport and froze, all tangled up in her thoughts and emotions. What was it about Nate that brought out such recklessness and made her throw caution to the wind, when all she'd wanted was a simple, unadorned life? He was some kind of wizard in disguise. That had to be it.

This whole experience got her so flustered, she lost all of her basic packing skills. She peered inside her suitcase. Four pairs of shorts, a tank top, six thongs, and a pair of mismatched socks. How was this supposed to do her any good?

After a few cleansing breaths, she stopped rushing around the apartment like a headless chicken and sat down on the couch. She sent a text to Todd.

Could you fill in for my shifts for the next 2 days? Pretty please?

He responded in a few minutes.

Of course, doll. But you owe me. *devil face emoji*

Thanks love! You get free cookies for life!

You'd better have those cookies ready when you get back cuz we're gonna have a major dish sesh. Take care and have fun!

Claire grinned and set her phone down. She loved Todd fiercely. The guy was more than qualified to lead a TED talk on friendship and loyalty. It was a shame she couldn't share her secret with her sisters, though. They spelled disaster for all her past boyfriends. Sam had a knack for pointing out the doomed parts of the relationship. Ro, on the other hand, always tried to convince Claire to be more daring and assertive. It only served to heighten Claire's uncertainty and resulted in a lot of strain on the relationship.

When she finished packing, she did a quick check of all the basics in her suitcase. The phone charger was missing. Just as she was unplugging the charger from the wall in her room, someone knocked at the front door. She rushed back into the living room and peered through the peep hole, wishing and hoping it was Nate somehow. Disappointment set in when she saw a stranger standing there. She opened the door slightly.

"Good evening," the man said. "Are you Miss Claire Ventura? I'm Craig Haverford, Mr. Noruta's assistant."

Claire looked up at him, surprised by the pleasant formality in his tone. Craig was about the same age and height as Nate, but his build was much slimmer. He was dressed impeccably in a blue-and-white floral print polo shirt and form-fitting navy slacks. Craig could definitely have been a runway model for one of those artsy fashion houses. Regardless, Claire liked his warm expression and sharp eyes. He seemed trustworthy.

"Hi, Craig, it's nice to meet you."

"Likewise. Do you have your passport?"

"Yes…" She reached into her purse. Her heart skipped when she realized it wasn't there. "Wait. It's not in here. Hold on a sec."

Claire unzipped her suitcase and did a frantic search

through her belongings but couldn't find it. Just when she was about to flip her lid, she saw it lying on the side table near the couch.

"Oh thank God." She grabbed the passport and lifted it up into the air. "I found it."

"Found what?"

Everything came to a grinding halt at the sound of Ro's voice.

"Ro!" Claire spun around and saw her sister standing beside Craig. "What the hell are you doing home? Aren't you supposed to be at work?"

Ro's eyes appraised Craig from head to toe. She cocked her eyebrow in approval, then turned her attention to Claire.

"I forgot my wallet at home." She stepped into the apartment. The sight of the suitcase and passport lit up her face in intrigue. "Where are you going, Ate? And who is this young man?"

Claire's eyes shot back and forth between Ro and Craig as she rapidly contemplated her next steps.

"Craig, could you please excuse us for a second?"

"Of course." He nodded politely and remained outside as he shut the door.

Once they were alone, Claire started to panic. No words would even come to mind to explain this strange turn of events.

"Well?" Ro asked, hands on her hips. "Who was that? Are you dating him?"

"Um...no. I'm not dating him. He's just taking me to the airport."

Ro gasped, her eyes wide with excitement.

"I know what you're doing! You met some guy on a dating app, and he's flying you out to meet him. I'm right, aren't I?"

Claire froze.

Ro's guess sounded preposterous. However, Claire wasn't ready to spill the truth, so she nodded.

"Ate, don't be ashamed," Ro said as she reached out and

rubbed Claire's arms reassuringly. "My friends do this all the time. Well, not all the time, but this is a common thing."

"It is?" Claire squeaked.

"Absolutely. Sometimes if you're lucky, you can get someone to fly you out to meet them. I can totally see why you'd want to keep this to yourself, but you can trust me. I don't judge. If you've gotta get yours, go and get it. I'm kind of relieved. I was afraid you'd end up alone forever, but there might be hope for you yet."

"Thanks," she said, blinking in disbelief.

"This isn't the Stone Age," Ro replied. "Things are different now. People are meeting through apps and the internet, and a lot are even ending up married. You never know. This guy might be the one. But if your Spidey-sense starts tingling, get the hell out of there. And don't be disappointed if he doesn't look one hundred percent like his profile picture. As long as he looks at least seventy-five percent similar, it's all good. That's the threshold for catfishing."

"Seventy-five percent?" Claire repeated.

Ro grabbed her wallet off the kitchen counter and opened the front door.

"Okay, she's ready," Ro said, beckoning to Craig.

"Allow me," he said, grasping Claire's suitcase handle.

Claire shot a nervous glance at Ro.

"Aren't you going to go back to work?" she asked.

"I'm going to walk you to the car first," Ro answered. "I know how this works. I have to take a picture of the license plate. Just in case. You don't mind, do you?"

"Of course not," Craig answered as they headed away from the apartment.

"It's fine. You don't need to walk with us," Claire said as her anxiety kicked up a notch. "I can text you a picture of the license plate later."

"Oh, I insist," Ro replied, keeping up with Craig's brisk

pace. They headed down the stairs and across the parking lot toward the curb, where Craig had most likely parked. "You have to scope out the rides these dudes send to pick you up. It says a lot. One time, instead of an Uber, this guy sent my friend Georgie a stretch Hummer. Kind of cheesy, if you ask me. He ended up being a total creep, but luckily, he was harmless. So Craig, is the guy you're working for a total creep, too? Fill us in."

Claire held her breath as she waited for Craig to respond.

"He's not a creep," Craig replied.

"Do you know his name? What kind of job he has?" Ro prodded.

Claire bit her lip to refrain from telling Ro to shut it.

"I'm not at liberty to say."

"Come on, Craig," Ro said, turning on the charm. "You can tell me—*holy shit.*"

Ro's emphatic exclamation startled Claire. Craig stopped in front of a black SUV and opened the trunk with his remote.

"This is a fucking Lamborghini," Ro cried. "Did the guy rent this or does he own it?"

Claire stared at the car. She couldn't see it very well in the darkness, but the lamppost did a good enough job of illuminating the sleek, exotic beauty of the car.

"Okay, it's time you went back to work," Claire insisted, attempting to turn Ro away.

"Take a picture of the guy," Ro said excitedly, trying to peer at the interior of the car. "I wanna see what he looks like. And call me right after your date!"

Claire nodded and darted into the car. She stewed in awkward silence for a moment as Craig started up the engine and headed off into the night.

"I'm sorry about my sister," she said. "She's kind of intense."

"No worries," Craig replied.

"So what's the plan? Are we going to meet Nate at the airport? Where are we going, exactly?"

"He had to depart on an earlier flight. But don't worry. He chartered a private jet for you."

"A private jet?" Claire repeated in shock. "Isn't it...expensive?"

"You don't have to worry about the cost," Craig replied. "Mr. Noruta will take care of it."

"Are you at liberty to say where that destination is?"

Craig hesitated. Even though he didn't respond right away, Claire could hear the grin forming at his lips.

"I can't," he replied. "He wanted it to be a surprise. But you're more than welcome to ask Mr. Noruta anything you want. He might not be able to respond immediately, but you can reach out to him any time."

Claire pulled out her phone and shot another text to Nate. *Can you please tell me where I'm going? I'm dying to know.*

Her heart sank when he didn't text back immediately like he normally did. After a few minutes, though, he finally responded.

Do you really want me to ruin the surprise?

Claire's heart tittered, and her face lit up.

Give me a hint.

You already know where.

She gasped and almost dropped her phone. "Are we really going to Paris? As in, France the country?"

Her eyes connected with Craig's through the rearview mirror. His expression was unreadable as he said, with a twinkle in his gaze, "I'm not at *liberté* to say."

Instead of driving to the International terminal like she had many times as a child, either departing to the Philippines or waiting for relatives returning from the motherland, Craig drove her to a place called the Private Terminal. It was a cobalt blue, futuristic building separate from the main terminal of LAX.

From there, she went straight through the TSA checkpoint, through a plush lounge with a full bar and swanky furniture, to the tarmac where a BMW drove her and Craig directly to the private jet.

All in less than ten minutes.

Claire exited the car and gaped at her surroundings. The night skies seemed wider and more wondrous out here, with the majestic airplanes and jets dotting the runway. The roars of the engines seemed to drown out the gallop of her heart as she approached the steps leading up to the airplane.

Private jet, rather. She had to keep telling herself this was real life and not some parallel dimension where dreams she hadn't even had yet came true.

Craig reached the top of the steps and turned, offering a hand to Claire. She grasped his hand for a moment and stepped into the cabin. She didn't quite know how to feel as she stared at the interior, with its cream-and-beige leather seats, woodgrain details, and tiny star-like lights lined up and down the central aisle.

"Welcome, Miss Ventura. I'm Brooke, and I will be your flight attendant." A statuesque blond woman in a crisp burgundy skirted uniform smiled at Claire. "Please have a seat anywhere. May I get you a drink?"

"No thanks." Claire sat down immediately in the nearest seat, clutching her purse tightly in her lap as the trepidation crept back up on her. She cursed in silence, regretting her decision to refuse the drink. She glanced across the aisle at Craig, who was settling down in the chair and getting comfortable as he ordered a drink from Brooke.

"What are we supposed to do now?" Claire asked.

Craig removed his laptop from his bag and placed it on the table in front of him.

"I'm going to check my emails," he replied. "We're taking off soon, but I suppose you can do whatever you want. There's no password for the wifi."

Claire leaned back in her seat. Brooke came by again and offered her a plush burgundy blanket, which she took even though it wasn't cold at all. She reached into her purse and pulled out her eReader, figuring she should finish the last chapter of her latest Regency romance novel. Even as she opened the eBook, though, she couldn't concentrate. An abundance of nervous energy swirled in her veins.

"Craig, I'm sorry to bother you, but can I ask you something?"

He removed his earbuds and turned toward her. "Sure," he said.

Claire paused for a moment, struggling to form her thoughts into words.

"Nate's really interesting," she said. "He's a lot different than what I expected him to be."

"What did you expect?"

"I don't really know," she admitted. "But definitely not someone like him. I mean...he's really sweet and considerate. He's funny and charming, and he seems so normal. I wouldn't expect many guys in his position to act so down to earth. Do you know what I mean?"

Craig hesitated. "Yes," he said after a moment of consideration. "I suppose I do."

Claire wanted to get to the heart of the matter, which was to ask point-blank: *Why do you think Nate likes me? Why not someone else more beautiful, more wealthy, more sophisticated?* But she lost her nerve right when she opened her mouth.

"Um...does he ever talk about me?" she asked.

"No," Craig said. "That's not really the kind of relationship we have. However, I can tell you a few things I've observed. He's canceled meetings and moved his schedule around to accommodate his time with you. He's seemed...more cheerful as of late. Also, he's never asked me to charter a private jet to fly anyone out to meet him overseas."

"Really?" she said. "Oh my God. What do you think that means?"

"Well, I can't speak for him," Craig replied. "So I don't know for sure."

Disappointment rushed in, and Claire averted her gaze. She should have known better than to ask such a personal, intrusive question.

"Oh," she said.

"But..." Craig leaned a little closer. "This is between you and me. Mr. Noruta is one of the hardest working people I know. Perhaps if you're worth going through all this trouble for, you must be really special to him. You seem to make him...happy."

CHAPTER TWELVE

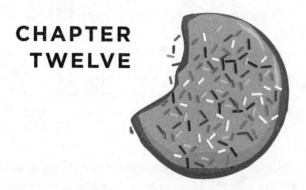

*W*elcome to Paris. I can't wait to see you.

The text message woke Claire from her nap, and she smiled. Even in a strange country, Nate made her feel like she was home.

Home.

The thought was like a splash of cold water to the face. There was no denying the powerful feelings Nate conjured within her. Actually, the word "powerful" wasn't even enough. He could make her forget herself. She'd left her home and responsibilities behind for...whatever this was. Regardless, she wanted to see where this journey took her. She only hoped her heart would emerge on the other side unscathed.

Craig escorted her from the jet and through the Charles de Gaulle airport. Her body protested with the stirrings of jet lag, but the adrenaline rush flooded everything else out. She was in Paris. The place she had dreamed of for years. It wasn't until they got into another fancy car (the make of which she was sure Ro would have been able to elaborate on) that the reality of everything sank in.

It was late at night, and the city twinkled like a star-speckled galaxy. The magic and beauty of Paris settled itself onto her skin. It was nostalgia and history, beauty and vice all thrumming through the city like an endless heartbeat. Her emotions heightened every time they passed by a famous landmark she recognized: the Eiffel Tower, the Arc de Triomphe, the Louvre, the Seine. Would they get a chance to visit those places together? Her entire body tingled with anticipation as she hoped *yes* with all her heart.

Claire forced her feet back to the ground and called Lola's facility. It was just after lunchtime back in California. Claire's worry eased when the attendant confirmed Lola was doing well. She shot off another text to Todd, confirming she'd landed safe and sound. A painful sense of guilt closed around her when she considered not contacting Ro. She wasn't upset with her. Ro could be intrusive, and Claire wasn't ready to talk about Nate yet. She still owed Ro a text, though. She figured there was nothing to worry about because Ro was probably still asleep. So she bit the bullet and texted her.

Claire's heart nearly froze when the response bubble appeared almost immediately

Who's the guy? Can you send me a pic?

She pursed her lips and shot off a final text.

Not right now. I'll get back to you soon.

She stuffed her phone back into her purse and ignored the next rapid succession of texts from Ro. A part of Claire was afraid her sister would actually call, but to her relief it never happened.

Instead, she turned her attention back to the Paris nightlife as it whizzed by in a blaze of lights and shadows. She drank everything in and tried to take pictures of beautiful buildings whenever they stopped. Even at this time of night, there was a healthy dose of bumper-to-bumper traffic clogging up the gridwork of the bustling city streets and highways.

Finally, the car pulled up in front of a building. Craig stowed his laptop away as the driver of the car opened the door for Claire. She thanked him and gazed up at the building in awe. The gold-plated sign said HOTEL LA JEUNESSE DE CREPSCULE. It was not the biggest hotel she'd seen, but it was still formidable. The gorgeous modern architecture and strategically placed lights along the building gave an updated, yet classically beautiful sense of style to this *arrondissement*. A bellman in a flawless navy blue uniform loaded the suitcases onto a trolley as Craig led Claire into the building through the revolving doors.

The splendor of the decor stole her breath. The low romantic lights twinkled spectacularly against the glistening dark granite floor, making it look like a sea of starlight. There were so many upscale artistic details built into every wall panel, sconce, and lush flora situated throughout the lobby that she couldn't keep up with it all. Dignified-looking hotel employees nodded in acknowledgment to her and Craig as they stepped into the elevator with the bellman.

"Mr. Noruta is already upstairs," Craig explained. "He's currently on a phone conference but he will be done shortly. The suite itself has five bedrooms. You're welcome to choose where you want to stay."

"Five bedrooms?" The thought of such a huge suite made her somewhat uncomfortable. "How many people are staying there?"

"I'm afraid I gave you the wrong impression," Craig said. "The only people staying at the executive suite are you and Mr. Noruta. I have my own room down the hall. We're here for the Technology Live summit. Have you ever heard of it before?"

Claire shook her head.

"Technology Live is the biggest tech and start-up summit in Europe. Influential speakers from all across the world and different businesses come to speak about certain topics, brainstorm innovations, and hear pitches from fledgling start-ups. Mr. Noruta is one of the keynote speakers and will be on several panels. Did he extend an invitation to you yet?"

"No, he never mentioned it at all."

"Don't worry. You'll get a VIP pass to access the summit. It will give you unrestricted access to all of the keynote speeches, panels, and workshops."

A spark of excitement ignited in her. Although she knew practically nothing about the tech industry, this was the perfect opportunity to get a real glimpse into Nate's passion and his life's work.

The elevator stopped at the top floor, and Craig used a keycard to access the executive suite. She barely registered the opulent, modern surroundings of the enormous room as she stepped inside. All she could think about was the one person she'd flown ten thousand miles for in the middle of a work week.

Her pulse sped up again. She got light-headed. Maybe it was the proximity to Nate—she couldn't see him, but her body knew he was near. In the meantime, she gazed through the huge windows overlooking the stunning vista of Paris and the gilded lights of the Eiffel Tower shining in the distance.

A door opened somewhere in the room. Footsteps approached.

"Claire."

She turned, and there he was. His simple outfit of faded jeans and a cable-knit gray sweater did nothing to obscure his hotness. Just as she feared, Nate's spell made her swoon even harder than she had before. The moment she laid eyes on him, all of the worries squeezing her chest vanished as if they'd never existed.

He closed the space between them with a few tentative steps. She met his gaze with bold curiosity. Would she see hunger there? A demanding, intense gaze with the power to scare her away and convince her this was all an epic mistake?

Instead, she saw the man she knew. He was simply Nate, the man who'd helped her decorate cookies and cared about her and the wellbeing of her family. Nate, the handsome man with soulful eyes, who could do amazing things with his mouth and hands. Nate, the man who respected her and treated her like a queen, even though she didn't feel she deserved it.

Nate, the one who she could see herself…falling in love with.

Claire stepped toward him, too, until they were in each other's arms. She held him tight for a brief moment, and she reveled in his solid warmth pressing against her chest, his large hands spanning across her lower back. When they broke apart, he smiled down at her with an excited gleam in his eyes.

"How was your flight?" he asked. "Were you comfortable? Was everything okay?"

"Yes. Everything was perfect."

He smiled and laced his fingers with hers, leading her to the rust-colored sofa in the living room. Craig and Nate nodded in acknowledgment of one another as Craig rolled his suitcase with him out the front door. Now they were alone, and Nate's presence was like a catalyst to her senses; everything was so vivid and clear and beautiful when she was with him.

"I figure this is probably an intense experience for you," Nate said. "Why don't you have something to eat? I had room service bring up a tray of their best desserts." He gestured to the bar behind him. Claire spotted a silver platter laden with an enticing array of artful sweets and pastries.

"Oh, how sweet of you. Literally and figuratively," Claire said, squeezing his hand with a warm smile. "But I'm not hungry."

"No, you should eat something." Nate got up and headed to the bar. He plucked a dessert off the tray, bringing it back to her on a delicate ceramic plate. "And something to drink."

He went back to the bar to fetch her a flute of champagne.

She was speechless for a moment. The refreshments looked amazing, but she had no appetite…for food. Rather than hurt his feelings, she took a sip of champagne and a bite of the delectable, flaky napoleon he'd offered her. Maybe it was the champagne mixing with the delicious pastry in her belly, but she felt like she was on top of the world, and nothing would ever tear her down. She gave him a peck on the cheek and wrapped her arms around him in a powerful hug.

Nate hesitated a moment before his arms wrapped around her, too.

"Where's this coming from?" The satisfied smile Claire heard in his voice warmed her tired, jet-lagged heart.

"You're the nicest person I've ever met." She pulled back and looked up at him. "I just thought you ought to know."

"If you could tell my board members and the rest of my employees that, I would really appreciate it," he replied, tucking a lock of hair behind her ear. "Craig told you about the Technology Live Summit, right? I would be honored if you'd be my guest. I'm speaking on a few panels, and I'm the keynote this year. There will be a lot of downtime for you, so you'll be free to explore the exhibits. But if you need anything, you can let me know."

"It sounds fun," Claire replied. "I've never been to any kind of tech convention. I'm excited to see you in action. I have a feeling your talents go farther than being an assistant cookie decorator."

A warm silence stretched between them. Nate smiled at her and took her hand in both of his. She released a contented sigh and leaned her head on his shoulder. For all the fanciness of this astonishing hotel, cuddling next to Nate on the sofa was the highlight of her trip so far.

"Are you tired?" he asked. "Maybe you should take a nap. We can postpone our date until you're feeling up to it."

"No." Claire shook her head vigorously. "I'm in Paris. I don't want to waste a minute. I'm fine, actually. I slept a lot on the jet, but I should really take a shower."

"Of course. There are five rooms here, but I chose one for you I thought you'd like the best."

Nate guided her from the living room to a staircase that spiraled up to a second floor she hadn't even noticed. The top of the staircase opened up to a landing that led to one of the most gorgeous bedrooms Claire had ever seen. The decor here mirrored the entire theme of the hotel, down to the beautiful pieces of custom-made furniture. Framed art depicting the moon and nighttime hung all about the room. There was also a large walk-in closet and a private bathroom with a giant sunken tub and enormous shower with three huge rainwater heads inside.

"I want to show you something," Nate said. He led Claire into the closet. At first she couldn't understand why they went there, but then her eyes fell on something that took her breath away.

A stunning pale blue and silver gown hung on a rack, its flowing train spread out like a sprawling lake upon the ground. An open jewelry box sat on a bureau beside the dress. Claire held her breath and approached it to get a better look. Nestled inside the box was a necklace that looked like it belonged in the Crown Jewels collection. The diamonds shimmered under the lights so brightly they made her squint. A pair of huge teardrop diamond earrings hung on a little display beside the necklace.

Claire's words lodged painfully in her throat. She had no idea what to make of all of this. The gown, the jewels, the private jet, the suite... It was too much, and she had to sit down.

"What's the matter?" Nate asked as she released his hand and settled on a footstool.

"I can't accept this," she said. "You shouldn't feel the need to splurge for me. That's not necessary."

Nate crouched in front of Claire and gently placed his hand on her knee.

"But this was your dream date," he said. "Your fantasy. The one with the duke's son and the teacher. I didn't mean any harm by it. I thought you would enjoy it. I even arranged for a candlelit dinner on the terrace."

Claire leaned forward and captured Nate's delectable lips

with her own. It was a gentle kiss, soft and exploring. Even still, Claire's craving for him spiraled unchecked as always.

Her eager fingers trailed from the satisfying roughness of his beard, and her arms encircled his shoulders. Their kiss grew more urgent and hungry—full of a desire that held them both in thrall. Fully aware where this was headed, Claire mustered the power of a thousand stallions and abruptly ended their kiss.

"Shower. First," she breathed, slowly pulling away from his grip.

"I already showered, but I don't mind jumping in there with you," he teased.

"If you continue to impress me during our date, you might get a chance later on."

Nate leaned in and gave her another breath-stealing kiss.

"I'll see you soon." He cast her a fleeting, sexy smile, then turned and left the room.

CHAPTER THIRTEEN

The shower in her room was so huge, it reminded Claire of an empty warehouse. She didn't want to think about how many people probably fit themselves in here all at once.

After her shower, she stood in front of the mirror, staring at someone who looked like her but was dressed in a gown that probably cost twice as much as her rent. She had always romanticized dressing up like a princess. Yet, as the confines of the bodice squeezed her ribcage, pushing her breasts up to unnatural heights, she wondered how a woman could be in the mood for love when she had to struggle to take a normal breath.

This was definitely *not* how she envisioned the romance heroines felt when they were about to get ravished by a duke.

Her hands shook as she fastened the diamond earrings and necklace on. The thought of how much money she wore on her body turned her stomach. It was enough to feed an entire family for a year—maybe enough to open a clinic in a foreign country where they lacked access to regular healthcare.

"Oh my goodness, stop it." Claire frowned at herself in the mirror. Sometimes her wayward thoughts got the better of her. Sam and Ro would tell her to "get out of her head" whenever she stressed herself out. It was much easier said than done.

Claire's hands shook so badly it took almost five minutes to clasp the necklace. Even when it was in place, she was scared it would fall off because it was so heavy. But after a few shallow breaths in her corset cage, Claire convinced herself she was ready.

With the utmost care, she gripped the banister and headed down the stairs. It took a great deal of coordination and strategy to negotiate each step without tripping and tumbling down the stairs like a big blue snowball.

Nate met her at the bottom of the stairs. Claire's knees almost buckled when she laid eyes on him. God almighty, the man was finer than fine. He stood before her, dressed in an impeccable black tuxedo and bowtie. He looked so good she had trouble believing he was real. But when his eyes swept over her and he took her hand in his warm, strong one, she knew he was very real.

And for tonight, he was hers.

Nate pressed a gentle kiss to her hand.

"Claire," he said, his voice low and reverent. "You're so pretty."

Claire's hand tingled where Nate's soft lips met her skin.

"Thanks," she replied with a coy smile. "You look amazing, too. I mean—you look absolutely dashing."

Nate led Claire across the living room toward the open doors leading onto the sprawling terrace. It was her first glimpse of the city in all its glory. The night skies made the Paris cityscape and its thousands of lights even more stunning and awe-inspiring. The essence of romance and whispers and stolen kisses rose up from the foundations of the city. Claire could feel it all seeping into her soul, and the sensations were made all the more potent with Nate by her side.

"I can't believe I'm actually here," she said, her voice filled with longing. "I would never, ever get tired of this view."

"Neither could I." Nate's eyes stayed only on Claire as he led her farther down the terrace toward a table set for a candlelit dinner for two.

"You're doing very well for yourself, Mr. Noruta," she said, sitting down across from him. A twinge of pain hit her side as the dress squeezed her.

"Are you okay?" he asked.

"Yes"—*breathe*—"I'm okay."

"If you're not comfortable, we can sit somewhere else."

"No, I'm fine," Claire replied. "I love it out here. The weather is fantastic, the city is just so beautiful…it's beckoning me and I want to sit out here and enjoy it."

A waiter in a white uniform appeared from a side door, carrying a tray. Claire watched in anticipation as he set down two elegant white bowls of pale green-colored soup in front of them.

"Oooh, what is this?" she asked, her eyes wide with excitement.

"It's a French soup called *vichyssoise*," Nate replied. "It's made of leeks and potatoes. Aside from the fact it's served chilled, it's actually pretty good."

Claire eyed the dish. She was a tad dubious about cold soup, but she knew Nate was pulling out all the stops to impress her.

"It looks good," she replied, reaching for the silver spoon. "I can't wait to try everything. Especially the rest of those desserts you ordered earlier. They look amazing."

"Of course." Nate started to get up. "I'll bring them to you now—"

"No! You don't have to do that." Claire implored Nate to sit back down. "Stay here with me."

She leaned forward to eat, but the dress stopped her short. The bodice was so stiff and tight she couldn't even sit at ninety degrees. Nate's spoon paused halfway to his lips, and he raised an eyebrow. Claire smiled and made a dismissive gesture with her hand. As gracefully as she could, she scooted her chair forward once…then twice. On the second scoot, her heavy diamond necklace slithered off her neck and fell into the *vichyssoise* with a resonant *plop*.

Claire froze. Her mouth stretched into a silent O as she stared at the fortune in huge diamonds resting inside a pool of liquefied leeks and potatoes.

"Oh my God, I'm such a klutz!" Claire fumbled the necklace out of the soup and shook it over the ground, sending drops of soup flying. "Nate, I'm so, so sorry. I hope I haven't ruined it forever. Do they have jewelry cleaner here? Maybe if I run it under some hot water and wrap it in a towel it'll—"

The sound of deep laughter stopped Claire's tirade. She looked up in surprise and saw pure delight flickering in Nate's eyes.

"Don't even worry about it," he said. "I don't care about the necklace."

"What do you mean you don't care about the necklace? This thing must be worth a fortune. Give me a second and I'll fix it."

"Leave it." Nate stood up and approached Claire. He reached for her free hand and guided her to stand. "Let's get out of here."

"But...what about the necklace?" Claire stuttered. "What about our candlelit dinner? God, I messed this one up, didn't I? Nate, you are the sweetest guy I have ever met, and I love this. I really appreciate you..."

Claire's words trailed off as Nate leaned in to kiss her. His gentle, warm lips stole every wandering thought, leaving her body pliant and melting with desire. He pulled away but kept her firmly in the circle of his strong arms.

"Something tells me you'd rather be out there, exploring the city," he said. "I'm more than game to play out your fantasy, but I'd have just as much fun walking the Paris streets with you. What do you think?"

"I think...that's the best idea." She threw her arms around Nate, holding him tight. She had no idea what she'd done to deserve someone like him. Even though her sensible side told her things were moving too fast, the swooning, love-drunk teen in Claire clung to Nate with every fiber of her being.

"I'm glad," he murmured into the strands of her thick, dark hair. He pulled away and gazed at her. "We can change into comfortable clothes. But beforehand, let's dig into the desserts. I think you'll really enjoy them."

Claire made a little squeal inside her throat. Her trip to Paris was off to an amazing start. Excitement lit her up from the inside out as she wondered what other amazing things this trip had in store for them.

Hand in hand, they struck out onto the romantic streets of Paris. She'd been liberated from the confines of the dress and now wore comfortable jeans and a loose shirt. With her sneakered feet on solid ground, and her ribs no longer crushed in a vise grip, Claire could feel the essence of the city capturing her heart and soul.

It was almost three in the morning. Despite the lull of the early morning hour, the city was still alive with adventurous, jet-lagged tourists looking to catch the thrills only Paris could give them.

"Where do you want to go?" Nate asked as he and Claire darted across the street.

"I'm starving," she said. "Let's keep walking until we find something. Are there twenty-four-hour places here in Paris, too?"

"Not like *Donizza* back home, but I think we'll find something that will suffice."

She laughed and squeezed Nate's hand tighter. She didn't think there was a level of happiness higher than this. Cloud nine? The term had lost all meaning. With Nate by her side, Claire knew how it felt to fly off into the stratosphere and get lost in the galaxy.

With every step they took within the picturesque backdrop of the French *arrondissements*, they finally got to know each other. Claire was able to delve deeper into Nate's life. She found out he was the only child of Patricia Noruta, a third-generation Japanese-American woman. She lived in a suburb just outside Seattle, and worked as a diner waitress. She'd raised him on her own because his father was not a part of the picture.

As a child, he was obsessed with video games. All he wanted was to plug into his game system and take a deep dive into virtual worlds. The only sport he liked was swimming, which came naturally. His mother had been concerned his obsession with video games would stunt his social and academic growth, but that wasn't the case. He managed to excel in school and swimming, even when he took up coding as another obsession.

Eventually he got accepted into Stanford on a full-ride scholarship for computer science. He was a division-one freestyle swimmer, and he graduated with honors. All the while, he worked with other computer savants like himself to develop programming platforms to help change the world and bridge the gap between technology and social needs. During college, he and his colleagues developed the prototype of *MyConnect*, which would eventually become one of the biggest social media platforms in the entire world, second only to Facebook.

Nate paused his tale as he stopped in front of a café. The sudden pause surprised Claire and jolted her from Nate's past life right into the present.

"*Claire de Lune Café*," he said, gazing up at the sign. "We definitely have to go in here."

The small, cozy café immediately enveloped them in an old-world ambiance reminiscent of bed and breakfasts from the French countryside. Claire took a seat across from Nate at a small round table topped with a slender vase containing a single, tiny red rose. Claire tried out her high school French by ordering hors d'oeuvres and espresso from the waiter.

After enjoying their little meal at the café, they hopped into a taxi that took them farther north to central Paris, where they explored the river Seine and the Eiffel Tower under the watchful stars. Claire took a few pictures of the scenery, but she wanted memories of her and Nate. She started snapping selfies of them together, and some of Nate by himself. She was relieved he didn't seem to mind.

They reached the top of the Eiffel Tower, and Nate decided it was his turn to be the photographer. He leaned in and kissed her cheek, taking their selfie with the stunning city lights stretching out below them. Claire giggled as he pulled her against his chest. Together, they drank in the city from their vantage point in the heavens. The vista of Paris under the dusky skies of approaching sunrise stole her breath away.

The moment was perfect. *Too perfect.*

An unwelcome thought shoved its way into her brain, and she blurted it out before she lost her nerve.

"Are you seeing any other women?" she asked. "Or, are you more of a one-woman type of guy? You said you don't date many women. So how many are you dating right now? Am I the only one? I'm sorry if I sound silly. It's just that…I *like* you, and I want to know where I stand."

When Nate didn't respond right away, she pulled back to see his reaction. Soft starlight limned his gorgeous face. He didn't look upset at all. As always, he appeared amused whenever she rambled on.

"You're the only one." He looked down at her, the darkness behind his eyes bold and enigmatic. "How about you? Are you dating other guys?"

"Of course not," she replied. "I'm—"

She suddenly remembered something she had tried so hard to forget. That damned dating app, *VioLit,* was such a nuisance. She only did it show support for Sam, but it made her feel guilty. Who was she to question Nate when she was the one who was casting her net far and wide?

"No," Claire said. "I'm not dating anyone else."

"Why the pause?"

"Because…okay. I'm not dating anyone else, but I created a profile on *VioLit*. Don't get the wrong idea. I did it for my sister. She got divorced six months ago, and she wants to try dating again, but she wants me to start dating, too. The problem is, I don't like dating. And I hate dating apps. I mean, I'm not trying to insult you, because I know you own *VioLit*. Am I offending you? Maybe I should stop talking."

"So I've got competition," Nate said, raising his eyebrows. "Open the app. I want to see who you matched with."

"What? No! That's ridiculous," Claire said, holding her phone away as Nate reached for it. "I'm deleting the app right now."

She swiped to the app and noticed she had a new alert.

"Would you look at that," Nate said. "You can't delete it now. It looks like you have a match."

"That's weird. I never even check this thing. I turned off all the notifications."

"You're not curious at all?" he asked.

"No."

"Don't you feel sorry for the poor guy? He matched with you, fair and square. He probably saw your gorgeous profile picture, fell head-over-heels, and swiped right without a second thought."

Claire narrowed her eyes in suspicion and opened the app. Sure enough, on the front page, she had only one match. Interesting. He looked a lot like the mischievous man standing in front of her.

"You know what? This guy is pretty hot," Claire said. "I think I'd rather be with him."

"He'll have to fight me for you." Nate swept her up into his arms. She yelped, startling another couple standing nearby.

"I'm so sorry," she said, her voice full of laughter. "Je suis desolée."

She clung to Nate, closing her eyes and hugging him tighter. He walked the both of them to a far corner, away from the others on the tower. He set her down in the shadows and bent down, covering her mouth with his own. The kiss was slow and passionate, his lips hungrily sliding over hers, his tongue dipping in to taste her. His actions pulled a moan out of her, and she pressed herself more firmly against his body.

Something heady and potent hit Claire at that moment, and from the way Nate looked at her, it probably hit him, too. Maybe it was the first inklings of the Paris sunrise creeping over the waning twilight of the city, or the way the shadows caressed Nate's face and made him look like a fantasy lover straight out of Claire's deepest, darkest dreams.

The kiss morphed from passionate to hungry. Wanton. The reins of control slipped as her hands roamed freely over Nate's firm, muscled form, reveling in every dip and line of his athletic body. Nate backed her against a pillar, continuing to plunder her eager lips. The feeling of his hard body pinning her down, his erection hard and insistent against her belly, had her inhibitions dying a fiery death. She boldly slipped her hand down to grasp him through his jeans.

"I want you so bad," he whispered against her mouth. "Let's go."

CHAPTER FOURTEEN

Claire lost all semblance of space and time. All she could register was: Uber. Nate. Hotel. Nate. Elevator. Nate.

She figured he probably experienced something similar. The only sign of his barely restrained control was the wide, possessive hand he splayed over her hip as he held her close to him on the elevator ride back up to the hotel room.

"Aren't you tired?" she asked. "I thought you had to start getting ready for the tech summit."

The elevator doors slid open and Nate swept her into his arms again, wrapping her legs around his waist.

"There's only one thing I want to do right now." His voice was gruff as he strode purposefully down the hallway toward their room at the far end. "I think you know what it is."

With a deft swipe of his hips, he unlocked the door with the keycard in his pocket. He strode into the suite and turned left into a spacious bedroom lit only by the dim golden light from the lamppost on the street below. He set Claire down on the bed. Rising up on her knees, she kissed Nate as she eagerly yanked at his clothes.

She closed her eyes and let the ambiance of the darkened room wrap its spell around her. She heard the gentle rustle of clothing as he undressed. She opened her eyes when his hands wrapped around her waist, and she melted into his urgent, hungry touch. Gentle but insistent fingers drifted across her belly as he lifted her shirt above her head. He tenderly kissed the skin above her wildly beating heart.

"I've been waiting for this moment forever," he said. "Ever since I got a taste of you the other day, I haven't stopped thinking about it." Nate's lips trailed down the delicate line of her jaw to the tender, heated flesh of her throat. The sensation of his beard and its gentle roughness against her sensitive skin set fire to every nerve ending. His hands smoothed over her body, worshiping the lines and the shape of her. She guided his hands to her jeans, where he eagerly unclasped the buttons and eased them down.

Claire grasped his face and brought their lips together again. The way he kissed put her past exes to shame, and all she wanted was the sensation of his lips blazing paths of fire across every surface of her skin. Nate pulled her against his body and thrust himself against her.

"You drive me insane," he growled. "I lose control when I'm with you. Tell me what to do, Claire. Tell me what you want."

Hearing Nate practically begging sent throbbing heat straight to her core. Instead of answering, she guided his hand down to her sex. She rose back up to her knees on the bed, and he slipped a finger beneath her panties, gently running it up and down her cleft.

"You're so wet for me. Tell me what you want me to do. I'm all yours."

His words were too much. They were almost worshipful, and she couldn't get enough.

"I want you…to go deeper."

"Like this?"

Nate's finger slipped easily past her folds to the swollen bud at the crest of her sex. She whimpered as he traced steady circles around it, each stroke making her weaker. A tingling sensation started at the base of her spine and spread down to the tips of her toes. Her knees began to tremble.

"Wait," he said, withdrawing his finger and almost sending Claire into a fit. "I want to taste you when you come." He moved away from her and walked to the head of the bed. With all her inhibitions burned to cinders, Claire feasted her eyes on Nate's naked form. The soft light of daybreak filtered in through the curtained window, highlighting every masculine line and ridge of his sculpted body. Her eyes skimmed farther down, down past his rock-hard abs to the part she was eager to see.

Holy fuck.

He was a big boy, indeed. Claire had seen several penises in real life, and all of them were perfunctory enough. But this was not a regular penis. This was a *cock*—long and thick and beautiful all at once. He had the kind of dick that belonged in porn, and Claire was certain her eyes were deceiving her.

The movement of Nate climbing into bed snapped Claire out of her trance. He lay down and beckoned to her.

"Come here."

She crawled over to him, then straddled his hips, and she was surprised when he gripped her firmly and pulled her toward him until her pussy hovered over his face. She braced her hands against the headboard as he pulled her hips down, pressing his lips and tongue against her soft heat.

"Oh, Nate." Claire's voice was a breathy whisper as she closed her fingers around the headboard in a death grip. "Oh my God."

There was no other word to use to describe his mouth other than "magic." Blood thundered through her veins all the way to her most aroused parts, making her feel higher than the clouds. He reached up and plucked at her nipples, sending more jolts of arousal straight to her clit. Every nerve ending sparked, and every breath was a steady climb to dizzying heights.

Her hips began to move. They were tentative at first, but when Nate groaned in approval, she began to fuck his face in earnest. She rubbed herself against his mouth, the sensation of his tongue flicking her sensitive flesh driving every coherent thought out of her mind.

"Oh my God," Claire gasped. "You're making me come. You're making me—"

A scream of ecstasy tore from Claire's lips as the orgasmic rush hit. She could have held off for longer, but it was too difficult when she caught glimpses of Nate's gorgeous face buried in her sex, his expression almost worshipful. Her pussy contracted as delicious currents of pleasure speared their way through her body, making her limbs melt.

Even though it was one of the best orgasms of her life, she wanted more. The sight of him licking her one more time almost undid her all over again.

He rose up, cradling her in his arms and turning her onto her back. She was still in the throes of her post-orgasm glow, her limp body drifting in euphoria.

Nate gently notched himself between her thighs, rubbing his erection against her slick heat. Desire scattered her thoughts like feathers in the wind, but she managed to gather her wits for a brief moment.

"Do you have a condom?" she asked.

"Yes." Nate covered her mouth with his own, kissing her long and deep. He released her lips and trailed his tongue down the tender flesh of her throat, sucking and licking her. He finally reached into the drawer of the nightstand and pulled out the condom.

After rolling the condom onto his length, his strong hands gripped her thighs, spreading them wider. Claire looked down to the space between them, and saw him guiding himself to her sex. Fire blazed in Nate's hazel eyes as he locked his gaze with Claire's. And drove his cock deep inside her.

Her back arched as his thick length filled her. Mentally, she wasn't prepared for his girth. Physically, she was drenched and welcoming. She spread her legs more and wiggled her hips, trying to accommodate his size.

"Oh fuck." Nate paused for a moment. "You're so tight. Are you okay?"

The sight of their bodies joined together was more amazing than her best fantasies. He could stoke the flames of her desire like no one else. She pressed her heels into Nate's firm ass, urging him on.

Passion sang through her body as he began to move. The delicious friction of their skin and his groans of pleasure heightened every sensation in Claire. His thrusts began to build more force, and soon he was driving into her with abandon, each powerful stroke hitting that sensitive spot within her, pushing her toward another earth-shattering orgasm.

Nate seemed to be getting closer to his own release. Each pump of his hips became harder and more urgent.

"You're so perfect," he whispered. "So fucking perfect. I could do this forever with you."

He reached down and began to rub gentle circles against her clit. Claire gasped and jerked her hips up higher. That movement put her at the perfect angle for every thrust. Her thighs trembled as her release began to unravel.

"Yes, Nate, oh God, you feel so *good*."

She barely got out her last words as the orgasm hit. Wave after wave crashed over her as she clenched around Nate in rhythmic motions. Nate grunted and his hips thrust hard against her, nearly smacking her head into the headboard.

The breath left him in a rush as he came. Nate closed the space between their bodies, relishing their closeness as Claire's own orgasm left her floating in a state of pure bliss. A quiet, restful minute passed as their heated breathing returned to normal. Nate rolled off slowly and pulled her close against his chest.

Claire's drowsy eyes drifted to the golden morning light

spilling in through the window. Her eyelids fluttered as she tried to fight off sleep and remember every detail of their lovemaking. She fell asleep to the feel of Nate's warm, soft lips pressing a kiss to the base of her neck, and the wish that this moment would never end.

I forgot about Lola.

Claire awoke with a start, shocked she had overslept and didn't visit Lola. She fought off the grogginess as she pushed herself up in bed, struggling to get her thoughts together. It only took a second to get over the disorientation. Memories of last night flooded back into her brain, and peace settled over her.

Nate.

She gazed around the bedroom. He was nowhere to be seen.

Claire got up and found her clothes scattered all over the floor and the bed. After putting them back on, she crept to the door and opened it.

"Hello?" She peered out into the hallway and into the enormous suite. There was no response. "Is anyone here?"

She went back into the room and found her phone in her purse. To her relief, there was a message from Nate. But there were also a handful of phone calls and texts from both of her sisters and Todd. She opened Nate's message first.

Hey Sleeping Beauty. I had a meeting. I should be back by one thirty. Feel free to order room service. <3

She stared at the little red heart emoji at the end of the sentence. Part of her couldn't even believe last night was real, but the delicious ache between her thighs proved otherwise. How she had snagged a hot-as-hell guy with expert prowess in the bedroom was anyone's guess. She didn't even know it was possible to come twice in one night, but Nate proved it could be done quite well, like a consummate professional. Pun intended.

Nate was due to return in an hour. Eager to get the day started, she shook off the jet lag and hurried up the stairs to her suite. She eyed the large, lush bed as dirty images of what she and Nate could do there danced in her head. After a shower and change, she was ready to start making phone calls and taking care of business back at home.

A sense of guilt deflated her. What was she thinking, dropping everything at a moment's notice to fly across the Atlantic for a man she barely knew? She used to think that popping a squat on Highway 15 in the dead of night because she had to take a piss during a Vegas road trip was the wildest thing she had ever done. Turns out it really wasn't.

Claire switched gears to business mode. Just because she was living a literal fantasy moment didn't mean she could neglect her responsibilities at home. She set up her laptop at the desk and opened up her *Eclectix* vendor dashboard to check her orders. To her pleasant surprise, there were five new orders and two new positive reviews. She sent out order acknowledgment emails to her customers and responded to her direct messages.

Next, Claire made a phone call to the nursing station at Lola's assisted living facility. It was early morning back home. Fortunately, the overnight nurse on duty said Lola was fine, aside from refusal to eat her dinner the night before. Claire was concerned nonetheless. It was never a good sign when the elderly started skipping meals, especially the ones with Alzheimer's. At the very least, Lola seemed fine for now. Claire would request a family meeting to deal with the issue if it got more serious later on.

Now came the hard part. Ro. Her sister had sent her numerous texts demanding a response, and Claire could no longer ignore her. She closed her eyes for her mindfulness minute, hoping it would settle her nerves.

About two seconds into her mindfulness minute, someone

called her phone. It was none other than Ro requesting a video chat.

"Damn," Claire muttered. The only time Ro ever video chatted was when she was either in trouble or scared to death. Claire cleared her throat and answered the call.

"Hi." She pasted on her brightest smile and positioned the phone to prevent Ro from seeing the full surroundings. Ro's worried face came into full view as she peered intently at Claire.

"Ate? For fuck's sake, I've been scared shitless. I was *this* close to calling the police."

"You don't need to be dramatic," Claire replied, trying to keep her voice chipper. "I'm fine."

"Fine?" Ro repeated incredulously. "You never ever do anything like this. You're inexperienced with these kinds of dates. So many things could have happened, and I am so pissed at myself for letting you go."

"*Letting* me go?" Claire's voice hitched up in warning, and Ro's face instantly registered remorse.

"I was really worried about you," she said, "especially after you didn't return any of my texts. Where are you?"

"I'm...outside the country."

"Really? Where?"

"All you need to know is that I'm doing fine, and I should be home soon."

"When?"

There was a rustling sound so quiet Claire almost didn't hear it. She spun around and gasped when she saw Nate standing in the doorway, looking super hot in a black T-shirt and jeans.

"Ate? What's going on? You're really freaking me out."

Claire absentmindedly turned her phone over as he entered the room and headed straight for her. He gripped the armrests of her chair as he bent down and gave her a long, deep kiss.

"She sounds really worried," Nate said as he pulled Claire to stand so he could sit in the office chair. He pulled her down onto his lap and wrapped his arms around her waist. The delicious, male scent of him and his embrace turned Claire on all over again. "You should tell her where you are. That's your sister, right?"

"Yes, but...are you sure?"

"Of course I'm sure. Your family shouldn't worry about you like this. Why don't you tell her about us?"

Deep in her heart, Claire knew the answer. *Because I wanted to go as long as possible without any judgments and meddling from my sisters.* But she couldn't tell him that. It was too early in their relationship to start dumping her family issues on his head.

But Nate was right. She shouldn't leave Ro in the dark. She picked up the phone and centered her face in the frame.

"Ro, I am going to tell you everything, but I'll only do it if you calm down. Can you do that?"

Ro let out an indignant huff. "Yes. I'll calm down."

"Are you at work right now?" Claire asked.

"Yes, but I locked myself in the bathroom so I wouldn't get interrupted. Why are you being so secretive? What's going on?"

"Nothing bad is going on. I want to let you know..." She turned and looked to Nate for reassurance. "I'm dating someone."

"Okay," Ro replied, her tone dubious. "And?"

Instead of answering, Claire moved the phone away until the frame widened enough to capture her and Nate. He grinned at Ro as Claire sat awkwardly in his lap.

Ro's sharp gaze appraised the situation. Her look morphed from suspicion, to understanding, to confusion, then shock. Claire knew what was coming, but it was too late to do anything now.

"Oh my God!" Ro's voice was shrill as her image shook violently on Claire's screen. "The guy you're fucking is Nate Noruta? *How could you not tell me?*"

CHAPTER FIFTEEN

"Ro, please lower your voice," Claire said through clenched teeth.

"How can you expect me to lower my voice at a time like this? My sister is fucking Nate Noruta!"

"Watch. Your. Language," she warned. "Ro, this is Nate. Nate, this is my sister Ro. I apologize for her behavior."

"Hi," Nate said. To Claire's relief, he didn't react to the look of pure shock on her face. "It's a pleasure to meet you."

"Trust me, Mr. Noruta, the pleasure is all mine." She quickly recovered and flashed him a million-watt smile. "It makes perfect sense now: Ate's weirdness, the black Lambo... How did you two meet? Tell me everything."

"I would love to, but unfortunately I have plans," Nate answered. "We will definitely get a chance to connect later."

He leaned in and gave Claire's bottom an affectionate squeeze. "I'll see you at the conference," he mumbled in her ear.

Nate eased out of the chair but still held on to Claire's hand as he stood beside her.

"Hey, what are you two talking about?" Ro demanded. "Ate, I can't see you. Hold the phone up."

"Nate has to leave," Claire said, re-centering the phone. "He's speaking at a tech conference."

"It was nice meeting you." Nate smiled at Ro. Claire frowned at the captivated look pasted on her face. Clearly she was not immune to Nate's charm.

He brushed his thumb tenderly over Claire's hand. She couldn't blame her sister for being starstruck. Nate was looking like an absolute snack, and if he wasn't on his way somewhere, she would have hung up and taken the untouched bed in her suite for a test run with him.

Claire was over being shy. She bit her lip and flicked her gaze to the very nice part of him obscured under his zipper. He gave her a panty-searing look right before he kissed her.

"You're making it very hard to leave," he said, his voice low and sexy and dangerous.

"Am I really?" She grasped the back of his thigh and gave it a possessive squeeze.

A squeal came from the phone. Claire let go of Nate, suddenly remembering Ro's presence.

"Okay, I'll see you later," Claire said, giving Nate one final, lingering kiss.

He sauntered out of the room and went downstairs. All the while, Ro simply stared at her older sister, her eyes wide with a thousand explosive thoughts she was probably keeping bottled up.

"Is he gone?" Ro asked.

"Yes."

"Oh God, Ate, oh my God *ohmygod*."

Claire grimaced and lowered her phone volume.

"Stop shouting. Someone at your work is going to notice."

"If there ever was a reason to shout the whole entire building down, this would be it," Ro said. "I cannot believe what is happening. This is wild. This is huge."

"It's not that big of a deal," Claire said unconvincingly. "People date each other every day."

"I'm sorry, but since when is dating *the* Nate Noruta an everyday occurrence? Do you know how much the man is worth?"

Claire prepared herself. Ro's brain was a supercomputer full of every trivial pop culture factoid that crossed her path.

"I don't want to hear it," she replied.

"Twenty billion dollars. Can you fucking believe it? You're dating a man who is worth *that* much money. Have you been to his house? Wait a minute. Holy shit. He flew you somewhere. Oh my God! Does he have a private jet? Ate, *where are you right now?*"

"I'm in Paris."

Claire held the phone away as expletives tore from her phone.

"Ate, I am so proud of you," Ro said. "To think, after years of no men, no action, no nothing, out of nowhere you hit the jackpot."

"Gee, thanks a lot," Claire said, ignoring her sister's subconscious jab. "We're just dating. It's not like we're getting married or anything. We haven't known each other for very long."

"Our whole family is going to freak when they find out. You haven't told anyone yet, have you?"

"The only one who knows is Todd. I don't want you to say anything, either. To anyone."

"Why not?"

"Because I said so. Please respect my wishes and keep this between us for now. Please, Ro. And…"

Ro blinked in confusion. "And what?" she asked.

Claire hesitated. There was no tactful way to tell Ro how she really felt without hurting her feelings. *You and Ate Sam are experts at sucking the joy out of my relationships.* Or maybe she was shit with confrontation. Maybe a little bit of both?

"Never mind," Claire said. "Just make sure you keep it zipped."

"Fine, I won't say anything. But if I were you, I'd be proclaiming that shit to the whole world. I'd go viral in a second. Oh, what I wouldn't give to step in your shoes for a day. Wait.

How *was* he? Is his body every bit as luscious in person as it is in the magazines? Does he have a big—"

"Don't go there," Claire interrupted, her cheeks going hot. "I'm planning on coming back Thursday night or Friday morning. While I'm gone, can you please visit Lola every day? It doesn't matter what time you visit. Make sure you ask the nurse supervisor or caregivers how she is doing. Ask if she's eating enough of her meals or if she's having any behavioral issues."

"Okay, no problem. When you guys get back, can you introduce me to Nate? Invite him over and we can all have dinner together. Or better yet, ask if we can go to his house! I bet he has a giant mansion somewhere in L.A. I'll find out right now."

"Have you spoken to Sam yet?" Claire asked.

The question wiped the excited smile right off of Ro's face. "No. Why should I? She's being impossible."

"That's not nice," Claire said. "You're not understanding the full picture. She has a good game face, but you don't know how badly this divorce affected her. I really think she's depressed and should get help, but she refuses."

"Depressed? So that gives her the right to act like a b—"

Claire's eyes widened in warning.

"Fine. I'll try calling her again. And FYI, I did call her a few days ago and she didn't answer."

A little burden lifted off of Claire's heart. Every minute she spent in Paris with Nate was a thrill. A guilty one. There had to be consequences for stealing away in the middle of the night to a foreign country with a handsome man. None that she could think of at the moment, but she knew there just had to be.

Ah, yes. Family. Work. Dreams. Obligations. All the things that had no place in the romance that was unfolding before Claire's disbelieving eyes.

"I need to call Todd now," she said. "I'll be in contact soon. Love you."

"Love you, too. But try to call me right after your tech conference. Take a lot of pics of Nate. Pretty please?"

"All right. Bye."

Right after her call with Todd, she was going to head to the Paris Expo for the tech conference. Her stomach twisted in excitement and trepidation. What was going to happen? Would Nate publicly acknowledge her? Would they even get a chance to talk? How many people would attend? The only public conferences Claire had ever attended were for romance book fans, and another for baking enthusiasts. There were a few hundred people at each one. How big could this tech conference possibly be?

Claire was not used to underestimating things. She thought her internet search for the Technology Live conference was pretty comprehensive, and she was satisfied with the information she'd gathered. So when the Uber dropped her and Craig off at the Paris Expo, Claire was not prepared for what she saw.

None of the photos or blurbs did any justice to the sheer size of the event. The Paris Expo was an enormous compound that seemed to stretch on for miles. And the people? She guessed there were...thousands. Maybe even tens of thousands? It was hard to say when the spectacle of this place dazzled you with its bright lights, excited chatter, and energy of so many minds gathered to share their passion for all things tech. Claire likened the entire atmosphere to Disneyland, except the rides were replaced with conferences and vendors, and the crowds were comprised of mostly millennials and sharply dressed, rich-looking middle-aged men.

"Nate goes to this event every year?" Claire asked as Craig led her through the crowds to the check-in line. While in line, he secured tote bags full of swag and information for both of them.

"He tries his best to." Craig walked up to an electronic kiosk with a touch-screen. He keyed in some information, and out popped two badges imprinted with QR codes. He attached them on colorful lanyards and handed one to Claire.

"This is your VIP badge," Craig said. "It'll give you unrestricted access to all panels, keynotes, and special events. It's almost time for Mr. Noruta's keynote address. I have to meet him backstage. He reserved a seat for you at the front row."

Craig gave her a friendly wave and disappeared toward the back entrance of the Grand Expo Room, where Nate's keynote address was scheduled to be held. Claire paused a moment and pulled the schedule of events out of her tote bag. It was a glossy, vividly colorful book. She loved running her fingers over the smooth texture. But her favorite part? The pages with Nate's handsome face printed on them, featuring articles about his accomplishments and upcoming business endeavors.

Claire flowed with the stream of the crowd as everyone filed into Grand Expo Room, and she noticed a few people throwing curious glances at her. She sported a short baby-blue dress with a stylishly ruffled skirt and a denim jacket. Her look was a far cry from the hipster and business chic of the mostly male and young demographic in attendance.

The bright backdrop of the stage caught her attention and filled her with wonder. Hundreds were already gathered there, just to hear Nate speak. Even though she was just a guest, her heart started fluttering at the thought of him addressing all these people in public.

Claire walked to the front row and found the one seat with a "reserved" sign on it. As she tried settling down and getting comfortable, she cast surreptitious glances at the people closest to her. No one seemed too intimidating. She grinned at a white-bearded gentleman sitting to her right, who nodded in gruff acknowledgment. She said a friendly hello to the boy sitting to her left. He couldn't have been older than fourteen or fifteen.

"So, have you been to one of these before?" she asked the boy.

"Yes, I come every year," he replied in a thick French accent. "But I am the most excited for this year."

"Why?"

"Because Nate Noruta is a keynote speaker this year," he replied. "He is a tech icon. I want to be a coder and follow in his footsteps."

"Really?" His excitement made Claire beam. "In what ways do you consider him a tech icon?"

"Oh, in every way," the boy said enthusiastically. "He is inspiring. He came from humble beginnings and worked hard to get to where he is today. And best of all, he is a philanthropist. He never forgets to give back to the community."

The boy's words resonated with Claire. Nate was an accomplished man, to say the least. But for some reason she'd never given any thought to what extent his actions had affected the world. The weight of who Nate Noruta really was started to dawn on her.

Suddenly the lights went low, and the vivid backdrop of the stage surged into even brighter hues. Applause filled the room as an older, yet very polished gentleman walked on stage. Even though he started addressing the crowd in French, his warm presence transcended the language barrier. Claire looked him up in her program. His name was Charles Saint-Germain, and apparently he was chairman of a corporate entity called *Le Prix Unifié*.

"It is my honor to present to you our keynote speaker."

Claire's ears perked up when Charles suddenly switched to English.

"This young man needs no introduction, but I will do so anyway because it would be an honor to present him. In his thirty-three years of life, he has done more for the world than most people would hope to do in an entire lifetime. Not only has he built a vast technological empire that has connected the world in ways we could only imagine, but he is an amazing example of human generosity. We might know him as the mogul—the tech genius who helped create *MyConnect* and Trance Media—but I want the world to know the depth of the heart and soul of the man who has spent so much of his time and money to establish organizations for outreach to our underserved communities. This man has dedicated himself to using his power and influence to help others, and he is an inspiration to us all. With no further ado, I am honored to present to you Mr. Nathaniel Noruta."

Thunderous cheers and applause filled the huge auditorium, but it all faded to a distant rumble as Nate came into view. Claire watched, entranced, as the familiar Nate who stole her heart strode across the stage, his captivating smile shining at the hundreds of people who admired and adored him. For reasons she couldn't explain, she felt as though a huge chasm separated them from one another. It was as if she was viewing him across an immeasurable distance, and no matter how much she tried to reach him, she'd never come close enough.

Yet across the distance, Nate knew where she was. He made it a point to find her. A wink and a smile were all it took to remind Claire of a simple fact: he was the same Nate who had helped her make cookies. He was the same man who had held her close on top of the Eiffel tower, and the same man who made passionate love to her as dawn broke across the horizon.

That was the moment she realized, with unwavering certainty, she was the star of her own modern-day fairy tale, and she'd found a hero who blew all the other princes out of the water.

CHAPTER SIXTEEN

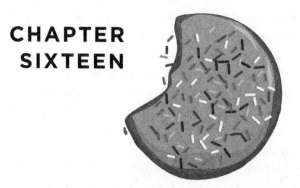

When the keynote speech was over, Nate was whisked away to an interview at the other side of the Expo. Even after the last of the applause had subsided, Claire remained seated, blown away by what she had just witnessed.

Nate had a whole other side. The face of *MyConnect* and Trance Media was an outgoing, charismatic, intensely smart man who could answer questions with incredible ease. He knew his business and industry like the back of his hand. On top of that, he was a literal hero. He had started several programs dedicated to bringing STEM education to inner-city and marginalized youth. He donated tons of money to organizations combating human trafficking and underage sex workers. Claire could easily see why the entire world was in love with him.

She still struggled to understand how she fit into his life. To say he was busy was an understatement. He'd already done so many wonderful things for Claire, let alone for the community. Didn't something have to give somewhere?

She wandered out of the grand room and pulled out her phone. It was fairly early in California, but she needed a chat with Todd.

Hey, u awake yet?

After about a minute, Todd's response came back.

I am now.

I'm so sorry to wake u, but I need help. Is it absurd to think Nate and I can be together?

The sudden ring surprised her, and she picked up immediately.

"Hello?"

"Claire, honey, there aren't many things in the world powerful enough to rouse me from my beauty sleep," Todd said in a raspy voice. "Jason Momoa tapping on my windowsill in the dead of night, wearing nothing but a smile is one of them. The other one is the notion that my best friend is seriously considering dumping her hot-as-hell rich boyfriend."

"What?" Claire said. "Where did you get *that* from?"

"Oh." He paused. "What did you mean, then?"

"It's…complicated. When I met Nate, I didn't even recognize him. To me, he was this handsome, sweet, and charming guy. I'm just having a hard time accepting all of this. His fame, his status, all the fans…everything."

Todd sighed. "You know I love you to death. Really, I do. So please do not take offense to what I'm about to say next. You're a beautiful, kind person, but you've got some…quirks."

"What do you mean, quirks?"

"Anyone who knows you knows you're the biggest sweetheart. But you tend to get too lost in your own head sometimes. You can't see past the weeds."

"Like how?"

"It's hard to pinpoint exact instances," Todd said. "Besides, it's not my objective to pick on you. All I can say is sometimes you get distracted and you don't focus on the big picture. Maybe this will ring a bell. Your sister Sam. You told me how she felt alienated from you and Ro."

"So what?"

"So…you said it came out of left field. Claire, you should have seen this coming from a mile away. You know Sam is really sensitive. You said so yourself. She's always been that way, and you and Ro have had to tiptoe around her sometimes because you were so scared of offending her. Her reaction shouldn't have surprised you, is all I'm saying."

"Well...she's hard to predict sometimes," Claire said.

"You see? That's what I'm talking about."

"Are you trying to say I'm stupid?"

A sense of regret stole over her as she said those words.

"I would never," Todd replied, his voice dead-serious. "You already know I think the world of you, but sometimes you let your anxiety get the better of you. Case in point: Mr. Nate 'Prince Charming' Noruta. You fell in love with one side of him while subconsciously disregarding his powerful, famous billionaire persona who rubs elbows with Mark Zuckerberg and Elon Musk. The thought made you uncomfortable, and you don't know how to handle it. I'm sorry to break it to you, sweetie, but you have to learn how to put aside your reservations and embrace the whole man."

He stunned Claire into silence. She wanted to be furious at Todd's level of intuition. How could someone else know what was going on in her own head before she did?

"Here's a simple homework assignment," Todd continued. "I want you to hop on Google, or your boyfriend's search engine competitor Tango, and look up as much information about him as possible. I'm guessing you probably haven't done all your research. Ignorance isn't bliss. You have to do it."

Claire paused as she let Todd's words sink in. Her eyes drifted across the Expo, watching crowds walk by, their excited chatter and smiles somehow dulled by the doubt sitting like a rock inside her gut. She began to question what she really wanted. Did she want Nate? Without a doubt, one hundred percent yes. But falling for someone so fast couldn't be a good thing. Could it?

Her revelations suddenly brought all her hidden yearnings to the surface. It made her wonder what was really important in her life, and all of a sudden she could see it with clarity:

Her business. Her dreams. Her independence.

Nate took the ultimate leap of faith in his own dreams, and look where it got him. Did she have the courage to break free from her family's expectations and do what she'd been too afraid to do on her own?

She let out a cleansing sigh, attempting to gather some serenity in the midst of the chaotic energy of the tech conference.

"Thanks, Todd," she said, her heart filling with gratitude. "You're amazing, you know that?"

"No question about it," Todd replied. "I'm gonna get back to sleep. I want you to enjoy yourself. It's not every day you get swept away to Paris by a hot rich guy. Soak it all up."

After ending the call, Claire knew what she needed to do: lighten up, allow herself to enjoy this whole experience, and have fun with Nate while they were here.

She pulled out the schedule and perused the events and vendor list. She was determined to take Todd's advice by immersing herself in whatever experiences this Technology Live had to offer.

If Claire had planned her excursion through the Expo efficiently, she wouldn't have wasted her time getting lost in exhibits she had no interest in. For example, she could not understand the fascination with robots. The extent of her A.I. knowledge went as far as the Roomba that Sam had given her for Christmas a few years ago. The huge thoroughfare of robots here at the convention all but blew her away. Looking for a cello-playing robot? One that could repair a web server? Fly around like a drone to record video? There were robots for that. To her horror, there was even one that could drive a car. Claire shuddered at the thought and hurried past the exhibit as fast as she could.

"Excuse me, *mademoiselle*. Have you ever tried VR before?"

Claire stopped in her tracks. A tall, athletic-looking woman in a black polo shirt smiled at her as she held out a shiny set of black VR goggles. The woman was standing in front of an elaborate, high-tech looking exhibit featuring full-body gaming suits, weapons, gloves, and even an array of treadmill-like contraptions made for running and exploring through virtual worlds.

"Oh, no I haven't," Claire replied. "I don't know if I have the time—"

"Your badge is VIP, so you don't have to wait in line," the woman said with a smile, gesturing to the ridiculously long line for the general audience. "Come. I guarantee you will enjoy it."

"Okay," Claire said hesitantly. She walked into the exhibit and put her tote bag down. "What do I do?"

"We put the haptics on you, and you'll get to step into the virtual landscape," the woman said. "My name is Dominique. Welcome to Virtuosa, the new horizon of virtual reality."

She proceeded to outfit Claire with a black shiny-paneled vest with wires crisscrossing over it. She gave her matching gloves and an electronic rifle that felt surprisingly light in her grip. Grasping her hand, Dominique helped Claire step onto the interactive gaming platform, then clipped the tethers on her vest securely to the side rails to prevent her from falling as she ran around in the game.

"Place the visor over your eyes," Dominique said. "The ear pieces should fit securely over both ears."

"And then what should I do?"

"It will come naturally," Dominque replied. "There are already several others plugged into the world who you will play alongside with. It is very intuitive. Trust your gut."

Claire's nervousness kicked up a notch as she lowered the visor over her eyes. The darkness only lasted a split second until a hyper-realistic world of vivid color rose up around her.

"Oh my God," Claire gasped. "This is amazing!"

She found herself in a huge cavern filled with piles of gold and treasure. Torches lit the perimeter, casting warm illumination over the glittering riches. She looked down and saw herself clad in skin-tight green cargo pants, a tiny white tank, and knee-high black combat boots.

She walked around the cavern, absorbing every vivid detail: the flickering flames of the torches, the echoing drip-drop of water somewhere in the distance, and the clanking of coins as she trod upon them. Her surroundings were so stunning, she lost track of time just walking around. A sudden menacing growl startled her out of her calm exploration.

She spun around. An enormous, rhino-like beast charged toward a man in the distance. The man was so preoccupied with trying to pry something out of a wall, he didn't notice the charging beast. Claire raised her rifle, aimed, and fired. The monster roared and collapsed as its body burst into flame.

Claire's heart raced in her chest as she hurried over to the scene. She still wasn't over how real the VR was. She was fully immersed in the world—with her feet treading on the ground, and the haptics sending sensations through her body, she could almost believe the game was more real than the world she came from.

"Are you all right?" Claire asked the man.

He straightened up, and Claire cocked her eyebrow at him. Tall, tanned, with brooding blue eyes and a lock of black hair falling over his forehead, he was the quintessential sex-idol hero. His black shirt was unbuttoned to show off the tops of his spectacular, sweat-sheened pecs. There was almost something familiar in his stance and the way he gazed at her.

"I sure am," he replied with a sexy smile.

The shock of familiarity in his voice spiked through Claire's body.

"Nate? What are you doing in here? I thought you were supposed to be getting ready for your next panel."

"I was, but when I saw the sexy girl in a short dress getting plugged into the VR, I wanted to join her."

"Sounds like you get distracted way too easily," Claire replied, trying to hide her smile. "And didn't you hear that thing coming after you? Why didn't you run?"

"The Shard of *Feyndari* is surrounded by an energy vortex," Nate explained. "Once you step inside, you become completely immersed in the energy field, and thus unaware of anything in the outside world."

"Okay," Claire said, delight coursing through her body. Dominique was right: this was a lot of fun. "What's so special about this shard, anyway?"

"It's one of the five shards you need to collect to make a superweapon to fight against the Scorpion Queen. We can't let her win, or else she'll shroud the world in evil and darkness for all eternity."

Claire gave him a sly look.

"You know this game really well," she said. "You're either a full-on gamer nerd, or you had something to do with all of this."

Nate's avatar took a step toward her, and she looked up into his ruggedly handsome face. Even though they were a stranger's eyes, Claire could have sworn she saw down to Nate's soul in their depths.

"Both," he replied. "I lived on adventure and RPGs practically my whole life. And *Virtuosa* is a subsidiary of Trance Media."

A ribbon of heat ran through her as he grasped her hand, holding it up in front of both of them.

"The magic protecting the shard can't be broken," Nate explained. "Unless two of the most powerful voyagers in the world joined forced to remove the shard together."

"Together?" Claire asked. "As in, you and me?"

Her heart skipped in awe as Nate guided her hand toward the vibrantly purple jewel embedded in the rock wall. His hand cupped the back of hers as they reached for the jewel. The moment they made contact, a deep vibration buzzed through the haptic vest and gloves, filling her with breathless energy. A brilliant light flashed forth from the jewel, and it dislodged from the wall into Clare's hand.

She felt a light touch on her arm. Applause and cheers filled the air as she removed her headset.

"We won."

Claire's head whipped toward Nate, who stood beside her on an adjacent gaming platform. Looking down, she noticed they were still holding hands.

She scanned the crowd. There were probably two hundred people lined up, and every single one of them was staring at her and Nate.

Claire's windpipe constricted. She struggled to swallow past the dryness in her throat.

"What's wrong?" Nate asked.

She couldn't answer. Claire and the crowd were in a staring stand-off, and she was losing. She observed women throwing hostile stares at her and whispering to one another.

"Oh. You are Mr. Noruta's...friend," Dominique said in surprise.

Heat rushed up Claire's neck. It was as if an invisible tidal wave was rising up above her, threatening to sweep her away into a cruel, lonely sea.

"I need to go." Her hands shook as she set the rifle down with a clatter and hurriedly disengaged herself from the tethers on the platform. Dominique rushed forward to help as Claire practically tore the vest and gloves off.

"Are you okay?" Nate asked. "Do you want me to go with you?"

"No. No, that's not necessary, but thank you. You need to do your panel. Everyone's waiting for you." Claire leaped down from the platform. "I'll see you in a little bit."

She tried to disregard the hundreds of eyes on her as she turned and rushed out of the exhibit.

CHAPTER SEVENTEEN

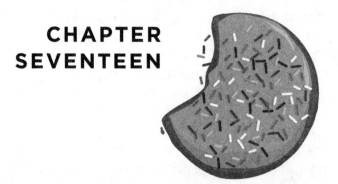

Thirty minutes later, Claire found herself back at the hotel. She took a few shameful steps into the suite and closed the door, then her phone pinged with another text from Nate.

Are you ok?

I looked everywhere for you.

Are you still here?

Claire sank down onto the couch and tried to gather her thoughts. She wanted nothing more than to talk to Todd or Ro, but she felt guilty bothering them again. The next best thing she would have done to calm her nerves was to start baking and decorating cookies, but that was out of the question. And she certainly wasn't in the right headspace to start reading a book.

The last resort? A nice, warm bubble bath with a glass of wine. In all her life, Claire had never taken a bath for relaxation. She'd always dreamed about it. In fact, she had a whole Pinterest board dedicated to the various ways people set up their tubs for a good soak. Unfortunately, the bathroom in her apartment didn't have a tub. Now was the perfect time, because she never knew when she'd get the chance to do this again.

Claire headed to the bar. She grabbed a bottle of red wine, a corkscrew, and a glass, and headed upstairs to her room. The sooner she could relax, the sooner she could sort out her feelings and try to convince herself she wasn't a total asshole for ditching the convention.

A few minutes later, she was sitting in the tub full of suds, chugging the glass of red wine. She looked ridiculous in the big mirror on the wall next to the tub. She had overdone it with the bubbles. It looked like she was getting throttled by a gang of fluffy clouds. It was a tad awkward in the enormous tub by herself, but she needed some time alone—some time to think.

As the alcohol loosened her muscles and her mind, she thought back to the scene at the VR exhibit, and the underlying reason for her reaction. Some delusional part of her wanted to keep their relationship a secret from the rest of the world. Why was she having such a difficult time accepting reality? Why did she have a problem with being labeled as Nate's girlfriend in public?

She already knew the answer to these questions—she was a fucking mess. Todd was sugarcoating it when he told her she had "quirks." It was just a nice way of saying she didn't have the ability to get her love life right. Sam and Ro always questioned why she never had a boyfriend, and why every guy she dated in the past was all wrong for her. Maybe Claire was the one with the problem.

She took another gulp of wine just as she heard a soft knock. "Claire?"

Through the mirror she saw Nate peering hopefully at her in the reflection. The butterflies in her belly fluttered into chaos.

"You left the Expo?" Claire asked. "I thought you had two more panels to attend."

He took a few steps toward her. "Tell me what's going on," he said. "Something's really bothering you, and I want to know what it is."

She averted her eyes, fidgeting with the stem of her wineglass. "You didn't have to leave the Expo early. All those people paid a lot of money to see you."

"I don't care about the Expo."

Claire stared wide-eyed at him. She couldn't move even as he crouched beside her by the tub, burning her with his gaze.

"I don't care about any of that," he said. "You should know by now there's only one thing I really care about."

Claire's heart was racing fast enough to burst out of her chest. "Don't say it," she whispered.

"Why not? Everything's moving really fast, but I know you feel the same way I do."

"You're right," Claire said, looking into Nate's eyes. "You are absolutely right. And that's what terrifies me. We've known each other for less than a week, and we're already spending the night together in Paris. You're foregoing all these major obligations and meetings just for me. This is wild. Irrational. Can't you see that?"

"The rest of the world might see it that way, but we know the truth. You don't want me to say it, but I have to. I'm falling for you, Claire."

The earth crumbled beneath her feet. She felt weightless. "Really?"

"Yes."

"But why?"

His eyes softened, and he leaned in closer. "Because…every time I'm with you, I'm happier than I've ever been. I look at you, and not only do I see the woman of my dreams, I see truth. You're genuine and real. There are no dollar signs in your eyes. There's no agenda. When you look back at me, I know you like me for the man I am, not for the things I own."

The water swished around Claire as she scooted closer to Nate. Without a word, she reached for his hand and entwined their fingers together.

"Claire," he whispered, closing his eyes and touching his forehead to hers. "What are you afraid of?"

I'm afraid of falling in love too fast.

I'm afraid of losing myself.

I'm afraid of what my family will think of me.

"I guess...I need more time," she replied. "I think it's best if I go home."

Nate pulled gently away from her, but kept her hand securely in his.

"All right," he said after a spell. "I'll tell Craig to arrange a flight."

Claire's heart nearly broke at the confusion and hurt in his eyes.

"Nate, this isn't goodbye," she explained. "When you come back home I'd like you to call me. All I need is a few days to get my thoughts together, tend to my family, and get back to work. This time with you has been like a beautiful dream. I'm so grateful for you, and I'll never forget this."

Nate exhaled and looked away for a brief moment. The pain in his eyes pierced Claire's heart like a dull ice pick.

"I want you to stay," he murmured. "This hurts. But if you have to go, you can go."

Nate was about to stand, but Claire squeezed his hand tighter, pulling him back. She pressed her lips to his, hoping and wishing he could feel her love for him pouring through the kiss. When they pulled apart, Nate glanced briefly into her eyes. The tense silence thrumming through the air displayed his pain more than words ever could.

He broke his gaze, and left the room. Claire lost track of how much time went by. Finally, she drained the last drops of her wine. Tears gathered in her eyes, trickling in silence into the lukewarm bathwater.

Claire touched down in Los Angeles on Thursday night. Despite the bone-deep exhaustion, her passion for cookies won out. She ended up pulling an all-nighter, mixing up icing, baking, and decorating until sunrise on Friday morning. Then and only then did she fall asleep for several hours, but forced herself to get up in time to pay Lola a visit before her shift at the bookstore.

Ro was fast asleep when Claire left in the morning. Ro had written a note in large block letters ordering Claire to wake her up immediately to give her an update before she left. Claire paid no attention to it. She chose to visit Lola and let Ro get some rest after her late-night shift at the bar.

As Claire entered Lola's facility with another cart full of magazines and cookies for the staff, she was already feeling better. Settling back into her routine and taking care of her family calmed her nerves and soothed away the guilt of abandoning everything to fly to Paris with Nate. She sighed wistfully. *Ah, Paris.* Every moment she had spent with Nate— every look, every touch, and especially when they...

A rush of heat filled her cheeks at the memory of Nate's hands and mouth working their magic on the most intimate parts of her body.

"Okay, Claire, focus," she whispered. She knocked and gently opened the door. "Lola, it's Claire. I missed you so much. How are you?"

Lola was snoozing in her armchair again with the morning news blaring on the TV screen. From the looks of her breakfast tray, the nurse had only been able to feed her very little food. Claire's lips turned down in a disappointed frown as she picked up the remote and muted the TV.

"Lola, wake up. It's time to eat breakfast." Claire knelt beside her and patted her hand until she woke up. Lola blinked groggily at her, but smiled when she focused on Claire.

"Clara," she said with a smile.

"Yes, Lola, it's me. It's time to eat now."

Claire rolled the bedside table closer and spread a little bit of strawberry jam onto her pancakes. She sliced the pancakes and fed a portion to Lola. As she ate, Claire couldn't help but notice the hollowness of her cheeks. The gauntness was more pronounced. It filled her with worry, but as always, she tried not to let any of her fears show.

"I cut up all the pancakes. Go ahead and feed yourself. Can you do it?"

Claire placed the fork in Lola's hand. It took her a minute, but she eventually started to feed herself at an extremely slow pace.

"I have more magazines," Claire said as she reached into her tote bag and pulled out the latest issue of *Trend*, an infamous tabloid known for their sensational, far-fetched stories about celebrities. To her relief, there weren't any stories or photos featuring Nate in this particular issue. She tried her best to flip through the magazine and read to Lola, but her mind kept straying back to Nate. Suddenly, an idea popped into her head. She put the magazine down.

"Lola, I have a confession to make," she said. "I want to let you know that I...sort of have a boyfriend."

Lola made eye contact for a few seconds, then stared at the TV.

"Well, at least I think I have a boyfriend," Claire continued. "I might have messed things up between us, but I'll get to that later. Anyway, he's the best. His name is Nate, and I really think you'd like him. He's one of the nicest, most loving people I've ever met. He stopped by a few days ago. Remember Nurse Vickie? She's Nate's aunt. Wasn't it so nice of him to have her stay with you?"

Lola didn't answer. She took a long time to chew her mouthful of pancake. Claire stuck a straw in the glass of water and held it out for Lola to take a sip.

"Anyway...he's an amazing person. I feel horrible because I think I hurt his feelings. Nate flew me out to Paris to spend time with him. I think he was trying to win my heart by re-enacting my silly fantasy, and it worked. I mean, from the moment I met him I really liked him, but after seeing how far he went to impress me…I couldn't resist. It's only been a week, and I think I'm falling in love with him. Do you think this is too fast? Am I stupid for thinking this could possibly work out between us? Do you think Mom and Dad would be disappointed?"

To Claire's surprise, Lola stared back at her with clear, focused eyes.

"Did you get it?" Lola asked.

Claire blinked, totally caught off-guard.

"Get what?"

"My treasure chest," Lola replied.

"What are you talking about? I have no idea—" The memory from a few days ago hit her. "Oh," she said, furrowing her brow. "I remember. I found it, but there was nothing inside. What was supposed to be in there?"

"You find it," Lola said. "Open it."

Claire sighed in resignation. The most remarkable thing she remembered from that day was disappointment. She still didn't really understand why the emptiness in the chest affected her so much, but she didn't want to keep focusing on the irreparable things in her life.

"Okay," she said with a sad smile. "I'll try to find it."

Claire worked the closing shift that night. Nate hadn't contacted her all day, and the loneliness was unbearable without Todd working.

In short, she was having a shit day, and she only had herself to blame.

When she finally pulled into the parking stall at her apartment building, she sat in her car for a long time.

"Let's get to the heart of all this," she said to herself. "You're grumpy and lonely because you told Nate you needed some space, and he actually respected your wishes? Jeez, Claire, you really are messed up."

She cut the engine and got out of her car, slamming the door harder than she meant. She paused again as the answer to her question smacked her in the face like an open palm.

She was *definitely* the asshole here.

Nate went out of his way—extremely out of his way—to win her heart, and what did she do? She freaked the hell out and hopped on his private jet back to L.A. She was a terrible human being. She had to make it up to him somehow and pray he wasn't bitter and averse to second chances. Claire dialed his number and waited.

He's not going to answer. It's going to go straight to voicemail. He probably blocked me and is on to the next girl in line. He probably hates my g—

"Hello."

Claire's heart lodged in her throat. She almost choked trying to respond.

"H—hi Nate," she stammered. "How are you?"

"I'm good. How are you?"

Claire cringed. His voice was pleasant, but she could sense everything underneath.

"Hello?" he asked. "Claire, are you still there?"

"Nate, I am so sorry." The words flowed out of her like water bursting through a broken dam. "What you did for me was amazing. Beyond amazing. I could live a thousand lifetimes and never deserve the beautiful trip you gave me. It was the most romantic thing I've ever experienced, and I'm so sorry I didn't tell you how I felt earlier. I guess I was scared. Everything was moving so fast, and I'm not used to the spotlight. The truth is…I'm simple. I'm a family girl. All the glitz and glamour scared me because I don't belong in that world. I wanted to pretend we lived in our own little world, where it was just you and me enjoying each other's company. Underneath it all, I realized all I wanted was you. I wanted to watch movies, and snuggle, and eat, and explore every corner of France with you. I'm so sorry I ran away, Nate. Can you give me another chance?"

Silence filled the other end of the phone. Claire's heart lurched with every ticking second.

"If something is bothering you, you need to tell me." Nate's voice was firm, and it pulled her in with its force. "Don't run away from me, Claire. That's the worst thing you can do to me. Promise me you'll be open and honest. Don't hide anything. I'll do the same for you."

"Of course I will," she said. "I'm so sorry. I promise I'll be open with you from now on."

There was a pause, and the breath of a sigh on the other end of the line. Hope teetered on the edge of her heart as she waited for Nate to respond.

"I really miss you," he said. "I wish you were here."

Joy tingled across every inch of Claire's skin. "Me too," she said.

"You owe me another game of *The Shard of Feyndari*. We never got to finish that level. You have no idea how hot your VR avatar is, but the real version is even better."

Claire swooned in silence, beaming so hard she thought her face would crack.

"When are you coming back home?" she asked.

"I'm going to be traveling for a little while longer, unfortunately."

"How long?"

"About two more weeks. It depends on how well everything goes."

"You'll still text or call me, right?" Claire asked hopefully.

"I guess I can."

"You *guess?*"

"I'll have to see if I can fit you into my busy schedule," Nate teased.

"Okay, I'll ask Craig to pencil me in," Claire replied.

"See, you're already getting used to being my girl. It was just a matter of time."

Claire laughed out loud. She clamped her hand over her mouth when one of her neighbors peeked at her through their window.

"Oops, it looks like I'm bothering my neighbors," Claire said. "I'm going to head inside."

"Okay. Bye."

"Good night."

Claire practically floated up the stairs and to her apartment. It was a damned miracle Nate forgave her. There was no mistaking the pain and anger in the undertone of his voice. It might take a while to truly earn forgiveness, but Claire was up to the task. Now she knew why people always said "Rome wasn't built in a day."

She unlocked the door to her apartment and opened it. Standing before her were both Ro and Todd, their faces ablaze with excitement.

"For the love of Jesus, you scared me!" Claire cried.

"Get your ass in here and tell us everything," Ro said, pulling her into the apartment. "Spare no details."

CHAPTER EIGHTEEN

Ro and Todd sat Claire down on the couch and shoved a can of spiked seltzer into her hand. They planted themselves on either side of her. Todd reached out for a bowl of popcorn on the coffee table, and Ro took a swig of her beer.

"What the hell is going on?" Claire demanded. "It looks like you guys were getting ready for a movie marathon."

"Screw the movie marathon, we have the real deal," Ro said.

"A real-life fairy tale," Todd concurred.

"If you're expecting me to spend the entire night dishing with you, you've got another think coming." Claire set the can down with a loud *thunk*. "You see all these cookies? I have to get these wrapped and shipped off, and then I have more orders to fill."

"Ate, please give us just five minutes, *please,*" Ro begged. "We are *dying* for an update."

"Aren't you supposed to be at work?" Claire asked.

"I called in sick. There was no way in hell I was going to miss talking to you again."

"Fine. If you want information, both of you have to help me wrap and package the cookies for delivery. Deal?"

"Deal," Todd said, leaning forward eagerly. "How. Was. Paris?"

Claire immediately got up from the couch and started

bustling around the kitchen, taking out the cellophane wrapping and shipping materials. She was no fool. She had to get Ro and Todd cracking on the work first before she gave them even one of the juicy details, or else they'd never follow through with their promise.

Once she had an assembly line going, she was satisfied enough to start her story. She only gave them what she thought they needed to know, and nothing more. Starting with the private jet and ending with the fiasco on the VR platform, Claire had to fight a cringe when she re-lived that roller coaster of emotions all over again.

"You haven't seen it yet, have you?" Todd asked.

"Seen what?" Claire asked.

Todd pulled up a photo on his phone and showed it to Claire. It was a blurry image of her awkwardly removing the haptic gear on the VR platform.

"Where did you get this?" Claire asked.

"They're all over," Ro replied. "There are a whole bunch of videos recording you and Nate playing the game together. It was super cute."

"Yeah," Todd agreed. "See the caption for this one? It says, '*Nate Noruta plays a sexy game with mystery girl*.'"

"Nate has a fan account on Instagram." Ro showed her phone to Claire, too. Her eyes widened at the multiple photos of them playing the VR game together. Her throat went dry.

"Ro! Don't show her that," Todd said, making a cutting gesture with his hand.

"She didn't see anything," Ro said. "I only showed her the thumbnails."

Claire snatched the phone out of Ro's hand and clicked on one of the photos. Right before Ro grabbed the phone back, Claire was able to get a brief glimpse of a few comments:

Romeo0407 *Is that his gf? She hot*

JazzHandsX2001 *That dress is too SHORT. Kinda slutty*

N0T_a_V1BE *Another member of the gold-diggers club!
#luckyb!tch*

Myko112 *He could do way better. Sry not sry*

Claire's hand went limp, and Ro grabbed it back. Her eyes grew unfocused, and she reached for a chair.

"I think I need to sit down."

"Ate, are you okay?"

"I told you not to show her Instagram!"

Claire could barely hear Todd and Ro bickering as those nasty comments continued to slice their way through her mind. She knew she shouldn't have been bothered by any of it, but she wasn't ready to see that kind of hate posted up on the internet for the whole world to see. They were at the beginning of their relationship and already people hated her. It made her heart ache.

"Ate, I am so sorry," Ro wailed, wrapping her arms around Claire. "I didn't mean for you to see any of those comments. I am so sorry."

"Don't let any of it bother you one bit." Todd's voice was gentle but firm as he patted Claire's arm. "Seriously though, seeing you two play the VR game together was like watching a romantic movie. And the part when he held your hand..."

Todd and Ro squealed, clapping like two giddy schoolgirls.

"Did anyone else say something about it?" Claire asked nervously. "Did Sam or Mom and Dad see it?"

"I doubt it," Ro replied. "None of the pictures show your face really well because of the visor. And even when you took it off, nobody was able to get a good picture of your face."

"Why are you nervous about your family finding out?" Todd asked. "Wouldn't your parents be proud of you for pulling a guy like Nate? Don't you think Sam would be happy for you?"

Claire hesitated, her glance falling on Ro.

"In theory they should be," Claire said. "But it's about more than just snagging a rich, famous guy. Commitment is important in my family. You don't take someone home to meet family unless you're serious about them. And even then, it takes more than just a few days or even weeks to really get to know someone in order to be serious about them."

"Says who?" Todd asked. "Listen. It is up to you and you alone to decide if and when you're serious about someone. No one can tell you how you feel. Not even your own family."

"Ate, I have your back one hundred percent," Ro said. "If you're in love with the man, I'm all for it."

Claire frowned.

"What?" Ro demanded.

"You see, that doesn't exactly instill any confidence in me," Claire said. "Do you remember what you said about my ex Steven?"

"No."

"You told me that you were one hundred percent certain he was my future husband," Claire replied. "You said that Mom and Dad were wrong to think he wasn't the right one for me, and that Steven and I should fight for our love."

Ro's eyes widened as the memory came rushing back. A burst of laughter escaped from her.

"Oh my dear Lord, no you didn't," Todd said. "I think I remember this guy. Was he the one who had that weird job? The one where he drove around in that old van with the chipped teal paint?"

"He was a professional aura cleanser," Claire said. "He didn't have an office. He was mobile and worked out of his van."

"And he lived in it, too." Ro couldn't hold the laughter in any longer. She and Todd burst into giggles.

"That's rude," Claire muttered.

"Steven had his own apartment," Ro sputtered. "But he chose to live in his van because he said the spirits in his room were too powerful, so he was forced out of his own home."

"And yet you were all for our relationship."

"You win some, you lose some," she responded with an innocent shrug. "I was wrong about Steven. So what? Nate is different. I'm one hundred percent certain about him."

"I swear to God Ro, if you say one hundred percent one more time…"

"There you go again getting all worked up," Ro said. "Steven's old news. Oh my God. My sister is the girlfriend of Nate Noruta. I will never get over this. What if you two end up getting married? Ah! It will be the most decadent wedding ever. It'll make Harry and Meghan's wedding look like a backyard barbecue. Can you imagine all the celebrities who will attend? I'm seriously dying right now."

Claire closed her eyes momentarily, praying for serenity.

"Now do you see why I didn't want to tell you about us?" she said. "You're getting way too ahead of yourself."

"I'm sorry Claire-bear, but I have to agree with your little sis," Todd said. "People were hating because they were jealous of the way he looked at you. That is the way a man looks when he's in love. Trust me, I know. Lots of men have given me the same look, but little did they know: Todd Kingsley Coulson is not one to be tied down."

He passed his phone to Claire. There was a picture on it of Nate shortly after they won the VR game. Claire had to suppress a swoony sigh at the sight of his strong, handsome profile and the fullness of his parted lips as he stared longingly after her while she jumped off the platform.

Claire bit her lip. Could Todd be right? Nate was the best boyfriend she'd ever had. No one had ever come close. And the way he made her feel when they were together? She existed in a space where there was no limit to happiness.

"When is he coming back home?" Ro asked.

"Not for another two weeks."

"That's a long time." She frowned. "What's he doing?"

"A whole bunch of business trips, I guess," Claire answered.

"Aren't you curious about what he's doing?" Todd asked. "Like, where is he going exactly, who is he talking to, what kind of business he's conducting?"

Claire paused, then shook her head. "No," she said. "Not really. I figured he did his own thing, and I did mine."

Todd and Ro exchanged silent looks with one another.

"What was that all about?" Claire demanded.

"Like I said earlier. You're quirky," Todd replied.

"I shouldn't be required to know everything about his business," Claire said defensively. "He owns so many companies and does so many things—it's hard to keep track of it all. And frankly, I don't want to intrude."

"That's probably why he likes you so much." Ro taped up a box of cookies with a flourish as she gazed at Claire. "You're the only girl he knows who isn't all up in his face about everything he does. It makes so much sense. You're the most un-materialistic person in the world. Leave it up to one of the richest men on the planet to be attracted to someone who's the complete opposite of all the women chasing after him."

"Wait. What is that supposed to mean?"

"Ate, I wasn't trying to insult you," Ro said. "What I mean is you're really not with him because of his money."

"Some people seem to think otherwise," Claire said, thinking back to the mean comments on Instagram.

"Don't even give them a second thought," Todd said. "You snagged your Prince Charming. That's cause for celebration. Let's raise a toast to our beautiful Claire. May she and Nate live happily ever after."

"And have tons of babies," Ro said, raising her beer.

Claire was tired of arguing. Instead, she played along, raising her own drink along with Todd and Ro. She looked at the flavor and noticed it was black cherry. It brought back memories of Nate, and her lips curved up in a secret smile as she indulged in memories of their times together.

...

Claire awoke to a video chat call.

A twinge of confusion ran through her as she stretched her arm out, blindly feeling for the phone. What the hell time was it anyway? It was still dark outside. Who would be calling her now?

Her screen lit up. It was five in the morning, and the caller's identity flashed across the front.

Nate.

Clearing her throat, she swiped the hair out of her face and propped herself up higher in bed. She switched on the lamp and reached for her glasses.

She accepted the call, and there he was. Claire was not at all prepared for the villainously hot man before her, absolutely drop-dead in suit and tie. Granted, she could only see the top part of his outfit, but that totally did it for her. Who was she kidding? He was so fine he'd look good in a burlap sack.

"Hi."

Nate's lips stretched into a gorgeous smile as he gazed back at her.

"Hi. I'm sorry I woke you up."

"I—uh, it's okay," Claire stammered. "I should be getting up soon any way. Is everything all right?"

"Yeah," Nate answered. "I called because I missed you. I wanted to see your face."

"I miss you, too," Claire said, her heart filling with lightness and warmth. "I wish you were here with me now."

Claire wanted to fall into a comfortable silence with Nate—to gaze into each other's eyes and try to enjoy some semblance of intimate peace, despite the thousands of miles separating them. But then she remembered her earlier conversation with Ro and Todd. Maybe it would be a good thing to show him her support by asking him about his business. That was the kind of thing a good girlfriend would do.

"So...why are you all dressed up?" Claire asked.

"I just got back from a meeting," Nate replied as he loosened his tie.

"With who?"

"An Italian politician."

"Oh. You're in Italy right now?"

"Yes. Rome."

"What was your meeting about?"

"It was about bringing some of my education programs to his city. I'm sorry to change the subject, but you look so fucking beautiful."

His sudden compliment derailed Claire's train of thought.

"What? Seriously?"

Nate didn't reply. His eyes were dark and intense as they drank her in. She never knew she could have this kind of effect on someone.

"Your hair and glasses are so sexy," Nate said, his voice a husky growl. "And your top—I remember you wearing it the first night I came to your apartment. You looked so hot in it."

Claire looked down at her thin white camisole. From the way her nipples poked eagerly through it, there was no hiding the effect his words were having on her.

"Do you ever touch yourself when you're thinking of me?" he asked.

Her pulse sped up. A flush of pleasure stole up her neck. There was no question he was turning her on, but she felt strange talking about it out loud.

"Nate... What are you doing?"

"Show me how you touch yourself." Nate's voice went from yearning to commanding. Hungry. "Please."

Her left hand flexed beneath the bedsheet. Now, this was new. She'd heard the term "cybersex" in old movies before. Was the word still applicable in the age of face chats and teleconferencing? From the look of pure lust in Nate's eyes, she would hazard the answer was "fuck, yes."

"I don't know," she said, her voice filled with uncertainty. "Are you alone? Do you think anyone can hack in and record this?"

"I'm alone in my hotel room," Nate replied. He placed his device on a stable surface, and centered himself in the frame. "This is not being recorded. I would never put you at risk."

Nervous laughter bubbled up in her throat.

"This is crazy," Claire whispered. "I don't know how to do this. What if I do it wrong?"

"Babe, you won't do anything wrong," Nate said, his eyes growing darker and sexier by the second. "You're so fucking hot. I can't stop thinking about the last time we were together in Paris."

There was definitely something magical at the sight of Nate in his work clothes, going from proper business man to a dirty, hot sex god in the space of a few seconds. Claire turned the phone on its side and placed it carefully on her nightstand beside her bed, propped against the lamp. She lay back down and centered herself so that only her bottom half was visible.

"What do you want me to do?" Claire asked.

"Show me how you touch yourself. Don't hold back."

Claire turned her head away to avoid seeing herself on the screen. As turned on as she was, her nervousness kept sending her heart into overdrive. Did she look awkward and weird? Was she doing any of this right?

She pushed the bedsheet away to expose her body. She was wearing shorts and the camisole. Uncertain whether or not she should get naked, she just went for it and slipped her hand beneath her shorts. A sharp gasp escaped her lips as her fingers skimmed across her already slick flesh.

"Tell me what you feel, Claire."

"I'm feeling...how wet I am."

"Is it because of me?"

"Yes," Claire breathed.

"What am I doing to you?"

"I'm imagining...you between my legs, with your mouth on me."

She flicked her gaze to the phone for a moment. She caught a glimpse of Nate, his eyes hungrily drinking in her body and the things her hand was doing. The look on his face sent a thrill of satisfaction through her.

Her free hand strayed to her breast, and she started teasing her nipple. She imagined Nate's tongue lashing at it as his fingers expertly played with her clit, pushing her ever so close to another orgasm. She pulled down the neckline of her camisole, exposing her breasts as her hand kneaded them more aggressively.

"You're so gorgeous," Nate said, his voice a strained whisper. "I could come just looking at you."

"I want to see how turned on you are, too." Claire surprised herself. The moment had swept her away, and left in its place someone brazen and demanding.

Nate threw her a sultry look, then took off his jacket. He aimed the camera down to where Claire could see the remarkable bulge in his pants. She slipped her hand back into her shorts, finding that perfect sensitive spot once more.

Nate stood up, making his lower body visible in the frame. He quickly shucked off his white dress shirt and unbuckled his belt.

"You have no idea what you do to me," he said as he unbuttoned his pants and drew out his erection. "I can't get enough of you. Being so far away from you is killing me."

A surge of heat careened through Claire as she laid eyes on his cock. She thought she'd lose her mind when his hand fisted around it and gave it a stroke.

"Do you see how much you turn me on?" Nate asked, his

voice little more than a seductive growl. "What are you thinking?"

"I want—I want to taste you," Claire gasped, working her fingers faster. "I want to make you come with my mouth."

Claire's words drew a deep groan of pleasure from Nate. Every sensation of desire soared higher, and suddenly she was balancing on the edge of the precipice, about to fall.

"Yes. Oh God, yes," she panted. Claire got to her knees in front of the camera, her thighs spread for Nate. All the noise and inhibitions in her head dulled to a distant roar. The power of the rush toward completion and the thrill of desire were much too strong. Her breasts bounced freely as one hand pulled her shorts and panties to the side, and the other played with herself the way she did when she fantasized about Nate.

She vaguely heard Nate groan as she opened her eyes briefly to the sight of his fist pumping over his rigid cock. It was enough to push her to the brink, and her orgasm exploded out of her, drawing out a cry she couldn't control. Wave after wave of sensation passed over her, surrounding her in languid warmth. As she floated back down, her body went lax and she slumped against the headboard. It bumped loudly against the wall, and the dog next door started barking.

"Oh shit." Claire closed her eyes, her breaths coming in heavy as she slowly descended from her amazing orgasm. "Oh my God."

After a spell, her eyelids fluttered open, and she saw Nate putting his shirt back on. He sat down again in front of the camera, looking as composed and handsome as ever, but Claire recognized the telltale flush of pleasure on his cheeks. So this was what it felt like to be a bad-ass bitch in bed. An invisible glow filled her from the inside out as she pulled the covers back over her body and straightened her glasses.

"Wow," she said with a smile. "I've never done that before."

"As much as I enjoyed this, I hope we won't have to do it again," Nate replied. "Because next time I don't want us to be apart for this long."

Claire's smile faded.

"I know, Nate, but if you have to go away on business all the time, then how are we going to prevent it?"

"I'm not sure. Maybe in the future, you'd consider coming with me."

"That would be nice," Claire said, unable to keep the reluctance out of her voice. "But I don't think it would be feasible all the time. I have a life here, too. And obligations."

"I see," he replied. "Look. I don't want to force you to make any kind of decision right now. Let's just see how everything goes, okay?"

Claire nodded.

"I'll call you later," Nate said.

They said their goodbyes and hung up. Nate's words continued to gnaw at her despite the afterglow of their cybersex session. As much as she wanted to make Nate happy, something held her back. Maybe it was all the different facets of her life: her job, her family, her passions.

Claire's mind turned back to her cookie business. She couldn't deny its growing success. Thoughts of her business and the mini-boom it was experiencing filled her mind almost as much as Nate.

Claire settled back onto her pillows with a sigh. Things were changing so fast. First, Nate entered her life, and his presence somehow acted as a catalyst for her business. Where once she was uncertain and floundering, Claire was developing a vision and a plan. She wanted to take steps toward making her dream come true. Being with Nate made her realize she could change her life for the better.

She only wished she had the courage to tell her family about what she really wanted to do with her life. That would definitely be a bridge she'd cross when she reached it, and not a moment sooner.

CHAPTER NINETEEN

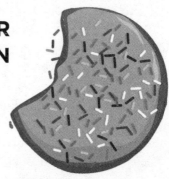

One week later

Claire's frustration mounted with every pass she took around the crowded block, looking for a parking spot. She had already circled the area four times with no success.

"Why Sam couldn't have picked an easy place like Olive Garden or Black Angus is beyond me," she muttered, even though she knew full well Sam wouldn't be caught dead in those places. "She picks the most crowded place in Long Beach at the busiest time. Thanks a lot, Ate."

Claire eventually settled for a tiny spot about two blocks away, wedged in between a two-story high Ford truck and a black Hummer with a pair of saggy testicles hanging from the back. It really put her parallel parking skills to the test. She got out of the car and cursed herself twice for settling on a pair of platform sandals she had no business wearing on any given day. Sam had told her to dress "cute" because she had reservations at a swanky eatery on PCH called *Sway*. Next time she would just wear her flip-flops, and if the restaurant had a problem, she'd leave and it would be for the best.

Claire's feet were in full-on agony by the time she reached *Sway*. Sam was waiting out front with her phone in hand, looking immaculate in a pair of black shorts that accented her great legs. Black ankle boots and a cream-colored blouse rounded out her pretty ensemble.

"There you are," Sam exclaimed. "What took you so long?"

"The parking situation is not great," Claire replied, kissing her cheek. "You look amazing."

"So do you," Sam replied. "I love your dress. Cute shoes."

Sam led the way into the crowded restaurant. Claire turned sideways to avoid brushing up against people. Loud conversations, laughter, and the sounds of the restaurant hustle filled the air, competing with the ambient music beating in the background. It all made Claire a little nervous for what she had planned. Sam originally wanted to meet with Claire to strategize their dating app situations. Claire's priority, however, was to get Sam and Ro to finally reconcile after weeks of not speaking to one another.

The hostess led them to a table beside the window facing the street. Sam and Claire took seats across from one another and perused the menu for drinks. Once they made their order, Sam got right down to business.

"Okay, so you've been really evasive with this whole dating thing," she said. "Every time I text you about it, you never give me a straight answer. I thought we were supposed to be doing this together. It would be so much easier for me if you did it, too."

"Ate, we should be focusing on you," Claire countered. "How are you doing with your matches? Have you found anyone you're compatible with?"

Sam shot her an exasperated look. "Yes," she said. "I told you already. I've matched with a handful of guys, but I haven't agreed to meet them yet because I don't want to be alone. We're supposed to be double-dating."

Claire opened her mouth to answer but stopped cold. Through the window, she saw Ro crossing the street toward the restaurant.

"I have to use the restroom really quick," she said, getting up from her chair. "Be right back."

She didn't wait for Sam to respond. Claire scurried on her

precarious shoes through the crowd and out the front door.

"Did you have to park far?" Claire asked as Ro sauntered up to her.

"I got lucky," Ro said. "There was a good spot right across the street from the restaurant. So you like this place? I heard their appetizers suck, but I'm so hungry I don't care."

As Ro chattered on, Claire positioned herself directly behind her to cut off her path of escape once she saw the real reason she was there.

"Keep going. Make a left here," Claire said as they maneuvered themselves through the crowd.

"This used to be a teppanyaki place before it was closed down due to health code violations," Ro explained. "The owner got bought out, and it re-opened as *Sway*, but I hear it's still not very g—"

Ro stopped and Claire crashed into her back. Claire's stomach flipped in anxiety as she witnessed the exact moment Sam and Ro caught sight of one another.

"Oh hell no," Ro said. "You didn't say anything about Ate Sam being here."

Sam's face was as beautifully unbothered as ever, but Claire could read the volumes of rage seething in her eyes. She was going to pay for this big time.

"So this was your plan all along?" Sam said. "This was a ruse for Ro and I to finally meet up."

"This has been going on long enough," Claire said. "You two need to talk this out."

Neither of her sisters said anything. She took advantage of the silence and steered Ro toward their awkwardly small table.

"Can we have one more chair?" Claire asked one of the servers.

Once the chair was placed at the table, Claire gently pushed Ro to sit, and she took a seat beside her. Ro made quite a show of scooting her chair very close to Claire's side, as if Sam had some kind of contagious bug she was afraid of catching. Ro picked up her menu and perused it in sullen silence.

"Ro, what are you in the mood for?" Claire asked.

"I'm not really sure," she replied. "Just as long as it isn't bitter."

"Congratulations on mastering the art of subtlety," Sam retorted.

"Ate, I don't know how many times I need to apologize to you," Ro said. "I've tried calling you multiple times. You don't even respond to my texts."

"I know sincerity when I see it," Sam said. "You're not sorry for what you did."

"Maybe at the time I wasn't, but now I sure as hell am. If I knew dating Jack would have this effect on you I would have steered clear."

"Wow. So sincere," Sam drawled.

Claire could feel the situation spiraling, and the last thing she wanted was someone storming out of the restaurant.

"Okay, let's get to the bottom of this," Claire said. "Ate Sam, Ro did not know you had feelings for Jack. If she had any kind of inkling, she would have never hooked up with him. She would never intentionally hurt you."

"Oh come on, Claire, it's a lot more complicated than that," Sam said.

"How?" Ro asked.

"If you really want to know, I'll tell you. You're inconsiderate. You do whatever you want, whenever you want, regardless of the consequences. And you just don't care."

"What?" Ro's face scrunched into disbelief.

"You've been this way since we were kids. Every time Claire and I had something, you wanted it, too. You'd throw a fit until you got it. You're constantly trying to one-up everyone, and it's annoying. Remember my college graduation, when I brought home Bobby? My boyfriend at the time? You were crushing on him and practically throwing yourself at him. You were a minor, and you were making him uncomfortable to the point he wanted to leave early."

"That is so not what happened," Ro said. "Bobby was really nice to me and we both had a common interest. He was a cross-country runner in high school, too."

"Facts are facts, Ro," Sam said.

"You're really going to hold that against me?" Ro demanded. "This happened forever ago. Let it go, for Christ's sake."

"I can't let it go when it's an established pattern of behavior," Sam replied. "There are other examples, but the incident with Jack really crossed the line. Jack is my CFO. I work closely with him, and I respect him. Taking advantage of him was really low. I would have expected better behavior from you."

The server came to take Ro's order, which provided a temporary reprieve in the sisterly shit storm.

"Jameson on the rocks, and make it a double," Ro said. "I'll also have the carnitas street tacos and the seared ahi salad."

Ro glanced at Claire.

"I'm not letting her ruin my night," Ro said. "If I have to take her verbal abuse, at the very least I can be drunk with good food in my belly."

"Excuse me for a moment." Sam's voice trembled as she got up from the table.

Claire almost stopped her, but she spied Sam's purse still hanging on the chair. She sat back in relief and turned toward Ro.

"Okay, Ro, it's time to be the bigger person," Claire said. "This has gone on long enough. This isn't about pointing fingers and laying blame. Sam is really hurting. Can't you see that?"

A worried look crossed Ro's face.

"Yeah," she agreed reluctantly. "She's really off. I didn't realize how truly upset she was."

"You have the power to end it," Claire said. "Please. Just be sincere. She's our ate, and she's done so much for us."

Ro didn't look happy, but she nodded in agreement.

A minute later, Sam returned to her seat. Her makeup and hair were still immaculate, but there was a sheen over her eyes. Claire's heart wrenched at the thought of her strong sister crying by herself in a corner.

"Ate Sam, I am really sorry," Ro said. "You're right. I was careless and inconsiderate. I promise from now on I'll work on those things. Please don't be mad at me anymore. I want to go back to the way things were. Claire and I miss you."

"You do?" Sam asked.

"Of course we do," Ro said. "Things have been…really different since your divorce. It kind of forced us to grow apart, but I think it's time we bury the hatchet. Will you please forgive me?"

Sam hesitated, squaring her shoulders.

"Yes I can," she murmured. "I'm sorry, too."

An entire gospel choir sang a resounding *hallelujah* in Claire's head. The tension between her sisters had affected her more than she wanted to admit. The truth was she felt responsible for her family's well-being. If she wasn't the one to help ease tensions, especially between her close family members, chances were they'd hold grudges for years. Her family was everything to her. She couldn't let them fall apart.

"Now that Ro's come to her senses, let's talk about the dating app," Sam said, quickly taking control of the conversation. "I'm not sure if Claire's filled you in, but we've agreed to try dating apps together."

"Really?" Ro said. "That's awesome. But…" She threw a confused look at Claire. "Why would you need a dating app if you have a boyfriend?"

"What?" Sam's ears perked up. "Who? Claire?"

"Yeah," Ro answered. "Ate, you didn't tell her about Nate?"

"No…I was trying to find the right moment," Claire said awkwardly.

Sam peered curiously at Claire. "You have a boyfriend?" she asked. "Why did you agree to create an account on the dating app if you already have a boyfriend? And why didn't you tell me?"

"Well...it was a brand new relationship and I didn't know where we stood."

"It's pretty damn clear where you two stand now," Ro remarked with a hearty chuckle. "Why don't you tell Ate Sam who you're dating?"

"Oh, it's someone I know?" Sam asked.

"Can I please tell her?" Ro whispered, leaning in toward Claire.

"Um, I'm dating a guy named Nate," Claire said, ignoring Ro.

"Oh. What does he do for a living?"

"He's an entrepreneur."

"What kind?"

"Oh for goodness sake Ate, just tell her!" Ro said in exasperation. "I know you wanted to keep this under wraps for as long as you could, but this is ridiculous."

The server approached and doled out the drinks and appetizers. Claire breathed another sigh of relief as she took a long pull of her mai tai. She tried to convince herself there was nothing to be afraid of. Sam would be happy for her, and she'd be impressed with Claire choosing a guy who was steadily employed. Sam's biggest gripe about all the guys Claire ever dated was their lack of a "real" career. Nate certainly did not fall into that category.

"Why so secretive?" Sam asked as she speared her fork through her salad. "Is there something wrong?"

"No, but I don't want anyone else to know about this yet," Claire replied. "Can you keep this a secret?"

"Of course I can," Sam said. "So who is it?"

"I'm dating Nate Noruta."

Sam stopped chewing. She glanced up at Claire.

"Wait a minute. The Nate you're dating is Nate Noruta? You're referring to *the* Nate Noruta?"

"Yes."

"The Nate Noruta who is the CEO of *MyConnect*?"

Claire nodded.

Sam finished chewing her mouthful of salad in thoughtful silence, her eyes turned to some distant point.

"Are you sure it's really him?" Sam asked. "What if you're being catfished?"

"Nope," Ro said, not caring about her mouthful of carnitas. "He's the real deal. She didn't meet him through a dating app. They've already been to Paris together. He flew her out in his private jet. Isn't it amazing?"

Sam's eyes widened in astonishment. She let out a breath of disbelief as she picked at her salad.

"Well that's…nice," she said. "I'm glad you've found somebody, Claire."

"But?" Claire asked. "You don't sound sure of something."

"I'm sorry," Sam replied. "That came out the wrong way. I really am happy for you. But…it sounds serious between you two already. And he doesn't really seem like your type."

"What?" Ro sputtered. "Not her type? Are you high? Nate Noruta is *everyone's* type."

"Look at her past dating history," Sam replied. "Nate is vastly different from the guys she's dated before."

"No shit, he's a hot billionaire." Ro took a gulp of her whiskey. "Those aren't exactly a dime a dozen."

"That is not what I mean," Sam said in annoyance. "He's a household name, Claire. There is practically no part of social media or the internet he hasn't touched or influenced in a huge way. Is he dating other people?"

"No," Claire replied, irritated at the hint of defensiveness in her tone.

"See, you didn't sound very certain," Sam said. "I sensed some hesitation there. It's only natural, because this is totally out of your comfort zone. You've never dealt with these high-powered alpha-male entrepreneurs before. They might seem enticing on the outside, but there's an ugly truth behind the facade. There's a reason they got to this point, and it's not pretty."

"Alpha male?" Claire said incredulously. "Nate has a strong personality, but I wouldn't call him alpha."

"He's a billionaire CEO," Sam said. "I don't even have to know him to know that he's alpha. Plus, you haven't known him for long. Trust me. As time passes by, you'll see I'm right."

"So you're trying to tell me Nate is an overbearing asshole, and that he's possibly cheating on me?"

Sam paused. A look of remorse flashed in her eyes.

"Claire-bear, I'm sorry," she said. "I'm not trying to be negative. I'm just trying to protect you. It's all about managing your expectations. Dylan was a highly paid hedge fund trader. He was the whole package, and look where we ended up. I want you to learn from my mistakes."

Claire's fist clenched tight around the skirt of her dress. She was surprised at the level of rage Sam incited by comparing her failed marriage to her new relationship. How dare she even draw a comparison between Nate and Dylan? Dylan was a two-timing jerk. Sam had no right to assume Nate would be the same way just because they both had money.

Ro must have sensed her anger bubbling over. She placed a calming hand on Claire's wrist. It was enough to help Claire calm down.

"Nate is on a business trip, but he's coming home really soon," Ro said with a brittle grin. "And when he does, Claire's going to introduce us, and you'll see he is nothing at all like Dylan. Not even close. Right, Ate?"

The thought of Nate meeting her family filled her with a

whole new type of worry. She was so certain Sam would approve, but she didn't react favorably at all. Would the rest of her family feel the same way?

"Yes," Claire said, hoping her grin hid the trepidation writhing beneath the surface. "I'm sure he'll be excited to meet everyone."

CHAPTER TWENTY

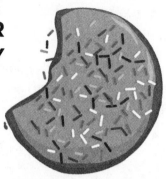

Another week later

Claire stood in the lobby of the Hilton Garden hotel, waiting patiently as the greeter for the convention checked off her name and handed her a name badge. Every year since she started her cookie business, she looked forward to the annual So Cal Bakery Arts Entrepreneurs Conference (who called themselves the So Cal BAEs for short). It was her opportunity to mingle and learn from like-minded people who were every bit as passionate about baking as she was.

She picked up a copy of the event map, taking a moment to peruse the schedule. She had some trouble focusing because Nate was scheduled to arrive early tomorrow morning. All she had left in her busy day after her conference was a dramatic reading event with her book club, the Dashing Duke Diehards, and then she'd see Nate first thing tomorrow morning. She was so excited she could hardly contain herself.

She entered the Gardenia Room for the first session: *Cookie Decorators unite! How to make your business boom with modern marketing.* The session was about three-quarters full, but she was able to find a seat in the front row. This was the session she was looking forward to the most. Her relationship with Nate seemed to be going somewhere, and it inspired her to critically examine her career and what she really wanted out of it. She hoped today's lessons would help spur her toward a concrete choice: continue her job at the Book Nook, or take a leap of faith by leaving her day job and plunging headfirst into her cookie business.

The decision made her belly burn with dread. Most of her family members worked in the medical field, engineering, or in the office in some administrative capacity, with the exception of Tita Chriss. Ironically, Claire had the most in common with Tita Chriss, because she was an entrepreneur, too. Granted, Tita Chriss had chosen to go into real estate, which was vastly different from Claire's chosen career. The last time Ro had brought up Claire's career in front of Tita Chriss, it was a disaster.

Cookie decorating? she had asked. *You can't be serious.*

"Good morning, So Cal BAEs!" A cheerful woman in her mid to late thirties with curly blond hair greeted everyone with a warm smile. The excitement bouncing off her was palpable, and it immediately passed on to Claire.

"I can't begin to tell you how excited I am to be here," she continued. "My name is Jasmine Rico, and I'm an independent marketing consultant specializing in social media. I'm not a cookie decorator myself, but I have experience and expertise in utilizing social media marketing to maximize the profit margins for your particular line of business. I'm well-known for helping Anne Jackson with her marketing strategy, which helped propel her bakery business into a booming success." Jasmine's slide show lit up the screen at the stage. She flipped through a dozen photos depicting her and Anne Jackson together.

Claire's jaw dropped. Anne Jackson of Lilly Anne's Desserts was arguably the most famous cookie decorator in the industry. Not only was her work stunning, but she ran an impressively successful business. She went from being a one-woman online vendor to opening multiple bakery locations across the United States. Anne Jackson was Claire's idol, and she could only dream of achieving a fraction of her success. She could not believe the woman responsible for Anne's success was standing right in front of her. It was a sign.

"I am so excited to share my tips and strategies with all of you," Jasmine continued. "In theory I could make a profit by selling my information, and I did this in the past. However, Anne and I became very good friends in the course of our business together. I came to develop a love and respect for the artistry behind cookie decorating. Innovative women were responsible for the culture that brought cookie decorating to the forefront. They wanted to make their mark in the world in a unique and joyful way. These women are professionals from different backgrounds. They're mothers, wives, sisters. No matter what role they have or what background they come from, they all held the same core belief: that they could spread joy with their cookie creations. For that, I commend and respect you all. For that, I have decided to share my secrets with you today."

A round of applause and approving murmurs filled the room.

"Before I begin, I have something else important to mention. I'm a feminist, through and through, but I have to give credit to the person whose business philosophy helped spur me toward success in my own career, thus allowing me to help many others. I owe a lot to Nate Noruta for his *Hope in an Uncertain World* lecture, because it helped me tap into the most powerful innate forces found in all of us, hope and positivity. If you haven't listened to it yet, I highly recommend it."

Claire's eyes widened in surprise as the room filled with applause again. Nate's influence wasn't restricted to the tech world. It spilled over into hers, too.

Determination filled Claire's heart. The signs were all there. She would start forging a path to entrepreneurship, starting today. She'd been floundering on deciding when the time was right, but she realized no time was more right than now. *Claire's Enchanted Confections* would be a real business, and she'd show her family, especially Tita Chriss, that she could be successful on her own terms.

• • •

The conference ended at five in the evening. It was, in a word, amazing. Claire got exactly what she wanted out of it. She had the inklings of a solid plan toward the formation of *Claire's Enchanted Confections* as a self-sufficient business.

She pulled into a parking spot near the Book Nook. Thursday nights were scheduled for her book club discussions. However, once every other month, the Dashing Duke Diehard event chair and director, Francine, arranged for a dramatic reading of a chosen romantic scene from their favorite books. These reading events were very popular in their group because Francine made it a point to hire handsome actors to read the part of the hero live, while Francine herself read the part of the heroine. Claire absolutely loved the readings, and she'd never missed one since joining the group three years ago.

Right before she reached the front door of the Book Nook, Nate texted her.

Claire—there's been a delay. I'll be home late tomorrow, maybe Saturday morning at the latest. I'm sorry. Will call you in a little bit. <3 Nate

Claire's spirits fell. She read the text a couple more times to make sure she wasn't mistaken. She missed Nate so much, it was almost physically painful.

Like he had said a few weeks ago, they would take it a day at a time. That was exactly what they did. Every day they texted and called each other, and video chatted when they could. To Claire's surprise, their feelings for one another didn't wane with the distance. Quite the contrary. Instead, Claire found herself growing more and more attached to Nate. His absence was like a void in her life, and she wanted nothing more than to have him back with her. She vowed she would never take that for granted again.

"Yoo-hoo, Claire."

She stopped in her path at the sound of Todd's voice.

"Oh, I forgot you were working tonight," Claire said with a smile. "How was it?"

"Busy today," Todd replied. "The weather was nice. It brought out a lot more people. Oh, you're here for the reading, right? Who's scheduled for today? The hot blond dude with long hair? Good Lord, that man was fine."

"I'm not sure who Francine got today," Claire replied. "I think I remember her saying it was going to be Jake LaFleur."

"Oh hell yes, I remember him," Todd said excitedly. "Jakey. Damn. He's the one who models for all those romance book covers, right?"

"Yes. That's him."

"Francine is a riot," Todd said with a laugh. "Doesn't she ever let any of you ladies read the role of the heroine?"

Claire smiled and shook her head.

"Half of us don't really mind, but the other half causes a scene about it," she said. "It's mostly Francine's friends who give her grief. But then she reminds them she's a sixty-five-year-old retired librarian divorcee whose passion is Regency romance, so it's only fair she gets to be the heroine every time."

"I ain't mad at that," Todd remarked. "What are you doing after? Isn't Nate coming home soon?"

"He was supposed to come in tomorrow morning," Claire replied, trying to hide her disappointment. "But he texted me a few minutes ago to tell me he was delayed."

"Oh no. For how long?"

"He probably won't be home until tomorrow night. Maybe Saturday morning at the latest."

"That really sucks. I'm so sorry. Well, I'm crossing my fingers he comes home sooner rather than later. It's been too long since you've been in each other's arms." Todd leaned in and gave Claire a peck on the cheek. "Hang in there, babe. Gotta get back to work before Margie shits a brick. Enjoy the reading."

Claire headed to the rear of the bookstore, where there was a large open area designated for event gatherings. A small refreshments table was set up in the corner, and she grabbed a bottle of water and took a sip. She perused the area and noticed the peculiar lack of attendance. There were about twenty people in the DDD, but a little less than half were present, which was surprising.

"Hi, honey, it's good to see you."

Claire turned toward the voice and saw the sweet smiling face of her friend, Norma.

"You too," Claire said, giving her a hug. "What happened to everyone?"

"Oh, it's because the male reader canceled last minute," Norma replied. "I think Francine is going to ask one of the employees here to do the reading with her instead."

"What? How strange," Claire said. "Why not just cancel the whole thing? The point of the event is to hear Francine get all dramatic with the male model. If he's not going to be here, it's no fun."

"I know," Norma said with a laugh. "But Francine always has something up her sleeve."

"The only male employee working here tonight is Todd," Claire said. "Can you imagine him reading as the duke with Francine? Oh my God, that would be hilarious."

Claire and Norma dissolved into fits of giggles as they made their way to the seating area. They sat down in the folding chairs as Francine swept into the space, greeting everyone with a magnanimous spread of her arms. She reminded Claire a lot of Mrs. Roper, an eccentric character from one of Lola's favorite shows, *Three's Company*. Francine's vivacious caftan collection definitely rivaled Mrs. Roper's.

"Good evening, my darling Diehards, and welcome to our event." She gently patted her platinum blond curls into place, then cleared her throat. "Tonight's dramatic reading is a passage from one of our favorite books, *Sinful Nights with My Duke,* by the illustrious Shana Winter. Some of you might have heard our beloved Jake LaFleur had to cancel last minute. We will certainly miss him, but the agency said they would be sending someone else in his place."

"He'd better be as handsome as Jake, or I'm out of here," one of the members quipped.

"Cool your jets, Ruth," Francine said. "Roberta, don't get a crick in your neck trying to see if he's coming in through the front. I told him to come in the back."

Several of the members, including Claire, fought to suppress laughter at Francine's unintentional innuendo, but failed miserably. Francine narrowed her eyes at the small crowd.

"You ladies knew exactly what I meant," Francine said. "I guess I shouldn't be surprised your minds are in the gutter. Ah, it looks like our handsome duke is here."

Claire took a swig of water as the stand-in for Jake LaFleur walked in—then it all came out in an ungraceful spray all over the floor as Claire laid eyes on the male actor. For a hot second, she thought she was hallucinating. The tall, gorgeous man looked exactly like—

"I'll be damned. That guy looks like Nate Noruta," Norma said. "I'm digging it. Hey, you okay, Claire?"

She could not even formulate words. Her lips pursed again and again like a goldfish, as she tried and failed to ask him what the hell he was doing here.

One of the ladies in the front row let out a high-pitched yelp.

"Agnes, what has gotten into you?" Francine asked.

"For heaven's sake, Francine, don't you recognize him?" Agnes screeched.

Claire's eyes widened in shock. Agnes was well into her eighties, and she'd never been a big talker in the group, but Nate's presence seemed to send a surge of miraculous energy through her.

"Oh my. Honey, you bear such a strong resemblance to Nate Noruta," Francine crooned, eyeing him with blatant appreciation. "Has anyone ever told you that before?"

"Yes, definitely," Nate said with a charming laugh.

Francine's appreciative eyes morphed into surprise. "You really are him!" she exclaimed. "What—I mean, how did you end up here with us tonight?"

"I'm actually here to surprise someone." Nate's dashing grin made the entire room release a dreamy sigh. "I was hoping that if I do a good enough job during this reading, she'll be impressed enough to leave with me tonight."

Nate's eyes settled on Claire, and he gave her a sexy wink.

The entire room fell into stunned silence. Everyone turned as a singular entity and looked directly at her.

CHAPTER
TWENTY-ONE

E ven when Nate and Francine were well into their dramatic reenactment, Claire still hadn't recovered. She really shouldn't have been so shocked. It was Nate's M.O. He took every opportunity he had to surprise and excite her, even if it meant lying and telling her that he was delayed in coming home. Claire wanted to be upset at him, though, because it had really hurt when he said he wasn't coming home tomorrow. But seeing him here now soothed the hurt away. It was especially helpful witnessing Nate read the part of a wicked rake attempting to seduce Francine with whispered promises of sensual fulfillment.

"I might have acted like the gentleman society expects me to be," Nate said to Francine as he read from the open novel in his hand. "I nod in polite acknowledgment, and I maintain a respectable distance. But make no mistake. The very sight of you ignites my desire. Every time you're near, I imagine how you'd feel in my arms. I fantasize about your soft, gorgeous curves beneath the whalebone and lace. I might be a gentleman on the outside, but I am mad with longing over you. The next time we're alone together, make no mistake—I'll be taking what belongs to me, and I'll leave you begging for more."

Francine drew in a ragged breath as the entire room erupted into applause.

"Lucky Francine," Agnes complained.

Claire grinned. Nate played the role of the wicked rake quite well. But she'd been away from him for far too long, and her priority was latching on to him and never letting go. Their gazes met, and Claire made a beeline for him. Before she could take another step, three members of the DDD converged on her.

"Darling, I am so happy for you," Roberta said, grasping Claire's hand. "How long have you been dating him?"

"He is so handsome," Agnes said. "You lucky girl, you."

"Did you know he was going to come here?" Ruth asked. "You looked surprised."

"Um...not long, thank you, and no, I had no idea he was coming," Claire said politely as she cautiously sidestepped around them.

"How did you two meet?" Agnes asked. "My husband and I met at the beach. I was one of the first girls back then to be brave enough to wear a bikini. Howard was a police officer on patrol that day, and he was in love the moment he laid eyes on me. He made love to me a week later, which was absolutely scandalous back then. We celebrated our fifty-ninth wedding anniversary in January."

"That's remarkable," Claire said. "Congratulations, Agnes. I'm so sorry, but I haven't seen Nate in two weeks, and I need to talk to him. But I want to hear more about Howard later. Please excuse me."

Claire broke away from the small gathering of women, but they ended up trailing after her as she approached Nate. She stopped a few feet away when she saw Francine and several other DDD members conversing with him. She started fidgeting impatiently as she waited for her moment to finally speak to Nate. His eyes were apologetic as they flicked up to hers.

Claire did not like all the obstacles standing in the way. She didn't really know how she'd ever get used to this, and she really didn't want to think about it at the moment. It was hard to focus with Nate standing so close after being gone for what seemed like forever.

"I'm sorry, ladies, but this young woman has waited her turn long enough," Nate said, his mischievous smile directed toward Claire. "If you'll excuse me."

"Wait, let us get a picture with you," Francine protested as she whipped out her camera phone. "Ruth, will you take our picture please?"

"Me too," Agnes said.

More choruses of the women requesting pictures with Nate rose up from the crowd, and Claire bit back a grunt of frustration.

None of it seemed to faze Nate. Ever the charismatic celebrity, he smiled graciously and accepted their requests for pictures. He even signed a few autographs, including Francine's bra strap.

After what felt like an eternity and a half, the starstruck ladies of the DDD finally let Nate off the hook. He immediately went to Claire and laced his fingers with hers, drawing her close to him. She sighed and let herself get swept away by the warmth of Nate's body finally next to hers. The fresh, subtle scent of his soap mingling with his skin stole into Claire's senses, and suddenly the world was right again.

"I'm sorry about all this," he said, leaning in close. "I wanted to surprise you."

Claire was about to respond, but she felt oddly exposed. She glanced around Nate's shoulder and noticed everyone's stares.

"Come this way," she said, pulling Nate along with her. She led him along the back wall, away from the prying eyes that seemed to pop up everywhere. Her first thought had been to lead him outside, but she wanted to avoid exposure to the public. Instead, she took him to the break room in the back corner of the bookstore.

She pushed open the door, and luckily it was empty. It was a small room with dingy white walls covered in bulletins and breaker boxes. There were three folding chairs set up near a rickety old table. It wasn't ideal, but it would make do.

When they were finally alone, Claire let his hand go and wrapped her arms around him, burying her face into his chest. A wave of emotion came over her, and she hugged him tighter.

"I missed you so much," she murmured. "God, I missed you."

Nate returned the hug. As he lovingly stroked her back, that familiar feeling of indescribable happiness enveloped Claire once again.

"Hey, are you all right?" he asked. He pulled away slightly and peered down into her face, stroking her cheek with the backs of his fingers.

"Yes," she answered with a smile.

Nate bent down and kissed her. Pleasant heat spread through Claire's body, seeping into her bones. His beard tickled her chin as his soft lips parted her own, allowing his tongue to dart in and taste her with deft, sensual strokes. Claire groaned and pulled away from him.

"Is there a lock on the door?" Nate asked, grasping her hips possessively. "I can make this quick."

Claire's face pinched into a playful frown as she lightly swatted his arm.

"How in the world did you pull this off?" she demanded.

"What do you mean?" Nate asked innocently.

"This—this whole *thing*," she said. "How did you know about any of this? How did you replace Francine's male model?"

"Well, if you didn't already know, there's not much I can't do," Nate said with a cocky grin. "But seriously, I have a good memory. You mentioned your meetings on Thursday nights, and you said the reading was scheduled for tonight. As for the details of the operation: Craig took care of it."

"Poor Craig," Claire said. "I'm sure that infiltrating a group of spicy romance fans wasn't in his job description."

Nate's phone rang. He glanced at it, then silenced it and put it away.

"Do you need to get that?" Claire asked.

"No. I spent the past few weeks working, and all I want right now is you."

His words melted Claire's heart all over again and threatened to turn her knees into melted butter. But now that Nate was home, it was time to start strengthening the foundation of their relationship. She gave his hand a squeeze and smiled sweetly up at him.

"I want to hear how your trip went. Where did you go? Did you get to do everything you had planned?"

"I did. The main reasons I went were for the Technology Live conference and the visit to Rome. Afterward I had some meetings in Barcelona and London, and then New York to meet with my literary agent and publisher."

"Literary agent? Did you write a book?" Claire asked, trying not to sound shocked.

"I'm in the process," Nate replied. "A while back, I sent in a proposal for a memoir. It's more of an inspirational book about business and innovation."

"That's great. Congratulations. It must be an amazing feeling to publish something."

"I imagine it will be. I'll find out for sure when it gets released in October."

Nate's phone buzzed again, but he completely ignored it this time.

"I can't believe you came home early," Claire said. "You tricked me. I had a little welcome back celebration planned for you. Not a big party with a bunch of people, or anything like that—just you and me, with home-cooked Filipino food and desserts by yours truly."

"Can we still plan on that?" he asked, his face brightening. "I can't wait to try your cooking. And I'd love to try more of your desserts."

"Of course," she said. "How about tomorrow night I cook?"

"Okay, but what do you want to do tonight? You want to go somewhere?"

"No. I already know what I want to do."

Nate leaned forward and raised his eyebrow at her. "I hope it's the same thing I want to do," he murmured, brushing his lips against hers.

"We'll have time for that later," she said with a grin. "I want to order takeout, go back to my place, watch movies, and cuddle on the couch. Like a normal couple."

Nate gently tucked Claire's hair behind her ears and planted another kiss on her lips.

"Of course," he said. "But let's go to my place. As fond as I am of your sister, I'd prefer to be alone with you tonight."

"Yes," Claire agreed as joy bubbled up inside her chest. "I'd love to."

Later on that night, Claire found herself in Nate's black SUV with bags of Italian takeout that filled the car with delicious aromas.

"For some reason I always thought you lived in Long Beach," Claire said as she glanced out the window at the gorgeous houses lining the street. "I've never been to this part of L.A. before. What's it called again?"

"Los Feliz," Nate replied. "We're almost there. My house is just up ahead."

Claire trained her eyes on the iron gate Nate drove up to. The gate slowly rolled open, as if somehow recognizing Nate's car or some device inside of it. As soon as the gate was open enough, Nate eased the car through and drove up an elegant, paved driveway that curved smoothly around a grassy knoll topped with a big tree.

Claire started fidgeting with the seatbelt. She didn't know

what to expect from Nate. Did he live in some kind of extravagant, gaudy estate reminiscent of Trump's awful Mar-a-Lago? Or a gothic monstrosity like the Playboy Mansion?

She crossed her fingers, hoping Nate didn't have an awful sense of style. It was one of the things she could find potentially off-putting. It had nothing to do with socioeconomic status. It was more about the choices and the details. Were there a lot of photos of friends and family? Plants? Artwork adorning the walls? Quirky knickknacks scattered about? Even if the space was plain and minimalist, it would make an impression on her. She knew it wasn't right to judge people by their homes, but the details said a lot about a person. She prayed there was nothing bizarre in there, like velvet wallpaper and disco balls.

The driveway emptied into a large courtyard in front of a three-car garage. Claire blinked and stared at the house in surprise. It was a large home, but not nearly as big as she thought it would be. The style was Spanish colonial, with sharp and artistic lines and wrought-iron detail. Even from the front of the house she could peer into the crevices hinting at various outdoor areas mimicking the classic style of Spanish courtyards.

"Nice house," Claire said as she got out of the car. "How long have you lived here?"

"About three years." Nate opened the trunk and grabbed the bags of food.

"Let me help, too," Claire said, reaching for two bags. "You'd think we're about to feed an army with all this food."

Nate led the way toward the double front doors. Claire hesitated when she noticed the lights on inside the house and a flash of movement through the window.

"Uh, does somebody else live here, too?" she asked.

"Yes," Nate answered as he unlocked and opened the door. "This is Maisy."

A very excited dog bounded toward them. It looked like a golden retriever, except for the fact it was covered in soft brindle fur with a tuft of white on its chest. Claire gasped, flinching as she expected the dog to start barking, but it didn't. Instead, it whimpered excitedly and stopped short, wagging its tail as it sniffed the bags in Claire's hands.

"You don't mind dogs, do you?" asked Nate.

"No, not at all," Claire said with a smile. "I love dogs."

"Good, because she likes you."

Nate guided Claire into the house before he shut the front door. She found herself in a tastefully decorated space. The walls were plain white with few adornments. Neutral-colored rugs were situated in the different living spaces atop the pale hardwood floor planks arranged in an attractive zig-zag pattern. Even though it was nighttime, Claire could tell the space would be light and airy during the day due to the many windows throughout the home. And she was right—every few feet, she could see numerous courtyards through the windows where there were fountains, gas lamps, fire pits, and comfortable seating.

"Let me give you a quick tour." Nate led Claire to the spacious kitchen where he set the food on top of the large rectangular island. "You can access the backyard through these doors." Nate flipped a few light switches and opened the framed glass doors onto a breathtakingly stunning space.

Claire's jaw dropped as she surveyed the pool and spa surrounded by a gorgeous latticework patterned concrete and turf hardscape. Trees lined the perimeter of the sprawling yard, showcasing the glimmer of the L.A. city lights through the gaps.

Nate continued showing her the rest of the house. When they were done, he led the way back to the kitchen, where they both set up the food, plates, and utensils on the countertop. Claire took a seat as Nate poured her some red wine. Maisy sat beside Claire and nudged her hand. She smiled and gave Maisy a good scratching. She loved the feel of the dog's luxurious fur beneath her fingers.

"So what do you think of the house?" Nate played some soft music through one of the hidden speakers, then sat down to serve himself some of the meat lasagna.

"It's impressive." Claire took a sip of wine and grabbed a garlic knot. "This house is stunning. It's not really something I would have envisioned for you."

"Why not?"

"I didn't mean it in a bad way. All I mean is, you're a single man. I would have thought you'd be living in a big penthouse in a high rise, or something along those lines. This house has six bedrooms and a lot of bathrooms. To me, it seems like the kind of home you could spend the rest of your life in."

Nate's gaze broke away from Claire as he sipped his wine.

"It could be," he said. "That was definitely on my mind when I bought the house. It's close to my offices downtown, and I liked the vibe and design. And it is big enough for a family. For a long time I was lonely, and I believed buying a house like this would put it out into the universe that I was ready to find someone and settle down."

Claire took a bite of her chicken marsala. The flavor was amplified by the wine and the heart-felt admission from Nate about his plans for the future.

"You were right," Claire said when she finished chewing. "This food is to die for."

Maisy whimpered and put her paws up on Claire's knees.

"Aw, Nate. Is she hungry?"

"No. Craig was here earlier and he fed her. That's her way of saying she likes you. She's a friendly dog by nature, but she usually doesn't ask to be pet by strangers."

Claire's heart filled with joy as she gave Maisy's soft fur another good scratching. As she gazed into the dog's pretty brindle face, her spirits elevated. This was exactly what she wanted: to sit with Nate in his cozy kitchen enjoying a nice dinner, with the beloved Maisy keeping them company. It was a simple, beautiful moment she wanted to repeat over and over again.

"I like you, too, Maisy," she whispered. "A lot."

"That was the best Italian food I've ever had." Claire ambled into the den. "I should do a few thousand meters on the rower in your gym, but your sofa's calling me."

Claire was about to plop down on the sofa, but stopped when her eyes landed on a large framed photo on Nate's wall.

"Oh my goodness," Claire breathed, moving in for a closer look. "This is gorgeous."

"Hmm? Oh. That's a picture of Cappadocia in Turkey," Nate said. "You've never seen it before?"

"No. I can't believe how gorgeous it is."

Claire drank in the photo of vibrant hot air balloons dotting a star-speckled deep blue sky. They floated serenely over a glimmering, ancient city fashioned from stone embedded in the hills. It captured Claire's heart in a warm, heady embrace.

"I've always wanted to ride in the famed hot air balloons of Cappadocia." Nate brought over their wine glasses and a slice of cake. Claire settled next to him on the sofa and snuggled underneath his arm.

"You've never been there before, right?" Claire asked.

"Not yet," Nate answered. "I promised myself I'd go one day, but there's one problem. I'm afraid of heights."

"No way," Claire said. "But you went with me to the top of the Eiffel Tower."

"I do my best to hide it, but heights scare me. The moment I finally take the leap and get into one of those balloons is the moment I conquer my fear. But I don't know if I could ever do it."

"You don't have to do it on your own. You're never alone.

That's what family and loved ones are for. They uplift you when you need them the most."

Nate's eyes grew troubled for a brief moment, but then it was gone.

"It's movie time," he said. "You have to try the butter cake. I guarantee you'll love it."

Claire dug her fork into the cake and took a bite as Nate flipped the TV on. The sudden shift in topic puzzled her, and she tucked it away to bring up at another time. Maisy jumped onto the couch and nestled beside her, nuzzling her thigh.

"This is so good," Claire said. "I'm more of a chocolate person, but I would change my tune just for this cake."

"What do you feel like watching?"

She skimmed the content on the screen, but nothing really jumped out at her. "How about something thought-provoking?" she suggested.

Nate chose a critically-acclaimed Korean drama film and hit play. Claire had every intention to immerse herself. She loved foreign films, and she had always wanted to see this particular one because it won so many awards. But being here, with Nate all to herself, was something precious and rare. The thought was a little sobering, and she found a little bit of sadness seeping into her day.

"You really don't get many chances to take a break, do you?" Claire lifted her head and looked at Nate. "Are you sacrificing a lot to be here with me?"

"No, not right now," Nate said with a reassuring grin. "You're not interrupting anything. I move things around on my schedule to make time."

"But you're really busy," Claire said. "You control this huge tech empire. You have thousands of employees, and you give speeches, and you're always expanding your business. I want to be respectful of that. I don't want you to resent me or anything because you feel obligated to spend time with me to make me happy."

"Where is this coming from?" he asked.

"I've just been thinking about a lot of things. I've never dated a guy like you before, and I'm not quite sure how to make it work."

"You don't have to worry about any of that." Nate gently stroked her cheek with his thumb. "I spend time with you because I want to, not because I have to. Being with you is like a break in a timeline of chaos. I'm a workaholic. It's not good for me to be this way, and it's started to take its toll. But then you came into my life and everything changed. None of this was planned. You dove headfirst into my life and stole my heart, and made me forget about all the things weighing me down. When I'm with you, I can slow down and enjoy the moment. I never knew anything was missing from my life until I met you."

Claire's breath left her in a rush. His words resounded in her head, making her heart feel so unbearably full and light all at once. She couldn't believe Nate was real. He was so pure and wonderful and loving. The world didn't deserve him, and least of all her. But he wanted her, and she was going to take advantage of that for as long as she could.

She kissed him. Nate returned the kiss, deepening it and drawing her body closer to him. She was drunk on his touch, and all she wanted was to experience this feeling forever.

"I'm guessing you're over the thought-provoking movie," Nate said with a sexy smile.

"Screw the movie," Claire whispered. "I want you."

"I like the sound of that. Maisy, go to your bed."

The dog obediently snapped to attention and bounded away down the hall.

Claire trailed slow, languid kisses down Nate's jaw and his neck. Her hands ran down his chest, smoothing over the chiseled planes of his muscular torso. She settled down on her knees between his legs as her fingers worked to unfasten his jeans. Pausing for a moment, she ran her hands up and down his hard, lean thighs and gazed up at him. He was completely in her thrall, and she loved the power of sensual anticipation she exercised over him.

Claire unbuttoned his jeans, and he lifted his hips to help her slide them down. Her palm rubbed up and down his rigid length before she reached into his boxer briefs and pulled out his erection. Nate drew in a sharp hiss as Claire leaned forward, drawing her tongue slowly over the swollen head. She didn't waste time putting him out of his misery. In the next moment, she took his dick as deep as she could into her mouth, moving up and down, as her hand pumped along his length.

Nate's hands fisted gently in her hair, drawing it up so he could see her. She lifted her gaze and stared directly into his eyes as her mouth suckled voraciously at him.

"Oh my God," Nate groaned, throwing his head back for a moment. "Take it easy, Claire. You feel so fucking good."

His hot shaft stiffened even more, and she knew he was getting close already. She tightened her grip on him and sped up her movements, using her tongue because she loved her ability to drive him wild with desire.

Suddenly Nate grasped her face, stilling her. She paused for a moment, then slowly suckled her way off him.

"As much as I love fucking your mouth, I've been waiting to get inside you forever." Nate pulled Claire forward until she was standing up. He unfastened her jeans and hooked his thumbs into her underwear, then slid them off. Claire straddled him, and he reached blindly into the pocket of his jeans for a condom.

"You don't need that." Claire lowered herself and pressed her slick core to his erection.

"Why not," Nate panted as she teased him with little thrusts of her pelvis.

"Because I started the pill a few weeks ago after I got home from Paris."

Nate looked up at Claire. She lifted her shirt over her head and tossed it away.

"Really?"

Claire paused. It was kind of a big moment for both of them. She prepared herself for some kind of doubt or hesitation on Nate's part. Claire knew she could trust Nate, and from the open and passionate look in his eyes, he trusted her, too. It was all she needed before she guided his hands to her breasts and positioned the head of his cock at her entrance.

"Yes," she whispered. "I've never trusted anyone the way I trust you. I wanted to show you I'm serious."

Nate pressed a soft, sensual kiss to her lips. Heat skipped across her flesh as his tongue tasted her in gentle strokes. It was in shocking contrast to what he did next.

He grasped her hips and drove himself up into her. They both cried out at the same time. The feeling of him stretching and filling her abruptly sent sparks of pleasure shooting through her entire body. She began to move on top of him, rising up on her knees and coming back down again in a gentle but rapid rhythm, savoring the feel of him inside her slick, sensitive flesh.

Nate grasped her ass as she rode him. He leaned forward and suckled her breasts. He stroked her lower back and thighs, and brought his thumb down to press on her clit. Her body went into a quick spasm as the jolt of pleasure shot straight to her core. Her rhythm sped up, and she began to tremble with the promise of release.

Soon, they fell into a synchronous rhythm, and every thrust pushed Claire closer and closer to her orgasm.

"That's it, baby," Nate whispered against her ear. "Come for me. Come hard."

She rose up on her feet and continued to bounce up and down on him, but with more vigor and force. She gripped his shoulders, squeezing hard as the release bore down on her. She gritted her teeth and vaguely realized she was digging her nails into Nate, but he didn't seem to care. Her legs began to shake, then suddenly the orgasm ripped through her body like a bolt of lightning.

With an almost animalistic grunt, Nate flipped Claire onto her back and slung her ankles over his shoulders. With his hands braced on the back of the couch, he began pumping fiercely into her. Claire moaned at the hot as hell sight of Nate taking pure pleasure in her body, his muscles straining and perspiration gleaming on his brow. He stilled with a groan as he found his own release, and spent himself inside her.

Once he was done, he held Claire in his arms tenderly and rolled her back on top of him. She clung to him with her eyes closed, her breathing deep and slow, allowing the sweet sensations to completely envelop her. Nate pressed a kiss to her temple.

"I love you," he whispered.

Her eyes flew open. She slowly leaned back until she was staring into Nate's eyes.

"I'm sorry if it's too early to say it," he said. "But I'm not afraid. I've never been more sure of anything."

A thousand fireworks were going off in her heart right now, and it took everything in her being to refrain from shouting in joy to the rooftops. Instead, she gazed into the eyes of the man she had already fallen hard for. The truth was, she already knew how she felt long before he confessed his love for her.

"I love you, too, Nate."

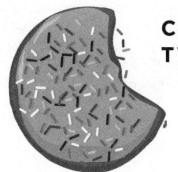

CHAPTER TWENTY-TWO

Claire awoke to a heavenly golden glow streaming in through the billowy white curtains. A moment of déjà vu suddenly struck as she remembered waking up in Paris after she and Nate had made love for the first time.

She checked the time. A quarter past six in the morning. Even though Nate wasn't in the room with her, she wasn't concerned. She knew he was nearby.

The memories of what they did the night before made her flush. At some point during their intimate activities, they'd somehow made it to Nate's bedroom. She'd pretty much lost count of how many times they'd had sex throughout the night. Even early in the morning, before the sun rose in the sky, her body roused her from sleep as it responded to Nate's heavy arousal pressing against her bare butt.

After she used the restroom, she got up and wandered into the hallway. She followed the sound of Nate's voice and found him on a video conference call in his office. Snooping in on his business was the last thing on her mind, but she wanted to get a sense of his mood. She really couldn't follow what he was talking about, but based on his tone, he sounded fine…maybe even chipper.

Peering through the crack, she noticed he was already freshly showered and dressed, but he had no coffee or anything to eat with him. For a hot second she considered asking him if he wanted breakfast, but then thought better of it. She didn't want to interrupt him, *and* she didn't want any of his colleagues to see her in the background wearing one of his T-shirts, which looked more like a dress on her small frame.

Instead, she quietly backed away and crept over to the kitchen. Maisy followed, tail wagging, as she opened the fridge and pulled out the eggs, shredded cheese, and a pack of turkey sausage.

"Let's be very quiet, okay Maisy?" Claire said as she carefully searched through his pantry for coffee. "We're going to surprise your wonderful daddy with breakfast."

Claire switched herself to cooking mode, easily finding everything she needed to make a nice breakfast for her and Nate. She wasn't sure how he liked his eggs, so she made scrambled and over-easy. She fried up some sausage, and even mixed up some pancake batter she found while riffling around the pantry for condiments.

Nate was still in his meeting when she finished making breakfast. She plated everything and laid it out nicely on the kitchen counter, hoping the aroma would be enough to beckon him to the kitchen. After a minute of waiting, Claire took her mug of coffee and opened the doors to the backyard. In the daylight she could see how beautiful his home really was. The night didn't do justice to the details, like the gorgeous city vista past the vivid trees, or the bold blueness of the water shimmering in the pool.

It was the tail end of August, and the heat was already coming in strong despite the early morning hour. The heady warmth of the summer weather latched onto Claire and pulled her in, beckoning her to wander out barefoot in the backyard to sit in the sun. She hoped there would be a chance to take a dip in the pool in the near future.

"Good morning, beautiful."

Claire turned around. Nate stood inside the kitchen doorway, looking handsome as sin.

"Me or Maisy?" she asked.

Nate walked over to Claire and wrapped his arms around her waist.

"You and only you." He leaned down and kissed her. "You look really good in my clothes."

"I hope I'm not being too presumptuous, but I went ahead and made you breakfast. Is it too early?"

"No, not at all," he replied. "That was so sweet of you. Let's have our breakfast outside."

Nate found some trays for them to put the dishes on and brought them outside to the covered seating area by the pool. He also brought out a bottle of champagne, glasses, and a jug of orange juice.

"Mimosas," Claire groaned as he poured some into her glass. "You're the best."

"I know," he replied. "What do you have planned today?"

"I'm going to visit Lola around nine. I don't work at the bookstore today, which is good because it will give me time to fulfill cookie orders and work on some plans I have for my business."

"Are you cutting back on your hours?" he asked.

"Um...yes. I'm trying to." Claire cleared her throat. It was a big moment for her. Nate would be the first person she'd be making this confession to, but she figured it was either now or never.

"I'm taking the leap," she said. "I'm going to quit my job to focus on turning *Claire's Enchanted Confections* into a real business."

Nate's face lit up.

"That's amazing, Claire. If you're passionate and this is what you want to do, you should go for it."

"Really?" she said. "You don't think this is a stupid, impractical thing to do?"

"Of course not," he replied. "You've got a solid product, and your customer service is great. You're one of the top sellers on *Eclectix*. I think you've got an excellent eye for business, and you should run with it."

A huge smile spread across her face. "Wow," she said, her heart filled with adoration. "Thank you. Your support means so much to me. If only my family could be this supportive and have the same level of faith in me, it would make all of this much easier."

"That's part of what's holding you back?" Nate asked as he passed her a flute of mimosa. "Your family?"

"Well...kind of. It's hard to say. I'm just afraid they'll tell me it won't work out, and I should go back to school to do something more practical, like be a nurse or a teacher. Not that there's anything wrong with those ideas, but they're not my dream. This is what I really want to do."

"This is your life." Nate sat across from Claire and took her hand in his. "I know your family means a lot to you, but you're the one who has to live with your decisions every single day. Not anyone else. And if they really love you, they'll come to understand. It won't be an easy road, but they'll eventually get there."

Nate's thumb stroked across Claire's skin. His words soothed her fears and made her believe, for just a moment, that her dream might actually be within her reach.

"I think this calls for a toast," Nate said, raising his flute. "To your new career as an entrepreneur. You deserve to be your own boss."

They clinked their glasses together and took a sip.

"You can ask me for help any time," Nate said. "Like hiring staff, or any kind of consultation or advice, I'm here for you. But before I forget, I'm hoping you're free tonight. I'm meeting up with some of my friends for dinner and I wanted you to come with me. They want to meet you."

Claire took a long sip of her mimosa to help dislodge the

ball of food that seemed to stick in her throat.

"You told your friends about me already?" she asked.

"Of course I did. They're excited to meet you. I think you'll like them. Can you come with me?"

A sudden wave of guilt hit Claire at her first instinctual response: refusal. She was flat-out afraid they wouldn't accept her. She wasn't even scraping the lowest levels of rich, glamorous, and sophisticated: all the criteria Claire knew they'd be expecting out of Nate's girlfriend. They'd be disappointed to see a nervous, overly-chatty Plain Jane in their midst.

But she couldn't let Nate down. It was only right to be there for him, like he was there for her every single time.

"Of course," she said, feigning delight. "No problem."

Nate hesitated. His eyes turned dubious. "Claire, there's nothing to be nervous about," he said. "Everyone is nice, and they will love you. Don't worry about anything. I'll be right there with you." He reached across the table and squeezed her hand again.

Claire loved it when this man touched her, but even his hand upon hers couldn't completely quell the anxiety stirring inside her like a distant storm.

"What do you have planned today?" she asked, shoving aside her discomfort.

"Meetings. Work, per usual."

"Are you traveling any time soon?"

"Not for a while."

Claire finished off the rest of her mimosa and dabbed at her mouth with a napkin.

"Okay, I'm going to take a quick shower," she said as she got up from the table. "Can you wait for me?"

"No," Nate replied. "I'm going to join you."

He lunged at her and swept her up in his arms. Claire squealed with delight as he rushed her back into the house for his second shower of the morning.

. . .

Later that night, back at her apartment, Claire finally got the chance to work on her cookie orders. She had arranged for a couple of assistants to help her with a few final details.

"I cannot thank you guys enough for all your help," she said.

Claire gazed down in abject love at her two younger cousins, Jaydee and Marco, who sat at her dining table filling plastic piping bags with colored royal icing.

"You're welcome," they both said. Jaydee and Marco were thirteen-year-old twins who had graciously agreed to help Claire with some of her orders. She offered to pay them, but her Tita Jovy had refused, saying it would be her kids' honor to help their cousin. Claire didn't want to argue with her aunt, so she paid Jaydee and Marco anyway and swore them both to secrecy.

"What are you going to do with all this icing?" Jaydee asked.

"I'm trying something new," Claire answered. "I scored a cookie decorating class gig for someone's birthday party tomorrow night. If it goes well, I'm going to start offering more classes."

"You're teaching classes now?" Marco asked, sounding a little disappointed. "You're not going to make cookies anymore?"

"Don't worry, I will make you all the cookies you want," Claire said with a laugh. "I'm trying out a few new things because I want to expand."

Marco grinned in satisfaction, clearly relieved he still had a steady source of free sugar cookies.

"What time are you leaving for your date?" Jaydee asked.

Claire checked the time.

"He'll be here any minute," she replied. "You two are here for one more hour. Be sure to sort the cookies into the boxes the way I showed you earlier. All the royal icing bags can go into the fridge, but make sure to sort them by color. Your mom is going to pick you up, right?"

"Right."

"When she comes, lock up the apartment with the key I left you. Just keep the key safe and I'll pick it up from you later on. Will you guys be okay here?"

"Yes," they replied simultaneously.

Claire checked herself in front of the mirror hung up on the wall by the front door. She had chosen a simple sleeveless knee-length maroon work dress with a black cardigan. Earlier she had trouble settling on a theme: fancy and stylish versus professional and practical. After debating with herself for nearly an hour, she finally went for professional and practical. It was better for Nate's friends to think she was plain as opposed to giving the impression she was trying too hard to impress them with her fashion sense when it was painfully clear she possessed none.

There was a gentle knock on the door.

"Okay, guys, remember what I told you," Claire said as she slung her purse over her shoulder. "Icing in fridge. Lock up. Don't lose the key. Oh, and you can help yourself to the chocolate in the pantry, but don't tell your mom. Call me if you need anything."

"Okay. Thanks Ate," the twins replied. They popped their earbuds back in their ears and trained their eyes on their phones as they went back to work. Claire opened the door just enough for her to squeeze through, then she closed it behind her.

"Hey." Nate bent down and kissed Claire, sending a shot of heat straight through to her toes. "What's going on in there?"

"Child labor operation," she replied, pulling him along the hallway. "Don't look at me like that. I hired my twin cousins to help me package some of my products."

"Oh. Why didn't you want them to see me?"

"Because I don't want them telling their mom about you," Claire replied. "I want to be the one to tell my family about us."

Nate didn't reply as they walked hand in hand to the front of the apartment complex where he had parked in one of the guest spots. This time he was driving a pearly-white Tesla coupe. He opened the door for Claire and she settled into the passenger seat.

"Did you get a chance to visit Lola today?" Nate asked as he started up the car.

"Yes," she said. "There's nothing new to report from the staff's point of view. The caregivers say she's doing well, but I've noticed she's eating less and sleeping more. Every once in a while she'll actually talk to me. Even though it's mostly nonsense, I love hearing her talk because it reminds me of how she used to be."

Nate merged into the traffic on the main road. He planted a kiss on the back of Claire's hand and gave her a sidelong glance.

"I like your outfit," he remarked. "You look like a hot school-teacher."

"What? You're into that?" she asked with a laugh.

"Hell yes."

"Good to know," she replied. "But seriously, that wasn't my intention. I wanted to make a good impression on your friends. Who's going to be there?"

"Only a few," Nate answered. "I keep a small circle of friends. You'll meet Aaron and Sawyer, who I've known since college. Then Jake, who's also the CFO, and then Ryder, my executive VP."

"Oh," Claire replied in surprise. "You're close friends with all of your board members?"

"No way," Nate answered. "Not all of them. Only those two. They're bringing their significant others, too."

Anxiety fizzled in Claire's belly. So she was going to a fancy restaurant in Hollywood to be paraded in front of a group of wealthy men and their glamorous wives. She assumed Nate was the ring leader of this powerful group. She expected to be scrutinized from head to toe and judged for anything and everything. Would they be welcoming to her? They'd been Nate's friends for a long time. How would they think Claire stacked up against his ex-girlfriends? Would they take her seriously?

Claire's heart galloped in tortured silence. She wasn't typically insecure, but being with Nate—fully coming into the understanding of his pivotal role for millions, perhaps billions of people in the world—conflated all of her shortcomings.

She said a silent Hail Mary, praying it would be a quick and painless evening.

CHAPTER TWENTY-THREE

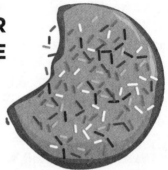

They drove to a restaurant called *Mariano's* in downtown Hollywood. It was the epitome of hip, fashionable, and trendy. Claire wouldn't be surprised if this was the epicenter for celebrities and rich people.

That was exactly why she felt like the odd one out.

But not with Nate. Being with him was easy and natural, and he made everything better. He drove up to the valet and escorted her out of the car and into the bright, stylish restaurant. She knew people were staring at Nate, and perhaps her, but she tried her best to ignore it. Instead she focused on being present with Nate and enjoying his company. She concentrated on the objective at hand: surviving the night with as few battle scars as possible.

And here she was jumping to conclusions again. Why did she automatically assume Nate's friends wouldn't like her? She couldn't help being worried. She'd been a natural worrier since childhood. Sam was the stern one, Ro the free-spirited one, and Claire the anxious one.

Nate held her hand, guiding her through the restaurant toward a private room with walls full of wine bottle racks. There was even a private bar in the room with their own bartender and server. Claire forced a smile onto her face and stiffened as Nate's friends approached with spirited greetings. The only one she recognized was Craig, whom she greeted with enthusiasm. But when she saw the women in the group, her stomach tightened in fear. Just as she expected. All gorgeous and glamorous. She even recognized the most beautiful one in the group.

"Hi, it's so nice to meet you," she said, giving Claire a dazzling smile. "I'm Kendall. I've heard such nice things about you."

Claire had a hard time concentrating. It was funny she didn't recognize Nate when she first met him, but she certainly knew Kendall. This was Kendall Greyhart, supermodel and Victoria's Secret angel. Her pictures were everywhere.

"Hi," Claire said, forcing herself to snap out of her thoughts. "It's a pleasure to meet you, too."

"The infamous Claire. It's nice to see you're actually real and not a figment of Nate's dreams," a handsome man with dark hair and bright blue eyes said as he sauntered up to them. He laughed good-naturedly and enveloped Claire in a warm hug. It caught her off guard, but she smiled and returned the hug as well.

"Sorry, Claire, this is Jake, my CFO," Nate said. "Jake and Kendall are engaged."

Claire liked Jake and Kendall's vibe, but Nate swept her along to introduce her to the rest of the group.

"This is my best friend from college, Aaron," Nate said. "And this is his wife, Sophia. Over here, we've got Ryder, my executive VP, and his wife, Nicole. And last but not least, Sawyer the lawyer. This is his wife, Nousha."

Claire's heart thrummed nervously as she stood there, smiling graciously, as eight new sets of strange eyes appraised her from head to toe. To her great relief, every single one of Nate's friends and their significant others were nothing but warm and friendly toward her. Everyone was relaxed and jovial. No negative energy whatsoever. They all had drinks in their hands, (save for Sophia and Nicole, who were twelve weeks and six months pregnant, respectively). They included everyone in the conversations, even Claire, despite her being a practical stranger to them.

Through it all, Claire found solace and strength in Nate's arm around her. He kept her close and didn't leave her side, holding her hand and touching her affectionately any chance he got. Soon the tension began to ease from her body. To her surprise, she started incorporating naturally into Nate's group of friends, especially the women.

"Nate, you don't mind if we steal Claire while you guys talk shop?" Sophia asked with a grin.

"Sure," he said, removing his arm from around her waist.

The women moved to the other end of the bar while the guys congregated at one end of the long dining table.

"Nicole, please have a seat," Claire said, moving aside and pushing the barstool closer to her.

"Thank you," Nicole said. "I've been standing for so long. I had a lot more stamina during my first pregnancy, but with this one, it's like my body is rebelling against me."

"This is your second?" Claire asked.

"Yes. I have a two-year-old daughter. Camilla is the apple of her father's eye, but Ryder is super excited this one's a boy."

"Aaron's the opposite," Sophia remarked. "He wants a girl. He has three brothers, so he's been traumatized growing up. He said his house was practically a war zone, and knowing his brothers, I can totally imagine it."

"Nousha, you're not drinking anything," Kendall said with a sly look in her eyes. "I wonder what that means."

An innocent look stole into Nousha's dark, beautiful eyes.

"No baby yet," she replied. "I swear. I'm planning on drinking, but I want some food in my belly first."

The conversation fascinated Claire. So it seemed the wives of Nate's close friends were all at the stage where they were having families, or seriously contemplating the notion. Maybe it meant Nate was serious about her, and that he was approaching the same stage in his life as well. The thought sent her stomach fluttering in conflicting waves of joy and nervousness.

"You know who'd probably be an amazing dad?" Sophia said. "Jake. He's hilarious, and he gets along with kids really well. Don't you think so, Kendall?"

"Yeah, he really would be a great dad," she agreed. "I can't wait."

"So you're planning on having kids right away?" Nousha asked.

"Pretty much," Kendall said. "He's really excited to have kids. He said he wants five. I'm not sure about that, but we'll see what I can tolerate—I mean, handle."

"You're not an Angel anymore, right Kenni?" Nicole asked. "I heard you quit."

"Yeah, I modeled for Victoria's Secret for five years," Kendall replied. "I'm twenty-eight now, so I'm considered old. It's okay, though, because I just got picked up by Balmain and Dior. My agency's great. They don't have any problems getting work for me."

Claire stared at her in mild surprise. Kendall was giving her agency credit? The woman was a beauty in its rarest form. No agency would have a problem scoring jobs for her.

"After you and Jake get married and have kids, would you still go back to modeling?" Nousha asked.

"No," Kendall replied. "Jake and I agreed I'd stay home and raise the kids."

"Hold on," Nicole said in suspicion. "Was this Jake's call or yours? You have to agree with it, too."

"It was a joint decision. I'm ready to move on to the next part of my life. I don't need to go back to modeling anymore. I've been doing it since I was fifteen. And Jake makes plenty of money, so I don't feel insecure at all."

"Here we are talking about getting married and having kids in front of Claire," Sophia said apologetically. "I'm sorry if this is tedious for you."

"Not at all," Claire replied.

"Tell us the story of how you met Nate," Sophia said. "I heard a little bit of the story from Aaron, but he didn't know any of the details."

"Oh, well, it's not all that exciting," Claire said. "It's kind of embarrassing, actually, and I haven't told many people about it. I was trying to park in a spot by the sidewalk in Long Beach, and I almost hit Nate with my car."

All four women's eyes flew open wide. Nousha and Kendall gasped. Nicole and Sophia laughed in disbelief.

"Aaron certainly did *not* tell me that part," Sophia said. "All he told me was he met you at his restaurant."

"I guess that's the short version of the story," Claire agreed. "Luckily, Nate had quick reflexes and jumped out of the way just in time. I felt terrible, and I even offered to bring him to the ER, but he refused, so I gave him my contact information."

"What happened after that?" Nicole asked eagerly.

"I had lunch at his restaurant, then he joined me a few minutes later," Claire answered. "We had a nice chat. He was really sweet."

"Aw, how cute," Kendall said.

"Aaron said you didn't recognize him at first," Sophia said. "Is that true?"

Claire paused as a flush stole up her neck. "Yeah," she admitted reluctantly.

"Don't worry about it," Kendall said reassuringly. "Maybe you didn't recognize him out of context. Don't be embarrassed about it."

Claire smiled gratefully. She didn't know it was humanly possible to be out-of-this-world beautiful, sweet, and sympathetic all at once.

"I love that story," Nousha remarked. "It gives the term 'meet-cute' a whole new meaning."

"But on a serious note, we're so glad you and Nate are together," Sophie said. "He's so much happier."

"Yeah." Nicole nodded. "He used to be a grump, but ever since he started dating you, we've noticed a difference."

"A grump?" Claire repeated. "Really?"

"Nicole's exaggerating," Kendall replied. "Nate's always been more serious than not. But Jake said Nate's been acting different lately. Like, happier and more upbeat, I guess. And now that he's here, I can totally see it's true."

"The whole thing is a trip," Sophie said. "Girls go to extreme lengths to get Nate's attention. They've gone full-on stalker: leaving him flowers, sending him letters, sending him nudes, following him everywhere. It would drive them crazy to know that the girl who caught his attention was the one who didn't even recognize him."

"Okay, Soph, let's not go there," Kendall warned. "I'm sure Claire doesn't want to hear about all that ridiculous stalker stuff."

"Oh you're right," Sophie agreed. "Let's change the subject. What do you do Claire? Do you work?"

"Right now I work as a bookseller. I absolutely love the job, but I think I'm going to quit pretty soon to start my own cookie decorating business."

"Cookie decorating? I've heard about that before," Nousha said. "Kind of like the online famous baker—what's her name again? Lilly Anne something."

"Oh, I know her," Sophia said. "Lilly Anne's Designs. I ordered custom cookies from her for my sister's baby shower. Is that the kind of cookie decorating you do Claire?"

"Yes, it is," Claire said, delighted they were familiar with her line of business. "Lilly Anne is my idol. I'm trying to grow my business similar to hers."

"That's awesome," Nicole said. "What a great hobby to have. And even if it doesn't pan out for you, it's okay because you have Nate."

Claire stilled. Her smile faded slightly. "It's not a hobby," she said. "Becoming an entrepreneur has been a life-long dream of mine. It's something I take seriously, regardless of whether or not I'm with Nate."

A moment of uncomfortable silence descended on the group.

"I didn't mean anything negatively," Nicole said. "I'm sure you'll do great, but it's nice to be able to fall back on Nate if the worst-case scenario happens. I mean…I eventually quit my job as a dental hygienist after Ryder and I got married."

"Yeah," Sophia replied. "I had plans for law school, but when Nate bought out Aaron we figured I didn't have to worry about working anymore. The same thing happened with Nousha when Sawyer made partner at the firm."

Nousha nodded in agreement.

Claire took a sip of wine and stayed quiet. She didn't like what she was hearing—all of them gave up on their careers and dreams after they got married. Even Kendall, who had built an amazing career for herself, resolved to hang up her runway shoes the moment she got knocked up. It was as if their whole lives boiled down to marriage as the ultimate objective.

The women started chatting again, but this time Claire listened politely even though the topic disturbed the hell out of her. She had no intention of making Nate her fail-safe backup plan. And what about life goals? Nicole could argue that being a dental hygienist wasn't her dream, but it wasn't right for her to assume Claire would want to give up her own career to settle down with Nate.

Claire took another sip of wine and willed herself to calm down. There was nothing wrong with any of these women. They were genuinely nice and interested in befriending Claire. Just because they were all derailing their lives for their men didn't mean Nate would expect her to do that, too. Would he?

"Hey." Nate gently placed his hand on Claire's neck and planted a kiss on her cheek. "Are you ready to order dinner?"

Claire nodded and followed him to take a seat beside him at the table.

"I told you they were nice," Nate murmured in her ear. "Weren't they? It looks like you were all getting along really well."

She cleared her throat. "Yes, they really are sweet. They made me feel welcome."

Nate smiled and wrapped his arm around her. She sensed absolute delight in his kiss and the way he held her in his embrace. Introducing Claire and integrating her into his close circle really meant a lot to him. The joy on his face made her heart melt.

"I love you," he whispered.

And just like that, with his hands on her and his voice in her ear, his magic spell enclosed them in their own world again, and she was safe. She longed for this feeling every single moment, even with the chaos of other people's expectations surging all around them.

CHAPTER TWENTY-FOUR

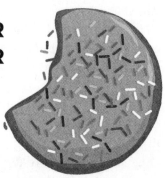

One week later

"I am so excited you guys are finally going to meet Nate," Claire said as she drove Ro and Todd up to his house in Los Feliz. "I'm really disappointed Sam couldn't come."

"She'll get plenty of chances to meet him in the future," Ro said. "Damn, Ate, he lives in such a nice neighborhood."

"He is so sweet to let us into his home," Todd said as he peered intently at the houses streaming past the windows. "Is he still at work?"

"Yeah, he feels bad he won't be able to greet you when we get there, but he gave us the go-ahead to order dinner."

"No ordering," Todd replied. "We have everything we need to make him a nice, home-cooked dinner. Ain't that right Ro-Ro?"

"Yup," she replied excitedly. "No one can resist our chicken adobo and lumpia."

Claire smiled as thoughts of Ro and Todd practicing their cooking skills in their kitchen came to mind. With tons of practice, they had actually become good cooks. They had perfected their recipes for chicken adobo and the Filipino fried egg rolls after multiple iterations. Before they drove up to Nate's house, they had stopped by the market to pick up all the ingredients they needed.

"You're sure Nate has a rice cooker?" Ro asked.

"Yes," Claire said. "I saw it in his pantry."

She drove up to the gated entry and checked the code scrawled on a crumpled receipt from her purse. Once the gate opened, she eased the car up the familiar curving driveway to the secluded courtyard in front of the garage doors. A disconcerting silence filled the car.

"Are you guys okay?" she asked, killing the engine. "What's—"

"Jesus Christ, Claire, what is this madness?" Todd cried.

"Ate, I cannot believe this is where he lives!"

"For the love of God, you don't have to shout," she scolded, pressing a hand to her chest. "You might freak the neighbors out."

Ro and Todd got out of the car and helped gather the groceries, eyes wide and mouths gaping the entire time.

"Nate has a dog named Maisy." Claire led them to the front door, where she unlocked it with a numeric code. As soon as she opened the door, the happy dog came skittering down the hall and merrily greeted her visitors.

"Take off your shoes," Claire reminded them as they entered the home and headed toward the kitchen.

"This house is sickening," Ro said. "How many bedrooms are there?"

"Six."

"How many bathrooms?" Todd asked.

"Um...I think five. I'm not sure," Claire answered.

"Ooh, the kitchen is gorgeous," Todd gushed as they set the groceries down on the island. "Claire-bear, take us on the grand tour."

Claire obliged, promptly walking Ro and Todd through the first level of the house, then upstairs to Nate's master bedroom.

"So this is where the magic happens," Todd said, taking a graceful sprawl on the edge of the king-sized bed. "Lucky girl."

"Aw, Ate, he has a picture of you here," Ro said.

Claire went over to Nate's nightstand. "Oh my gosh," she

said, a pleasant warmth spreading through her chest. "That was when I took a selfie of us at a café in Paris."

"I'm telling you. The guy is in the kind of love Beyoncé sings about," Todd replied. "Don't be surprised if he proposes soon."

"That's not going to happen," she said. "Come on. Let's go back to the kitchen."

"Anything's possible," Ro said as they headed down the stairs together. "Let's say Nate proposes to you tonight. What would you say?"

When they reached the kitchen, Claire shook her head and started unloading the groceries. "You two have the wildest imaginations."

"Come on Claire, you have to answer," Todd insisted. "Would you say yes?"

The question sent little quivers of anxiety through her belly.

"We've only been dating a couple of months," she said. "And he has to be very practical about these kinds of things. I figure he'd have to consult with his whole business and legal team if he ever wanted to get married. Right? It's really complicated."

"In other words, yes, you would marry him," Todd said. "Just as I suspected. You can't hide your feelings for him, Claire-bear. I can tell you have some reservations, but you're every bit as crazy over him as he is over you."

"Reservations?" Ro asked incredulously. "How is that possible? A fine-as-hell billionaire is in love with you. And he's a good Asian boy—he has a rice cooker in his pantry and a no-shoes policy inside the house. What's the issue?"

Claire could tell Ro was being facetious, but her question struck a chord in her anyway.

"Nothing." She averted her eyes and started searching for pots, pans, and cutting boards. She paused in surprise when Todd laid a gentle hand on her arm.

"Claire. All kidding aside. What's bothering you?"

She gazed up at him. It would have been easy to shrug off her worries if he didn't look so concerned.

"I'm afraid to tell you because if I do, you're going to think I'm crazy."

Todd and Ro snapped to attention. She sighed and continued on.

"Our relationship is moving really fast. The practical side of me tells me this is wrong. People aren't supposed to fall in love like this. Relationships take time to cultivate. And I don't fit in with his group of friends. Last weekend when I went to dinner with them, I was shocked at how different their perspectives on life were compared to mine. They were really nice, but they're so different than what I'm used to. The women were dressed to the nines, with perfect hair and makeup, sporting designer handbags and shoes. They quit their jobs to become housewives and to dedicate their free time to their husbands' causes.

"And remember what I told you about Kendall Greyhart? The woman was more than willing to leave behind her career to settle down with her fiancé. The truth is...I don't know if I'm willing to do that. I finally came to this epiphany with regard to the direction I want to take my career, but being in a relationship with Nate has made me unsure of myself—of the things I'm capable of doing. The only thing I'm sure of is I'm in love with him. It might have happened too fast, but it's the truth."

Claire averted her gaze again, turning her attention back to dinner. She didn't like the pity sparking in Ro and Todd's eyes.

"Did Nate ever tell you he expects you to give up your dreams to be with him?" Todd asked.

"No. But—"

"Do you think he would ever put you in that position?" Todd interrupted, holding a finger up. "In your heart, do you think he is the type of man who would do that to you?"

Claire hesitated. She thought back to what Sam said—that men like Nate hid their true nature, but it would come out eventually. Even still, she wanted to believe Sam was wrong.

"I don't think so," Claire replied.

Todd crossed his arms and nodded in satisfaction. "See?" he said. "You just solved your own problem. Okay Ro-Ro, let's get this Filipino cooking show on the road."

Even as they continued with dinner, Claire wasn't convinced she was close to solving any problems, but she tucked it all away for the sake of having a nice evening.

"I'm impressed Nate has a full kitchen," Ro said. "He has everything we need. It's weird for a single guy to have all this stuff. Does he cook?"

"No, not really," Claire replied. "I asked him about that, too. It turns out he has another assistant who cleans and cooks for him on a regular basis. Nate didn't want me to meet him at first because he was afraid I would think it was weird."

"Well, it might be weird to you, but to the rich people it's normal," Ro said. "You've got to get used to this lifestyle now, Ate."

Almost a couple hours later, when the food was ready and set up on the table, Nate still hadn't arrived. He sent Claire a message apologizing for the delay. Todd and Ro did not complain. They were perfectly content to take another leisurely tour through the house and around the stunning courtyards and gardens, each with a hefty glass of wine in their hands. Claire spied on them through the windows having a blast taking selfies and documenting their antics for social media platforms.

"Hey, don't tag Nate or let anyone know you're at his house," Claire warned with a stern knock on the window. Todd gave her an exaggerated nod, then went back to hamming it up for the phone camera with Ro, lounging dramatically across the chaise as though he was a world-famous model on a photo-shoot.

Suddenly, Maisy let out a little yelp and ran to the front door. Claire rounded the corner and saw Nate entering the house. He flashed her a smile as he greeted Maisy. Before Claire knew what she was doing, she jumped at him and wrapped her arms tightly around his body. She pressed her lips to his, and he met the kiss with equal fervor, wrapping his arm around her waist and lifting her off the ground.

"What did I do to deserve this kind of welcome?" Nate asked, running his hand slowly down her lower back. Everywhere he touched sparked the kind of electricity that made her feel alive in every possible way. "God, every time I see you I just want to..."

He trailed off at the sound of the glass door opening and closing. Todd and Ro's voices carried through the hallway, and Nate promptly released Claire. She took his hand and led him to the kitchen.

"You guys?" she said, entering with Nate in tow. "Nate's here."

Ro and Todd froze. After a second of stunned silence, their faces lit up brighter than the sun itself.

"Oh my God, it's so nice to finally meet you in person," Ro said.

"Thank you for inviting us to your home," Todd said at the same exact time.

"Nate, this is my younger sister, Ro, and my best friend, Todd," Claire continued. "I know you said you wanted us to order food, but they have a surprise for you."

"We made you an authentic Filipino dinner," Ro said. "Come on. It's in the dining room."

She and Todd practically skipped down the hall into the dining room. Nate and Claire exchanged delighted smiles, then followed after them.

"Wow, this looks and smells amazing," Nate said as he and Claire took a seat. "Thank you. I can't wait to try it."

"Have you ever had chicken adobo and lumpia before?" Ro asked.

"Yes," Nate replied. "When I first moved down here after college my business partner and I used to order takeout from the Filipino restaurant nearby."

"I heard you own a new restaurant in Long Beach," Todd interjected. "That's so interesting. What made you go into the restaurant business?"

"To be honest, I'm a silent partner. A good friend of mine is the real owner. The media got wind of my involvement, but I'm not really a part of the day-to-day operations."

Todd and Ro beamed and took long sips of their wine. They were very clearly buzzed, and being in this house around Nate was enhancing the effect of the alcohol. Claire prayed they would behave themselves and not say anything that would embarrass her.

"Ro-Ro, you've done it again with the adobo." Todd covered his mouth with a prim hand as he finished chewing and looked at Nate. "I don't know how she does it. Every time she makes it, it gets better and better."

Nate took a bite of rice and chicken. He nodded in agreement, and Ro practically swooned.

"You're right," Nate said. "This is the best chicken adobo I've ever tasted."

"So...you love food, right?" Ro's eyes went a little hazy after she took another sip of wine. "How do you stay in such amazing shape? And I mean...*amazing*."

"It's all an illusion," Nate said. "You'd be surprised at what a good spray tan and a lot of plastic surgery can do."

Todd and Ro exploded into laughter. Claire beamed, appreciating Nate's easy ability to handle the wild fan-girling going on right in front of him. Who was she kidding? He was probably so used to it by now, dealing with it was like second nature.

"I'd love to get to know you both," Nate said, making a smooth transition. "Tell me about yourselves."

"You are such a sweetheart," Todd gushed. "There's not much to know about me. I met Claire five years ago when we started working at the bookstore together, and it was love at first sight. From her, not me. Just kidding. I love you Claire-bear. Anyway, we got along like peas and carrots from day one. That's how I met the other love of my life, Ro-Ro. I work part-time at the bookstore, and as a freelance makeup artist."

"And I'm Claire's favorite sister," Ro said, winking at Claire. "Sorry, I'm just playing. Claire hates when I say things like that. Let's see…I have two steady jobs as a bartender and Pilates instructor. And I also…" She trailed off, giving Claire a bashful look. "I've been trying my hand at stand-up comedy."

"I knew it!" Claire said. "I was getting this vibe that there was something going on. That's so cool, Ro. How has that been going so far?"

"So-so. I'm a total novice. Right now I'm at the stage where I'm learning what works on the audience, and I'm taking improv classes."

"I'm so proud of you. When can we come and see you perform?"

"Not quite yet," Ro replied. Claire could almost see a blush forming on her tanned cheeks. "Give me a month or so, and then I'll be ready. You've always been so supportive of me. Isn't she amazing, Nate?"

"Absolutely," he replied.

Todd and Ro waited until Claire took a big bite of food, then they exchanged sly glances with one another. Claire picked up on it and narrowed her eyes in suspicion.

"So Nate, how did Claire catch your attention?" Ro asked.

"I mean, besides the fact she's gorgeous. Have you noticed the family resemblance between us?"

Amusement glimmered in Nate's eyes as he gave Claire an appraising glance.

"I won't argue with you there," he replied. "You are both gorgeous."

Ro went starry-eyed.

"I don't really know how to describe what I felt," he continued. "I just knew."

"You knew what?" Todd asked.

Nate's gaze roved over Claire, and it made her melt like royal icing at room temperature.

"That she was the one," he said.

Todd grinned, casting a smug look at Claire. She could almost hear his voice in her head. *You see? I told you the man is in love and he is about ready to propose.*

"I, uh, have a little announcement to make," Claire said, attempting to shift them toward more comfortable territory. "I'm about to give my two weeks' notice at the bookstore. As of next month, I'm going to be a full-time business owner."

"Really? That's great, Claire-bear!" Todd exclaimed.

"Ate, I'm so happy for you." Ro came around the table and gave Claire a big hug.

Nate reached out and squeezed Claire's hand. The pride shining in his eyes made Claire feel higher than the sky.

"Congratulations," he said, lifting his wineglass. "Let's drink to my Claire. I have no doubt you're going to be successful. I see it in you. Cheers."

As they clinked their drinks together, Claire let the moment carry her away. Being here in this bright house with an amazing dinner and loved ones who gave her their unconditional support—she had no idea this level of joy was possible. She scooted a little closer to Nate and planted a kiss on his bearded cheek. As she did so, her phone rang. She checked the caller, and a slight frown formed on her face.

"What's wrong?" Nate asked.

"Oh no, nothing's wrong," Claire said as she forced a smile. "It's Tita Chriss. She never calls. Excuse me."

She got up from the table and moved down the hallway to answer the phone. A tiny thread of unease tugged at her heart, and she had no idea why.

"Hi, Tita Chriss. How are you?"

"I'm good. Do you have a minute to talk?"

"Yes."

"Okay, good. I have something very important to tell you, but I want to do it in person. Can you meet me tomorrow? Lunch or dinner. You pick one."

"Um…can we do brunch?" Claire asked. "I have to visit Lola in the morning, and then I work the closing shift afterward. That leaves me a small window in between to have brunch." She braced herself for whatever negative reaction Tita Chriss had in store for her any time she mentioned her job at the bookstore.

"That should work," Tita Chriss replied. "I'll meet you tomorrow for brunch at La Soledad."

"All right," Claire said. "Is everything okay?"

"Of course everything's okay. As a matter of fact, everything is great. I have wonderful news for you. Don't be worried. I'll see you tomorrow."

Claire returned to the table with an unnerving tightness in her chest. Her past experience with Tita Chriss told her to be on full alert whenever she told someone not to worry about something. She hid the anxiety and pasted on a smile as Ro grilled Nate about his life, asking him to dish about famous people.

Claire grinned and enjoyed the positive vibes buzzing through the air. She marveled at his pure charismatic energy. He was definitely a people person, and the yin to her yang. Despite their differences, there was no one else she would rather be with—no one else she'd rather sit with and simply watch the sun rise and set every day of her life, well into old age.

The realization shocked her. Squeezing Nate's hand a little tighter, she rested her head on his shoulder, trying to draw strength from him. She only hoped that whatever Tita Chriss had in store for her wouldn't do anything to ruin the perfect balance of her life right now.

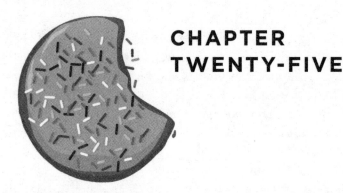

CHAPTER
TWENTY-FIVE

T he next day, Claire strolled into La Soledad. The aroma of carne asada fajitas overcame her senses and nearly hypnotized her into walking past her aunt's table.

"Psst! Claire, I'm over here."

She backtracked and joined Tita Chriss at her booth. She already had mimosas poured for them and a pot of coffee sitting on the table. Claire kissed her on the cheek and sat down.

"This is nice," Claire said, putting her purse down beside her. "So what's the good news?"

"No, you first," she chided. "We heard you have a new boyfriend."

Claire paused and forced a pleasant smile upon her face. "Um, what did you hear exactly?"

"That you had a boyfriend," Tita Chriss repeated. "That's all we know. I heard it from your Tita Jovy. The twins said they saw you leaving the apartment with a man."

Claire let out a sigh of relief. The twins probably put two and two together, but they didn't see Nate's face, so they didn't actually know anything.

"Yes. I am dating someone."

"Nice," she said. "How long?"

Claire paused. Technically, they'd been dating for about twelve weeks, but she figured it wouldn't hurt to round up.

"Almost three months."

"What does he do for a living? He has a real job, right? Not like your last boyfriend…the one who was like a ghostbuster?" Tita Chriss slapped the seat as she laughed at the memory. Claire had to laugh as well, because it was sort of true.

"He did what's called 'spirit cleansing,'" Claire explained. "It's a real thing to some people. And yes, my current boyfriend has a real job."

"What does he do?"

Claire knew this was coming. She cleared her throat and went for it.

"He works in the tech industry."

"What's the name of the company?"

"*MyConnect.*"

Tita Chriss's eyebrows raised. "Really? What does he do there?"

Claire took a sip of her mimosa. "He works as a…supervisor." It wasn't technically a lie. Nate did a lot of supervising…as the CEO of the company. Claire figured she could have told Tita Chriss about Nate's identity, but not after the way Sam had reacted initially. Her aunt could be a hundred times more judgmental than Sam, and Claire wasn't in the right frame of mind to deal with it.

"Oh," Tita Chriss said, nodding in approval. "He probably makes a lot of money then."

Claire didn't respond. She took another sip of the mimosa instead.

"I'm happy for you," her aunt said. "Good for you, Claire."

"So tell me your good news now," Claire said. "I'm dying to know."

"Let's get something to eat at the buffet first. When we get back I promise I'll tell you everything."

Claire bit back a groan of impatience. Sometimes her aunt had the capacity to frustrate others by making everything more dramatic than it had to be. Claire pasted on a smile and followed Tita Chriss to the buffet line.

"Okay, I'm ready," Claire said when they returned to the table. She picked up her bacon and nibbled the end. "Tell me your news."

"Remember how I've been talking about getting into the healthcare industry?" Tita Chriss began. "Well, that's why I've been so busy these past few months. I bought three houses and had them converted to the ADA standards. All the licensing I applied for finally went through, and I hired all the staff. I am the owner of three board-and-care homes."

"Awesome," Claire said. "Congratulations, Tita."

"But that isn't the best part," Tita Chriss said. "The best part is this: I'm hiring you to be the supervising administrator for these homes. Do you know what this means? You will finally have a steady job making a lot of money."

A sick, roiling sensation squeezed through Claire's stomach, and all of her hunger vanished. It was almost as if she was watching a strange drama unfold before her—that it was happening to someone else even though she knew this was all completely real. Tita Chriss's excitement faltered.

"Claire? What's wrong? Aren't you happy?"

"I—um, it just caught me off guard," she stammered. "I'm grateful, but don't you think this job would be better suited for someone else? I have no experience in the healthcare industry. Did you ask Arvin or J.P. about this, too?"

"Your cousins already have good jobs as nurses," Tita Chriss replied. "And they don't have your kind of talent. We've all seen the way you are with Lola. You have an excellent sensibility working with these kinds of patients. You don't see your own potential, but I do. You're smart and caring, and you need a steady job. Not only is this job steady, but it's high-paying. You would be making just as much, if not more than Arvin and J.P. with your starting salary, and they've been nurses for a long time."

Claire didn't respond. The standoffs in the Wild West had nothing on the one between her and Tita Chriss. There was no possible way she could turn down this opportunity without sounding foolish and ungrateful. What was she going to say? "I'm sorry Tita, but I don't want to make a high, steady income because I am planning on decorating cookies for the rest of my life." Claire dropped the bacon on her plate and braced her back against the vinyl seat.

"I am so grateful for this opportunity, which you offered to me first." Claire spoke in measured tones, choosing her words carefully. "But I'm not sure I'm the right person for this job."

"Why?" Tita Chriss asked through a mouthful of hash browns.

"For starters, I know nothing about board-and-care facilities. I have no managerial experience, and the thought of taking on this kind of job scares me. I might mess everything up, and I don't want to take that kind of risk."

Tita Chriss chewed with gusto, making a dismissive gesture with her hand.

"Is that what you're afraid of? It's all taken care of. I told you I hired staff already, and it includes a supervising nurse with many years of experience. A part of her job is to train you how to be an administrator, and she will stay for a few months to help you until you become used to the job."

"Then why don't you hire the supervising nurse as the administrator?" Claire asked, barely keeping her desperation in check.

"Because she's only temporary, and I created this job for you. After years of these dead-end jobs and playing around with baking and whatnot, you finally have a chance to make real money and make your parents proud. Can't you see what a blessing this is?" Tita Chriss's eyes shined with hope, and it made Claire feel even worse.

"Yes," she said with uncertainty.

"What's the matter, Claire? You don't sound excited."

She sighed. "I am excited. But...I'd like some time to consider. This is a really big decision, and a huge life change. I need some time to plan and give my two weeks' notice at the bookstore."

"Okay, fine," Tita Chriss said. "Give your two weeks' notice, and then let me know when you're ready to start. I am so excited for you. This is exactly what you need, and trust me, you will be so much happier."

Tita Chriss continued to enjoy her food while Claire fumed in shameful silence. The minutes ticked by, and she played every single scenario of turning down her aunt's offer in her head. Too bad she had no intention of playing out any of those scenes in real life...unless she miraculously grew a spine in the next half hour.

"Claire, keep eating," Tita Chriss said. "You don't want to get too skinny. Hey, what's going on with Sam? I haven't heard from her in a while. What's she been up to? How is her work? Has she started dating again?"

Claire's thoughts remained distant as she pasted on a weak grin and picked up her fork.

"She's thinking about it," she replied, staring forlornly at her plate of food.

Claire stood in her bathroom, hands braced against the counter, heaving deep, calming breaths. After that shameful display at La Soledad, she couldn't even look at herself in the mirror.

She was a thirty-year-old woman. She was by no means wealthy—nowhere close to it—but she was financially independent. Her dream was there, hovering just within reach, but she didn't have the courage to grab it.

"What in the world is wrong with me," she groaned.

What made things even worse? Her two sisters had the courage to forge their own paths, and they had the vision and foresight to go for what they wanted. They didn't flounder in self-doubt. No time wasted. Why couldn't Claire be that way, too?

She forced her head up, meeting her own gaze in the mirror. What did she see there behind the fear and self-doubt? There was determination. Persistence. Talent. She just had to believe it.

Now was the time to finally put *Claire's Enchanted Confections* to the test. Claire figured the only way she was going to learn, after all her careful planning and strategizing, was to jump directly into the deep end. Baptism by fire. That was pretty much how she described the situation of booking two cookie decorating classes back to back.

The first one was a mini team-building event with a group of ten employees from a local women's clothing boutique. The second class consisted of twelve young Girl Scouts who were excited to decorate flower cookies. This venue was about five miles away from the first one, and she had to haul serious ass to get there with less than two minutes to spare.

All in all, it was a success. Everyone had a blast and ended up with delicious treats they enthusiastically shared on social media, with the hashtag #ClairesCookies. She had charged twenty-five dollars per head for each event, and her overhead was nominal. Online she had sold three DIY cookie kits, and had about ten new orders to fill. Claire had what it took to make a humble living off her business, if she could just break free from her lifeline at the bookstore and fully commit herself.

By the time she hauled herself back into her apartment in the late afternoon, she was exhausted, but completely buzzing with excitement. This was just a small taste of being a real business owner, and it filled her with pride. It made life a hundred times more meaningful than it already was. And she fantasized about the look on Tita Chriss's face when she would finally be able to tell her she was a successful viral cookie queen making unprecedented sales due to word of mouth from her classes and delicious treats.

She wanted to tell Ro all about it, but she was still asleep, trying to catch the last hour of shut-eye before she had to get up and get ready for work at the bar. Claire went into her room and texted her news to Nate, who responded almost immediately with a smiley emoji and words of warm encouragement.

I'm so proud of you. You're getting closer to your goal.

Thank you. Can I see you tonight?

I'm still at the office. Won't get home until late. Wait for me at my place.

Claire was about to respond with an affirmative, but then a sudden idea hit her.

Can I visit you at the office?

She bit her lip in trepidation. Was it weird asking that question? Would he say no? The three little bubbles sprang up on the text, and she held her breath.

I would love that.

Claire had every intention of hopping into her car to speed up to Nate's headquarters in downtown L.A. right after they hung up, but the urge to do something sweet for him overpowered everything. She ended up leaving almost two hours later, after having baked her famous purple velvet cake. Well, it was famous to her family and friends, and now Nate would be the next lucky recipient.

As she suspected, the L.A. traffic was dreadful. She was practically bouncing with excitement when the imposing dark blue glass of the *MyConnect* headquarters finally came into view from the street. Taking Nate's previous instruction, she headed directly into the underground parking lot. She gave her name to the guard, who then let her through and notified someone inside the building of her arrival.

This place was more intimidating than she thought it would be. She could only guess as to what Nate did at work—he probably sat at his desk in his big office, supervised people, ran meetings, and managed projects. Her whole life was anti-corporate, which explained her complete lack of interest in working in an office. But now that she was going to be her own boss (if she ever had the nerve to turn down Tita Chriss), she figured she'd have to get used to doing office work in some capacity.

No matter how much she tried to bring the idea of Nate back down to earth at her level, it didn't work. He was no mere supervisor. He was the CFEO. The Chief Fucking Executive Officer of one of the biggest companies in the world. What would Todd have said to comfort her in this situation? Oh yeah. He wouldn't have comforted her. She could hear his voice in her head right now:

You are wasting time with your nervous energy. Nate is a snack and he is wild for you, so your number one priority is to get the hell over yourself and enjoy each other's rockin' virile bodies while you're still young.

She parked her car in a stall near the elevator, popped the trunk, and pulled out a paper bag. Inside was the naked purple two-layer cake and a canister of homemade cream cheese frosting. She had to give the cake time to cool before she put the frosting on.

"Hi," a man's voice said from behind her.

She turned and saw Nate approaching her from the elevator. His captivating smile made her heart skip every single time. When he reached her, he gave her a kiss and enveloped her in his arms. He smelled good enough to eat.

"I brought you something," she said.

"You did? What is it?"

Claire turned aside and showed him the cake inside her bag. His eyes lit up.

"It doesn't look too pretty because it's unfrosted. But it's my special purple velvet cake. You are going to love it. Are your employees here? They're welcome to try it, too."

"I can't wait," Nate said as he took the bag and led Claire toward the elevator. "But everyone's already gone home for the night. I'm the only one here, so the cake is all mine. How are you doing?"

Claire was about to deliver the automatic "I'm fine" response, but she didn't want to lie. The episode between her and Tita Chriss continued to haunt her. Nate detected the hesitation and cocked his head in curiosity.

"Babe, are you okay?" he asked.

The term of endearment surprised her. It was the first time he'd given her a nickname, and it amused her to no end.

"What?" Nate asked. "Don't laugh at me. What am I supposed to call you?"

"No, don't feel bad," she replied, stifling her smile. They stepped onto the elevator and Nate pressed a button. "You've never called me that before. I like it."

"Let's make it even," Nate said. "You can give me a nickname. Go ahead."

"I can't give you a nickname if you're pressuring me to do it. It has to come naturally."

"Fine. I can wait. But make sure you don't call me mahal. All my Filipino ex-girlfriends used to call me that."

Claire barely suppressed an eye roll.

"Don't even try me," she said.

Nate laughed and lunged for Claire, grabbing her around the waist and planting a scratchy kiss on her neck.

"That's why I love you," he said. "You're not the jealous type."

"And because I put up with you," Claire said.

The elevator opened at the eighth floor. Claire stepped into a vast, open office space perfectly designed for discerning millennial hipsters and tech enthusiasts. Stylish pods, couches, and modular workspaces dotted the entire area. The two far walls were made entirely of glass, giving the office a stunning vista of downtown.

"This place is amazing," Claire said, following Nate off the elevator. "It's like...a really sophisticated version of Google."

"Don't say the G word here," Nate admonished.

"Then what do you say when someone asks you a question you can't answer?"

"Ask Siri."

Claire smiled and shook her head. Nate led her to a portion of the office that appeared to be the break area. Nate set the cake down on the countertop and turned to Claire.

"Tell me what's bothering you," he said.

"I met with Tita Chriss for brunch today. She supposedly had good news. It turns out she recently bought three board-and-care homes, and she wants to hire me to be the overseeing manager."

Talking about it made her antsy. She took the cake container out of the bag, lifted the lid, and opened the canister of frosting.

"I see," Nate said. He sidled closer to her, watching as she skillfully spread the white frosting over the purple cake. "This puts you in a bad spot."

"Exactly," Claire said.

"What did you tell her? Did you say you can't do it?"

She pursed her lips, her knife pausing in its spread of the frosting.

"Claire? Babe, what happened?"

"I didn't refuse," she said in shame. "I just...let her believe I wanted to do it."

"What? Why?"

"I don't know," Claire replied. "I don't know why I'm like this. Do you have any plates?"

Nate opened a cabinet and produced a small stack of clear plastic plates and forks. She quickly carved out two generous slices for her and Nate, then took a big bite. As the delectably sweet, rich flavor filled her mouth, it worked like a magic spell and began to release some of the tension coiled in her body. She looked up at Nate, who was nodding in approval.

"I think this is the best cake I've ever had," he said. "I'm serious. Has your aunt tried this yet? Maybe she'd believe you if she tasted this. It's legit, babe. I would eat this every day if I could."

"She's not a sweets type of person," Claire said. "I think that's one of the reasons we clash."

Nate set his fork down and gazed at Claire with the mischievous eyes she had grown so familiar with.

"Uh-oh," she said as she gulped down her bite of cake. "You've got that look again. What's going on?"

"Claire. I love you, and I wish I could make all of your worries go away. Owning your own business is tough, but you've got what it takes. I have complete faith in your ability as a business owner, and I know you're going to thrive."

Little tingles of delight spread through Claire's body. How did he always know the right things to say to make her feel like she could conquer anything?

"Aw, you're the sweetest honey bunny ever." The words flew out of her mouth before she could stop them. Her eyes widened in embarrassment.

"Honey bunny?" Nate repeated. "I like it. I think it suits me."

"I don't know why I said that. I hate it. That is *not* going to be your nickname."

"It's too late. It came to you naturally, so that's what it has to be from now on. You made the rule."

Claire shook her head in exasperation.

"Anyway, I've got another surprise for you that I think will make you feel a lot better. You're coming with me tonight. To San Francisco."

Claire crossed her arms and knitted her brow. If Nate was any other man, she would have waved off the statement as a practical joke. But she knew him. This was the same guy who flew her to Paris on a whim—the same guy who popped in on her romance book group and played the impromptu role of a rakish duke. He was dead serious.

"How do you know I'm not busy this weekend?" she demanded.

"You're not busy," Nate said. "I know because I had access to some special intel."

"What do you mean?"

He held up a finger and shot off a quick text. A few seconds later, a nearby office door flew open, scaring Claire half to death.

"Hi Ate!"

Claire gasped as Ro scampered up to her.

"Ro? What are you doing here? Where did you come from?"

"You and Nate are going to San Francisco," she explained. "In exchange for some information about your schedule, he agreed to let me go with you. Don't worry. I won't interrupt you two, I promise."

"So you've been scheming behind my back?" Claire said, scowling at her sister. "Shame on you."

"It's going to be fun, and you know it." Ro smiled and took a bite of Claire's cake. Claire sighed in resignation, narrowing her eyes at Nate

"You got me again," she said. "Honey bunny."

CHAPTER TWENTY-SIX

Later that night, Claire ended up on Nate's private jet, flying off to yet another faraway place. She gazed out the window at the yawning darkness below dotted with the lights of distant cities. The moment of solitude helped lift her spirits in light of the problem Tita Chriss introduced to her life.

"Ate." Ro plopped down in the seat recently vacated by Nate. "What's Nate doing?"

"He had to take a call," Claire said. "Why, what's up?"

"First of all, I cannot believe I am sitting in Nate Noruta's private jet," Ro whispered. "And second of all, I cannot believe I am sitting in Nate Noruta's private jet. I can keep saying it over and over again, and I still won't believe it."

"Well, believe it because you sold me out," Claire said. "So that's why you were asking about my cookie orders and events this weekend. It was because Nate bribed you."

"How can you possibly be mad at me?" Ro asked. "Look where we are right now. I even packed for you, and if there's anything I missed you can have Nate get it for you later. Or maybe he'll send his cute assistant."

Claire glanced across the aisle where Craig sat quietly with his earbuds in and laptop open.

"He doesn't strike me as your type," Claire whispered.

"Why? Is he gay?" Ro asked.

"Shh! I don't know, but even if he wasn't, I don't think you two would be compatible. Whatever happened to the other guy? The one you brought home a few weeks ago?"

"Oh, him? That was nothing. Maybe I'll meet someone new in San Francisco. What's Nate going to do up there?"

"He's one of the speakers at the Innovator TED Talk. I forget where exactly, but afterward he has a series of meetings for the next few days. He said something about an acquisition."

Ro's eyes went wide.

"Wait a minute. Did that acquisition actually go through?" She didn't wait for Claire to answer. She did a quick search on her phone, and her eyes scanned the screen intently.

"How did you know about that?" Claire asked.

"It's all over the internet," Ro said. "How could you miss it? He's *your* freaking boyfriend. Um, excuse me, Craig?"

Craig looked up and removed one of his earbuds. "Yes? How can I help you?"

"I was wondering if you could fill me in. I read in this Daily Mail article that *MyConnect* acquired *TechKnowledge Industries* two days ago. Is that true?"

Craig hesitated for a moment, as if unsure how to respond. "To make a long story short, yes. It went through."

"Thank you, Craig."

He nodded politely and replaced his earbud. Ro grabbed Claire's forearm and squealed.

"Ow. What is your problem?" Claire demanded, wrenching her arm out of Ro's grasp.

"Your man just acquired a huge corporation," Ro whispered harshly. "Seriously, Ate, you are a sweet summer child. I will never get over how a hippie chick fell in love with a corporate monster. It's a love story that needs to be told."

"Monster? Nate's not a monster."

"I didn't mean it in a bad way. All I'm saying is he's like Pac Man, gobbling up unsuspecting companies left and right."

Claire settled into her seat, trying to ignore her sister's dramatic way of describing Nate. It wasn't how she perceived him at all. Corporate sharks wore fancy designer suits, smoked cigars, and drank hundred-year-old scotch out of fancy glasses. They gambled and caroused and frequented strip clubs, dropping tons of cash on women and drugs.

Nate wasn't a corporate shark. He wore hoodies and sneakers and T-shirts. He played video games and D&D with his nerd friends. He cuddled with her on the couch as they streamed romantic movies and comedies. He was, in essence, the love of her life. She would never have fallen for a "corporate monster." It didn't make sense.

Nate strolled up and paused in the aisle, grinning down at Claire and her sister.

"Having a little chat?" he asked.

"Congrats on your new acquisition," Ro said brightly. "Ate? Aren't you excited, too?"

"Oh yes," Claire said. "Congrats...honey bunny."

"Thanks, babe."

"Okay, I'll leave you two lovebirds alone." Ro sprang up from her seat and went back to her spot in the row across the aisle behind Craig.

Nate sat down. He put his arm around Claire, who immediately burrowed into his body like a bear curling up for hibernation.

"Are you doing okay?" he asked, running his hand in circles over her back. "Has your aunt contacted you again?"

"No," Claire said, her voice muffled against Nate's shoulder. "I'm dreading talking to her. I don't know why I let her scare me so much. I need to get over it, but I don't know how."

"Have you talked to your parents about it?"

"No. That won't do any good. They wouldn't understand where I'm coming from."

"The way I see it is, it all boils down to one question: What's important to you?"

Claire paused.

"In general? My family. Lola. Work. My cookie business. And obviously, you. Why are you asking me this? Don't you know what's important to me already?"

"Listen. These are the five pillars your life stands on, and each of these things ultimately is a foundation of hope. Hope of finding and maintaining happiness, hope of finding success, hope of seeing your dreams become reality. Here's the part that eludes you—you can have it all. Don't wish for perfection. Embrace everything that comes to you. The world is yours."

Claire raised her head and gave Nate a lopsided grin. "I'm pouring my heart out to you, and you're giving me snippets of your world-famous lecture," she said.

"It's never steered anyone wrong," he said, returning the smile.

"But the problem is…I don't want to work for my aunt."

"You just told me family is important to you," Nate replied. "Try finding a happy medium. Maybe work for your aunt and see if you like it, and you can still do your cookie business on the side."

To admit defeat and give in to Tita Chriss, while turning away from her true passion? Claire didn't know if it was possible to live that way for the rest of her life.

"No," she said. "I can't do that. I just—"

She sighed and buried her face in Nate's shoulder again. He put his arm around her and squeezed her tightly to him. It was funny how his touch had the power to do amazing things. It chased away all the shadows clouding her thoughts and wrapped a warm embrace around her heart.

"Claire. Babe, look."

She peeked at Nate's phone. There was a familiar image of vibrant hot air balloons levitating in the sky.

"Oh. I remember that. It's the photo on your wall."

"It's more than just a photo on my wall." Nate nuzzled Claire's hair with his cheek, his deep voice rumbling pleasantly through her body. "It's a promise I made to myself. If I found the right person who brought out the best in me and made me see all the beauty and wonder this world has to offer, they would make me realize I'm strong enough to conquer my fear. Claire Ventura, will you ride in the hot air balloons of Cappadocia with me?"

"If you're telling me this plane is headed to Eastern Europe right now, I think I just might lose it," Claire said.

"No," he said with a laugh. "Not this time. But promise me. Say you'll go with me on my grand adventures."

Claire's chest swelled with love, overflowing until it colored everything with its dazzling warmth. She didn't know what kind of magic he had to dispel her fears and worries, but she was glad to bask in its heady afterglow every single time.

"Of course I will," she whispered, entwining their fingers together. "Always."

By the time they touched down in San Francisco and got settled into their hotel rooms at the Hilton at Union Square, Claire was exhausted. She sat down on a cushy couch in the master bedroom of their suite, and she awoke at nine in the morning, buried in blankets in the middle of the huge bed, alone.

She vaguely remembered Nate's hand skimming up her leg in the middle of the night, and all she did was swat it away. At the time, she thought he wanted to have sex, but it looked more like he was trying to pick her up and put her in the bed, which he eventually succeeded in doing. She picked up her phone and found a few text messages from Nate.

Good morning beautiful. I had an early meeting with Jake and Ryder. I'll call you when I'm done.

Claire sat up and shot off a text to Ro. A few seconds later, there was a knock at her door. Ro opened the door and crept into the room, sitting at the edge of Claire's bed.

"Good morning," Claire said. "Wow, you're all dressed already. How long have you been up?"

"I've only been up for two hours and already this is the most fun I have ever had on a trip." The words tumbled from Ro's mouth in a rush of excitement. "This is the nicest suite in the nicest hotel I have ever stayed in. And last night Nate offered to get me my own room even though there are four rooms in this suite. Incredible."

"You have far too much energy this early in the morning," Claire said with a yawn. She threw the covers off of her and stretched.

"How can I not have this much energy when I'm living in the lap of luxury? Ate, did you know that Nate said I could order anything I wanted from room service? Or if we wanted to eat at the restaurants in the hotel, to just charge it to this room? Fucking hell, I could get used to this."

"Ro," Claire said, her voice tinged with warning.

"I'm sorry." Ro approached Claire and gave her a crushing hug. "I'm so happy for you. Nate is amazing. You're perfect for each other."

"I can't breathe," Claire rasped.

Ro let her go and backed out of the room.

"Hurry up and get ready," Ro said. "San Francisco awaits the Ventura sisters!"

Claire showered and changed into a long, flowy Bohemian skirt and a plain white tank top. Nate called her the moment she left her room to meet with Ro.

"Hey, babe," he said. "There's been a change of plans. I'm so sorry to spring this on you."

"What's going on?" Claire asked.

"My mom's here," he said. "Originally she said she couldn't

come, but she was able to make it last minute. Her flight came in, and I told her to meet us for brunch downstairs at the restaurant near the bar. Ro is welcome to join us."

An overwhelming sense of trepidation froze her in place. Nate's mom was here? And they were going to meet? She was not prepared for this in the least.

"Oh. Okay," Claire said. "W-what time should I go down there?"

"She's down there now," Nate replied. "I'll be on my way in the next few minutes, but if you could go down and meet her, I would really appreciate it. I told her all about you. She's really eager to meet you."

They said goodbye, and Claire's heart continued to pound like a marching drum. She was usually good with parents, but Nate's mom was a different story. Claire would crumble into dust if Nate's mom didn't like her for any reason. She stood up from the armchair as Ro came into the living room, in the middle of a phone conversation.

"Yes, that sounds fantastic!" Ro said. "Yes. Absolutely. I'm so excited. Okay. Bye. Ate, you will not believe who that was."

"Who was it?"

"Do you remember Ray-Ray? My cheerleader friend from high school? Well, he moved up here a few years ago and I was able to get in contact. We're meeting up and he's going to show us around. But don't worry, if Nate calls you and needs you to go to his TED talk thing, it's totally fine. Come hang with us in the meantime."

"Actually, I can't," Claire said. "Is there any way you can cancel with Ray-Ray? Nate's mom is here and he wants me to meet her. I was hoping you could come with me for moral support."

"Whoa," Ro said. "Nate's mom? I shouldn't be there when you meet her for the first time. This is something between you and Nate and his mother. I don't want to be in the middle."

Claire bit her lip in frustration. Ro's reaction made perfect sense, but she was terrified of meeting Nate's mom. *Alone.* Especially with no advanced warning.

"Please Ro? For me?"

Ro took a deep breath.

"Ate, I love you to the moon and back, but you're a big girl. This is a Noruta family affair, and I shouldn't be involved this early on. This is your chance to make a good first impression. Be strong. Show his mom you're serious about him. And since when are you nervous about meeting parents? You love old people. They're your jam."

"But Nate's mom is different," Claire said. "I'm nervous."

"Don't be," Ro said. "You're great with parents. Get down there and charm her. I know you can do it."

Ro's abandonment frazzled Claire, but she also knew her sister was right. They rode the elevator down to the lobby together, then parted ways. Claire's fingernails clacked nervously together as she headed toward the restaurant. She couldn't believe Nate put her in the position to meet his mother by herself for the first time. Should she have refused? Honestly, she didn't know the right answer, but it was too late. His mother was expecting her, and now it was up to her to make a good first impression.

She didn't know much about Nate's mom. All she knew was that Patricia Noruta was a Japanese-American woman who raised Nate as a single mother, and she worked part-time as a waitress near Seattle, Washington. She knew nothing else. Claire hoped to God she didn't screw this up.

She walked into the restaurant and up to the hostess's podium.

"Excuse me, I'm here to meet someone," she said. "Her name is—"

"Claire. Is that you?"

Claire turned toward the voice. It came from an older Asian

woman sitting at a nearby table. She was strikingly pretty with long black-and-silver hair that hung in a shiny cascade around her shoulders. The resemblance to Nate was so strong, there was no mistaking this woman's identity.

"Ms. Noruta?"

Nate's mother smiled warmly and stood up, spreading her arms.

"Call me Patti." She enclosed Claire in a tight hug. "It's so nice to meet you finally. Have a seat, dear. You're all Nate can talk about."

"Oh really?" Claire smiled and tucked a lock of hair behind her ear.

"Yes. Do you know if he's on his way now?"

"He said he was a few minutes behind. Sorry about that."

"Don't apologize for him," Patti said. "What with all his work, he tends to be very busy. Let's go ahead and order first. I hope you don't mind."

"No. Not at all," Claire replied.

Patti flagged down the waiter and they submitted their drink orders.

"So, Claire. Tell me about yourself," Patti continued. "Where are you from? Where do you work?"

"I'm from Long Beach, a city a few miles south of L.A. Right now I'm a bookseller, but I'm planning on quitting to start my own online business. I'm a baker. I do cookie decorating and things like fulfilling special orders, making DIY kits, teaching decorating classes. It's a lot of fun, and it's my passion. I was scared to do it for a long time, but I finally told myself to stop doubting, and start doing. So I came up with a plan, did my research, and the last step is to quit my job and jump into this full-time. I don't think I would have been able to get this far without Nate. He was so wonderful. He motivated me and made me believe in myself."

"I see. Are you saying that my son helped you get your

business off the ground? Financially?"

"No, that's not what I meant," she said. "I was doubting myself, but he told me he thought I had a solid product, and that I was one of the stronger performers on *Eclectix*. He gave me confidence that I could potentially succeed as a business owner."

The warmth in Patti's eyes dissipated. Claire paused in surprise. It was like watching a cobra preparing to attack its snake charmer.

"Claire, I'm going to be blunt with you. As Nate's mother, I'm always looking out for his best interests. And it's going to sound very cliché for the mom to be overprotective of her billionaire son, but that's the reality we're facing. To put it bluntly: if you're with my son for his money, I suggest you cut your losses right now, because you're not getting a cent."

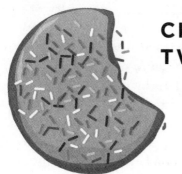

CHAPTER TWENTY-SEVEN

Claire was stunned. Words failed as she withered under Patti's sharp gaze. Heat swirled in her cheeks as she fought to defend herself—fought to prove to this woman that she was dead wrong.

"You—you think I'm with Nate because of his money?" she stammered. "No. That's not true at all."

"How are you going to convince me otherwise?" Patti asked. Her demeanor softened somewhat. "Look. I'm sorry I came across so harshly. You seem like a very nice girl, and you've done nothing wrong that I know of. I just wanted to manage your expectations."

Claire fought to keep calm. Patti could not be more wrong about Claire's intentions, but she wanted to be respectful. Lola would kill her if she heard Claire had raised her voice to Nate's mother.

"Patti, Nate means a lot to me," she said. "I've loved and cherished every single moment we've spent together. It's those moments I crave. They mean more to me than anything. I've never asked him for money or expensive gifts. I'm telling you the truth. I swear it on my family."

Patti paused a moment. Her eyes lingered on Claire's clothes and her worn black shoulder bag.

"I have to admit, you're a lot different than his last girlfriend,"

Patti said. "The girl was dripping in expensive jewelry. She was shameless."

"I'm sorry you had bad experiences with Nate's last relationship, but I'm not like that," Claire said. "The best things about him are his kindness and his loving, considerate heart. He's the sweetest man I've ever met, and he's so respectful. It's a shame most people don't get a chance to see that side of him. They're always distracted by the money and power, which, as far as I'm concerned, don't even make the list of his top ten attributes."

Patti didn't respond. Her gaze was different this time. Instead of trying to flay Clare with her eyes, it was as if she were gently unpeeling her layers, one by one.

"If Nate asked you to sign a prenup, would you do it?" Patti asked.

The question stunned Claire. It took her a few seconds to recover.

"Prenup? We're nowhere near getting married."

An annoyed look crossed Patti's face. "I need you to answer the question, please. Theoretically, if Nate asked you to sign a prenup, would you do it?"

"Of course," Claire said. "I trust Nate. Implicitly. If he asked me to do something, it must mean a lot to him, and I would respect that."

Patti gazed intently at Claire a few seconds longer, as if rolling her response around in her mind to test its validity. At that moment the server came with their drinks. It took a considerable amount of strength for Claire to refrain from chugging the entire wineglass.

"It takes a long time for me to trust people," Patti said. "I've been that way since I was young. But with you…there's something different. I can't explain how, but a mom just knows certain things."

"Does that mean you believe me?" Claire asked hopefully.

"I'm getting there," Patti replied. "But let me tell you one thing. I like you a hell of a lot more than his ex. Her problem was that she was an actress. Not a literal actress, but the underhanded kind that wholeheartedly believed she could pull the wool over everyone's eyes."

"How did she and Nate eventually break up?" Claire asked.

"Nate's very smart," Patti replied. "Even though he's the type to become emotionally attached, he eventually began to see the things I warned him about. Little signs here and there. The truth always comes out. It's all about catching it before it's too late."

Claire let out a shaky breath. Patti was definitely a force to be reckoned with. She only hoped that one day, when she was a mom, that she had half of her savvy and bold intelligence when standing up for the best interests of her future children. At the very least, Patti said she liked her a lot more than the ex. It wasn't much, but Claire took it as a win.

"Nate told me you're Filipino," Patti said. "Filipino desserts are my favorite. Do you know how to make them?"

A sense of triumph thundered through Claire. "I sure do," she replied. "I wish Nate told me that. I would have made some for you. Which ones do you like?"

"I haven't met one I didn't like," Patti replied. "But you can't go wrong with ube. It's delicious."

"I love ube, too," Claire gushed. "I have this amazing recipe for ube cake and cupcakes. I will make them and ship them to you when I get home. Or maybe you can come and visit soon, and I'll show you everything I can make. How does that sound?"

"I would like that very much," Patti said.

Claire's heart lifted when Patti's mouth curved up in a smile. It was more than just a smile. It was a sign that Claire was driving toward the right direction, and away from the danger sign signaling a steep drop to her demise. She had a long way to go, but at least she knew one of Patti's weaknesses.

Claire's senses tingled, and she glanced up. It took her all of two seconds to realize the stunningly gorgeous man walking into the restaurant was none other than her honey bunny. He flashed her a big smile when their eyes met. Patti turned and stood up when she saw her son approaching.

"I hurried as fast as I could," Nate said, giving Patti a big hug. "Sorry. I missed you, Mom. I'm so happy you could make it."

"I missed you, too, sweetie," Patti said. She pulled away and held him at arm's length. "Let me look at you. That beard is getting out of control. I thought you were going to shave it off."

Nate embraced Claire and kissed her right before they both sat across from Patti.

"I've decided to keep it," Nate said. "Claire likes it. Have you two been getting along? Isn't Claire the best?"

"She is a remarkable young lady," Patti said, with a knowing gleam in her eye.

Claire took a deep breath and squeezed Nate's hand tightly under the table. If her looks could scorch, all of Nate's hair would have gone up in flames. Why he hadn't warned her about his mother's, for lack of a better term, strong personality, was beyond her comprehension. But that was a discussion best left for later. In any case, Claire tried shaking it off. She was here in San Francisco with her love, and she was determined to make the best of this trip.

After brunch was over, Nate's mother went up to her hotel room (she had her own room reserved, much to Claire's relief) and said she was going to the TED talk with some local friends. Nate, on the other hand, had no time to do anything else except head over to the venue, which was located a couple miles west of the hotel.

"The talk doesn't start for a couple hours," Nate explained

as they walked hand in hand out of the restaurant. "In the meantime, I have some interviews and meetings scheduled."

"What should I do?" Claire asked. "Should I stay here at the hotel?"

"I was hoping you could come with me," Nate said. "I wanted to introduce you to a few more people. Is that okay?"

"Okay," Claire said, even though her stomach filled with butterflies once again. "Are we going to get a chance to spend some time together? You know, explore the city like we did in Paris? Don't get me wrong. I'm excited to see your TED talk and meet more of your colleagues, but..." Claire closed her arms around Nate's waist and pulled him close. "I can't wait to get you all to myself."

"Really?" Nate said, grinning mischievously. "Me too."

"I wish you didn't have all these events this weekend. I wish you weren't that busy."

Nate's eyes softened as the light of concern gathered in them. "Hey," he said. "Are you okay? You seem upset."

Claire loosened her grip on him, but placed her head against his chest. "I'm fine," she said softly. "Let's just go to the venue. We can talk about it later. Promise."

Nate's hand caressed Claire's face, and he tipped her chin up toward him with a gentle press of his finger.

"Are you sure?" he asked. "Because you have to tell me if something's bothering you. You can't keep holding things inside and pretending everything's okay. I'm here for you."

Claire paused. She considered talking to Nate about the things weighing on her mind—his mother, and the women in his group of friends who abandoned their dreams to become wives—but she simply didn't want to. It was too much to deal with at this moment.

"I'm sure," Claire said.

There was still worry brimming in Nate's eyes as he took Claire by the hand and led her to the hotel exit. This was what she did best. Even with her family, when there was turmoil, she pushed aside her own feelings to make it easier for others. She made peace, brought people together, and spared feelings when she could...even if it meant pushing aside her own needs.

Craig drove Nate and Claire to the venue, where they met up with the CFO, Jacob, and his fiancée, Kendall. Ryder was also there with his wife, Nicole. Everyone was delighted to see one another again. There were no hard feelings whatsoever with Kendall and Nicole. They were happy to see Claire, and they carefully steered any chit-chat away from career-oriented talk.

Spending time with his friends was the smoothest part of the event. Shortly afterward, Claire was whisked away and introduced to a procession of people whose names she would not be able to remember for the life of her. She was introduced to countless other tech influencers and entrepreneurs. Businessmen and women, motivational speakers, innovators, authors, Nobel Prize winners... Claire met so many of them her head was spinning.

Despite being overwhelmed, she smiled and played her part. She lost count of how many times she failed to grasp the complicated subjects people were discussing, but she continued to act engaged and interested. She observed Kendall and Nicole's behavior and mirrored it to the best of her ability. How? With charming smiles, polite laughter, nodding, and the occasional "that's fascinating" thrown into the mix. All the while, one part of her was content to be by Nate's side as his support, while the other side was lost amongst the clouds, hopelessly tangled in the messy thread of his inscrutable tech world.

Claire breathed a huge sigh of relief when the TED talks finally started, signaling the end of socializing. To her surprise, she enjoyed the first two speakers very much. Even though their tech and business acumen were worlds apart from her own, she could certainly relate to the topics. Inspiration. Creativity. Taking your dream and turning it into reality. Finding joy and purpose in using your talents to help others.

Nate was the third of five speakers that night. When he took the stage, Claire's heart fluttered in suspense. This was the famous talk that inspired millions of people. His perspectives on the harmony between hope and innovation had won him awards and accolades. Elements of his speech had even been incorporated into the business culture of many successful companies.

He began to speak, and Claire found herself enraptured—not by the man she fell in love with, but with the man whose passion and intellect had taken the world by storm. It wasn't merely his words. Confidence and wisdom exuded from his entire being. In an hour-long lecture, he captured the audience by illustrating his expertise on the role of hope in igniting the spark of innovation.

The entire audience rose to its feet at the end. The applause was deafening. Pure, unbridled energy coursed through the crowd as Nate's words wound their way into her mind and heart. When the applause died down, she had to sit for a moment and marvel in the fact that he was only thirty-three years old. He was a visionary in the truest sense of the word.

And he was in love with her.

Claire floated on a cloud the rest of the night as she thought of Nate. He was so much more than simply the man who loved her. He was the sum of his parts, in the truest sense, and she slowly began to realize that she really was in love with him—all of him. Would she ever be enough for a man like him? Was it possible to fall hopelessly in love in just three months?

At the end of the evening, she met Nate backstage. He grasped her hand and pulled her close again.

"Are you ready to go back up to our room?" she murmured in his ear.

Nate looked down at her, his eyes filled with surprise.

"Our room? It's still early," he said. "A friend of mine invited us to a little get-together. Dr. Kumar was the last speaker. Remember him?"

"Oh yes," Claire said. She liked his speech, but was less than thrilled to have to socialize again.

Nate leaned in, giving her a dubious look. "Babe, I know this isn't your cup of tea," he said. "But please, come with me to Dr. Kumar's. It'll be quick. You have no idea how happy I am when you're with me. You make all of this a thousand times more bearable. I swear I will make this up to you."

"Okay." Claire flashed him a smile that she prayed looked one hundred percent genuine. "No problem."

They went with a large crowd of people, many of whom Claire vaguely remembered from initial introductions, to a large estate in Nob Hill for a fancy early dinner party. Claire, who usually didn't pay any mind to what people thought of her, felt unbelievably self-conscious in her casual skirt and tank top. It was slob-chic versus wealthy elegance, and she was losing by a long shot. Nevertheless, no one gave her the side-eye or any disparaging remarks. She had a feeling it had a lot to do with her very powerful boyfriend.

Nate followed through on his end of the bargain and only stayed at the party with Claire for an hour—enough for a few drinks, but right before the actual dinner started.

"Are we going back to the hotel now?" Claire asked. It was around six in the evening and the sun was starting to set, casting the city in a stunning pale pink glow. They were in the backseat of the car as Craig drove them down San Francisco's lazy, curving streets.

"Not yet," Nate said. "I wanted to show you something."

Claire held his hand in hers, their fingers twined tight. Even in the silence, she knew Nate was casting off the stress and high-energy of the day and sinking into her presence. He was in the now and enjoying a moment of peaceful rest with her. It was as if everything was in perfect balance, and nothing could ever go wrong as long as they were together.

Craig dropped them off at the peak of a large hill, inside a park nestled into a picturesque neighborhood. The sun had set even farther, and the blue of the once bright sky faded into a dusky, dark gray. Lights started coming on all over the neighborhood, and from their vantage point on the hill, the city seemed to glow like a convergence of fireflies.

Nate held Claire's hand as he led her through the park. Claire gazed around in appreciation of the beauty around her, but she gasped when she saw what lay up ahead.

"Oh my God," she said. "What is this place?"

"It's called the Palace of Fine Arts," Nate replied. "Do you like it?"

"Like it? I love it," Claire whispered. The sandy brown structure rose from the grass like the ruins of some castle straight out of a fairy tale. There was a lake at the base, fringed with lush greenery and verdant flowers. Twinkle lights hung across the columns and arches, making the place look alive with unearthly magic. Claire could almost believe she was stepping into the pages of a fantasy romance as the mortal heroine falling for a sinfully gorgeous fae king.

"Claire. I'm so grateful you came with me today," Nate said, looking down earnestly into her eyes. "Full transparency—things haven't been going great. This acquisition was the biggest challenge I've ever experienced in my professional life. It really threw me for a loop, and I was really stressed out. That's why I was insistent that you come to San Francisco. You have no idea the effect you have on me. When you're with me, it's like you're the calm in the eye of the storm. I don't have to worry when you're around. You have this amazing energy that centers me and helps me find my balance."

His words melted Claire's soul like candle wax. She had to hold his hands tighter for fear her knees would buckle.

"Meeting you was the most…transformative thing I've ever

experienced," Nate went on. "It's hard for me to explain my feelings, because that's what love is. You can't really make any sense of it. You can only feel it. And I felt it the day you almost ran into me with your car. I felt it when I first looked into your eyes. I knew that my heart belonged to you, and you alone."

He released her hand and dropped to one knee. At first, Claire thought he was being playful again. But then he looked back up at her, a tiny open box in his hand, with a diamond in it that put all the stars in the sky to shame.

"Maria Clara Ilagan Ventura, will you marry me?"

Claire was free falling. His question echoed over and over again in her mind, the deep cadence of his voice sweet and alluring. The diamond seemed to draw in the remaining illumination, leaving the night barren. It was the only source of light left in the world, and it was all she needed.

Earlier that night, he had seen how uncomfortable she was with socializing and being out of her element. Instead of becoming frustrated, he was patient. Attentive. He didn't write her off as a spoiled, antisocial brat. Instead, he made up for putting her in that situation by planning a romantic night topped off with a proposal. She couldn't imagine a more perfect night. She didn't care about anything else in that moment, except one thing: the man she loved with all her heart.

"Yes," she whispered as fresh tears began to fall. "Yes. I will marry you."

Nate took the ring and stood, slipping it tenderly onto her finger. Claire captured Nate's bearded jaw with her hands and brought his mouth to hers. She held him tight as they kissed beneath the twinkling lights. The joy of the moment filled every space and made her heart feel like it would burst at the seams.

"Marry me tonight," Nate whispered.

Claire stilled. "What did you say?"

"I want to get married tonight," he repeated. "I know a judge who would do it. Holy shit—this is perfect. This is a sign,

Claire. Marry me tonight."

Her grip tightened on his arms as she struggled with the gravity of his words. "But...we just got engaged," she said with a nervous laugh. "Why the rush?"

Nate took a step back. His eyes glowed with the fire of conviction. "This is how I live my life," he said. "I jump in headfirst."

"That doesn't exactly instill more confidence in my decision."

"This is a part of my philosophy. You have to listen to your heart and your head. The very first answer that pops into your head is the decision that your instinct and psyche both agree on. It's the answer you would regret if you didn't take the chance. That's why I know without a doubt. I want to marry you tonight. I don't want to go on one more day without you as my wife."

Claire was already lost to feeling. The inspirational words from his lecture filled her mind, fueling her courage and awakening the boldness she never knew she had. Just when she thought she couldn't fall deeper in love, he proved her wrong once again. She didn't think and didn't allow herself to doubt when she finally answered him.

"Okay," she said. "Let's do it."

CHAPTER TWENTY-EIGHT

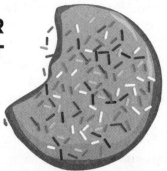

Craig dropped them off at yet another gorgeous home, this time farther north in the neighborhood known as Russian Hill. Intruding on a stranger's home at eight o'clock in the evening was strange to say the least. An elderly woman with a halo of frizzy white hair opened the door and gave Nate a hug.

"Judge Nina, it's good to see you," Nate said. "I'm so sorry for calling and bothering you out of the blue. This is my fiancée, Claire. Claire, this is Judge Nina. She's Sawyer's grandmother."

"It's a pleasure," Judge Nina said. "Shall we do the ceremony right here?" She gestured to her expansive front porch.

"What do you think?" Nate asked, looking down at Claire.

She gazed around the porch. Nate wasn't kidding when he said everything was perfect. Not only did he happen to know a judge in this very city, but the beautiful bay area and the twinkling lights of the city shining brightly made it seem like everything was set up especially for this one particular night.

"Yes," she said. "This is perfect."

Nate and Claire were married on Judge Nina's porch, with Craig as a witness. They recited their vows, holding each other's hands tight. Claire kept waiting for some sign that this was wrong, and that she shouldn't be too hasty. Her conscience screamed at her to stop—to not get married unless her family was there, and unless it was in a church.

But she didn't let anything stop her. This was the new Claire. Bold Claire, the kind who had the courage to grab life by the balls. The kind who was brave enough to quit her day job, tell her aunt to kick rocks, and follow her dreams.

Okay, maybe not the "kick rocks" part. But she promised herself she would start making all the right moves when she got home. She owed it to herself.

They decided to skip any kind of formal celebration that night, and instead returned back to their hotel room. It was Claire who pounced first. As soon as the door closed behind them, she grabbed Nate by his belt buckle and yanked him toward her, crushing her lips to his in a possessive kiss.

Words didn't need to be exchanged. Nate complied with all of Claire's demands, and did so eagerly. As his wife, she felt entitled to take advantage of her husband's sculpted, made-for-sex body, and she did so to the best of her ability.

The next morning, Claire woke up in Nate's arms. She blinked a few times in the moment of silence, with Nate's warm, strong body enveloping hers. A rush of emotion suddenly overwhelmed her. This was the first time she woke up with Nate still sleeping beside her, but this time, he was her husband.

Husband.

Claire gasped. Nate stirred, releasing a deep groan as his arms tightened around her. She squirmed against him, struggling to sit up in bed. Apparently he liked the feel of her bottom rubbing against him, because his hand strayed down between her legs, and he began planting kisses to the back of her neck. A shiver of pleasure ran through Claire, but she forced herself out of it.

"Nate." The sound of her voice stilled him, and she sat up in bed, covering her mouth with her hand. "We're married. Holy shit. We're married."

Nate blinked sleepily up at her and propped up his head on his hand.

"Are you happy?" he asked.

The morning light felt like taking a bucket of ice water to the face.

She, Claire Ventura, had gotten married on a stranger's front porch, without any of her family present. To a man she'd known for only three months.

She recalled Patti's strong suspicions about her motives, and the question of whether or not she would sign a prenup. Her heart thudded in fear when she thought about telling Patti they actually did get married. Or…maybe Patti had already had an inkling of Nate's intentions?

"Did you tell your mom you wanted to marry me?" Claire asked. "You never warned me about her, by the way. She told me I'd better not be with you for your money."

"I didn't exactly tell her I wanted to marry you, but I told her you were The One. And I'm sorry if she was harsh. I didn't realize she'd come on that strong right off the bat. That's my bad. She really hated my ex, and maybe she was a little traumatized by it."

"And what did she say when you told her that…I was The One?"

"She was doubtful," Nate replied. "But that doesn't matter. She already knows how I live my life, and she knows what I do when I feel strongly about something or someone."

Claire lapsed into silence again. Last night she had been so sure of everything, but now…

"You never answered my question." Nate's eyes filled with concern. "Are you happy?"

She hated making Nate worry, but she really had to think. She didn't want to weigh him down with her reservations, so she told him the truth, the only thing she was sure of in that very moment.

"I love you," she said, planting a kiss on his hand. "With all my heart."

Nate grinned and wrapped his arms around her waist, giving her an affectionate squeeze.

"I'm going to look for Ro," Claire said. She untangled herself from Nate's arms and threw on one of the fluffy dark blue bathrobes from the closet. After brushing her teeth, she crept quietly down the hallway toward Ro's room, but it was empty. She headed to the kitchen area, where she found Ro standing by the counter, drinking a cup of coffee.

"You're awake already?" Claire asked. "I didn't even know you were here. You're so quiet."

"Ate, you missed an epic night." Ro's eyes were still half closed as she managed a weak smile and took a sip of coffee. "Ray-Ray and I were—"

Suddenly, all signs of sleepiness and hangover vanished. It was as if she were hit by an invisible bolt of magic. Ro's eyes went wide, and her brown skin paled slightly.

"Oh my God," she whispered. She set down her coffee and rounded the kitchen counter, her eyes glued to Claire's hand. "What is this? What is this, *whatisthis*—"

She grabbed Claire's left hand.

"Don't freak out," Claire said, trying to loosen Ro's death grip on her hand. "That's why I was looking for you. I have some news."

Ro screamed. "See? I told you so!" She started skipping around the kitchen. "Todd and I were right. You didn't believe us, but we knew. We knew it. You owe us an apology. Oh my God, you're engaged to Nate! Congratulations, Ate. I am so excited for you! Did you tell anyone else yet?"

Claire grabbed Ro's wrist and pulled her to the living room, forcing her to sit on the couch.

"Ro, I have to tell you something, but you have to promise not to freak out. When I say freak out, I mean no screaming, yelling, cursing, or any type of inappropriate outbursts. Got it?"

Ro nodded.

"Nate and I are not engaged. We're…married."

Ro didn't move. Didn't even blink. Claire quirked her head in concern, wondering if this was the epic tea potent enough to finally short-circuit her gossip-hungry brain.

"Hello? Are you okay?" Claire asked.

Ro screamed. Louder this time. A door opened from down the hall and rapid footsteps approached. Nate appeared, naked except for the bedsheet held around his waist, which, Claire had to be honest, didn't cover up much.

"Is everything okay?" he asked.

Ro's jaw dropped to the floor at the sight of Nate dressed in nothing but a very thin sheet.

"Everything's okay, honey," Claire said. "We're fine."

Nate went back to the room. Ro's jaw was still gaping when she finally turned and looked at Claire.

"You think this was stupid, don't you?" Claire whispered. "Was this a mistake? Oh my God. I cannot believe I did this. You can understand where I'm coming from, though, right? He's so wonderful and romantic, and he really loves me. It's only been three months. Oh God. This is bad. Very, very bad. You think I'm an idiot, don't you?"

"Idiot?" Ro repeated. "Ate. You're not an idiot. You're a freakin' badass."

"What?"

"You are such a badass. You've always been pretty mild-mannered. I never knew you had the balls to do something like this. I'm in awe of you. If there is anyone in the entire world it's okay to marry after three months, it's Nate Noruta. Trust me. You're golden."

Claire stared at Ro incredulously.

"Are you serious?" she asked. "You don't think this was a mistake?"

"I would have done the same damn thing if I were you," she said. "Actually, no. I take that back. I would have trapped his ass much earlier than three months."

None of what Ro had said instilled even an atom-sized amount of confidence in Claire.

"Oh my God. When are you going to tell Mom and Dad?" Ro asked.

Claire groaned and buried her face in her hands. Tita Chriss had already mentioned to them Claire was dating someone, but they had no idea how serious they were. What would they think when she brought a stranger home and introduced him as her husband?

"This is too much to deal with right now," Claire said. "I'm going to shower and figure out how to approach this."

She headed down the hallway back to her and Nate's room. Nate was already in the shower. As nontraditional as she was, she still held her family in high regard. The guilt of not being forthcoming about her and Nate's relationship was like an elephant sitting on her chest. She knew what she had to do.

"Honey, I have to tell my parents about us," she said, wandering into the spacious bathroom. "I want you to come with me so I can introduce you to them. When are you coming home?"

Nate turned off the shower. He opened the door and grabbed the towel off the rack.

"Tuesday," he said as he toweled off.

"Is there any way you can come home tomorrow night? I know it's an inconvenience, but it's really important to me."

Claire watched in the mirror as Nate emerged from the shower. She suppressed a groan of appreciation as his lean muscles flexed with every movement. Would she ever get used to how fine this man was? Probably not. He approached and wrapped his arms around her.

"Of course I will." A mischievous look stole into his eyes as he untied her robe.

"Really? You're not joking, are you?"

"I'm serious." Nate's eyes stayed locked onto hers as his

hands strayed under her robe. "I'll do anything you want me to do." Her knees almost buckled when one hand closed over her breast, and his expert fingers went to work between her legs.

"Nate, I'm serious about this," Claire panted as she fought to gain control over her wild desire, which was hard to do as she watched her husband bend her over the counter and hitch her knee over it. "I really need you to commit to this."

"I will commit. I promise."

With a smooth, powerful stroke, he slowly eased into her. Claire moaned, tightening her grip on the counter. Once he was all the way in, he withdrew slowly, then started thrusting. The feeling of Nate pounding into her at this angle drove her mad, and it wasn't long before she was close to orgasming.

Claire's inhibitions vanished as Nate's fingers strayed down again to where their slick flesh was joined. She couldn't hold in her cries of ecstasy as her climax crashed through her like a raging storm. Her joints went weak, but Nate was there to hold her as the amazing sensations streaked through her veins. He planted a tender kiss on her neck and lifted her, taking her into the shower where there was a repeat performance of his lovemaking prowess.

At the end of the shower, Claire thought she heard a sound coming from the hallway. She threw her robe on again and cracked open the door. Ro was standing in the hallway with a worried expression on her face.

"Ro, what's going on?"

"I'm so sorry to interrupt your newlywed activities, Ate, but there's a big problem."

Her stomach dropped. "What's wrong?"

"You've been ignoring your texts and calls," Ro said. "I just finished speaking to Ate Sam. She knows you're married to Nate. The whole family knows. The news recently broke on TMZ."

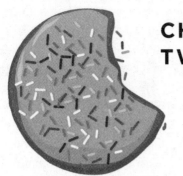

CHAPTER
TWENTY-NINE

Claire flew back down to Long Beach that day with Ro. She was furious with herself. This was the second time she'd allowed her whirlwind romance with to Nate distract her from real life. Now that she was home, she was way too high-strung to work on her cookies, let alone think about the process of moving in with Nate. One look at the long queue of orders demanding to be fulfilled, plus the prospect of packing up all her belongings, and she wanted to run. Her mind was a jumble, and her emotions were turning her into a train wreck of a human being. But she couldn't let her ratings fall. Scraping together the dregs of her resolve, she got to work baking and decorating.

She hadn't planned adequately for staffing, or anything else for that matter. She had let herself get swept away by Nate once again, instead of keeping her priorities straight.

But Nate was a priority now, too. He was her husband.

Husband.

Claire had to scrap several cookies because her hands shook so badly, the icing came out all wrong.

A few agonizing hours later, after she was done with most of her work for the day, Claire headed to her parents' house. They lived in a neighborhood a few miles north of Claire's apartment, close to where Lola's house had been. Only Claire's immediate family was supposed to be there, but word had spread like wildfire, and soon the whole extended family wanted in on the action.

As she drove up to the modest one-story home, there was already a horde of cars clogging the driveway and the curb stretching out in both directions. Claire let out a shaky breath as she parked and stared at the house, its windows completely lit up from within. Grasping her phone, she pondered sending out another call to Nate. He had been busy all day long doing business and whatnot. Claire wasn't in the frame of mind to retain any of the explanation Nate had offered via text. He had been so busy he didn't even have time to speak to her.

She did not like that one bit.

She shot off another call to Nate. This time he answered on the second ring.

"Hey, babe," he said. "What's up?"

"Are you still coming down?" Claire asked, barely managing to unclench her teeth. "I'm here parked in front of my parents' house right now. This morning you said you would be flying down tonight so I could introduce you to them."

"I'm trying my best," he replied. "It's a hectic time for me with all the projects going on."

"Where are you right now?" Claire held her breath, hoping he was doing that thing where he was going to surprise her again.

"I'm still in San Francisco," he said. "I have one more meeting to attend, and I'm not sure how long it's going to run. Why couldn't you have just flown down with me later on? Why are you in such a hurry?"

Claire bit down on a sharp retort. Nate was considerate and understanding, but only up to a certain point. She shouldn't expect him to understand the nuances of her family dynamics, but the frustration still stung.

"Because I have to face my family," she explained. "It's really bad that they found out about our marriage through

TMZ. I'm not trying to lay the blame on anybody. I have a duty to face them and introduce you to them. This is really important to me, and I was hoping you could be here. The longer I let this go, the worse it's going to be for us in the long run."

Claire's heart twisted at the silence stretching between them.

"It was wrong of me to make promises." The regret in his voice made her chest ache. "I'm so sorry, babe. But I can promise you I will try my best."

They said goodbye. Claire resisted the urge to throw her phone down the street. So this was the hard-edge, corporate heart of steel side of Nate. Of course he would make promises during the throes of sex. Why was it that he seemed perfect during certain times, but when it really mattered, he wasn't there?

Claire kept a firm grip on her courage and walked up the driveway to the side entrance of the house, her steps rigid and resolute, as if she were approaching her execution. She slid the glass door open and entered the kitchen.

The entire house was full. They hadn't wasted any time firing up the karaoke as the beginning strains of Bruno Mars's timely tune, *Marry You,* tinkled merrily through the air. As soon as she set foot inside, a hush fell over everyone. Her cousin muted the TV. Mom and Dad were standing together in the kitchen. Her aunties and some of their husbands were scattered through the dining room and living room. The younger and older cousins were also present, and she assumed the rest of her relatives were either in the other rooms or in the garage.

Claire put on her bravest smile. Suddenly, her family seemed to sort themselves into three teams based on conflicting ideologies. The first team clearly disapproved of Claire's shotgun wedding. Those team members wore their disapproval on their faces, ranging from scowls to stern looks of disappointment. The second team was happy. Overjoyed, even. These members cheered and hooted, sending hearty congratulations toward

Claire. Most of them consisted of cousins close in age, and surprisingly, her aunts Lianne and Lissabeth. Claire had not expected any of her aunties to approve. The third team...well, they were comprised of the little kids, who were completely oblivious that a stranger had just joined their family. Claire found herself wishing the disapprovers would join the kids' team and just happily go with the flow.

"Congrats, Claire." Her cousin Arvin enclosed her in a strong hug.

"Thank you."

"Where's Nate?" he asked. "Are we going to get to meet him?"

"Yeah, where's Nate?" her other cousin J.P. asked.

"That can wait till later." Her stomach clenched when she looked up and saw Sam. "Hi, Ate," Claire said.

"You owe Mom and Dad an explanation," Sam replied, her face the sternest of all.

Claire's shoulders were hunched as she approached her parents and gave them solemn kisses on the cheek. They didn't say anything to her, which made her stomach ache even more.

"Let's go out front," Claire said.

She walked with her parents and Sam through the front door. The front yard was enclosed in a tall wooden-slat fence, which gave them a lot of privacy. There was nowhere to sit, so they stood on the front walkway facing each other.

"Mom. Dad. I owe you an apology," Claire said. "I didn't mean for you to find out this way. I meant to tell you everything, but things happened so fast—"

"Where is Nate?" Sam interrupted.

"In San Francisco."

"You married him in San Francisco?" her mom asked.

"Yes."

"Did a priest do the ceremony?"

Claire winced and shook her head.

"This is the same man who owns that company?" her dad asked. "*MyConnect*?"

"Yes."

"Is he a good man?"

Claire looked up at her dad. Every time she was with him, her heart overflowed with love. They had been very close when she was younger, and she liked to believe, deep down inside, she was his favorite child. Her dad had always been a gentle soul. Her whole family said Claire had the soul of her father, with her mother's looks. That was the reason she felt horrible facing him now. She owed him so much more than a shotgun wedding to a man he had never met. Nate should have asked him for her hand in marriage first. She really should have done this a different way.

"Yes, he is a good man." Her voice caught as her eyes filled with tears. "I'm so sorry, Dad. I'm so sorry, Mom."

She reached out, and her dad enveloped her in his arms. She sobbed onto his shoulder as her mom stroked her hair.

"It's okay, anak," Dad said. "What's done is done. If he is a good man, and he works hard, that's all that matters."

Claire squeezed her father harder. He was trying to be supportive, but she heard the disappointment in his voice. She noticed her mother's silence, and it cut deep. Mom was clearly upset, but she was never the type to yell and scream and make a scene. It wasn't necessary when her eyes could express a thousand words that had the power to strike fear into a disobedient child's heart. Claire straightened up and forced herself to look into her mother's eyes.

"You're grown up now, and you can make your own decisions," Mom said. "I hope you made the right one."

Claire nodded, but didn't respond.

"I think you guys are missing the point," Sam said. "I think we can all agree this happened way too fast. How can you marry someone you've only known for three months? And I don't care how rich he is. This is about marriage. You have to be compatible in every way. Look at me and Dylan. We were both well-off, and you know how that ended up."

"I hear you, Ate," Claire said. "But—"

"He's not even here with you." Sam's eyes were sharp. Accusatory. "Doesn't he know how important your family is to you? Don't you think this is really disrespectful?"

"He's trying his best to come down," Claire replied, even though she knew he probably wouldn't be able to show up.

"He might be trying his best, but this isn't good enough," Sam said. "It sounds like I'm being harsh, but I'm just trying to protect you. Life isn't a fairy tale. You can't allow yourself to get swept off your feet by a guy simply because he's hot and has a lot of money. You have to be sensible. This is your future. This is real life, and there are consequences to marrying this kind of man."

Sam's words choked Claire like toxic fumes. There were some truths to what her sister said, but she was wrong about so many things—the things that really mattered.

"I am *not* with him because of his money."

Mom, Dad, and Sam stared in surprise at Claire. She hadn't meant to sound so angry, but she couldn't help it.

"I know this is hard for a lot of people to believe, but it is possible to fall in love with a person," Claire said. "It's possible to fall in love with a soul, free of money and possessions. Nate and I are in love. We don't have to justify how and why we feel the way we do."

A look of disbelief filled Sam's eyes. "Come on. You say you fell in love with Nate 'the person,' but you can't separate him from his money and power. Not at his level. Maybe you could do that with a guy who owned, let's say, a few retail franchises, but not with a guy who owns a billion-dollar global empire. Even when you're talking about him, you don't sound very convinced about the way you feel."

"I hate it when you say I don't sound sure," Claire said, even though Sam's words forced her to face her deep-seated fears. "You don't know what's going on in my head. And you can't make these assumptions when you haven't even met Nate yet."

"Fine. I can see you're emotional right now, and I don't want to upset you." Sam squeezed Claire's hand in reassurance. "Tomorrow, when you're feeling better, you should really take a look at what happened. Ask yourself if this is really what you want—to be married to someone you barely know, who has the power to destroy your life."

Destroy? That was going too far. Claire yanked her hand free.

"Okay," she said, her anger threatening to boil over. "Excuse me."

She went back inside the house and headed straight to her parents' master bathroom, which was the only place she could really be alone at this moment. She closed the door and took a few deep breaths. Even though she wanted to go home and sulk in silence, it wouldn't look good at all. She didn't want anyone thinking she was ashamed or afraid. She had no choice but to put on a brave face for her family.

Claire stayed in the bathroom for a long time, trying to compose herself. People were texting her, asking where she was. When she finally decided to come out, she went to the garage first. The uncles and an assortment of cousins usually hung out there, smoking and drinking and eating. She opened the door and everyone greeted her with genuine cheer.

"Hey, congrats, Claire!"

"Wow, you're so lucky. What a catch."

"You're rich now, iha. Good for you."

Claire moved through the house gradually, mingling with her family and chatting with her cousins. Soon, a sense of comfort filled her heart. Unlike the earlier conversation with Sam and her parents, her relatives had positive things to say.

It was hard to believe, but most of them were actually happy for her.

At a quarter past ten in the evening, the mood shifted. That was the moment Tita Chriss finally arrived. Claire cursed herself to hell and back for staying to sing two karaoke songs instead of cutting out early for the night. And yes, ten p.m. was considered early for one of her family parties.

She felt like a deer getting caught in the headlights once Tita Chriss entered through the front door. The karaoke was set up right there, and Tita Chriss's eyes fell on Claire immediately. She gave Claire a polite, auntie-like smile and came over to hug her.

"Congrats, Claire," she said. "Or should I say, Mrs. Noruta? This is quite a surprise. Quite a surprise indeed. Where is your husband? I'd love to meet him."

"He's not here," Claire replied. "He's out of town at the moment, but he'll be back on Tuesday."

"That's too bad. Come, let's have a word outside."

Claire followed Tita Chriss through the front door and into the yard.

"This is so shocking," Tita Chriss said. Her smile was brittle, and Claire didn't miss the disapproving edge to her voice. "I think this is what they call a shotgun wedding. And to Nate Noruta of all people. I don't know if I should be disappointed or impressed."

"I think happy would be a good choice," Claire replied.

"I am happy for you," she said. "You have to admit this is kind of sudden, though. And getting married to someone so quickly isn't always wise. But I guess if you're going to get married quick, Nate Noruta would be the best choice."

Claire braced herself because she knew where her aunt's train of thought was heading.

"This actually makes a lot of sense to me now," Tita Chriss said. "Now I know why you seemed so hesitant to accept my job offer. Why would you need to work if you're married to Nate Noruta?"

"I wasn't married to him at that time," Claire replied. "Nate doesn't control the decisions I make in my professional life. And the reason I was hesitant was because..." She clenched her fists at her side, determined to rise above her fear. "Because I am going to start my own business."

A condescending grin curved along Tita Chriss's lips.

"If you're married to a billionaire, you don't really need a plan," she replied. "You can do any little side hobby you want and call it a 'business.' In the end you know you always have someone to fall back on when it doesn't work out the way you want it to. The stakes are very low for you when you have all that money. There is little risk in anything you choose to do from this moment forward."

Claire was convinced she was stuck in some kind of maddening déjà vu loop. Nicole had said something similar just a few weeks before. Why did everyone think she was suddenly worth a lot less because she was married to Nate? Something inside her snapped.

"I have always been my own person, first and foremost," she said. "Being in a relationship with someone doesn't mean I'm changing myself on a fundamental level. I've always dreamed of having my own business. Whether or not I'm with Nate doesn't change that. Being married to him does not define me."

Tita Chriss looked taken aback by the heat, but she recovered quickly.

"Whether you like it or not, that's what has happened to you," she said. "You marry a billionaire, and you become a billionaire's wife. Plain and simple. How could you not understand that?"

A heavy sense of weariness fell upon Claire. Even though the nonstop activity of the weekend was finally catching up with her, a spark of something white-hot burned in her chest.

Hope. Taking chances. Nate wasn't here with her, but his words lingered. If she continued to deny what she really wanted in life, maybe people would continue to underestimate and undervalue her. It was time to start standing up for herself. She bit down on the apology that automatically came to her lips, and she forced something else out entirely.

"I'm not going to work for you, Tita. Not because I married a billionaire. Not because I have a fail-safe. It's because I've dreamed all my life of being my own boss and doing something that makes me happy. Cookies make me happy. If you can't understand or support me, there's nothing else left to say."

She had no courage left to look into Tita Chriss's stunned face, so she turned to leave. But a gentle knock at the front gate stopped her. Her relatives never knocked. They simply opened the gate. Unless…

"Who's there?" she asked hopefully.

"Claire? It's me."

The sound of that voice made her gasp. She hurried over and opened the gate. A tall figure stood there, limned in the pale golden glow coming from the street light.

"Nate?"

Claire's heart raced in her chest as Nate came forward. Pure joy and disbelief exploded around her, and she threw her arms around him so forcefully he stumbled back.

"How—what—I can't believe you're here," she stammered, looking up at him. "How did you get down here so fast? Were you here this whole time?"

She looked up into his face and saw the shadows under his eyes.

"I knew it was important to you, so I made time to fly down," he replied, his smile masking the weariness in his voice. "It wasn't easy, but I did it. For you."

She grasped Nate's hand and drew him into the yard, her spirits so light she was practically walking on air. Her relatives were spying, and soon everyone was spilling onto the front porch with cries of excitement. Her parents also emerged from the house and approached them. She swallowed nervously and squeezed Nate's hand for reassurance.

"Mom. Dad. I'd like you to meet Nate. My husband."

Dad shook Nate's hand, and Nate kissed Mom's cheek. He introduced himself with the easy grace of his charismatic persona, but Claire couldn't help but notice the adorable way he smiled nervously as he was finally faced with meeting his in-laws for the first time.

"I guess I should welcome you to the family," Dad said, giving Nate a hearty slap on the shoulder. "What do you want to drink?"

"I'll have whatever you're having, sir," Nate said.

"No more *sir*," Dad said. "Like it or not, I'm *Dad* to you from now on."

The crowd of Claire's family converged on Nate as Dad guided him into the house. Claire smiled as everyone began to chatter excitedly. She could always count on her father's warm and generous personality. Her mother, on the other hand, grinned politely but remained guarded. Claire's cousins and aunts gushed over him and congratulated her again, commenting on how charming he was.

On her way into the house, Claire locked eyes with Sam. She stood there in silence for a brief moment, but that was all it took to remind Claire that nothing came easy.

No matter how much she tried to forget it, she and Nate still had a long way to go.

CHAPTER THIRTY

Claire prided herself on being a patient person, but the parking situation in this part of Long Beach had her cursing up a silent storm. She circled the neighborhood once again after spotting not even a sliver of a spot where she could wedge her car in, and she broke into a sweat. Todd texted her again, but she was in no position to stop and read it. She hit the call button.

"Todd, I am trying my best," she said, all the while scanning the streets like a hawk. "I have circled this place a million times, but there is absolutely nothing."

"Girl, make a U-turn right now," Todd said. "Somebody just left. I'm standing in the spot so nobody takes it from you."

Claire busted a U and hauled her butt down the road. Todd barely jumped out of the way before she barreled into the spot beside the curb.

"So this is how Nate felt when he stared death in the face the first time he met you," Todd said breathlessly as he clutched his chest. "I'm fine, by the way."

"I'm sorry." Claire popped the trunk and hurriedly unloaded her boxes of cookie samples. "Todd, we are so late. Please help me with these."

He helped her stack the boxes of cookies into her fold-up trolley, then unloaded the folding table from the back of her car. They trekked half a block down the residential road and into the foyer of a large apartment building, where they hit the button for the tenth floor.

"I haven't even congratulated you in person yet," Todd said. "Congrats Claire-bear. You're a married woman now." He leaned in and gave her a quick hug.

"Thanks."

"You don't sound thrilled," Todd said in surprise. "I would think you'd be the happiest woman in the whole world."

"I am happy," Claire replied, dabbing the sweat off her forehead. "It's hot as hell outside and we've been running around, and I'm super stressed because I hate being late for a client consultation."

A troubled look stole into Todd's eyes. "Is Nate still down here?" he asked.

"No. He left for San Francisco again after my family's party on Saturday night."

"Damn! So you're telling me he flew all the way down here for you, stayed for a couple of hours, then flew back up there?"

Claire nodded.

"When's he coming back?"

"Tomorrow night."

Todd lapsed into a moment of silence. It looked like he was struggling to find the words to say, which was strange because words never escaped this man.

"I know you're working right now, but after this, let's talk okay? I think some Todd time is exactly what you need."

"Sure," Claire said, shrugging off his concern. Now was not the time for Todd's friend instincts to be kicking in. If she gave one more thought to how overwhelmed she was, she would burst into tears right before the biggest client meeting of her life.

They got off the elevator on the tenth floor and turned right to head to apartment 1022.

"This is a really important consultation," she explained. "I want everything to be perfect. This is my very first wedding order, and it's going to be huge. This could possibly be the turning point in my career. We'll ask the bride, Cynthia, where she wants us to set up the table so that we can show her the samples."

"Got it," Todd said.

Claire knocked at 1022, and a brunette woman with a pixie cut opened the door.

"Hi," she said. "Claire, right? I'm Cynthia."

"Yes, it's so nice to meet you. This is my friend Todd. He's helping me out today."

"It's a pleasure," Cynthia said, opening the door wider. "Come on in. Oh, you have your own table. You can set that up right here behind the couch."

Claire and Todd entered the spacious apartment. Cynthia introduced them to her mother, Grace, and her maid-of-honor, Stephanie.

"I want to offer my sincere apology for being late," Claire said as Todd set up the table and the cookies. "I was having trouble finding parking, but I promise you this will not be a problem next time."

"Please, no apology is necessary," Cynthia said. "I totally understand. And it's super hot outside. Steph, can you get them waters, please?"

"I want to thank you so much for choosing my services," Claire began. "As promised, I brought a generous assortment of wedding-themed sugar cookies that you can choose from. Everything is completely customizable, from the shapes, to the themes, to the colors. Here's a price sheet with everything itemized. Now that Todd's got the display boxes set up, I'll show you what I've brought."

Claire led the three ladies to the table, where Todd had beautifully laid out the display boxes showing the sample wedding cookies. Cynthia, Grace, and Stephanie admired her work as Todd handed her a small, separate box.

"Hopefully some of these designs are to your liking," Claire said. "I also have a little surprise for you. I made a few custom samples with your motif colors and initials on them." She opened the small box, showing Cynthia an assortment of cookies custom-made for her wedding.

"Oh my gosh, these are gorgeous." Cynthia took the box reverently in her hand and peered into it. "I love them. Mom, aren't they beautiful?"

"They really are, honey," Grace replied. "This assortment is lovely. Absolutely lovely. I'm very impressed."

"Thank you so much," Claire said as pride filled her chest.

"Wait a minute," Stephanie said.

Everyone paused as she checked something on her phone. She glanced up and gave Cynthia a look that Claire couldn't decipher.

"What's the matter?" Cynthia asked.

Stephanie opened her mouth to respond, but shut it when her eyes swung over to Claire.

"I'm so sorry, but we're going to need a minute to talk," Stephanie said as she grasped Cynthia's wrist. "Let's have a word in the bedroom real quick. Grace, you should come, too."

Claire and Todd stared in confusion at one another once the other women had retreated into the bedroom at the end of the hall.

"What was that all about?" Claire asked.

"I don't know," Todd replied. "That maid-of-honor gave you a weird look."

They lapsed into silence for a few seconds.

"Can you hear anything?" Claire asked.

Todd crept quietly across the living room towards the hallway leading to the bedroom. He listened intently for a few seconds.

"No, I can't hear a thing," he whispered, returning back to

the cookie table.

"They're taking longer than I expected. What do you think they're discussing?"

"Girl, I have no clue. This really is strange."

Claire fidgeted with her skirt as she leaned against the sofa, her mind swimming with puzzlement. She and Cynthia had hit it off online. She'd been so enthusiastic about Claire's services that she hired her on the spot. What could be the problem now?

Suddenly the bedroom door opened. Claire and Todd snapped to attention as the three women emerged. Claire waited eagerly for someone to talk. Cynthia gave a look of uncertainty to Stephanie, who nodded to her in encouragement.

"Claire…are you the same Claire who married Nate Noruta?" Cynthia asked, her voice hesitant.

"Um…yes, that's correct."

"Okay. See, that's the reason we had to confer for a moment," Cynthia replied. "We thought we recognized your name, but we had to be sure. I guess…congratulations are in order for you, too."

The air thickened with a strange, awkward tension. A nervous grin spread over Claire's lips.

"Thank you," she replied. "What does this have to do with my services, if you don't mind me asking?"

"So…Claire, you know I like you very much." Cynthia's voice was pleasant, but it still filled Claire with a sense of foreboding. "It's evident you've got this amazing talent and passion for what you do. That's why I'm so sorry to tell you…I've decided to hire someone else to do the custom cookies."

Claire felt like someone slapped her across the face. She blinked in confusion.

"You're firing me?" she asked. "Why?"

"Please don't look at it that way," Cynthia said, her voice practically pleading. "I'm not firing you. You've done absolutely nothing wrong. It's just…well, I'm a supporter of small businesses. I was trying to choose between you and Lilly Anne's Designs, and I went with you initially. But now that I know you're married to Nate Noruta, I have to go with Lilly. She's a small, self-made business. You're the last person in the world who needs business because…I mean, you're Nate Noruta's wife. Do you understand where I'm coming from?"

Claire was convinced she'd fallen into a parallel universe—one in which everything was wildly, ironically unfair. Lilly Anne's business was far more advanced than hers—she had three successful brick-and-mortar locations!

"But I'm self-made, too," Claire argued. "I wasn't born into wealth, and Nate's money doesn't belong to me. This was a dream I had for a long time, and with a lot of hard work and dedication, I made it come true. On my own."

Cynthia, Grace, and Stephanie were looking at Claire like she'd just sprouted horns.

"Claire, honey." Todd gently touched her arm. She noticed he'd packed up all the sample cookies and folded the table. "We should go now."

"But I'm not done here," Claire replied more loudly than she intended.

"You are," Todd whispered. He turned and flashed a polite, apologetic smile at Cynthia as he handed the rolling cart handle to Claire and picked up the table. "Thank you so much. It was a pleasure meeting you. Have a wonderful wedding, and I hope y'all don't choke on Lilly's dry-ass cookies. Bye-bye now."

They briskly strode out of the apartment and headed back to the elevator. Claire didn't say a word, even as Todd gazed at her with concern.

"Hey," he said. "Are you okay?"

Emotions of every color crowded into Claire's brain, making everything sound distant and muffled. She crossed her arms, desperately trying to focus on what went wrong.

"No," she answered. "I don't understand what happened

back there. Why were they looking at me like that?"

"Because you were clearly distraught and saying things that didn't sound right," Todd answered.

"What do you mean by that?"

"Claire." Todd's voice was cajoling, and it grated on her nerves. "Let's forget about this. Let's concentrate on the next client and use this as a learning experience. It's not healthy to dwell on negative things."

"No, I don't want to forget about it." Claire hit the stop button on the elevator. Todd's eyes bulged. "Explain to me what I did wrong, because I do not recall doing anything to lose that client."

Todd gazed intently at Claire for a moment, and seemed to draw strength from an invisible power source before he spoke.

"So this is what happened," he said. "You married Nate a few days ago. It means you two united as one, and you agreed to give up a piece of your independence. Wait, let me finish. It goes both ways. You're a huge part of *his* life now, too. So when you try to tell people that Nate—who is one of the richest, most powerful men in the world—has nothing whatsoever to do with any stake in your business, it sounds a little bit...inaccurate."

Claire wanted to scream. It had been her life-long dream to blaze her own path, free from the constraints of her family's expectations. She wanted to be brave and strong and independent. It was almost within reach, but Todd's words were like a sobering bucket of ice water dumped on her head.

"So you're saying it's impossible for me to be a business owner while I'm married to Nate? I have to abandon my dreams in order to be his wife, following him all over the globe while he travels on business, and make him my only reason for being?"

Sympathy filled Todd's eyes. "If you were anyone else, I'd tell you to snap the hell out of it," he said. "I'd tell you that millions of people out there would kill to be in the position you're in—to be the love of Nate Noruta's life. But I'm not going to say that. Instead, I'm just going to say that you need to find a way to accept this change. Like it or not, everything's shifted, and it all happened so fast. Maybe you need to take a moment to figure out what's really important to you now."

Claire didn't move for a long time. She stared off at some distant point, turning Todd's words over in her head. Todd leaned forward and hit the resume button.

By the time they reached the ground floor, Claire still didn't know what to do, and it scared her. She was supposed to be secure in her new marriage, but the truth was she felt more lost than ever.

CHAPTER THIRTY-ONE

Things were getting stranger by the day since Claire and Nate got married. Yesterday, Claire's client dumped her with no warning whatsoever. Then today, when she got up in the morning, she looked through her window and saw a peculiar handful of people standing on the sidewalk near her apartment complex. As soon as she left the apartment to visit Lola, it became very clear that these people were paparazzi and they were there for her.

"Hey, are you Claire Ventura? Or should I say, Claire Noruta?"

Claire frowned at the lanky, intrusive guy lingering at the bottom of the steps leading to her carport. Annoyance flashed through her at the camera phone he brazenly pointed at her. She ignored him, but all it did was spur the handful of other paparazzi to approach and start photographing and filming her.

"What are you guys doing?" she asked, laughing nervously. "This is ridiculous."

"Where's Nate?" someone asked.

"Why aren't you living with Nate?"

"Why did he marry you? Are you pregnant?"

"Aren't you worried about him cheating on you?"

Claire threw hostile looks at the paparazzi, or whatever the hell they were, and kept walking to her carport. She was tempted to fire right back at them, but she knew that's what they wanted. They were trying to bait her, and she didn't want to give them the satisfaction.

"Hey, Claire, I looked you up online and saw that you're a cookie decorator," one of them said as she finally reached her car. "Do you still plan on pursuing that while married to Nate?"

"Yes," Claire said harshly. She threw open her door so hard she almost hit someone. Dropping into the seat, she fired up the engine and her anger flared up at the same time. These people had some nerve. She could not fathom the rudeness and intrusiveness. Was this what Nate had to live with? When they were dating, she'd somehow been spared from this, but now that news of their impromptu wedding became public, she was pulled unwillingly into the harsh spotlight.

When she backed her car out of the spot and drove down the road, she was deathly scared they would follow her. Fortunately, they didn't follow her, but that didn't mean anything. They could easily camp out, waiting to accost her the second she got home.

She dialed Nate's number immediately. It rang until it went to voicemail.

"So he picks up every time I call, except when I really need to talk," she muttered, hanging up. "Thanks for the warning about the stalkerazzi, honey bunny."

When Claire finally got to Lola's facility, she was on edge. This was not the frame of mind she wanted to be in when she saw Lola. Even though Lola had pretty much lost her normal awareness, Claire believed she could still feel positive and negative vibes. That was why Claire made a vow to never bring any baggage with her during her visits. It was like showing up with a raging cold and being careless enough to pass it along to an unsuspecting victim. Instead of entering Lola's room, Claire chose to take a seat in one of the comfortable armchairs in the hallway to calm herself down.

"Claire?"

She turned to see Lola's nurse, Allison, walking up to her.

"Hi," Claire said. "How are you?"

"I'm doing well," she replied. "I'm glad I caught you before you went in to visit your grandma. Do you mind if I have a word with you?"

"Not at all. Is something wrong?"

Allison sat in the armchair beside Claire.

"This is never easy to say, but I wanted to have a serious conversation with you about your grandma. We've noticed she's taken a sharp decline in her health over the past month. Dr. Tran discussed her concerns with you a couple weeks after she moved in, but your grandmother has actually declined a lot faster than we anticipated."

A painful heaviness pressed down on Claire's chest.

"Decline?" she repeated. "What do you mean by that exactly?"

"She's not eating very much at all, and she sleeps a lot more. We've been tracking her closely. She's eating less than ten percent of every meal, and she spends about eighty to ninety percent of the day sleeping."

"But what about the activities?" Claire asked as the fear spiked within her. "I thought someone was supposed to wheel her down to the activities so she could participate every day."

"We do wheel her down to as many activities as we can," Allison answered. "But she sleeps through most of it."

"Well…is she too sedated? Maybe her meds are too strong."

"I could ask Dr. Tran to cut back on some of her meds," Allison offered. "But with the advanced state of her dementia, cutting back on her meds might cause her behavioral issues to come back."

Claire sat in stunned silence. She thought maybe discontinuing her meds might make Lola more alert, but she knew that wouldn't be the case. She would likely get more confused and combative, and she'd end up having to go to the ER to get knocked out. Claire closed her eyes for a moment and shook her head.

"So what does this mean," she murmured, even though she already knew.

"This is nature's way of telling us her body is shutting down. It's hard to say how long the process is going to take. We just want you and your family to be ready when the time comes."

Claire's heart twisted into a knot. The sensible part of her knew that Lola's days were numbered, especially after her dementia diagnosis. There was no way to prepare for this. She couldn't imagine a world without this once vibrant, vivacious woman—the woman who inspired her to stay true to herself and follow her dreams.

"Thank you, Allison," Claire whispered as she stood back up. "I'm going to see her now."

"Of course. If there is anything you need at all, please don't hesitate to reach out to us."

Claire opened the door to Lola's room and walked inside. Lola was sitting in her armchair, looking as peacefully regal as ever. Even though she was dozing, she didn't look very sick. Granted, she appeared quite thin, but nothing too extreme. She wasn't pale, and her curly, short silvery hair was still relatively thick for someone her age. Claire didn't want to believe this was happening. She sat on a stool beside Lola and gently placed her hand on top of hers.

"Lola, I wish you could hear me right now. I wish you could understand my words—"

Claire paused as a sob escaped her. The emotion hit hard without warning, wrapping around her heart like a tightening fist.

"If I could turn back the clock to a time before all this happened, I would have told you that you were my favorite person. My hero. You were the only one who didn't laugh at me when I told everyone I wanted to be an entrepreneur. You pulled me aside and told me not to listen to them. You said I could do anything because I was smart and loving, and I deserved good things in my life."

Claire paused a moment to swipe away her tears. The heaviness of her wedding ring caught her attention. It refracted light in a million different directions. It really was so beautiful, but for some reason she never gave it a good look until now.

"Lola, I got married to a wonderful man. He's amazing in so many ways, but…"

Her tears began to fall faster as the words caught in her throat.

"I don't know if we are going to work out. I'm so in love with him, but there's this part of me that thinks this might have been a mistake. I wish you could tell me what to do. I really wish you were here with me right now, because you would have all the answers."

When Claire realized she was speaking to her grandma as if she were already gone, she gave in to her tears, breaking down and letting the words wash away in the flood of her sorrow.

The phone rang.

Claire's eyes flew open, and she was momentarily dazed. She sat up as the phone continued to ring. A soft, furry dog ear twitched against her hand, and then she remembered: she was in Nate's house in L.A., sitting on the cushy sofa in his family room, waiting for him to finally fly in from San Francisco. He was due to come home soon. She reached over and picked her phone up off the side table. It was Sam.

"Hello?"

"Hi. How are you?" Sam asked.

"I'm fine. How are you?"

"You don't sound fine." Surprisingly, there was a hint of sympathy in Sam's voice, and Claire found it perplexing. Sam should have put two and two together and understood how her negative feelings toward the marriage affected Claire. But Claire didn't feel like opening that can of worms right now—not after everything she was going through at the moment.

"You're right. I'm not fine," Claire replied. "Actually, it's Lola."

Claire updated Sam on what the nurse said, and about Lola's prognosis. At the end, Sam stayed silent.

"Hello?" Claire said. "Are you still there?"

"Yeah," Sam said, her voice weary. "I'm sorry. I...this is a lot harder than I thought it would be."

"The nurse told me we should start preparing for the inevitable," Claire replied. "It's such a morbid, terrible thought. I mean...I know she's ninety-three years old, but I'll never be ready for this."

"Where are you?" Sam asked.

"I'm at Nate's house."

"How are things going with you two?"

Claire sighed. Sam's question was both easy and hard to answer.

"It's funny you should ask," she said. "I've been thinking about what you said a few days ago—about us moving too fast. I was angry that you were making assumptions, but then I really thought about it. The truth is, I am so madly in love with Nate. I've never loved anyone the way I love him, and I know he feels the same way for me. But..."

Claire couldn't finish. Was love enough to sustain a marriage? There had to be more to it, but she was too weary to think about it. Maybe that was the reason things didn't feel right: she didn't put enough thought into any of it. She let herself get swept away in the romance of it all. It was easy to get swept away because Nate was overwhelmingly attractive, in more ways than one. He had this magnetism that possessed people. Instantly. He was the closest thing to a real-life prince charming she could think of.

"Claire," Sam said gently. "I'm here for you. I might not have been the best big sister these past few months, but I'm going to make up for it. Okay?"

Headlights flashed through the window as a car drove up the private driveway. Nate was home.

"I've gotta go, Ate," Claire said. "Thank you for being there for me."

They disconnected the call. Maisy, who had been resting peacefully beside Claire, bolted up and wagged her tail. She leaped off the couch when the front door opened.

"Maisy! I missed you, girl. How's my good girl?"

The sound of Nate's joyful voice drifting down the hall made Claire's heart skip. Their connection was so strong, on both an emotional and physical level. He affected her in ways she didn't understand, which was why her conflicted emotions made no sense to her. She emerged from the family room and walked up to Nate. A huge smile broke across his face as he dropped his backpack on the floor and swept Claire up in his arms, pressing his lips to hers.

"I missed you," he whispered as he pressed passionate kisses to Claire's neck. He reached down and wrapped her legs around his waist. His hands gripped her thighs possessively as he backed her against the wall. A sexy grin lit up his face. "Do you want to do it here or in our room?"

"Let's talk for a little bit," Claire answered, fighting back her instinct to give in to her desire for Nate. "I feel like we never get a chance to talk."

"You're right." Nate eased her down and grabbed her hand. "Have a seat on the couch and I'll bring us some drinks. What do you want?"

"Anything."

Claire waited for Nate on the couch as he bustled around at the bar area near the kitchen, fetching a few drinks for them. She shifted nervously on her seat. He seemed to be in a jovial mood for some strange reason.

"How was your trip?" she asked as Nate returned. He placed a glass of prosecco in her hand as he took a sip of whiskey on ice.

"It was amazing. At first I was nervous about the acquisition. It was our biggest one to date, and a lot of people said I was in over my head. But our team did it. Everything's going smoothly for once. Tech has a completely different mindset and culture from *MyConnect* and Trance, but after a lot of hard work we finally came to a compromise. The Tech CEO's a pain in the ass, but we were able to schedule a retreat to settle on terms and get our two teams on the same page. I'm flying out to New York tomorrow morning."

"Wait, you're leaving again?" Claire cried. "You just got back."

"I know, babe, but this is my job. This is a really important time in my career. Don't worry, you can just come with me. You're always welcome. I'd prefer you were with me anyway. You can bring your sisters and Todd if you want. While we're up there, we can look at some real estate. I'm thinking of relocating us over there part-time since that's where the Tech headquarters are located."

Claire felt like she'd been swept away in a flash flood. Her mind had trouble comprehending everything. She squeezed her eyes shut to gather her thoughts.

"Nate, you can't expect me to drop everything to fly off with you at a moment's notice," she said. "And what are you talking about now? You want to move to the East Coast? That's such a big decision. It's so disruptive to our lives here."

"I know it'll seem that way at first, but you'll get used to it. That was the hardest part for me, too. But with all the work I do, I can't avoid it. Sometimes you have to be everywhere all at once, and you do the best you can."

Claire set her glass down. A solemn feeling settled on her shoulders as she struggled to maintain eye contact with Nate.

"Nate. I don't think I can get used to this."

A look of alarm appeared on Nate's face. "What do you mean?"

"I love you. I really do. But when we decided to get together, things happened so fast. We've only known each other for three months, and we were engaged for all of five minutes before we got married on a judge's front doorstep."

"What are you saying?" Nate asked. "Are you telling me that getting married was a mistake?"

"I think we moved too fast. The truth is...I'm not ready to move anywhere. I'm not ready to drop everything to become a rich man's wife, and I don't want to leave my family. My Lola is really sick, and I don't want to be far away from her."

Nate's body stiffened. He leaned forward, resting his elbows on his knees as he stared intently into some point in the distance.

"Okay. We'll find a way to make this work," he said, switching to problem-solving mode. "You can fly out to see me when you're ready. I'll hold off on looking at real estate for now, and maybe next month, when we see how Lola's doing, we can think about it again."

"It's not just my family," Claire replied. "It's so many things. I lost a client because they found out I'm married to you. They said I was rich, so I didn't need clients as much as my competition. I've wanted to be a business owner since I was a child. It was my dream. And it's really hard to do that now. On top of that, all your friends' wives gave up on their careers once they married rich men. I'm not okay with that. After all of this, I feel like...I've lost all sense of who I really am."

"I don't understand," Nate said. "I thought you were happy. When I asked you to marry me, you said yes. You were excited to move in and start our lives together. Marrying you was the best thing that's ever happened to me. Do you not feel the same way?"

Claire's chest was splitting open. An excruciating pain radiated out from her center, wrenching tears from her eyes. She wanted to stay. Every part of her soul reached out to Nate and wanted to take simple pleasure in being his wife. But Claire knew this was far more complex than she could have ever imagined, and she had to work hard to stay strong. Resolute.

"It was a mistake," she whispered. "We shouldn't have gotten married. I'm just a simple girl, and I don't belong in your world. I can't handle the paparazzi and the reporters. And I'm not willing to give up on my dreams to support yours. I'm so sorry, Nate. This is killing me, but it has to be this way. I don't think…I don't think this is the life I want."

Claire stood up on shaky legs. She didn't feel like herself. How could she when her soul had been ripped apart, leaving every wound raw and exposed, with no hope of healing ever again?

"Wait, you're leaving?"

Claire stopped. She'd never heard such despair in Nate's voice, and it had the power to reduce her to dust.

"Are you seriously doing this to me, Claire? You're walking away from me?"

Claire looked away as tears flooded her vision. She stayed planted as Nate's footsteps approached. Her body screamed to go to him—to wrap her arms around him and never let go—but she stayed still. Instead, he reached out and gently grasped her hands.

"You're not thinking clearly," he said softly. "You're just overwhelmed by everything, and all these changes happening at once. But this is how life is. There are ups and downs, and we'll go through them together. It's you and me now. We're in love. Everything we have is real and true. Don't walk away from me. Don't walk away from us."

Claire simply stood there, her hands trembling as agonizing

silence speared through her. Even as the words finally came, she couldn't look into Nate's eyes.

"It all moved too fast," she whispered. "I didn't realize until it was too late that we're not compatible. I'm not poised and glamorous like your friends' wives. Your job keeps interfering—"

"*Bullshit*, Claire."

Claire gasped as Nate dropped her hands and stepped back, running his hands through his hair as tension poured out of his whole body.

"That's all bullshit, and you know it," he snapped. "Kendall and Sophia and all the rest...they're nothing to me. Why are you so hung up on that? And my job? You might not have recognized me at first, but from day one you knew who I was. And even though my job is a priority, I do my best to put you first. Everything that's important to you is important to me, too. How could you not see that? You're willing to throw everything away for what? Some bullshit insecurities you can't get past?"

His words crashed through Claire like a sonic boom. Anger and fear and despair rose up in waves, clawing at her throat.

"Don't make me feel like that," Claire whispered. "My insecurities are not bullshit."

"They are when you let them get in the way," Nate retorted. "You're throwing our relationship away for nothing."

"It's not nothing," Claire said. "See? This is what I mean. You don't know how I feel. This isn't the way things are supposed to be."

"How am I supposed to know how you feel when you don't talk to me?" Nate demanded. "You keep everything bottled up inside. You want to please everyone, and you avoid confrontation. Life doesn't work that way. You have to communicate. You can't let things build up until the wall gets so high you can't climb over it anymore."

The tears fell in silence, burning a brand of sorrow across her skin.

Fear. It was so simple. She was so scared of everything: disappointing her family, standing up for herself, and pursuing her dreams. It was time to be brave. But if she was being brave, why did it hurt so bad? Why did her heart scream that this was wrong, when her head told her it was the right thing to do?

Claire dropped her gaze to the floor. Her feet started moving of their own accord. She felt as though a tether was guiding her, pulling her away, leading her where she was supposed to go. She was almost to the door when she felt Nate's presence right behind her. She spun around and was shocked to see he was still far away, at the other end of the room. He hadn't moved. His eyes were glazed over. Claire couldn't stand seeing him this way, but she forced herself to look—to see what she'd done to him.

"Every time you'd ask me about my family, I'd only talk about my mom." His voice was distant, but his eyes burned right into her. "I know family is everything to you. It killed me to keep things from you, but it was too painful to talk about. Did you know that Noruta wasn't my birth name? It was Carter. My mother changed my last name to hers when my father walked out on us. I was only five, but I remember like it was yesterday." Nate's voice caught, and he cleared his throat.

"I was standing in the garage, and my dad was leaving after he and my mom got into an argument. She told me he wasn't coming back. I started crying and begging him to stay. He turned back to look at me, and I was so hopeful. The way he looked at me—I could have sworn there was so much love in him, and he was going to stay. But then he walked away. He turned his fucking back on me like I was nothing. Just—gone."

Silence stretched between them. Claire's sorrow engulfed her as she continued to drown in the silence. Nate blinked and took a deep breath.

"You're doing the same thing," he said with a rueful grin. "Walking out on me. You promised me you'd always tell me what was on your mind, and that you'd always be here. You said you'd never walk away, but you didn't mean it."

Claire fought against the weakness that told her to give in. She loved Nate, but she didn't know in what universe their relationship would work. It was a beautiful fantasy while it lasted. But that's what it was—a fairy tale, and fairy tales weren't real. She lifted her hand and opened the door.

"I hope this makes perfect sense to you, Claire, because I don't understand this. I'll never understand. You'd better be fucking sure this is what you want. Because if you leave, I don't ever want to see you again."

Nate's voice resonated in her head—conflicting warnings telling her to run away *and* stay. She made her decision.

It was done.

Claire didn't remember leaving the house. She didn't recall walking down the driveway to her car, or the curse of despair that came from inside the house as she got into her car and drove away. She barely remembered the stream of city lights flashing by on her way home.

It wasn't until she got back to her apartment that everything hit her.

She was alone. She was strong, and she was going to see all her dreams come true. She was going to be practical and independent, and keep on the path she'd always wanted to travel.

She went into her room and logged into her laptop. A new, shiny batch of orders and inquiries waited for her. With numb determination, she went to work. It was strange how there was no joy in anything she did. There was no sense of excitement, no hope—

Hope.

Claire shoved her laptop away and buried her face in her arms, crying and crying until there was no strength left in her body.

CHAPTER THIRTY-TWO

Claire woke up on the floor beside her laptop. Her neck and shoulders were killing her. Despite the pain, nothing hurt worse than what happened the night before.

She went through the motions like a programmed robot until she was dressed and ready to start her day.

She figured she should be grateful for her business. It was the only thing saving her right now. Baking and decorating and mixing helped suffuse some semblance of comfort into her tortured state of being. She tried as hard as she could to find the joy and hope that had once filled every space of her business, but to no avail. This was probably all normal. It was a rite of passage she had to endure, and it was all part of breaking up.

Claire gasped at the sharp pain elicited by the thought of Nate. Tears stung her eyes again, and a surge of anger went through her. She tried to be strong every moment of her life, and when she was really being tested, all she could do was curl up into a ball and cry alone in her room, feeling sorry for herself. She needed to focus. Her business was her dream. The most important thing in her life.

Wasn't it?

Claire closed her eyes and let out a big sigh of frustration. This was exactly what she meant. She didn't know who she was anymore. Being with Nate confused her and sent her life into a tailspin. He was so intoxicating that he drew her away from her goals and ambitions. He drew her into this fantasy world like a siren tempting sailors with their alluring songs. And for the love of God, Nate was intoxicating. She could spend countless hours gazing deep into his beautiful hazel eyes. What was one of the main tenets of the feminist manifesto? Don't ever choose a man over a career.

She figured all this wallowing was an essential part of the healing process. Post-breakup was the hardest part. All she had to do was survive past it, and things would somehow find a way to go back to normal. Yet, even as she tried to convince herself of all this, she didn't buy it. Her sadness was all-encompassing. It held her captive. It wouldn't let her function, wouldn't let her think. She wanted to go back to Nate and find solace in his embrace, the way she always could, but the practical part of her vied for control—and won.

Feeling a tad bit stronger, she picked up her phone and faced the onslaught of whatever she would find. To her dismay, there was nothing from Nate, but there were multiple missed calls from her mother. She returned the call, and Irene picked up almost right away.

"Hi, Mom, sorry I missed your call. What's up?"

"Anak, you need to go to the hospital now. Something happened to Lola."

The world stopped spinning. Claire had to take a moment to pause—to gather her wits at the worst possible thing that could be happening at this moment. This was the one day she had decided to forgo a visit to Lola, and the guilt was so strong it threatened to bury her. She felt sick to her stomach.

"Is she—is she okay?" Claire asked.

"I don't know, anak," Mom answered. "You need to meet us there now."

• • •

Claire parked at the visitor lot of St. Frances Medical Center. She gripped the steering wheel, telling herself that this was not the time to be weak. Even though evil forces out there conspired to take her grandmother away from her only the day after she lost Nate, she had to hold it together. Be strong for herself and her family.

She walked in through the lobby and was directed to Lola's location. ICU, bed eighteen. The threads holding her together threatened to unravel with every step toward her destination.

The lights, the smells, and the sounds assaulted her. All around her, people were lying in cold, hard beds, with beeping and sighing machines keeping them alive—alerting the nurses how close or far away from death they were. Claire drifted into the ICU as if caught in the web of some horrid dream that wouldn't let her go.

Room eighteen. She heard crying. Recognition dawned as she saw her aunts and uncles crowded into the room and spilling out into the hall. All eyes turned to her when they realized she was there. Claire, Lola's beloved grandchild. The one who visited her every day. The one who brought her books and magazines and watched funny old movies with her because on some level, Claire believed these things broke through the haze of her dementia and gave her a true sense of happiness. As long as Lola sensed the love, that was all that mattered.

A gentle hand grasped her arm, but she didn't look to see who it was. She saw Sam standing in the corner of the room by the window, her face solemn. Dad was there, too, sitting in a chair next to her, listening to something her Uncle Armando was saying. Tita Chriss stood beside the bed, facing Lola and blocking Claire's view. She didn't notice that Claire had entered. Claire stopped in her tracks, afraid to get any closer.

"She's not doing well, mahal ko."

It was her mother grasping her arm, her eyes filled with tears.

"What do you mean?" Claire asked. "What happened to her?"

"They found her unresponsive at the facility and called 911," Mom replied. "The ER doctor said she coded at the hospital. She had a heart attack. They performed CPR and were able to get her back, but..."

"Oh my God," Claire said. "So they were able to revive her."

"Yes, but—"

"There's no but," Claire said forcefully. "We almost lost her, but she's still here. She survived."

Relief coursed through Claire's body as she wove between the members of the family to stand beside Lola's bed. She looked so much more feeble and small with that voluminous gown draped over her. There were so many tubes running meds into her veins she almost looked like the victim of a twisted science experiment. A big plastic tube ran from a breathing machine into her gaping mouth, taking deep breaths on her behalf.

Claire approached and stood beside Tita Chriss as they both looked down into Lola's face. A flickering sense of hope bloomed within Claire. As long as Lola still had a heartbeat and had oxygen flowing into her body, she was still alive. She was still here.

"I didn't know it would happen so soon." Tita Chriss took a small step back and dabbed a tear from the corner of her eye.

"You didn't know what would happen?" Claire asked.

"This," she responded, gesturing to Lola's prone form. "I thought she had at least five more years to live. I was hoping she would live long enough to see my last child graduate from high school."

"There's still a chance," Claire said. "She's still alive. She might come out of this."

Tita Chriss paused, a puzzled look forming on her face.

"Come out of this?" she repeated. "Why in the world would

you say that?"

"Because…she's still breathing," Claire said slowly, irritated at Tita Chriss's attitude. "If we give her some time, she might wake up and recover."

Tita Chriss scoffed.

"Claire, you think she is going to wake up?" she asked. "I'm sorry, anak, but she isn't. Lola is not going to recover anymore."

Fretful stares turned toward Claire. She gulped in trepidation and faced her aunt.

"How do you know she's not going to recover?" she asked. "You need to give her time. We can't give up on her."

"It's not giving up when this is not what she would have wanted," Tita Chriss responded gently. "I take responsibility for this. As her power of attorney, I should have updated her end-of-life wishes, but I got caught up in so many different things, I didn't make it a priority."

"End-of-life wishes?" A knot of dread tightened in her stomach. "What are you talking about?"

"Lola wanted to be a DNR. Do not resuscitate."

Waves of painful shock stunned Claire.

"But the paramedics *did* perform CPR on her. Mom said they did."

"They never should have resuscitated her," Tita Chriss said. "That's what I was talking about, Claire. I never updated the paperwork to show Lola's status as DNR, so by default they were required to perform CPR. Lying here like this with a breathing machine keeping her alive…this is not what Lola would have wanted. In your heart you know this is true, too."

"So what are you saying," Claire demanded. "You're going to remove her breathing tube? You're going to *kill* her?"

"Mahal ko, it's not killing." Mom came up beside her and placed a gentle hand on her arm. "These are Lola's wishes. We have to honor them."

Hot tears burned Claire's eyes as the worst emotions

launched their attack on her. Fear, sadness, regret…she never knew the pain could be this bad.

"No, you can't do this to her," she begged as the tears ran freely. Her aunts and cousins started crying, too. "Please give her a chance, Mom. She's your mother. Our Lola. Don't do this, please."

Claire lost herself to the agony scorching her heart, her body, and soul. She was vaguely aware of arms encircling her, comforting her, and soothing words murmured in her ear. None of it could break through the immense haze of pain.

Hysterical sobs racked Claire's body. Mom, Tita Chriss, and Sam tried to gently guide her to a chair, but she pushed them away.

"When are you going to do this?" Claire asked. "When are you going to pull the plug?"

No one answered. Lola's children simply exchanged silent, bleary-eyed glances that Claire couldn't read.

"Give her two weeks at least," Claire begged. "Two weeks."

Only a few seconds of silence ensued, but it was like an eternity. Claire turned to her aunts and uncles, silently pleading with all her heart to give Lola a fighting chance.

"Okay," Tita Chriss said.

Claire's heart filled with hope as she turned and gave her aunt a fierce hug. In the midst of their adversarial relationship, it was easy to forget that Tita Chriss really did love her and want the best for her. She just showed her emotions in an unconventional way. Her sudden display of affection must have surprised Chriss, but after a brief moment she returned the hug.

"Okay, anak," she said, stroking Claire's hair. "We'll try."

It was hospital policy to allow only one family member to stay the night per patient. Claire's family was kind enough to allow her to be the one to stay with Lola.

The staff set up a little cot for her to sleep in against the wall. Claire sat on it, her knees tucked beneath her chin, as she watched the slow rhythm of the breathing machine. She had lost all track of time as the night progressed. Her mind raced with memories of Lola, and little dreams where Lola recovered within the two weeks and moved back into her facility, and things went back to the way they were.

"Knock-knock."

Claire looked up. Ro stood in the doorway, her eyes glistening.

"You made it," Claire said.

"It's almost four in the morning," Ro said, entering the room. "You should be sleeping. You look so tired."

"I can't sleep," she said. "I'm afraid if I go to sleep, Lola might stop breathing, or something."

"She's not going to stop breathing." Ro sighed wearily and settled onto a chair near her sister. "As long as that machine keeps going, so will Lola."

"Did Mom tell you everything over the phone?" Claire asked.

"Pretty much."

"When they first told me they were going to pull the plug, I went berserk," Claire said. "I don't know what came over me. I just wasn't prepared. But now that I've had some time to think, I understand the rationale. Lola was a strong woman, and I know she wouldn't want to live this way. But it drives me crazy wondering, 'what-if.' What if there was a chance she was going to recover? I mean, she already beat the odds when CPR brought her back to life. To me, that's a sign she's not ready to go yet."

Ro turned to take a good long look at her grandmother.

"I don't know, Ate," she finally replied. "I hope Lola survives, but it's not looking good."

"Of course the outcome looks grim, but it doesn't mean I'm

going to give up all hope."

"Where is Nate?" Ro asked, looking around the room. "Why isn't he here with you?"

The mention of his name twisted the knife in Claire's heart all over again. She did not want to be reminded of the other thing in her life she lost.

"He's flying out to New York," Claire replied.

"Did you tell him what happened to Lola?"

"No."

Worry bloomed in Ro's stare. Claire averted her eyes, even though she knew Ro sensed something was very wrong.

"Are you two doing okay?" Ro asked.

Claire's throat tightened. She couldn't bring herself to speak. Ro left her seat and sat beside Claire on the cot.

"Ate, what happened?"

Claire started to cry again.

"I left him. Ro, I couldn't stand the thought of giving up my dreams and my career to earn a place in his life. We weren't compatible, so I left. Do you think I'm stupid? Was this the worst mistake I ever made? Because even though it seems like the right decision—the practical choice—why does it feel like I'm falling apart? Tell me, Ro. Was I wrong? Why do I keep doing this to myself?"

Ro didn't answer. Instead, she wrapped her arms around her big sister and hugged her with all the fierceness her small body could muster. Claire clung to Ro and cried. She was in so much agony, it was impossible to believe she'd ever be happy again.

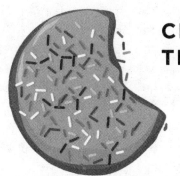

CHAPTER THIRTY-THREE

Five days later

Lola's favorite flowers were tiger lilies and dendrobium orchids. The church was full of them. They were woven into wreaths displayed at the altar. They were draped in graceful garland arrangements along the pews and down the aisles. Stunningly carved artistic glass vases filled with the most beautiful arrangements were displayed throughout the entire space, making the church seem alive and vibrant with the spirit of the woman that a hundred people had gathered to celebrate.

Carmelita Lorenzo Ilagan passed away five days ago. A few hours after Ro arrived at the hospital, she and Claire had drifted off to sleep. During that time, Lola suffered from a seizure and her heart simply gave out. There was no use for the breathing machine at that point. Claire watched in helpless horror as the nurses started the morphine drip and disconnected her breathing tube with a finality that made her heart shatter.

Claire had never mourned the death of anyone close to her before. It was a nightmare she couldn't wake up from. It consumed every moment and crowded out her normal life— even her business. She couldn't bring herself to even log on to *Eclectix* or bake anything, which was not like her at all.

She thought losing her grandmother was the worst pain she could imagine, but she discovered it wasn't true. Lola's death hit her harder than she expected because…she was mourning two losses at the same time, an event that no amount of warning could ever make her feel prepared for.

The crowd of attendants started to stream into the church. Claire stood outside in the shade of an old sycamore tree on the front lawn, thankful for the dark sunglasses hiding her swollen eyes. She was sick and tired of everyone asking where Nate was, and the shower of compliments at the flowers he'd sent. She was tired of pretending everything was okay when her whole world was burning down.

"Ate," Ro whispered, leaning in close. "Are you mad at me for telling Nate about Lola?"

Claire didn't respond. It was too hard to find the right words nowadays.

"I didn't know he was going to send all these flowers," Ro said. "He's amazing."

Claire's throat tightened as she fought the tears. Nate's tribute to Lola moved her beyond words. If Lola could see the beautiful flowers he had sent for her, she would instantly fall in love with him. Even after Claire left him, he still took his duty to her family seriously, and it made her feel like the most horrible person on the planet.

"You're not talking to me." Ro nodded in acknowledgment. "I understand you're pissed, but try to hide it because you're not going to believe who's here."

A car door slammed shut. She turned and saw Nate standing on the sidewalk as Craig drove away. Her heart went into shock as her vision drank in the pure splendor of his form, clad in an immaculate black suit that flattered his broad shoulders and athletic build. A pair of dark sunglasses obscured his gaze, and he wasted no time before heading straight to Claire.

She forced her legs to stand strong as he approached. He offered respectful greetings to her parents, aunts, and uncles. He greeted Sam and Ro. And then he was there, standing before Claire.

"I—I thought you were in New York," she said.

Nate's lips lifted in a humorless grin.

"I was."

Those were his only words as he offered his arm to Claire. They walked together into the church for the funeral service. She could feel the tension in Nate's body through the touch of his arm. This was not the joyful, hopeful man filled with humor and goodwill Claire once knew. No. This was a man devoid of everything that made him who he was. He was a beast of Claire's own making, and it made her want to cry all over again.

The funeral service crawled forward, each agonizing minute stretching out to what seemed like hours. The entire time, Nate sat patiently beside Claire, not saying a single word. Every part of him was dutiful, from his silent engagement during the mass and eulogy, to the last minute when he paid his respects to Lola in her open casket.

The crowd of attendants started streaming out of the church, and Claire lost sight of Nate. Guests offered her condolences, but she only half listened as she struggled through the crowd to find him.

"Ate, did you see where Nate went?" Claire tried not to sound panicked as she grabbed on to Sam's wrist.

"Ow, Claire, take it easy," Sam said. "He left already. I saw him get into a car a minute ago."

Claire stepped back, her hand lightly pressed to her chest. She should have known he wasn't going to stay for her. He was here for Lola. He was here to pay his respects because that was the kind of person he was.

Sam must have seen and understood the emotions in Claire's eyes. Her face softened and she took Claire into the gentle embrace of her arms. They stood there together for a long time as Claire took comfort in the solace that only her big sister could give her.

...

The laughter of children rang through the house as Claire's young cousins chased each other down the hall.

Claire had wanted nothing more than to go home after the funeral. She wanted to crawl into bed and fall into a dreamless sleep, except she would wake up in the past before everything got messed up.

But she couldn't. After the funeral, there was a big family gathering. The proper term was "celebration of life party," but she could not bring herself to call it that. All her relatives were at Tita Chriss's estate in Rancho Palos Verdes. There was plenty of food and drink for everyone. There was a karaoke machine set up in the living room, but so far no one could decide on what song to sing. Separate poker and mah-jongg tables were set up on the patio for those who wanted a semblance of normalcy during this somber occasion.

Then came torture in the form of the following questions:

Where's Nate?

What happened to Nate? Is he coming?

What's Nate doing right now?

How is the acquisition? How much money did he make from that?

Claire kept the frustration bottled up inside, along with the truth. It wasn't her relatives' fault. Their curiosity was only natural, but it made things a million times harder.

"Ate, do you want me to stay with you?" Ro asked. "I don't mind."

"Me too." Sam gave Claire's elbow a reassuring squeeze. It was a gesture she used to do when they were kids, and it filled Claire with a sense of warmth and comfort. "We'll stick by your side so we can deflect all these intrusive questions."

"Oh no, that's not necessary." Claire managed a weak smile. "I'll be fine. Please go and mingle. I know you all have a lot of catching up to do. I'm going to hide out in one of the rooms for a few minutes. I'll be fine. I promise."

"Don't leave, okay?" Ro asked. "If you do have to leave, let me know and I can take you home."

Claire nodded. Her sisters drifted off to mingle with their relatives and guests. Claire took that opportunity to head into the nearest empty room she could find—the laundry room. She closed the door and leaned her back against it. Now she felt safe enough to let her wall of strength collapse. As it crumbled, her body sagged in relief. She bowed her head and allowed herself to cry again.

That was when she made a startling discovery.

The pain of Lola's death defied explanation. There were not enough words to describe the depth of sorrow and loss. It was as if she lost a piece of her past—the part that anchored her to earth and served as her foundation. But Lola was ninety-three. She'd lived a long, fulfilling life. She'd raised eight children and seen the birth of her grandchildren. She even lived long enough to see five great-grandchildren born. But these tears, all the turmoil tearing up her soul into shreds—it was all because of Nate.

She released a ragged sigh and pressed her hand to her heart as if she could staunch the sadness bleeding from it. Why had she left him? It had all made sense at the time: it was the practical thing to do, and she didn't want to choose between him and her career. But some dark, uncomfortable part of her was filled with doubt. With every passing day, the question of whether or not she made a grave mistake loomed bigger and bigger until it threatened to block out every ray of light from her life.

Claire stood there for a long time, letting the silence and minutes tumble past her. It was time to face the music. She had two choices. Either she could let this moment destroy her...or she could make the best of it. Be strong for once in her life, and try turning her trials into opportunities. She logged on to her *Eclectix* app and saw a message that made her heart leap up into her throat.

Hello Claire

Sorry to slide into your DMs. I am getting married in Costa Rica in four weeks. I'm a veteran wedding planner myself, but none of my contacts has availability on such short notice (I do see the irony here, LOL). Since it's short notice, I am willing to compensate you accordingly. I will need at least five hundred custom cookies to be wrapped and shipped to Costa Rica, plus any other kind of dessert that can survive the trip. I will need to know in 24 hours. Thanks and sorry once again for the late notice.

Sincerely, Beatrice Cho

This was it. Maybe the gods were smiling down on her after all. Even after her first huge client was wrenched away, another one came along...with an even bigger order. And the fact that this client was a wedding planner? If Claire could fulfill this order and do a great job, she'd open the door to an immense wedding and event network that could boost her career farther than she'd ever dreamed.

Claire typed up a response and hit send. She didn't think twice.

Hi Beatrice,

Yes, I would be happy to commit to filling your order for you. I will reach out to you tomorrow with the contract and details.

Claire spent a few minutes putting herself together, physically and mentally, before she emerged from the laundry room. Head held high, she strode through the house and headed outdoors to her favorite part of the property: the gazebo and flower garden in a very secluded part of the backyard. Even though the house was full of guests, Claire didn't want to mingle. Strangely, the huge new client she'd gained didn't really put the skip in her step like she was expecting.

"Claire! Wait up."

She paused in her trek across the lawn as Sam jogged over to her.

"Where are you going?" Sam asked.

"I just wanted to sit in the gazebo."

"I'll go with you," she said. "I need to tell you something." They headed to the gazebo and sat down across from one another.

"This isn't easy for me to say," Sam began. "But I know when I'm wrong. I owe you an apology for this past year. While Dylan and I were going through the divorce, I wasn't the nicest person. I distanced myself from you and Ro. Instead of dealing with everything in a healthy way, I started throwing around blame rather than taking responsibility. You even tried to help me, but instead of being grateful, I shut you down."

"Thanks, but didn't you apologize about this already?" Claire asked.

"Yes, but it bears repeating." Sam paused and took a deep breath. "And there's no excuse for how I treated you when I found out about you and Nate. I'm your big sister. I should have been more supportive and encouraging, but I wasn't. Looking back, I can see how I might have been...a little bit jealous of you. It's because when I saw you and Nate together, and listened to the way you talked about him, it was clear that you two were serious about one another. Even more than that, I saw the love between you two. The real kind of love that everyone looks for, but might never find in their lifetime. I'm ashamed to admit this, but I was angry and jealous that you had found that kind of love with Nate after only a few months, when Dylan and I had been together for six years, and we ended up in divorce."

The distant strains of *Truly Madly Deeply* by Savage Garden came drifting across the vast backyard as one of the party guests·finally settled on a karaoke song that would be the least offensive during this occasion.

"That's why when you told me you left Nate, it took me a while to come up with a response. As your big sister, I'm going to give you my unsolicited opinion. I think you are too hard on yourself. You get so caught up in ideas, and it puts you in this rigid frame of mind that backfires on you. Yes, you're driven and passionate, but you have to see the big picture. I know you're sad about losing Lola, but that's not why you're crying. You love Nate. You two were perfect for each other. Why would you leave him?"

It took a moment for Claire to recover. Sam and apologies? The two concepts were not synonymous. It was practically a miracle she'd apologized a few weeks ago, but to voice regret again? Claire didn't think there was anything more rare than a miracle, but Sam proved her wrong.

"First of all, it's not easy being a relationship when I have you and Ro as my siblings," Claire said, finally finding her voice after all this time. "You two have to weigh in on every single thing, especially all the imperfections. Remember what you guys said about my high school boyfriend? And the guys I dated in college? Don't look so innocent. You got into my head about all of them and made me doubt and question everything."

"Even the spiritual cleanser guy?" Sam asked incredulously. "You really needed an outside party to tell you he wasn't right for you?"

"That's exactly what I mean," Claire replied. "Ro said he was the one for me, you said he wasn't…every guy I brought home was subject to all of your little judgments and it drove me up the wall. I couldn't deal with it. It's one of the reasons it was hard for me to get serious about dating…because no one was ever good enough. The chase was never worth the reward."

"So now you're blaming me and Ro for your failed relationships?" Sam asked, her brow cocked.

"Of course not," Claire said gently. "I know it sounds that way, but...all I'm trying to say is that I need you and Ro to be more supportive of me. From now on. What you said earlier about being a big sister...I loved it. That's what's been missing this entire time, and I appreciate you being there for me. But please—I need you and Ro to respect my wishes and relationships from now on. No more judgments and nit-picking."

"Agreed," Sam said. "You'll have to give Ro this whole spiel when you see her again."

"No she won't."

Claire and Sam whipped their heads toward Ro, who suddenly emerged from behind a bush. She bounded up the gazebo steps and threw her arms around her sisters.

"What in the world was that?" Claire demanded, her voice straining at Ro's intense hug.

"Sorry for snooping, but I couldn't help it," Ro said as she finally released them. "I saw you two headed over here for a private moment, and I wanted to know what was going on."

"You never answered my question," Sam said, fixing her gaze on Claire. "I know this is hard to talk about, but you have to face this. Why did you leave Nate?"

Their wide-eyed stares of anticipation practically suffocated Claire. She had very good reasons for leaving Nate, all of them focusing on being pragmatic and brave. But for some strange reason, the words wouldn't come out the way she wanted them to.

"His world and mine—they weren't meant to be," Claire said. "It was scary just letting him sweep me away from everything. Allowing myself to fall for Nate this hard and this fast...it reminded me I can't be weak anymore. I have to be stronger than that."

A look of intensity stole into Sam's eyes.

"Weak?" Sam scoffed. "Claire, you are anything *but* weak. You're honest, and true, and reliable. Do you think Lola would have survived as long as she did without you? She's been sick for a long time, but you gave her the will to keep on going. You made life worth living after Lolo died. You never abandoned her. You were with her until the very end, and you never, ever gave up on her. I don't want to hear you call yourself weak ever again. You're my little sister, but you're the strongest person I know. And if there is anyone who can manage it all: the career of her dreams and the love of her life, all at the same time, it's you."

Sam's words sucked the air out of Claire's lungs. Not only was Sam back to her wise, advice-giving self, but she was a source of validation. Claire had no clue anyone looked at her this way. Claire had fought for bravery and fearlessness, and it turned out it was in her all along.

"Hey, is everything okay with you girls?"

The three Ventura sisters looked up. Their mom approached with a cautious smile on her face.

"Yes," Claire said, dabbing away more tears. "We'll be okay."

"I know this is very hard for you, anak," Mom said as she took a seat next to Claire. "You were the closest to Lola. At least you know she is at peace now."

Mom paused as she reached for something tucked into the waistband of her slacks. She produced three worn envelopes and handed one each to her daughters.

"What is this?" Claire asked, examining the envelope.

"Gifts from your Lola," Mom replied. "These are letters she wrote to each of her grandkids a long time ago."

Claire flipped the envelope over and saw her name written in black sharpie across it. Her heart started racing at the sight of her name in Lola's handwriting.

"Oh my God," Claire whispered. "This is incredible."

"Lola actually wrote letters to all thirty of her grandkids?" Sam asked in disbelief.

"Well, by the time the youngest cousins were born, she was

already too old to write them letters," Mom explained. "You older ones are lucky because you all got letters."

"Where did you find these?" Claire asked.

"Lola kept them inside a wooden treasure chest," Mom replied. "A few months ago when we were cleaning out the house to sell it, I took the letters for safe-keeping. Lola wanted me to distribute them after she passed away."

"Wait...what did you say?" Claire's jaw dropped at the astounding news. "You mean, she had a real treasure chest full of letters to her grandkids from beyond the grave?"

"Yes."

Claire sat back, stunned. She reached back in time, dredging up the painful memory of Lola's empty treasure chest. It turned out Lola's ramblings weren't meaningless, and she was capable of fleeting moments of clarity. Clutching the old letter to her chest, Claire finally had the closure she needed. Even though Alzheimer's ravaged Lola's mind, there was still a glimmer of her true self within that Claire had never given up on. She gently tore open the envelope and removed the letter.

March 30

Dearest Maria Clara,

You are only 7 yrs old when I write this letter but already you are my favorite. I give you $10 per A grade, and everyone else gets only 50% of that. (It's our secret, do not tell anyone!!)

Thank you for being such a loving child. This is always what I remember of you, even if it is no longer apparent as I grow old.

Do not ever forget that you deserve so many things.

You deserve love and happiness. You do not have to choose.

When your prince charming comes along, and I promise you he will, let him sweep you off your feet. I found my prince 50 years ago. Even though Lolo is in heaven now, I have memories of love and my beautiful children and grandchildren to remind me of him.

I love you forever, my darling.

Be good to your sisters, and most importantly, be good to yourself.

And lastly, do not live a life of regret.

Hugs and Kisses,

Lola

Claire drew a sweet, deep breath into her lungs. She turned her eyes skyward where the blues had long since faded to a deep gray. She imagined Lola high above, looking down on her family, showering them with endless love. Lola's presence was so strong it chased away all the shadows of doubt, shedding light on everything that had been obscure up until then.

Do not live a life of regret.

Lola knew the secret to life. It was up to Claire to make the best of it and follow Lola's words of wisdom.

"I made a mistake," Claire said. "I messed up, and I need to get Nate back. Now."

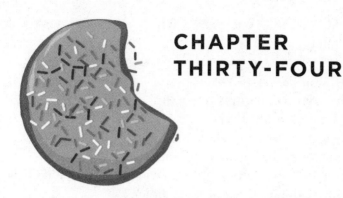

CHAPTER THIRTY-FOUR

Claire went into full-on strategy mode. She had to track Nate down, but his schedule was a mystery. The last she heard, he was in New York on business. He also had press conferences and an award ceremony to attend. She could sit there and stare off into space, wondering about the different possibilities of what could happen, or she could pull her head out of her ass and find out from the source.

She called Nate.

There was no answer.

Claire bit back a curse of frustration. The celebration of life party had been going on for hours. It was dark outside now, with only a few dim lanterns casting soft yellow light across the shadows. Most of her relatives were still inside Tita Chriss's house, but everyone had stopped pretending to be shy and were fighting over who got to sing karaoke next. "Hey Jude" started playing for what had to be the tenth time that night, and everybody groaned.

"Not again!" someone shouted.

"Shut up, it's a good song," came the retort.

"How goes it, Claire-Bear?" Todd asked as he ambled up to the gazebo with a heaping plate of pancit in his hands. Ro was also in tow, and they both took a seat near Claire as they munched on their food.

Suddenly the phone rang. Claire gasped and answered immediately.

"Nate?"

"It's Sam."

"Oh." Claire's heart plummeted.

"You're still in the backyard?"

"Yes."

"You haven't gotten ahold of Nate yet?"

"No. This is so frustrating. I even called his assistant, Craig, a few times, and he didn't pick up, either."

"So you really have no idea where Nate could be?"

"He could literally be anywhere," Claire wailed. "I'm just going to keep calling until one of them picks up."

"When you find out where he is, let me know," Sam said. "I'll be more than happy to help you pay for the trip."

"Thank you," Claire said. "I love you so much, Ate."

She said goodbye and started calling Nate again. After a few more tries, the phone stopped ringing and started going straight to voicemail. Not a good sign.

"Ate, what's going on?" Ro asked. "Did he hang up on you?"

"No, but I think he blocked me," Claire replied, dialing again.

"That's so rude," Ro said.

"The girl smashed his heart into a million pieces," Todd remarked. "Of course he's bitter." His eyes filled with contrition at her death-glare. "Sorry, Claire-Bear."

Voicemail again. Claire was not in a good place. Her fingers kept hitting Nate's number and coming up with the same result.

"Claire, honey, maybe you should take a break," Todd said with an alarmed look on his face. "Give me your phone for a minute. Let me and Ro help you."

"No, I'm fine," Claire said, dialing Craig's number this time.

"Mrs. Noruta."

Claire was so shocked at hearing Craig's voice she almost

dropped the phone.

"Craig? Oh my God, Craig, it's you. Thank God you picked up, I was trying to—"

"The only reason I answered is to ask you to stop calling," Craig interrupted, his voice firm. "You've made your feelings toward Mr. Noruta very clear. He's asked me to relay the message to you to stop calling."

"Wait, you spoke to him?" Claire said, heedless of Craig's request. "I am begging you. Please, let me talk to him. I've made the biggest mistake of my life and I have to let him know how I feel."

"Goodbye, Mrs. Noruta."

"Craig, do *not hang up on me.*"

Todd and Ro gaped at Claire. Her heart fluttered at an astonishing rate. She'd never yelled like that before, but it must have worked because Craig was still there. Either that, or he was still in shock at being rendered deaf.

"This is critical." Claire forced her voice back to normal. "I need to talk to Nate. Better yet, I have to see him again. Where is he?"

Silence. Icy fear ran down Claire's spine.

"Hello? Craig? Are you still there?"

And then...a weary sigh.

"I'm not at liberty to tell you his location," Craig replied. "I shouldn't even be talking to you right now."

"But I—"

"Do you have any idea what you've done to him? Mr. Noruta is one of the most generous, selfless people I've ever met. They're rare qualities for people in his position. It wasn't easy seeing how he was after you left. I know you're still his wife, and I respect that, but I will never understand how you could do this to him."

A lump swelled in Claire's throat. She fought for words, but none came to her.

"I just sent you an article about Mr. Noruta's recent trip to New York," Craig said. "Take a look at it."

Claire's hands trembled as she opened the link Craig had texted to her. It was a short online article about Nate winning an award. There was a photo of him accepting the award, and below the picture was a blurb that read: *Nate Noruta, CEO and founder of MyConnect, accepting the Humanitarian of the Year Award from the Universal Foundation. Through his acceptance speech he announced the new Carmelita Ilagan fund for the Alzheimer's Association, the cause for which he donated a staggering $1 million.*

"Oh. My. God," Claire whispered.

"What happened?" Todd demanded

"Is everything okay?" Ro asked, eyes wide with concern.

Claire had to take a few seconds to calm herself down. It shouldn't have surprised her. Nate was...a wonder. A miracle she let go. She put the phone back up to her ear.

"Please, Craig," she whispered. "I have to see Nate. I have to fix the mistake I made. I love him, and I don't want to go on another day without him."

"I can't tell you where he is. I'm forbidden." Craig's voice was firm, but Claire could hear a crack forming in his armor.

"This isn't about you or me," Claire said. "It's about Nate. It's about making all the wrongs right again. I am ready to drop everything, leave everything behind...to be with him. I have to show him that I'm willing to make sacrifices for him, just like he does for me."

Craig heaved a deep sigh.

"He's going to kill me," he groaned.

"He will not kill you," Claire said. "I give you my word. Tell me where he is. I will go to him right now."

"Mr. Noruta is en route to Eastern Europe," Craig replied. "He was going to surprise you with a trip there for your honeymoon."

Claire gasped. She immediately knew where Nate was headed.

"Cappadocia," she murmured. "Thank you, Craig. You've been amazing. I know how hard that must have been for you. I'll find a way to get there ASAP."

"Wait a minute," Craig warned. "You're planning on going there all alone?"

"Of course. My sister Sam will help me pay for the ticket. Don't worry."

"Do you really think Mr. Noruta would be happy if he found out I sent you off to Turkey all by yourself?" Craig asked. "There's no way I can do that. I'll arrange everything. He can't know you're planning on meeting him there. If he does, I'm afraid he won't want to see you, and on top of that he'll fire me. I promised I'd keep his location a secret, and here I am, breaking my word. But I believe in you. Many people care about Mr. Noruta and his well-being. I can't make any promises that this will go in your favor but...in my heart, I believe you're doing the right thing."

Warm emotions welled up in Claire's chest.

"Aw, Craig," she said. "You're so sweet. I'm so lucky to have you on my side."

"You're welcome," he said, his tone gentler now. "Give me a few minutes to arrange everything. I think our best bet would be to take Turkish Airlines out of LAX. It's a seventeen-hour flight, and there's usually a layover in Istanbul."

Claire arranged to meet Craig over at Nate's house in Los Feliz. When she finally hung up the phone, she felt like she'd just been whisked off by a tornado. Her thoughts tumbled around in chaos, and her emotions whipped in a frenzy inside her belly. Todd and Ro stared up at her as if they were watching the most dramatic scene unfold before their eyes.

"Did Nate change his mind?" Ro asked hopefully. "He wants you back, right?"

Claire shook her head.

"No," she said, her voice filled with determination. "But I need to let him know how sorry I am. I need to let him know...I was wrong."

The twenty-four hours it took to finally get on the flight to Turkey was the longest day of Claire's life. Even during the exceedingly long plane ride, as Craig dozed on and off nearby, Claire couldn't sleep. Not when every nerve in her body was crackling with excitement and nervous energy at seeing Nate again.

She kept replaying the scene over and over in her mind. Nate would be there, his fine self standing in the distance with the pale brown hills of Cappadocia surrounding him, oblivious to her presence. She would square her shoulders, take a deep breath, and walk up to him. He'd see her, his face would light up, and they'd fall into each other's arms, their lips locking in a passionate kiss rivaling Princess Buttercup and Westley in that iconic scene at the end of *The Princess Bride*.

A grating snore pierced through Claire's reverie.

It was fitting, really, because Claire knew that the likelihood of the real-life scene matching the imaginary one in her head was very, very low. Worst-case scenario? Nate would see her, glare, and storm off, immediately hopping on one of his private jets and hightailing it to whatever part of the planet was farthest away from her.

She wouldn't give up. The pain of a thousand cuts was nothing compared to the possibility that Nate would reject her, but then she thought about how much she'd hurt him when she left, and she allowed herself to feel that pain again.

The flight literally and figuratively flew by. It was amazing how mental anguish could make the time zip past you like a streak of lightning. When they touched down in Istanbul for the layover, it was nighttime.

The bright lights and sweeping modern architecture of the terminal weren't enough to brighten the dark shadow of Claire's sorrow. Even though Craig was traveling with her, she had never felt more alone. Not only was she mourning over Lola, she kept torturing herself with the possibility that Nate truly didn't want her. What if…he'd lost complete faith in her?

What if he didn't love her anymore?

The loss was great and infinite, shocking her senses. To imagine a world without Nate's all-encompassing love…it was too much to bear.

Right when Claire took a seat on the connecting flight to Kayseri, she couldn't hold it in anymore. She promised herself she was done crying because she'd shed enough tears in the past week to last a lifetime, but she couldn't help it.

"Mrs. Noruta," Craig said, his voice filled with such pity it made Claire cry even harder. "It's okay. Everything will be okay."

"No it won't," Claire sobbed. "We both know…it's not going to be okay."

Craig didn't respond. Claire curled up in her seat and pressed herself against the window, feeling the thread of hope tying her to Nate slipping away through her fingers.

It took an hour and a half to fly from Istanbul to Kayseri Airport. Afterward, Claire and Craig hopped on a bus bound for Goreme, a historic town at the heart of the Cappadocia region. During the bus ride, Claire finally slept. It was only for an hour, but she needed the reprieve.

It was exhausting being strong. Nate was an expert on

maintaining hope, but Claire didn't know how to do it when she was drained of everything that made her happy. How could she be hopeful when there was a good chance Nate had already given up hope on them for good?

Craig and Claire disembarked once the bus reached its destination. It was late morning, and the summer heat was building. Cornflower-blue skies framed the striking brown hills and stately architecture that spoke of innovation and beauty born from this ancient civilization's will to survive persecution. Claire felt the magic and history of the place imbuing her skin. Sadness flowed in right after, swift and sure, at the thought of experiencing this place without Nate by her side.

"Mrs. Noruta, you need to focus."

The fuzziness in Claire's head dissipated for a moment. The intense look in Craig's eyes startled her, and she forced herself to concentrate.

"Let's go over the plan one more time. I also emailed you all the details," Craig went on. "I arranged for you to stay here at the Dazi Hotel, while Mr. Noruta is staying at the one right across the plaza from you."

"Where are you staying?" Claire asked.

"At the Hilton on the opposite end of town," he replied. "Remember. It is absolutely crucial he doesn't know you're here. He wanted to be alone. The whole reason he came here was to try to get over you and start fresh. I don't know what you're planning to do, but whatever it is, make sure your timing is spot-on."

"When is he leaving?"

"I don't know," Craig replied. "He's pretty much gone off the grid. He's not in contact with anyone, and he won't contact me unless it's an emergency. He wants to be left alone. You'll have to find a way. You've got this, Mrs. Noruta."

Claire watched Craig leave. Her sadness was like a lead weight on her body, freezing all her joints, but she forced herself to move and finally check into the hotel. After settling into her room, she emerged again in her full disguise—light beige sweatpants, a loose, long-sleeved white shirt, with a pink bandana over her hair, and a facemask. She donned a large pair of shiny black sunglasses and struck out into the heat, hoping she'd be lucky enough to find Nate sooner rather than later.

The dryness made the heat somewhat more bearable. She would have preferred to wear shorts and a tank top, but she didn't want to risk Nate recognizing her. As tourists and citizens milled about the town, Claire took Craig's advice to heart and honed in on her mission: track Nate, learn his routine, and determine the best time and way in which to confront him. Then, if he didn't immediately turn his back on her, she'd apologize and confess her love.

She set herself up at an outdoor café a few doors down from the entrance of Nate's hotel. Posing as a casual tourist, she took out her laptop and placed it on the table, ordered tea, and took out the pair of binoculars Craig had loaned her. She felt absolutely ridiculous in her getup, spying on the entrance to Nate's hotel, but she didn't know what else to do.

After about an hour or so of observing, Claire still hadn't seen Nate come out of the hotel. Maybe he was already out and about exploring the town, or perhaps he could still be in his room resting? In any case, Claire couldn't risk overstaying her welcome at the café, and she decided to start packing up to gather her intel elsewhere.

A sudden flurry of movement at Nate's hotel entrance drew Claire's attention. She paused as a small crowd of people streamed out of the entrance. The very last person to exit the hotel was Nate. He was wearing a baseball cap and sunglasses, but she recognized him immediately. Her heart caught in her throat, then plummeted to smash in pieces at her feet.

He wasn't alone. A stunningly beautiful woman in a gorgeous red dress walked beside him, smiling and laughing.

CHAPTER THIRTY-FIVE

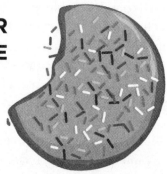

One of her worst fears was coming true.

Nate had moved on already. He found a gorgeous woman to love and adore him and fulfill his every fantasy without any of her insecurities or anxieties getting in the way of their happiness.

Claire held the binoculars up with trembling hands, forcing herself to watch them even though it hurt more than anything. Nate and the woman paused for a moment, exchanging a few pleasant words. Afterward, the woman waved farewell and headed back inside the hotel, but not before greeting other guests and exchanging pleasantries with them.

Oh. It was looking more and more like the woman was an employee at the hotel, and not Nate's clandestine lover he had replaced Claire with on what was supposed to be their honeymoon.

With a grunt of frustration, Claire packed away her belongings in her knapsack, left money for the bill, and hurried after Nate. She had lost him momentarily in her jealous delusions, but she spotted him again. It looked like he was going on a hike in the valley alone. Claire slowed her pace a bit, keeping a close eye on him. It was going to be difficult trailing him unnoticed. He'd be sure to notice some stalker girl following him on the remote trail if she continued following him.

Instead, she tracked him on foot for as long as she could

before he disappeared past a copse of trees in the valley between two large hills. Claire turned and scrambled back up a pathway leading up to a popular vantage point where a small crowd had gathered to do some sightseeing.

The word "stunning" didn't do any justice to the beauty of this place. Breathtaking. Majestic. Even still, these words barely scraped the surface of Cappadocia; its natural rock formations and shadowy forests making it look like the portal to an enchanted world.

Claire stepped up to the railing of the vantage point and trained her binoculars at the part of the valley where she had lost Nate. It took only a minute to see him again, continuing his hike deeper into the valley.

She lowered her binoculars, losing sight of him. Even though she wanted nothing more than to run after him, she left him alone in peace. She had to have faith that she would find the right moment to approach him, and when she did, she prayed with all her might he wouldn't turn her away.

The sun set late in the evening. By the time the soft glow of golden lights began to wash through the city, Claire's hope had dwindled to almost nothing.

Nate had returned from his hike a few hours after he'd taken off. All the while, he was alone. He retreated back into his hotel alone, emerged again after freshening up, and headed off outside the city again to another part of the valley filled with remarkable rock formations called Fairy Chimneys. That time, Claire was able to trail him farther because there were more people in this area, allowing her to blend in better.

Nate seemed to be...fine. He carried himself as though there was nothing wrong, appearing to enjoy his surroundings and solitude in his favorite place in the world.

Claire figured she shouldn't be surprised. Craig had told her Nate's objective was to move past her and try to heal from the damage she'd done to him. And it was quite strange to see him all alone. He'd always been an extrovert, drawn to people and craving human contact, whether it be conversation or education. He drew life and excitement from people, and others felt the same from him. To see him so alone, and trying his best to cut off ties from everyone...it unsettled Claire and made her feel lower than she'd ever been.

Even toward nightfall, solitude was the theme of the day for Nate. He had spent hours in the valley, immersing himself in nature. Afterward, he headed over to the Open-Air Museum and Kaymakli where he explored the ancient cave cities for a few more hours. Claire ached to be there beside him, holding his hand as they squeezed through the underground passages where ancient Christians hid to flee persecution from the Romans. She dreamed of hiking through the valleys and forests with him, exploring these beautiful places together—of the countless adventures they had waiting for them for the rest of their lives.

Claire's heart squeezed in agony. She had made a vow to Nate, and she'd broken it in the worst way. She was so focused on being strong, she lost sight of what she was being strong for. And now, the only thing she could see before her was a bleak path where she'd single-handedly destroyed every hope and dream they'd built before them the night they'd gotten married on the judge's front doorstep.

"Are you okay, madam?"

The waiter's voice startled her, and Claire jumped in her seat. She was sitting at the same café she'd been at earlier, trying in vain to enjoy the beauty of the Cappadocian night while waiting for Nate to emerge from his hotel.

"Oh yes," she replied, forcing on a smile even though she wore her mask. "I'm fine."

The waiter nodded at her and moved on.

Claire forced herself to look more relaxed. He'd probably been alarmed because she hadn't moved at all for a long time, and hadn't touched any of the food or tea she'd ordered. She grimaced after taking a sip of the tea, which had gone cold.

Nate suddenly emerged from the hotel. Claire sat up, watching intently as he headed over to...her location. She made sure her hair covering and mask were in place, and tried to be as nonchalant as possible, even though her blood simmered in response to his proximity. She breathed a sigh of relief as she realized his destination was the bar next door, and not the café itself.

He started up a conversation with the bartender as he ordered a drink. Claire would have given anything to be close by—to hear his voice and see what was making him smile, but she forced herself to stay calm and patient. For now, she was content to just watch him from afar, and hope he was finding some kind of peace from the turmoil she had caused in his life. Was there any way she could convince him he could trust her? That she was worthy of a second chance?

The horror of their breakup replayed itself in her mind automatically. She forced the thoughts away as Nate took a sip of his drink. After a few minutes, he finished his drink and headed back to his hotel.

The fatigue started to get the better of Claire, and she decided to rest for a while before emerging again. Time was slipping away, and she still had no idea how to even approach Nate. Craig had offered a few ideas, but she wasn't sure any of them were going to work.

She watched Nate enter the hotel. After a few moments of numb silence, she paid the bill for her untouched food and retreated back to her room.

...

Claire awoke, disoriented after her dreamless sleep. She couldn't figure out why she'd woken up so abruptly, but she was glad she'd gotten some shut-eye. Her plan was to sit on the rooftop lounge area of the hotel, where she would have a great vantage point of the plaza in front of Nate's hotel. Once morning came, she'd head back down to the café and resume her observation once again. Rubbing the tiredness from her eyes, she glanced at the clock.

It was half-past four a.m.

"Holy shit!"

Claire shot up from the bed and raced to the bathroom. After freshening up in record time, she threw her belongings in her knapsack and bolted out of the room. She'd only meant to doze for an hour or two, but according to the clock she'd slept for almost eight hours.

She raced up the steps to the rooftop. Perhaps it was silly flying into a panic. There was no rhyme or reason to anything she was doing. All she had was this plan, and sleeping past her scheduled time felt like she had failed again somehow. She had just reached the rooftop when her phone rang.

"Hello?"

"Mrs. Noruta, I have something to tell you."

Craig's voice sounded strange, as if it was difficult for him to force out the words. Fresh fear gathered in Claire's chest like a swarm of bees.

"What is it?" she asked.

"Mr. Noruta isn't there," Craig replied. "He left for the airport an hour ago."

"What?" Claire cried. "Why didn't you tell me?"

"Mr. Noruta didn't inform me until a minute ago," Craig answered, his voice filled with remorse. "He called and told me he was at the airport and arranged for me to pick him up at LAX when his flight arrived home. I have to leave now, too. I'm so sorry."

In the distance, dozens of colorful hot air balloons lit up the dusky horizon, preparing for flight. Claire allowed the vision to sweep her away, and she imagined her and Nate together, drifting away in each other's arms, as the balloon took them to the skies and beyond. But now she knew it was a dream that would never come true. She had lived a real-life fantasy, but let it go because she was too stubborn to believe she deserved it.

"Mrs. Noruta? Claire," Craig said, startling her out of her thoughts. "I need to know you're okay. What are you going to do right now? Where are you going?"

"I, uh..." Claire's vision grew fuzzy as she struggled to string her thoughts together. "The airfield."

Craig kept talking about the logistics of arranging Nate's ride home, and said something about buying her a ticket for whenever she wanted to return, but she wasn't listening anymore. After they hung up, Claire could do nothing but stand there in silence, realizing this was what it felt like to hit rock bottom.

Her phone pinged with a direct message from her *Eclectix* app. Claire stared at it for a speechless minute before she opened it.

Hi Claire,

I've sent you two requests for confirmation now, but haven't heard anything. Have you changed your mind about my wedding order? I really wish you'd respond. I'm willing to pay a premium because time is running out. Please respond. Thank you so much.

Sincerely,

Beatrice Cho

The message forced Claire back to real life. Her personal life was in shambles, but she still had a responsibility to her business. *Claire's Enchanted Confections* was her dream. It represented everything she wanted in life, and the chance to blaze a path of success that deviated from her family's expectations. She wanted to show them she could be successful as her own boss, in a profession she had built from the ground up herself. If she ignored this huge opportunity, would it make her a failure?

Claire looked up at the horizon again. The distant fires of the hot air balloons burned and pulsed, like dozens of heartbeats syncing together as one.

She read the message again. And again. The last time, she read it with open eyes, and an open mind.

Being Nate's wife did not define her. Being someone's wife was not a measure of her self-worth, or an indicator of the amazing things she was capable of. She was Claire Ventura, daughter of Filipino immigrants, proud granddaughter of a fierce woman whose legacy would live on forever. She was a sister, a daughter, and a business owner.

And a wife to the most amazing man on the planet. He'd probably never know the sacrifice she had made for him, and it wasn't fair, but she knew that actions defined you best when others were not watching.

Business opportunities would come and go. True love would not.

Claire deleted the message. She descended the stairs, determined to say her final farewell at the airfield.

The taxi dropped her off at a massive, grassy field, which served as the launch site. By that time, some of the balloons were already taking flight into the skies faintly lit by the awakening sun.

Claire turned her face toward the heavens, reveling in the warm summer morning, finally allowing herself to find some semblance of joy in this place that some people could only dream of visiting.

More of the hot air balloons were taking off into the sky. The bright boldness of the balloons drifting into the air was like witnessing dreams come to life. It was the most beautiful thing Claire had ever seen. The stunning photo in Nate's living room did no justice to the real thing.

The pain had morphed from fire engulfing her whole body to a dull ache balled inside her gut. It was a pain that would always be there, as long as she lived, but these were the consequences she had to deal with. What was that one saying? It was better to have loved and lost than never to have loved at all. She never understood the sentiment, and she figured the person who'd come up with that obviously never had someone as good as Nate in their life.

She took a step forward and lifted her left hand into the air, framing it amongst the hot air balloons lifting into the sky. Her wedding ring glimmered restlessly, as if desperately trying to capture the glow from the balloons. She wanted to keep it as a reminder of Nate, but she knew it wasn't right. Even still, she didn't have the heart to take it off.

"Goodbye, Nate," she whispered, cradling her hand to her heart. "I love you always."

A warm wind gusted across the plain. Even when it stopped blowing, and grass settled, there was a still a rustle of movement from behind her.

She turned around, and he was there.

Nate.

She froze, thinking this was some kind of dream—a madness born from her yearning and pain, a symbol of something she wanted so badly that Nate manifested himself in everything and everyone.

"Nate," she breathed. "Is that you?"

"Yes."

He simply stood there, making no move toward her. His face was hard, and his eyes impassive. He gave no signal that he wanted anything to do with her, or that he loved her at all, yet there he was. A hundred questions rose in her mind, demanding to be answered, but she wiped them all clean. Claire was tired of wasting time and opportunities. She was tired of living with regret. The time to make things right was now.

"I am so sorry for hurting you," she said. "It was the worst mistake I've ever made in my life, and I will never forgive myself. I don't blame you for hating me, or if you've stopped loving me. I wouldn't be surprised if you've lost complete faith in me and wanted nothing to do with me ever again. But I have to tell you that being with you made me happier than I've ever been. I'm so angry at myself for the way I treated you. Since day one, all you've done is try to make me happy. And that donation you made on behalf of Lola? There are no words to thank you enough. You've sacrificed for me time and again, and all I did was run away. I've done it more times to you than you deserve."

Claire paused, swallowing past the dryness in her throat. She took a tentative step toward Nate. To her relief, he didn't move away.

"I don't know why I fought against this so hard," she continued, her voice tight with despair. "Maybe a part of me didn't want to believe I deserved all the good things coming my way. My grandma and sisters helped me realize that I'm too hard on myself. I set up this rigid expectation of my success, and I didn't want to deviate from it at all. And when you came into the picture, I didn't know how you factored into my life. Especially when we fell for each other so fast. It happened so fast, Nate. Falling in love like this happens once in a blue moon. Even less than that. My mistake was thinking it was too good to be true—that there had to be some kind of caveat, or condition that would cause us to fail.

"But now I know I was wrong. Dead wrong. And I'm paying the price. Knowing that I hurt and betrayed you—I'll never live it down. I can spend the rest of my life trying to make up for it, but I know it's impossible. I don't know if you can ever forgive me, but I still wanted to let you know—"

Claire's voice caught as tears started to trickle down her face.

"I still love you," she said. "I never stopped loving you, and I never will. No matter what happens, I'll always have my business and my family, but my mistake was taking you for granted. I'm so sorry Nate. I don't blame you if you hate me…if you don't love me anymore…"

Claire buried her face in her hands and sobbed. She hated doing this in front of Nate, but the emotions were winning, taking over, and battering her into submission. She figured she deserved it—this overwhelming sorrow. This was her life now. She could have had it all—a successful business, Nate by her side—but she fucked up, and she lost the love of her life forever.

Warm hands settled gently around Claire's arms. She looked up in disbelief, and found herself staring into the green and gold depths of Nate's gorgeous gaze.

"I knew you were here," he murmured, the warmth from his hands soothing her. "I knew it was you waiting at the café, standing at the vantage point, spying on me with binoculars while I hiked in the valley."

Claire stared up at him, shocked into momentary silence.

"What? You knew it was me all along?" she asked.

"Well, not right away," Nate replied, his mouth cocked in the sexy grin Claire loved. "At first I was mad, but after I calmed down, I wanted to see what your plans were. And don't be upset with Craig. I infiltrated him."

"Oh," Claire said as realization dawned on her. "You made him lie to me. You never went to the airport."

"I guess we're even now," Nate replied. His hands came up and caressed Claire's face. She closed her eyes, loving the feel of his skin against hers, wondering if this moment was a dream.

"Claire. When you left…I was beyond hurt. Nothing will ever erase the feeling of you leaving me, but there's one thing I know for sure, with every fiber of my being. You're a part of me. It doesn't matter how long we've known each other. When you know you're in love, and you've met the person you want to spend the rest of your life with, you don't wait. You act on it. I had no doubts, Claire. I've had a lot of relationships, and it's given me perspective on what's true, and what's real. That's why I knew you were the one for me from the beginning. And you always will be."

Happiness swelled in Claire's heart, bringing a smile to her face.

"Really?" She held tight to Nate's shoulders to stop her body from shaking. "You really feel that way about me?"

"Of course I do," Nate said.

She threw her arms around Nate, holding him tight, remembering how it felt to have him caress her and hold her so close to him that they were practically one.

"I will never, ever ask you to give up your dreams for me," Nate murmured in her ear. "I would move heaven and earth to make sure you get what you want. I'd never stand in your way."

Nate's words were a miracle, healing the countless invisible wounds Claire had suffered since she left. Deep inside, she already knew he would always support her no matter what. It was up to her to realize her dreams might look different in light of Nate's way of life, but she knew she would never have to deny herself happiness ever again.

Hand in hand, Nate and Claire walked across the airfield. He led her to a brilliant crimson-and-white balloon, where he opened the door to the basket and guided her inside first. Once again, she found herself not surprised. It was Nate's dream to conquer his fear with the love of his life, and she was ready and eager to be his strength. She reached out and grasped his hands, pulling him on board with her.

"This is it," she said, gazing up into his eyes. "You and me, going on grand adventures for the rest of our lives."

"Always," Nate whispered.

The world fell away as the balloon lifted off into the air. Claire felt her spirits soaring alongside the balloon as she reached up on her tiptoes and pressed her lips to Nate's. It might have taken them only three months to fall in love, but Claire couldn't wait to spend forever loving the man who proved time and again they were meant to be.

And they lived happily ever after...

ACKNOWLEDGMENTS

My sincerest gratitude to Liz Pelletier, who championed my story and made my publishing career come true. Lydia Sharp, thank you from the bottom of my heart for your amazing editing skills. I learned so much from you!

Thanks to the Entangled Team: Riki Cleveland, Heather Riccio, Curtis Svehlak, and the rest of the amazing team for their help and support.

To my wonderful literary agent, Naomi Davis, who by some miracle picked me out of the slush and became one of my biggest supporters. Thank you for being the world's best business partner! I'm still pinching myself because I can't believe you're my agent!

Special thanks to Elizabeth Turner Stokes for the most gorgeous, eye-popping cover.

Thanks to the Author Mentor Match fam: Alexa Donne, Maura Milan, Alyssa Colman, Jessica Kim, Gretchen Schreiber and the Round 3 Fabocracy: Leanne Schwartz, Heidi Christopher, Graci Kim, Susan Kim, Dakota Shain Byrd, Debra Spiegel, Julie Abe, Chelsea Ichaso, Sajan Prabhakar, Brittney Arena, Susan Lee, and the rest of my lovelies: your support means so much to me.

Special shout-out to my beloved Lindsey Meredith, who was my first CP for this book and one of my biggest cheerleaders. Thank you for your unwavering friendship!

Thank you also to Jessica Kelley, my very first CP ever who introduced me to the world of romance back when I wrote my first YA manuscript.

Thank you to these amazing literary agents whose advice really made a big difference earlier in my writing journey: Uwe Stender, Veronica Park, Laura Zats, Sara Megibow, and Patricia Nelson.

Much appreciation to my wonderful mentor, Nina Crespo, whose sage advice and support helped guide me through my fledgling writing career.

Where would I be without my amazing fellow Filipino writers? Sarah Smith, Tif Marcelo, Mia Hopkins, Mia Manansala, and Pamela Delupio: you all inspire me with your hard work and talent. I have loved every minute of reading your stories, and you've inspired me to persevere!

To Rachel, my sister-in-law turned sister. You were my very first beta reader for this book, and the first one to ever believe that Nate and Claire had a chance. Thank you for your love and support and for being my best friend even though I don't deserve you!

To Mom and Dad: words cannot express how proud I am to be your daughter. This book is a love letter to your hard work and to show the world how grateful I am for you.

Lola and Ninong: I love you both so much! Thank you for your love and kindness.

To my family, especially my cousins: Mike, Melanie, Michelle, Merielle, Derrik, Rae Rae, Ronnie, and the rest. I love you guys!

To my kids: Sean and Maddie. You are still too young to read this book, but thank you for inspiring me and filling my life with love and joy.

To my beloved grandma Caridad: you left this world too soon, but I carry your love and wonderful memories with me everyday.

Last but not least, to my high school sweetheart, Oliver. I am so grateful for you. Without you, this book would never have been written. You are the reason I believe in happily ever afters.

How to Survive a Modern-Day Fairy Tale is a fun, heartwarming story about love and family, however the book contains some elements that might not be suitable for all readers. Mild body shaming, the illness and death of a loved one, explicit sexual content, and occasional use of profanity are included in the novel. Readers who are sensitive to these, please take note.

Sometimes the perfect arrangement can lead to something more, even when you least expect it.

CONSTANCE GILLAM

Rashida Howard has never been a one-night-stand kind of woman, but she has good reason for making an exception with Elliott after meeting him in a bar. Cliché? Yes. Utterly amazing? Absolutely. Regrets? None.

Elliott Quinn is a workaholic. The one night he decides to break his routine, he has an encounter with the woman of his dreams. But no matter how amazing they are together, work will always come first.

Both of their lives get turned upside down when they find themselves on opposite sides of an ongoing fight between Elliott's company and Rashida's community. Though their chemistry is undeniable, neither of them will risk their integrity...or their heart.

And just when they think they might have found a solution that benefits both sides, they uncover a secret that will change everything.

APRIL
may
FALL

April Davis totally has her life in order. Ha! Not really. Yes, she's the Calm Mom—a social influencer with a reputation for showing moms how to stay calm and collected through yoga—but behind the scenes, she's barely holding it all together. Raising tiny humans alone is exhausting, but that's just the chewed-up cherry on the melted sundae of her life. Her kids aren't behaving, her husband left her for his skydiving instructor, and her top knot proves she hasn't showered in days.

Then a live video of the "always calm" April goes viral...and she's most definitely *not*. Enter Jack Gibson, April's contact at the media conglomerate that has purchased April's brand. The too-sexy-for-his-own-good Jack will help clean up April's viral mess, and even work with her to expand her influence, but toddler tea parties and a dog with a penchant for peeing on his shoes were definitely not part of the deal.

Now April's calm has jumped ship quicker than her kids running from their vegetables. Not to mention, the sparks flying between her and Jack have her completely out of her depth. Forget finding her calm—April's going to need a boatload of margaritas just to find her way back to herself again.

Two powerhouse authors bring you a hilarious tale of one woman's journey to find herself again.

by Tracy Wolff
New York Times Bestselling Author
and
by Avery Flynn
USA Today Bestselling Author

Ever have one of those days where life just plain sucks? Welcome to my last three months—ever since I caught my can't-be-soon-enough ex-husband cheating with his paralegal. I'm thirty-five years old, and I've lost my NYC apartment, my job, my money, and frankly, my dignity.

But the final heartache in the suck sandwich of my life? My great-aunt Maggie died. The only family member who's ever gotten me.

Even after death, though, she's helping me get back up. She's willed me the keys to a house in the burbs, of all places, and dared me to grab life by the family jewels. Well, I've got the vise grips already in hand (my ex should take note) and I'm ready to fight for my life again.

Too bad that bravado only lasts as long as it takes to drive into Huckleberry Hills. And see the house.

There are forty-seven separate HOA violations, and I feel them all in my bones. Honestly, I'm surprised no one's "accidentally" torched the house yet. I want to, and I've only been standing in front of it for five minutes. But then my hot, grumpy neighbor tells me to mow the lawn first and I'm just...done. Done with men too sexy for their own good and done with anyone telling me what to do.

First rule of surviving the burbs? There is nothing that YouTube and a glass of wine can't conquer.

AMARA
an imprint of Entangled Publishing LLC